A SECRET LIES IN NEW ORLEANS

RON WALLACE

To Gary

Prose who'd a thunk it?

Ron

DORRANCE PUBLISHING CO
EST. 1920
PITTSBURGH, PENNSYLVANIA 15238

The contents of this work, including, but not limited to, the accuracy of events, people, and places depicted; opinions expressed; permission to use previously published materials included; and any advice given or actions advocated are solely the responsibility of the author, who assumes all liability for said work and indemnifies the publisher against any claims stemming from publication of the work.

All Rights Reserved
Copyright © 2021 by Ron Wallace

No part of this book may be reproduced or transmitted, downloaded, distributed, reverse engineered, or stored in or introduced into any information storage and retrieval system, in any form or by any means, including photocopying and recording, whether electronic or mechanical, now known or hereinafter invented without permission in writing from the publisher.

Dorrance Publishing Co
585 Alpha Drive
Pittsburgh, PA 15238
Visit our website at *www.dorrancebookstore.com*

ISBN: 978-1-6491-3191-1
eISBN: 978-1-6491-3688-6

1

AT NINETY-SIX, William Matthew Wallace still cut an imposing figure sitting behind my desk at C&I Investigative and Protective Services. He'd slipped down below 200 pounds trying to find a weight his knees would bear, but his mind was still razor-sharp at ninety-six, and I was willing to bet that he was armed. He always was. Most likely he was carrying his old Iver-Johnson hammerless Owl Head .32 in the front pocket of his khakis. His eyes were clear and the same grey as Momma's. I knew his hair was snow white beneath the New York Yankee cap; it had been as long as I'd known him. They tell me as a young man it was almost red, but since he turned fifty-three the year I was born, I relied primarily on hearsay for that tidbit of information.

"Morning, Dad," I said.

He grinned. "It was morning two hours ago, Bud; you're sleeping your life away."

I sipped my Coke and set a box of Krispy Kremes on the desk in front of him as a peace offering.

He took one.

"Pour me a damned cup of coffee," he growled. "I can't believe a grown man drinks soda instead of coffee. That shit will kill you someday."

I laughed.

"Yes, sir, boss, but I'm pretty sure *that* shit will kill you someday, too."

Last night he had called me to tell me to be in the office by nine this morning. He had something I needed to see, and there was a long story with it. That was William Wallace's way of dealing with problems, set 'em up and knock 'em down, just like his namesake, Braveheart. You'd think he was Mel Gibson riding that horse in circles around his fellow Scots, spurring them on. He definitely knew how to pick a fight.

I didn't even consider asking why we were meeting. I knew damn good and well it would take him a while to explain it all; otherwise he'd have simply told me right then over the phone without wasting any time.

As he selected a second doughnut, I poured him a cup of coffee from the pot I was sure he'd put on earlier. He had his own key and had made himself at home behind the desk, a massive dark walnut monster with my brass name plate sitting on it, Mickey Warren Wallace. It was his desk before it was mine, so I handed him his cup and sat in the nice leather client's chair across from him admiring the brass name plate that I had contributed as my part of the décor.

He took the cup and turned the painting I'd seen lying on the desk to where I could see it better.

"Take a look at that," he said, taking a long pull off the hot coffee as he pushed the painting across the desk.

"I had to roll out of bed early to come see an oil painting?" I grinned.

"Early? Oh, sweet Lord, you are hopeless," He shook his head and went on. "Got a phone call Wednesday night from my old buddy, Tommy Moon, retired U.S. Marshal down in New Orleans, said he had something with my name on it that I'd have to see to believe, and he was sending it to me, and I needed to call him back once I'd looked it over."

I took another Krispy Kreme and kept working on the Coca-Cola.

"It was this painting." He tapped the frame lightly with the heavy stick he'd carved into a walking cane. "And the water-proof canvas it was wrapped in when Tommy found it, UPS man brought it late yesterday. Take a good look at it, Mickey."

I took the painting by the frame. It was oil on canvas. The mottled background was full of dark greens and browns, a forest I suppose. The focal point of the work centered on two men with a team of four horses pulling long logs behind them. One man, dark-skinned with black hair, was bent over examining a horse's raised forefoot; the other man, a bit fairer-skinned, wearing a slouch hat, was touching him on the shoulder, pointing at a six-point star carved in a rock cliff slightly ahead of them with more dark trees growing all around on the side of a hill. The detail was masterful. Both men were dressed in dull white shirts, denim jeans and western boots. In the lower right-hand corner, the work was signed John William Wallace in a flowing hand and dated 1930.

I was surprised.

"John William Wallace, that was your father's name," I said, looking up at Dad.

"It was, but he died in 1916," Dad replied in a matter of fact tone.

"Then that can't possibly be our John William Wallace, can it?" I said looking across the desk at him. "I mean, it's an excellent work, but it couldn't be your father's painting with that date on it. And honestly John William Wallace is a relatively common name. No pun intended. What's the deal?"

He shook his head and raised both hands slightly in a sign of uncertainty.

"I don't know, Mick, but we've gotta find out. It's not just the name on the painting. It was originally addressed to William Wallace in Durant, Oklahoma. There are some serious questions suddenly rising late in the game, and I need to have answers. You know time is short. That's why I called you last night right after I hung up from talking to Tommy again."

I was trying to focus on the painting, but it wasn't easy with the eyes of Ira Bluesoldier and William Matthew Wallace peering down from the portraits that hung behind his chair. I found myself wondering if those eyes had felt as powerful to all those who sat before them, as I did now.

"You don't really think your dad, Grandpa Wallace, painted this do you, Pop?"

He smiled.

"There are more things in heaven and earth, Horatio than are dreamt of in your philosophy."

I unfolded the weatherproof canvas the painting had once been wrapped in that was lying on the desk. William Matthew Wallace, South 4th Street, Durant, Oklahoma was neatly lettered in paint.

"And it was wrapped in this?"

"Yep, of course that's my grandfather's name just like it's mine, and that was his address at one time, so the painting must have been intended for him if the 1930 date is legitimate."

I heard our office manager/secretary/boss enter the front door outside my office.

"Mick, what are you doing in this early?" her voice came through the open door.

"Dad drug me outta bed, darlin'. You know he's been up since dawn. The wicked never rest," I said, covering the Krispy Kreme box with the painting.

She stuck her head in the door.

"Will, my sweetheart, what's the best man I know doing, hanging out with such bad company?"

He laughed.

"Just trying to keep the boy busy and outta jail, beautiful. I hope you're feeling as fine as you are looking this morning."

I swear she blushed.

"I've got a nice pot of fresh hot coffee in the outer office, you sweet man. Can I bring you a fresh cup?" she cooed.

"I wouldn't want to have you fetching coffee for me, beautiful, but you know I'd love a fresh cup."

He winked.

I rolled my eyes as she walked back out of the office to her desk area. She never offered to bring me coffee. Good thing I don't drink that crap.

"Now tell me again, exactly where did Mr. Moon say he found the painting?" I asked.

"This may take a while," he said, lifting the painting and taking another Krispy Kreme.

2

JANIE, HER HAIR hanging in loose curls, wearing a nice little black dress covered in tiny, multi-colored flowers, brought in the coffee, looked at the donuts, frowned, and took the box before I could take another. I almost felt guilty about smuggling them past her in the first place.

"Save those for me, will you, darlin'," Dad grinned and winked at her again as she moved toward the door.

"They'll be right out here on my desk when you're ready, Will," she said smiling at him. "Just can't have you feeding the animals here at the zoo."

She blew a kiss at me and walked out with the rest of the box, unintimidated by my piercing glare.

"You really oughtta marry that girl, son," Dad said as soon as she was out the door. "She's crazy about you for some odd reason, and you're gonna keep screwing around until some old boy runs off with her."

Janie Holloway was a striking brunette. She was maybe five-six and moved with a dancer's grace. Mom and Ira's wife, Regina Bluesoldier, hired her as secretary/receptionist back in '93 when Mom had first gotten ill, and now almost ten years later, with Mom and Regina both having passed, she ran the office with an iron fist. She took crap from no one and worshipped the ground my father walked on.

"It's complicated, Dad," I grinned. "Besides I think she loves you best."

Dad sipped his coffee. "Your mom and Lauren have been gone for almost five years now, Mick. You're still a young man, and Janie's young, too."

"We're friends," I said. "We've been out a few times in the last couple of years. There's chemistry but…it's just complicated. We don't want to mess up our friendship and there's work…"

"All good excuses, son, but just that, excuses." He sat his cup down on a coaster and looked me in the eye. "But any fool can see you two care about each other."

"She's still dating other guys, Dad," I tried deflecting the subject. "I'm seeing other people, too. Give us more time."

He shook his head. "I've seen some of the 'other people' y'all date. You both need to quit wasting time. Besides that you know I don't have much more time to give. A good son would honor his daddy's wishes."

I laughed. "Okay, I give. I'll ask her to marry me as soon as you tell me what the hell is going on with this painting. Now can we continue?"

"I hate a smart ass," he said and paused to sip his coffee before he continued. "Anyway Tommy said he found the package with the painting still in it as part of an estate sale. Seems an old Cajun badass outlaw name of Marcel Fontenot finally died with no close heirs; old bastard was the major criminal in south Louisiana for years, the absolute baddest of the bad like his daddy, Anton, before him. Tommy wasn't looking for the painting of course," Dad continued. "He wanted Fontenot, even if he was dead. The painting was just an accidental small find in a much bigger pile."

I sat quietly as Dad glanced at the painting again.

"Tommy's retired now, but he figured something had to be out there at the Fontenot place that could tie Marcel to some really bad stuff, and he didn't want to see the old son of a bitch remembered as the fine upstanding member of the parish that Fontenot had come to be known as, so Tommy went looking. He wanted to hang Marcel, dead or alive, where everyone would see him as the walking, talking piece of shit he really was…just quoting my buddy there." Dad laughed softly.

"Uh-huh," I said and settled back into the leather chair. This wasn't going to be a short story. He was going to unwrap it for me a little at a time…might as well relax and listen.

"Fontenot had a nice big home in Lafayette, old historic place that Anton probably stole back before the twenties, as well as a nice piece of land out of town on the Vermillion River. Phillips or Texaco or one of the big oil companies found oil and natural gas there back in the early fifties. Shortly thereafter Marcel became semi-legit, a pillar of the community; he phased out the majority of the criminal side of his business bit by bit to other associates over the next ten, twenty or so years, took up golf and tennis, but Tommy Moon don't quit so easy."

I listened while I looked the painting over closely. Perhaps a clue would leap out, and I could say, "Ah-hah."

One didn't.

"Marcel's rural property was going to auction, so Tommy and his boy, Jeff, a high-powered Baton Rouge lawyer, pulled some strings and went to look the place over. Jeff is a golfing buddy with one of the lawyers handling the estate. He connived around a bit with the pretense his dad wanted to make an early purchase or two and was willing to pay top dollar. Apparently most of the remaining Fontenot descendants were sort of unaware of their relative's earlier occupation, or maybe they just didn't care and were simply a lot more interested in collecting quickly on their inheritance..."

"So out to the country go Tommy and Jeff in the company of friendly lawyers," I finished, trying to resist the temptation to rush the narrative along.

He chuckled again and continued, "Tommy and Jeff take the tour of the house. There are a few desks and filing cabinets in the farmhouse that they ask about buying in order to look inside them. And of course, they've been emptied, looks like a long time ago. Tommy makes a small offer on a nice mahogany desk and drops the word he's looking for older stuff, collectible maybe. The lawyers tell Jeff and Tommy there are several old cars and some farm and ranch items stored in some barns on the backside of the property, near the stables, apparently untouched for ages if he's interested. Being a trained investigator, much like myself, Tommy says sure, he'd love to have a look."

I admired my father's narrative ability and smiled as he grinned at his own wit. The man could tell a story, and his Scots-Irish blood was showing now.

"The first car they come to is a red 1938 Cadillac LaSalle under a heavy tarp. Jeff pulls off the cover, and sure enough, bullet holes in the driver's door and the glass is gone in the driver side window. Tommy looks at Jeff and looks at the lawyers. 'Let's see the rest of these,' says Jeff, and the next one, a '42 Olds, has bullet holes as well. There are four more cars lined up against the barn's back wall, all under tarps just like these, but one of the lawyers is nervous and balking now, so Tommy gets on the phone to his other boy, Jaxon, a U.S. Marshal in New Orleans."

"I assume the search continues," I said.

He nodded in the affirmative. "Yep, the lawyers are panicking at this point, but like I said, one is buds with Jeff, so they let Tommy keep looking as the Marshals and the State Police are on the way. In the back seat of a 1930 Ford Coupe under an old blanket, he finds the package with my name on it, and somehow he convinced the lawyers, Jeff included, that he knows me, that I, like him, was a retired U.S. Marshal. They would open it in Jaxon's office, and if it was of any importance, he'd give it back over to current investigators. Tommy's a highly respected and well-admired retired U.S. Marshal; they went for it, or it would still be in a Louisiana State Police evidence room somewhere."

"So the Moons open it, find this painting that may very well be evidence in any number of federal crimes, and just pack it up and mail it to you, that simple?" I ask.

Dad shrugged. "What can I say; I'm almost twenty years older than Tommy. He was just starting. I was winding down. I was his superior officer for a while. We got along. He liked me."

"Well enough to tamper with possible evidence in at least one felony case, possibly more, possibly homicides, and probably federal since Tommy Moon was a U.S. Deputy Marshal just like you?"

"Well enough," Dad grinned.

As he paused, looking at the painting again, I picked up the slack and said, "If my math is right, in 1930, you were twenty-four, Dad. Your father, John William Wallace, had been killed in 1916 when you were ten. Granny told me lots of the stories, but the dates don't jibe here. Who's 'this' John William, and why was he sending this painting to your grandfather in Durant, Oklahoma back in 1930 or '31?"

He looked across my desk, his desk, or our desk, whichever it was right then. "Well, it just may be that's why I called my brilliant detective son in on the case."

"Don't tell me you're thinking some of the old family stories may have been true?" I asked, a little surprised.

Dad leaned back in my chair, his chair, or our chair, whichever it was right now.

"A man's got to wonder, Mick. It just doesn't make much sense otherwise. Does it?"

I'd heard all the rumors, the whispers that my grandfather hadn't actually died in prison back in 1916, but I was under the impression that Dad firmly believed his mom (Granny to me) and his grandfather (William Matthew same as him) simply didn't want to believe their husband and son, his father, was gone. And like I said: someone was sure buried out there in the family plot, where Granny and Dad's grandparents had joined him, someone shipped back in a box from McAlester State Penitentiary with the name John William Wallace on it.

"How could he have escaped and no one knew it, Dad?" I asked. "And even if he did, how did the painting wind up in Lafayette, Louisiana on some old gangster's property?"

"Good questions, Boy, ain't you glad I taught you all those detective tactics? Let's grab a bite of lunch. I want you to drive me out to Highland in a bit."

"Lunch is on you? Good deal. I'm in the mood for some barbecue; how about you?" I chuckled.

"I don't recall saying I was paying," Dad replied. "But see if Janie wants to go get a bite with us. You can drop her back here before we drive out to the cemetery."

I rose from the comfortable leather chair. "At your service, Boss."

3

MCCURTAIN COUNTY, INDIAN TERRITORY, JUNE 1903

TWO WAGONS ROLLED *to a stop just east of Eagletown, Indian Territory late summer 1903. John William and Rena Wallace were in the lead wagon. Levi and Lucy Carroll were in the back one, their colicky baby, Isaac Carroll, crying loudly. It was still early, several hours before sunset, but they'd found a nice shady spot and stopped by a clearing off the track to camp before rising with the sun to push on for Fort Towson the next morning.*

They had left Murphreesboro, Arkansas only a few days earlier, armed with John William's plan for attaining land and starting their lives on adjoining lots in the Territories. Rena was quarter-blood Choctaw and Levi's mother was full-blood. They'd sign the Rolls and get their tribal allotments and begin a new chapter in their lives, leaving Arkansas, where they'd grown up together far behind.

The sun was shining, but the weather wasn't terribly hot, and birds were singing in the trees; outside of Isaac's colic, all was well in their worlds. There was even a little hint of breeze occasionally winding through the trees.

John William was unhitching the teams and hobbling the stock. Levi had gone to cut some long-bladed grass growing just off the wagon road to feed the animals while the girls got camp ready. They weren't more than ten miles outside of Eagletown. They'd make Fort Towson the next day after some hard rolling and an early start.

Rena was getting down from the back of their wagon, where she'd been looking for a skillet to cook supper with, while Lucy sat in their wagon nursing Isaac.

They both sighted Levi walking toward them from twenty or thirty yards away, carrying a full armload of long grass he'd cut from a nearby fencerow.

He smiled at Rena and Lucy and said, "Well, girls…"

But the shotgun blast rang out, ending his final words in mid-sentence. It was still echoing in the trees as he sank to his knees and fell forward.

Rena screamed and ran toward him with Lucy trailing right behind, still carrying baby Isaac. John William left the animals and came running with his 44.40 rifle, only to find them both kneeling beside Levi, stone dead when they had reached him, gone, simply gone; smiling and happy one second, then gone the next.

The hole in his back where the twelve-gauge slug had entered, exploding his heart, was an ugly wound, and Lucy was wailing, holding Isaac as Rena tried to roll Levi over onto his side. His eyes were closed as if he were asleep when John knelt beside Rena and gently turned the best friend he'd ever known in this world over onto his back.

Out of the corner of his eye, John saw a short, heavyset man dressed in a nice white shirt, black trousers, and high boots step out of the corn on the other side of the fencerow. He reached for the Winchester he'd laid down when he knelt beside Levi.

The older man leveled a long-barreled shotgun directly at them. A boy of eleven or twelve maybe stood right behind him.

"Young fella, you need to let that rifle lay right there on the ground, so no one else gets hurt. This is how we deal with thieves here in the Territories. No one, white or Injun, steals from the McBrides and gets away with it. Now stand up, lift your hands, and back away from that rifle."

John felt pure rage surge through his veins; he couldn't breathe and desperately wanted to kill this man. He and Levi had grown up together since they were old enough to walk. Their birthdays were only two days apart. John had never known life without Levi Carroll in it, but he contained the fury and did as he was told. He had Rena and Lucy to think of at the moment.

The man stepped between the wooden rails of the fence, keeping the shotgun pointed with one hand toward them, and the boy followed close behind.

Rena and Lucy were sobbing in shock and disbelief, causing the baby to join in the wailing.

"Mister, this man never stole a thing in his life," John William said, almost in tears himself.

"Don't lie to me, boy. Saw the brown bastard with my own eyes, cutting my corn. He just didn't see me standing over there in the corn rows," the man said. "That's all my farm over there on t'other of that fence, bought and paid for, and like I said, no one steals from me or mine."

Rena gathered herself and looked down where Levi lay on the ground; there was nothing but the long-stemmed grass that he'd cut for the horses and mules lying beside him, not a single ear of corn anywhere.

"Then where is this corn he was stealing?" she asked, tears pouring down her cheeks.

The farmer looked down and turned pale for just a moment. He nudged the boy and whispered to him, still holding the gun on the little group. The boy darted back into the cornfield. A minute later, he came running back with four or five ears of corn.

"Throw it down right there, boy," the man in the high boots said, and the boy did as he was told.

"Now, by God, he's stealing corn," the farmer growled.

John felt the blood rising in his temples and would have charged him right then if he wasn't worried about the women and baby Isaac. Good sense stayed his hand as his mind began to work rapidly. Justice could be delayed a while.

"Listen, mister, my daddy used to work for Judge Parker in Fort Smith. We're from Murphreesboro. We meant no harm. If you'll just let us load Levi here up and head out, we'll get back to Arkansas and never bother you again. I know you thought he was stealing. This was all just a terrible, terrible mistake. Let me take him and the women and baby and head back home. We'll be out of your life forever," John pleaded.

"I got friends here," the farmer said. "I'm Franklin McBride, and that Indian boy was stealing my corn as far as the constable or anyone else will say. I should have you all locked up right now. You were all..."

"I know. I understand. I just want to get the girls and the babe home, Levi, too. We'll bury him in Arkansas, and you'll never see us again. I swear it, Mr. McBride. We'll be out of your way in no time at all, no time."

"Well, then leave that rifle a laying for now; you women just stay right where you are, and you hitch them teams back up, boy, while I think."

The two girls clung to one another, Isaac between them while John William hitched up his mules and Levi's horses, tied his buckskin stud and Levi's grey *gelding behind the wagons, then brought a canvas tarp from one of the wagons and wrapped Levi's body.*

The farmer kept his shotgun leveled, moving it back and forth from Rena and Lucy to John.

"Okay, it's your lucky day. Load him up and git," McBride finally snarled. "Leave now while I'm feeling Christian. Lord knows you're thieving Indians, and I should take you all into the constable."

John felt the hatred surging through him again as he lifted Levi into the back of the wagon.

"Y'all can get yer sorry selves back close to Arkansas before dark if you don't stop. Now git."

John William reached for the Winchester lying on the ground from where he'd lifted Levi.

"Leave it layin', boy," came the growl in the bright summer light.

"I need it, sir; we're just going home, and I need it. I haven't got the money to buy another. Please, I'll need it for hunting when we get home, Mr. McBride."

"I know better than to give a thief his gun back, but I'm feelin' sorry for ya, boy, and I'm no thief myself. I'll put it in the back of the wagon with him. You drive the back wagon. You women get in the lead wagon and go, while I'm still of a mind to be rid of you thieves."

Lucy climbed up into the lead wagon. Rena held Isaac until she was seated and handed him up, then climbed up beside Lucy and took the reins.

The man gestured toward the east with his gun barrel, the boy standing behind him.

"Stop that wagon, even for a split second, boy, and I'll blast you straight to hell with your friend back there. Go on now! Git!"

John William saw him lay the rifle in the back of the wagon, but when he looked back again, McBride and the boy were gone back into the corn.

4

I PULLED THE GREEN Jeep Cherokee through the ornate gates of Highland Cemetery, just south of town.

This was the burial spot for my mother, my grandparents, and great-grandparents, Dad's first wife, Anna, and my half-brother, John William. Only one plot remained open there in the Wallace plots, between Mom and Anna, Dad's first wife, who had died after complications during surgery back in 1952.

Only my father could pull off eternal rest between two women he loved. I smiled at the thought.

"You know, son, if that signature on the painting is really Dad's, it means everything I've believed about him since 1916 is wrong, dead wrong, and I don't have a clue as to who's buried out here next to Gramma. Hellfire, I might be out here before summer comes again. I don't want to be lying with strangers, Mick. I have to know who painted this. If it was Dad, I need to know what happened and why. And I want whoever is out here with our family properly tended to. Understand, son?"

"I know, Dad," was all I could manage.

He looked me straight in the eye. "Mickey, I never once doubted Dad was dead. I'd heard Grampa and Grandma, even Momma, say little things that questioned his death, but for me, there wasn't any doubt. I just knew that if he was alive back then, he'd have found me and Robert and Shelby somehow, some way."

Robert and Shelby, both lost in World War II, were buried in foreign graveyards. The oldest of the three Wallace boys was my father, William

Matthew, with no Roman numerals to denote him as a second, a third, or anything else. Seems we don't use the I's, II's, or III's, but we do name first sons William Matthew and John William in alternating generations, all the way back to Scotland I'm told.

I'm not John William though, as my grandfather was. My older brother received that title, half-brother actually. He was eight years older than me. He was my hero, and he was killed in Vietnam back in '69. I walked over to the stone on his grave. I named my son after him just to further muddy the waters of our kinfolk, since by the rules and conventions of our family, I should have named him William Matthew. I figured what the hell, skipping a generation wasn't that big a deal.

Lost in thought for a moment, Dad stood at the north end of the eight plots where we had assumed his father, John William, was buried. I stood at the south end where my brother, John William, had filled the last plot in our family section, save the one reserved between Mom and Anna.

I wasn't sure what was running through his mind right then, and he wasn't sharing. I was thinking of the unusual grouping there before us, my grandparents (at least I had always thought so up to now), my great-grandparents, a woman I'd never known but was certain my father had loved, the spot where Dad would lie someday, Mom, and finally my brother.

Looking east he finally broke the silence, "They say time heals all wounds, Mick, but it doesn't. Maybe it dulls the ache, allows you to put the hurt in a box, wrap it up, and hide it on the back shelf of some closet, but some wounds never really heal."

I walked over and put a hand on his huge shoulder.

His eyes were tearing up a little. He wiped them with a finger and said, "As soon as I saw the signature in the bottom corner of that painting, I believed it was Dad's, no matter how hard my rational mind told me it wasn't, no matter how impossible it seemed."

In a moment of silence, under a perfect blue sky, the breeze stirred flags in the distance.

"Then I guess we better figure out who's lying over there next to Granny and how that all came about, huh?" I said.

He gave me a slight smile, nodded, and spoke, "Standing here over that grave, eighty-six years dissolved like an early morning mist, son, and for a minute, I was ten-years-old again, standing with Grampa and Shelby at the old KATY depot just off South 1st Street where the train had rolled in."

"My father, always the poet," I thought to myself.

"I remembered the two men unloading a long box from the freight car onto Grampa's buckboard, a box that held my father inside. I remember it was hot, really hot. The men were sweating, and one mashed a finger and swore as he slid the box out of the boxcar into the wagon. He asked Grampa to sign for receipt, and we took the crate back to his blacksmith shop, just off Market Square in Durant. I know Grampa opened the box sometime later because I heard him tell Momma, Gramma, and Aunt Sarah there was no way they could see him. Momma threw such a fit though, they finally did let her see him down at the funeral home, but they never did let me or Shelby or Robert see him, despite all our crying and pleading. I have to know, Mick. I don't have much time and I need to know, son. I'm counting on you. I'm too old to do it, or I would. I wouldn't put it off on you."

We both looked across the fence twenty yards away in silence at the seventh green on the Durant Country Club where a foursome was walking from their carts for just a moment before I spoke.

"I'm already on it, Dad, had a great teacher, ya know, inherited some of his investigative mind and all of his incredibly hard head."

He gave my shoulder a solid love tap that told me he still had some honest power in the old body, and we started our walk back toward the Jeep, Dad moving stiffly, using his cane carefully as we covered the soft ground. All I could do now was listen again. He was going to talk it all through on our way home.

"At the burial, I heard Aunt Sarah whisper that it wasn't Bud, her pet name for Daddy, in that box that they buried; it was someone else, and I heard Momma and Grampa tell her to hush before she upset the children. That was too late though; we were already confused and plenty upset.

That day, son, standing at the open grave before they lowered the coffin, I remember thinking about the baseball glove he'd made me for my birthday that summer before they took him away to McAlester. He loved playing catch with us boys, guess that's where I got the baseball bug. He'd promised to make Shelby one, too, for his birthday, but he was behind prison walls before that day came, so Momma gave Dad's glove to Shelby, and he became my new throwing partner. But I remember how angry I was that Dad would never play catch with me again, and I was pissed that I hadn't even got to see him one last time. I stayed mad at the world for a long time."

I kept a hand on his shoulder for balance as we crossed the soft earth.

"Later when I was a grown man," he continued, "Momma told me he was burned too badly for us to see, and she had only identified him by a silver ring on his finger, one that she'd given him when they were married. That was eighty-six years ago, Mick. It seems somehow inconceivable to me that my father avoided death and never returned to us, but that damned signature in the corner of that painting looks so much like his. The painting couldn't have been intended for me though. I finished West Point in 1927 and was commissioned a second lieutenant. By 1930 I had been promoted to captain and was stationed at Fort McPherson, Georgia, so logic dictates the intended recipient of our newly found package was my grandfather, William Matthew, not me."

We paused our walk and stood, looking out over the stones for a minute.

"If this phantom painter is my father, he'd been gone for nearly fifteen years when it was being prepared for delivery in 1930. That's fifteen years of blank space and eighty-six years of mystery and lies," he said to the air around him.

"We have to learn what prompted the painting in the first place, Dad," I said. "And what does 1930 have to do with it all? Why after fifteen years would your father decide to contact your grandfather again, and how did the painting wind up in the backseat of a car in Lafayette, Louisiana? Not to mention, if it was really from our John William Wallace, why did he choose to send a painting; why not call home or send a letter, or better yet, come back himself?"

He looked at me again. "All questions I've been asking myself, Mickey. There are at least two critical dates in the mystery. The answer is somewhere in those dates – 1930 and 1916. That's where we have to start looking; in those dates somewhere is the key."

"That's going back a long, long way, Dad, but if that's what it takes, we'll do it. We will find the answers. After all we're detectives, right?"

Dad grinned. "Yep; you, me, and Brantley – a whole covey of Sherlock Holmeses. Let's walk over to Ira and Regina and Lauren and Leigh's stones before we leave."

"We should've brought flowers, I reckon," I said. "I haven't been out here since JW and I came out on Leigh's birthday in March."

He put a massive hand on my shoulder. "They're not here, ya know, bud, but from time to time, I feel a need to come out. I'm sorry. I know you still hurt plenty."

I tried to smile as we walked to the section on the other side of the Jeep where Ira and Regina's stone lay next to my wife Lauren and our daughter Leigh.

Five years ago, Lauren and Leigh had driven Mom to a doctor's appointment in Plano, Texas, and all three were killed when a semi driver fell asleep and crossed the median, striking their car just south of the Red River.

It had been a beautiful Saturday afternoon. JW and I had been at a ball game in Hugo where he was playing for Durant in his junior year of high school.

We were shattered. Dad lost his wife of almost forty years, his daughter-in-law, and only granddaughter. I lost my wife, my mom, my thirteen-year-old daughter. JW lost his grandmother, his mother, and his much-loved little sister. I don't think any of us would have survived it if we wouldn't have had each other to lean on. Even now five years down the road, all of us can still see a movie or hear a song that one of them loved, and it's like the whole thing sneaks back in to hurt us again.

Dad touched the top of the black stone with an affectionate pat and moved over to Ira, and Regina's with his Yankee cap in hand, giving me a second to dry the mist in my eyes and join him before we would walk back to the waiting Jeep Cherokee and load up.

Once his aching knees had carried him back to where we had parked, he shook his head, looked me in the eyes, then just opened the door and took his seat.

I got in the driver's side, turned the key, and the straight-six motor came to life. As we prepared to turn right onto Cemetery Road out of Highland and head for our offices back on Main Street, he looked at me and smiled sadly.

"Never spent a happy minute in this place, bud," he said. "Let's go."

I looked over at him and saw the age that I had tried to deny taking him away from me.

"I'll call Brant as soon as we get back to the offices, Dad, let you give him all the particulars, and we'll get this done."

"Yep, we gotta get this right, son," he said, still looking east out his window. "If that's not Dad there next to Mom, she'd be a mighty unhappy lady, and I always tried to never make my momma unhappy,"

I punched Waylon into the CD player.

I been to Shreveport and down to New Orleans...

I looked ahead, straight over the steering wheel at the path through the field of stone. "I reckon so."

He looked over at me and adjusted his Yankee cap. "Yep, it's gotta be done, and you better not mess it up."

I laughed as we traveled the blacktop back to town.

5

I STILL LIVED IN our two-story house on Fourth Street, but since JW had started at OU, it was just too much. I never entertained. I slept in a different room from mine and Lauren's old bedroom when I was home, usually on the sofa in front of the television. I seldom entered Leigh's room anymore; it was pretty much as she left it, though Janie had offered to come over and help me pack some things away for storage. I knew she'd helped Dad with putting some of Mom's things away. I'd just been busy I guess, but I woke the morning after our Highland visit and decided it was time to sell if JW was okay with it. If he wanted the house, it was his, but I made a note to mention it in our next phone call.

Brant lived above our offices in four rooms that had been remodeled in the early twentieth century building. We were both on the road a lot. Maybe I'd talk him out of a room up there. It might be just like old times.

Usually I walked to the office down the elm-shaded streets of Durant, but I'd driven to McDonald's for breakfast this morning, knowing Mrs. Wyatt would be there instead of Janie, who had a doctor's appointment, and I could sneak the contraband breakfast past her.

Mrs. Wyatt, Janie's go-to temp, a stern-looking middle-aged woman, was at her desk next to Janie's. I wouldn't say she was barrel of laughs, but I liked her; she was efficient, all business, and had no time for any of our BS. I'd even tried to get Janie to hire her full-time to cut down on her workload, but she wouldn't have any part of it.

Mrs. Wyatt looked up over her glasses as I entered and smiled when I nodded. She didn't frisk me and confiscate the Mickey D's bag of goodies, but I tried to be inconspicuous anyway, one word to Janie and my ass would hear about it.

Brant was still on assignment somewhere in Texas, but Dad was back, firmly entrenched behind my desk again, the portraits of Ira Bluesoldier and himself looking down at me over his shoulder again. But today he was in full attack mode. The deed to the place may be in mine and Brant's names, but we both understand that as long as either set of eyes in those portraits open somewhere on this planet, neither of us are really in command.

The man has questions he needs answered, questions about his own father, a man I never met, questions that seek an ending to a story beginning almost a century ago, questions that he needs answered before he can rest, and some of those, the same questions that stumped us yesterday, were still circling like hunting hawks.

Sitting behind my desk, at least it has my name on it, Dad was scanning notes he'd made during the night. "About time you got here, boy. Big case like this and you're sleeping in."

"You're the early riser in the family, Pops, and I'm hell-bent on keeping it that way."

I polished off my sausage, egg, and cheese biscuit and chugged down my McDonald's orange juice, thankful that Janie was away from her desk and Mrs. Wyatt was the only one to see me carrying the Mickey D sack into the office.

"Can't believe you still don't drink coffee, son, and how many times have I gotta tell ya that fast food crap is gonna kill you. What am I gonna do with you, boy?"

He lifted his mug and sipped.

"I hate coffee... And since you're not going to let this soda and fast food stuff go, let's get down to solving mysteries," I grinned. "Think it's time we called Brant in on this?"

Brant was Ira Bluesoldier's son, our partner, my best friend, and a second son to Dad.

"He's still in Texas following that congressman, isn't he? Somebody's gotta make money for this place; let him take care of business for now," Dad said. "It'll wait a little while. We'll need him soon enough."

I nodded. "Okay, boss. I've been thinking about it all night. Assuming the painting is the real deal, why 1930? If your father had survived the incidents, which supposedly killed him in 1916, what was the trigger that moved him to finally attempt re-establishing contact with his family after almost fifteen years of silence?"

"I've been thinking about that, too, Mick. Consider this: Momma and Robert had returned to Oklahoma from New York to live with Grampa Wallace in 1930. Amos Buchanan, Mom's second husband, went from millionaire to pauper with the stock market crash of '29, stepped into his office a few weeks later, and shot himself in the head, bang! Not a jumper like some of his contemporaries."

I remained attentive, finished my second orange juice, and tossed the cup in the waste can beside the desk without a word.

Dad pushed his Yankee cap back and leaned forward. "With no visible means of support and all of Mr. Buchanan's property scattered right and left, Mom was forced to seek shelter with her father-in-law, who truly adored her, probably the only man she felt she could trust at the time. Again assuming that painting really is my father's work and assuming he found out about Buchanan's death, Mom's return to Oklahoma could be the contributing factor in the 1930 date..." he paused and sipped his coffee. "Or maybe...it's simply just a coincidence."

"I'm not big on coincidence, Dad," I interjected. "A great detective taught me to be leery of them years ago. The dates are too close, almost overlapping in that period. Considering your ideas, could something like this have happened? First, Mr. Buchanan kills himself in late 1929, when all the money is gone, poof, just like that. Your brother, Rob, has to leave the Point, and he and Granny have to come back to Oklahoma. It takes John William a few months to somehow learn his former wife is widowed and back home with his father. He decides he needs to re-establish a relationship with his family and sets out to contact his dad to test the waters, but something happens...sudden death, a change of heart, something...something we simply don't know about, maybe preventing the reunion and somehow the painting gets lost in events of the day, covered up and forgotten."

He appeared lost in thought for a moment. "That offers some possible answers, but it still leaves a lot of questions, bud. Once again why would he decide on sending a painting instead of a letter or coming himself? And how in the name of hell does it wind up in the back seat of a Cajun mobster's car in Lafayette, Louisiana?"

"What about Buchanan himself, Dad? Could he have played some part in all this?" I asked.

"I can't imagine anything not on the up and up with Mr. Buchanan. He was an amiable man, kind-hearted and good to me, Robert, and Shelby. He always gave us anything he felt we needed, almost anything we wanted, even got all three of us into West Point, and he treated Momma like a queen."

"Okay," I said, "let's take Mr. Buchanan out of the equation for the moment and think."

"I am thinking, boy, but we have eighty-six years' worth of time covering up any potential answers that might be lying around…good thing we're professional detectives, ain't it?"

"Damn good thing," I grinned. "Or else we'd just be sitting around as lost as Ned in the first reader."

He laughed softly.

"Okay, how about the location? How does John William get out of prison in McAlester, Oklahoma and wind up in Lafayette, Louisiana? Is he even physically there, or does the painting somehow wind up there without him? There's no return address on the wrapping after all. I'd reckon there are some traces of him still lingering in one or both of those places if he actually went to Louisiana."

"Good a place to check as any," he said. "I'll get a hold of Tommy Moon again, see what he thinks. I suppose you have some contacts at Big Mac, guess we're gonna have to figure in some travel expense, huh?"

I laughed. "No worry, I work pretty cheap, and I can just bill you. Will that be cash, check, or credit card, sir?"

"Take it outta what you owe me," he said and lifted his boots up on the desk.

"Ha… Don't think I'll ever get that side of the deal square. So you think we need to start in McAlester first?"

"I'm retired," he grinned. "You and Brant are the brains behind this operation now, but if I was you, I'd head there first, then hook it down to Lafayette, Louisiana. And I know if Momma was still here, she'd say Senator McBride was tied in to all this somehow, and we better check him out, too."

"According to Granny, the McBrides were responsible for everything bad that happened, from WWI to the present," I said.

Dad chuckled his soft chuckle again. "You ever know her to be wrong much?"

"Nope."

"Me either," he laughed out loud. "Me either."

"So since McCurtain County is McBride stomping grounds, it goes on the look-around list," I said, "Pittsburgh County as well. I want to see the records on the prison break when John William Wallace was allegedly killed."

He grinned. "I guess business is down right now, huh? You've just got nothing else to do?"

I tried to ignore him.

"We might as well go ahead pull Brant off the case of that Republican congressman chasing young unsuspecting males around the City, put Wayne Ray and maybe Debbie on it," I offered. "The congressman's wife's not in a big hurry to catch him just yet, until she's got all her ducks in a row anyway. We were looking at another week or two there regardless. You know Brant will want in on this, and I sure as hell want him with me when we head down south to Louisiana."

He gulped the last of his coffee down. "*I sure as hell* want him with you, too, boy."

"If there's even a hint of trouble, who else would you want to have my back, Dad?"

"Me," he answered quick enough, "but those days are gone, bud. Spenser had Hawk; I reckon you can have the most dangerous Indian on the planet."

"I think you're supposed to say Native American nowadays, Pops."

"Ira Bluesoldier was a full blood Osage, and he called himself an Indian; I'm a good chunk a Choctaw, I reckon I can say Indian if I want to."

I just smiled and nodded.

Dad reached for his empty coffee mug. "Anyway Brant's as good as Parker made Hawk out to be in all those Spenser books, so call him; get his butt back to Oklahoma pronto."

I took the mug and filled it with more coffee and handed it back to him. "I'll head up to Big Mac tomorrow. I don't need anyone with me yet, at least not in the relative safety of Pittsburg County."

"Much obliged," he said, taking the mug.

"That stuff'll kill you," I said and smiled at his low grunt. "I'll circle back and pick up Brant before heading to McCurtain County, that's still the Territories as far as I'm concerned. That should give him plenty of time to get the guys up to speed on our Republican friend."

"Good enough," he smiled. "But I wouldn't call Deb a guy. She might take offense and kick your tail."

"Payback for my 'Native American' remark, huh?" I grinned. "Well, I stand corrected...our employees."

He sipped his coffee. "Good boy, I'll feel better with the both of you heading for Louisiana together. Guess I better call Tommy back and let him know you and Brant are headed to New Orleans to see him and Jaxon. I've just got a funny feeling about this."

"Me and Brant on Bourbon Street, just like old times."

"Yeah, boy," he shook his head. "I'll keep some bail money on hand. And you two keep both eyes open and watch each other's backs."

"I'll be the one having to take care of him once we make the Big Easy, you know."

He snorted. "I don't think anyone has had to take care of Brantley since he was about five...you either for that matter."

"Yep, I'm cut from tough leather, or so I've been told anyway."

"Tough enough," Dad grinned. "But you don't have eyes in the back of that thick skull of yours, so be smart. Good Lord, you two boys are a perfect match. New Orleans may never recover. May God forgive me for unleashing y'all on 'em."

I sat back down in the leather client chair. "My skull is genetically designed."

"You better hope so," he said, rubbing the bridge of his nose with both hands.

"You ride in with Janie in the mornings. She'll pick you up and you can read, play on the computer, help her keep the riffraff in line in case Debbie and Wayne Ray run into any unforeseen problems or whatever, and I'll roll for McAlester in the morning if you'll bring Brant up to speed once he gets here."

"As long as you got cable in the office, we're in business. I gotta watch the western channel at least once a day. It's in the cowboy code somewhere."

"Not a problem, Kimo Sabe," I smiled to see him so alive. "We got cable in my office, and the Yankees aren't blacked out on the MLB channel. You'll be in hog heaven."

He leaned all the way back in my chair and smiled his big Okie smile. "Yep, my trusty sidekick, I will be, and Janie's not a smart-ass like you are. She loves and adores me. All will be right in my kingdom. You two yahoos just try to be safe way down yonder in New Orleans."

"Just don't get too used to it. Remember that's my desk that I always find you sitting behind in my office."

"Then get up earlier. If I could get my feet up on it a little easier, you'd find me with my boots resting here every day. I believe I was the one who bought it anyway, wasn't I? Uh-huh."

I couldn't think of a clever comeback, so I conceded the point and shut up before he made me feel any dumber.

I knew he was feeling better, feeling the sense of the chase about to begin, the adrenaline rush of attacking the problem physically since the mental part was winding down, but I also understood the urgency of time pressing him forward, the looming specter peering over his shoulder.

Brant and I had forever, but his forever was fading fast. This had to take the top of the list in our priorities. Other areas of interest would have to keep for the time being.

Still he looked damned good, strong and healthy, sitting there. Hell, I almost expected him to adjust his cap, light his pipe and say, "Quick, Watson, the game's afoot."

I picked the landline telephone up from the desk and dialed Brant's number.

6

MCCURTAIN COUNTY, INDIAN TERRITORY, JUNE 1903

RENA WAS PUSHING the mules hard with Lucy and the baby in the wagon beside her. John William was behind them in Levi and Lucy's wagon with Levi's body lying in the back, wrapped in a tarp.

They hadn't been gone from Eagletown much more than an hour when John spotted the riders in the distance coming hard behind them and called out for Rena to pull up.

"Whoa, Numbers, Leviticus; whoa, mules, whoa," she shouted at the big mules, tugging back on the reins.

Just days earlier, when they were leaving Arkansas, Levi had laughed at the mules' names and asked if Rena knew where Genesis, Exodus, and Deuteronomy were. The unexpected flash of memory made her tear up again.

She was almost as broken-hearted as Lucy. The terrible realization of life's uncertainty was overwhelming, and she found herself thinking she wanted to shoot that bastard, McBride, right between the eyes herself.

John hopped down, went to the back of the wagon, and retrieved his .44-40, still lying beside Levi where the farmer had laid it. He checked the tether to both Levi's gelding and his buckskin, then walked up to where Rena and Lucy were sitting in the front wagon.

"Riders comin'," he said. "Three of 'em, looks like."

"John William, what's happening?" Rena asked, her voice breaking slightly.

"I shouldn't a mentioned Poppa working for Judge Parker," John told her. "I think these men mean to take me back with them, or maybe worse."

He handed her Levi's Winchester.

"Put this where you can reach it, but don't touch it unless you have to."

"Oh, Johnny," Lucy said, starting to cry harder again.

Rena covered the rifle beside her leg with the folds of her dress and tried to keep a brave face.

"Both of you, be strong. Stay quiet and follow my lead. I don't aim to go nowhere."

He placed his own rifle along the leather straps of the trace chains and began to act as if he was working on the trace chain on the outside mule as the three riders came riding up.

Franklin McBride was on a nice bay horse with his shotgun lying across his saddle in front of him, another man wearing a badge with a big Colt pistol on his hip, was riding a good-looking sorrel mare, and a third fellow with a big droopy red mustache, wearing two guns, was on a little bay gelding.

John was pretty sure the smaller fellow with the mustache and gunfighter rig was "Little Red" Ivers, a known gunman in Indian Territory and Arkansas as well. The pistol on his right was a .44 Colt and the one on his left matched it but was inverted, with the back of the handle facing John William.

The smaller two-gun man crossed his arms in a relaxed manner and leaned forward on his saddle horn as the man with the badge dismounted while McBride sat quietly, his right hand on the shotgun.

"Howdy, Mr. Wallace," the badge man said. "I'm Constable Aldean from Eagletown. Mr. McBride here has informed me of the problem y'all had on his property back yonder outside of town."

Lucy and Rena sat, maybe too scared to speak. It was almost like they weren't even there. No one looked at them or spoke to them.

John William nodded to the men without speaking and held his ground beside the mules as if pausing a moment from the trace chain repair.

"We need you to come back to town and help us with a bit of paperwork, if'n you don't mind," the constable continued, smiling broadly. "Won't take but a little bit."

"Well, Constable," John said after a brief pause. "We got two wagons and only these two women to drive if I leave, and there's the babe to boot. It'll be getting dark soon, and we were looking to travel straight on through for a couple more hours, maybe camp in Arkansas. We got kin in De Queen. I can head back first thing in the morning once I get the ladies settled in place."

"Can't let you do that, Mr. Wallace, no offense, but you get to Arkansas and..."

"I reckon Mr. McBride told you my father used to be with Judge Parker in Fort Smith before the judge passed. Dad's a lawman in Arkansas now. I assure you, Constable Aldean, I'll be back tomorrow."

McBride sat silent in his saddle. The other fellow still leaned forward on his pommel where he'd been since they first rode up.

"The ladies could just camp here, Mr. Wallace, and..."

"I just don't see the urgency in my returning with y'all right this minute," John William broke in. "Shouldn't matter much when we do any paperwork. Mr. McBride made a mistake thinking my friend was stealing from him. I'll write out a document saying he had no ill intent. Bad things just sometimes happen, wasn't like he was laying for him."

"I know, Mr. Wallace, but..." the constable started again.

"We're wasting daylight, Aldean," the man with the mustache spoke for the first time, still without moving off the saddle pommel, "might as well get to it and..."

The rifle shot sounded out of nowhere, the second life-ending blast of that day, and the little gunman fell sideways out of his saddle, silenced in midsentence.

Without any warning, John William had whipped the rifle with one hand from behind the leather on the trace chains and shot him square in the breastbone. Constable Aldean was already whirling back toward John, drawing his Colt, and John had no choice. He levered another round into the chamber and shot Aldean in the chest before the constable could get his pistol up good but not before he discharged it once. The shell grazed John William's temple and left a deep burn back over his left ear.

It was suddenly quiet again. McBride lay in the dirt where his horse had thrown him, and two of the three horses were running hard back to the west. The gunfighter groaned once as McBride jumped to his feet holding the shotgun. Aldean was dead as dead could be, unmoving dead, his Colt Peacemaker still in his hand.

When McBride realized John was aiming the .44-40 at him, he threw his shotgun down and began to beg. "I'm sorry, Wallace, I'm sorry."

"I reckon you are," John William said in a hoarse almost-whisper. "You bastards were gonna kill me, and now you're not. I'm gonna kill you."

He was angry and he was hurt and he'd had enough. He kept seeing Levi's lifeless face and the farmer's remorseless eyes after he'd shot Levi.

McBride glanced at the gunfighter as the man's last breath rattled out.

"They were just gonna scare you, Wallace, that's all. I told Aldean, and he went and got Ivers, said U.S. Marshals outta Fort Smith would be on me if we didn't..."

"Kill me?" John finished for him.

McBride was near tears. "No, just scare you out of any ideas you might have."

"That man kills people." John Wallace pointed the .44-40 barrel at Ivers on the ground. "He doesn't scare them, and he doesn't do it for free, you sonuvabitch. Were you gonna kill the women and the baby, too?"

He was almost growling now.

"No!" the farmer almost screamed. "I mean I wasn't going to kill anyone... I just..."

"Was gonna let that bastard do it," John William finished for him again, gesturing with his rifle barrel again at the man on the ground who was now just as dead as the Eagletown constable.

McBride stretched his hands up even higher into the air as John William pointed the gun straight at his face

"No, no, no...I'm giving up," McBride began to cry. "I... I... You can't shoot an unarmed man, Wallace."

"You did," John said calmly, and the back of McBride's skull exploded. He crumpled beside the gunfighter.

There was a sudden, almost eerie silence, the smell of burnt gunpowder still hanging acrid in the air.

Reba and Lucy sat stunned into silence, holding each other, the baby between them. Thankfully neither team had tried to bolt during the melee. Both were visibly shaken by the sudden violence, but neither questioned the actions, at least not out loud. Lucy cried softly as the baby wailed for a few moments until she soothed it.

John William regretted that shot for the rest of his life; sometimes, years later, at night he'd wake up with the sound of the rifle shot ringing in his ears. But stone, once thrown, can't be called back and some things just can't be undone, a hard lesson learned.

John took the holster and guns off the gunfighter, picked up Constable Aldean's Colt and McBride's shotgun. He probably would have taken Aldean's mare that was still there, but she was just skittish enough that he couldn't get close enough to her.

As John stowed the weapons in the back of the wagon, Lucy continued crying softly, "Oh, Johnny, oh, Johnny," she sobbed, sitting beside Rena and holding Isaac.

Patting Lucy's arm softly, Rena breathed deeply and collected her strength. She knew she had to be strong. Their survival now depended on her doing what needed to be done.

She stepped down from the wagon seat and touched John lightly on his left cheek, tuning his face to better see the wound on his temple where the constable's shot had creased John's skin and took a strip of his hair back above his ear. It barely bled as he ran his fingertips gently down the furrow, but it was plenty sore to the touch.

"No time for anything else, girls," he said. "Those horses will show up somewhere soon, and there'll be somebody after us before we know it. We gotta roll for Arkansas right now."

"Let me put some salve on the burn, John William. It's gonna scar bad, and it'll hurt worse soon," Rena begged as he started to turn away.

He paused and kissed her lightly on the forehead.

"Just hand me the tin. I'll smear it on for now. Get the mules going and don't stop for anything, darlin'. We gotta make the Musgrove's place in De Queen before they catch us."

Rena climbed back up beside Lucy and tossed him the tin of salve. He took two fingers, dipped a swath of the balm, and winced as he coated the wound before mounting the seat in the rear wagon again while Rena secured the rifle behind the seat in her wagon.

They rolled hard for Arkansas without looking back, leaving the bodies lying in the dirt behind them, Aldean's mare still standing near the wreckage.

Life, for them all, would never be the same again.

7

BRANTLEY BLUESOLDIER was a striking man; he looked like a Charles Russell painting, brown-skinned, dark-haired, muscled and athletic, a former Navy Seal. We'd been friends ever since we were born. I honestly couldn't recall my life without Brantley in it.

His father, Ira Bluesoldier, a full blood Osage, was the Indian half of Cowboys and Indians Investigations and Protective Services while William Matthew Wallace was the cowboy half. Both men served together as Deputy U.S. Marshals, becoming best friends during the Civil Rights days of the Kennedy and Johnson administrations until they retired Dad in '71 and Ira in '73. My father called Ira a force of nature.

Brant's mom, Regina, twenty years younger than Ira, was the force behind the throne, along with my mom at C&I when it all started back in 1974. She endowed both Brant and myself with an early exposure to the classics: Willie Nelson, Johnny Cash, Kris Kristofferson, Jerry Jeff Walker, Jimmy Buffett, Jackson Browne, and of course, Waylon Jennings. Music started every day at C&I Investigative and Protective Services as long as she and Momma were there.

While Regina and my mom were becoming close, even before the business started, being only two months older than Brant, he and I became brothers. Mom was fifteen years older but instantly adopted Regina as a little sister, and they both became integral parts of the early C&I days. The business would never have made it if not for them.

Brant picked up his cell on the second or third ring. "You rang, boss?"

"Glad you finally figured out who's boss," I said. "Drop what you're doing as soon as possible and get into the offices pronto. Don't screw around. We've got a major change in agendas. New case, you're gonna love it, road trip, bro."

"Not a problem in the world, Mick, I'll be there in less than an hour. You know I wasn't serious about that boss thing, right, boss?"

No questions, no complaints, no bull, he just rolled with the punch and moved, one among the many reasons I was so fond of Brant. Absolute trust was another.

True to his word, he walked into my office about forty-five minutes later.

"It sure took you long enough to get awake," I said.

"Napping at some young unsuspecting girl's place no doubt."

"No napping was involved," he said as seriously as the man on the five o'clock news. "Nor was she unsuspecting or too young."

I just nodded.

"Actually I was just coming back from Sherman," he said, "where I was watching the local Republican lecher take his intern across state lines when you called me."

I opened a drawer where I usually kept my contraband candy bars hidden. They were missing. "Hard to keep up with you heathen Redskins just living off my paychecks and drinking my beer," I said. "And apparently stealing my Snickers bars."

"Racist," snarled Brant. "Janie found your stash last week, dude. You are busted."

"Damn it," I said. "Well, hell, get hold of Debbie or Wayne Ray, either one, and give them all you've got on our esteemed congressman. I want you with me on something new."

He smiled broadly.

"You and me together again, boy, this must be big. Someone take a shot at the president?"

"Not yet," I said. "This is about Dad."

He tossed me a Snicker out of his jacket pocket. "You know your Dad is my dad, too, now. Fill me in, brother."

"Okay, I'm going to McAlester in the morning to check on Dad's father, John William Wallace's prison records. You get Debbie and/or Wayne Ray up to snuff on our piece of shit you've been surveilling."

"That may take a while; he's a pretty sick puppy for such a stalwart, family-values Christian. If his intern wasn't of age and I wasn't sure the relationship was consensual, I'd have busted the sorry bastard myself already."

"One of or both, Deb and Wayne Ray can get it finished up. Me and you are both going to Broken Bow when I get back, then south to Louisiana to talk with an old colleague of Dad's."

"So I get the whole story from the boss and we plan out the details while you're not in our way, right?"

I started to toss the wrapper in the trash can, then thought it wiser to put it in my pocket. "I thought I was the boss?"

"Yeah, we try to let you think that. I been here almost ten years longer ya know. I just let you run some stuff because you're older and getting feeble, keep you safe in the office, outta harm's way," Brant said in his best stoic Redman voice. "Janie finds that wrapper, you're on your own," he grinned.

"Just shut up, and I'll give you all we've got right now, which isn't a whole helluva a lot, but first make sure everyone is up on the job switches. I don't want our people being surprised about the good congressman's habits."

"Won't take long, Wayne Ray can handle it by himself probably, but Debbie can help if we can spare her. She's about to wrap up the Jackson file, I think."

Both were competent investigators. Wayne Ray Marlow was a former Grayson County sheriff before losing the election after three terms when he arrested the son of the wrong guy. Debbie Reyes was about as average, mild-looking housewife type as they come but a former military police sergeant, capable of blending in or kicking butt whichever was needed, so we would be all right.

"Have you thought about Daniel?" Brant asked.

Our long-time buddy Daniel Letts was running for governor, and Brant or I one have been accompanying him as security on the campaign trail.

"There's a big fundraiser coming up, think you can get Dean Masters over to the Daniel's campaign offices tomorrow? We'll hire him to fill in for us as security chief for now. Get someone you trust to go with him; make him a big scary bastard, if at all possible, since Dean's only a little scary bastard. Assure Daniel we'll be back as soon as we get this taken care of. Tell him it's for Dad, and he'll be fine with the change."

Brant laughed, "Wow, takes two guys to replace me, and one of 'em has to be a big scary fucker."

"As long as one doesn't have to be uglier, we'll be okay. I don't think we could find an uglier one. I know we couldn't find two," I said.

"I'm telling your daddy you're being mean to me again," Brant grinned.

"Okay, run to the big guy," I laughed. "Might as well catch him now; he's on his way here."

"Keep it up and I'll tell Janie, too," he grinned. "And I know all your stash areas, too."

I grinned. "This is a big deal for Dad, Brant. The painting has brought up some things that might have been better off left in the past, but who knows. He'll fill you in for starters, at least as much as he's told me so far. I want to find out as much as we can and keep him constantly in the loop. Tommy Moon, his old buddy, is expecting us in New Orleans early next week."

We both stood. Brant gave me a shoulder punch and we eased out to the reception area.

"I'll check out McAlester, got a meeting set up there to research some of the details in John William's incarceration and the circumstances surrounding his death, see if I can uncover any discrepancies in the official report and family history," I said.

"Boy, ain't it cool when you break out the detective talk?" Brant whistled. "Makes me want to read a Mickey Spillane novel."

Rolling my eyes and exhaling deeply, I said, "After McAlester tomorrow, I'll pick you up here. We're meeting Mason McBride in his McCurtain County offices before we head on down to Louisiana."

"You seriously think McBride might be involved in this?" Brant asked, squinting one eye at me.

"I don't know. Anything is possible, I suppose. Reckon we'll have to figure it all out. Now go make some calls, get the other yahoos in place, then get with Dad and let him fill you in on what he thinks. He wanted to tell you himself, so listen and I'll get your take on it later."

"Whooo, Mickey, The Big Easy, Bourbon Street, and Dixie Beer, you remember the last time we were down there?"

"Yep, but the statute of limitations has run out. I don't think they'll remember you or prosecute now."

"Not me I'm worried about, bro, that Cajun girl's pa probably don't hold to no statute of limitations."

"Just talk to Dad, I got to make some calls before tomorrow."

"We'll get this done and have a blast doing it. I'm ready to have a Dixie already," he said as he walked out of my office heading for his.

"We'd be fools not to," I said in my best Robert Urich voice.

Brant closed the door behind him with a soft laugh.

8

I PULLED THE JEEP into the parking lot at "Big Mac," where I was supposed to meet Nola Munson. She was in charge of records and had been working on Oklahoma State Penitentiary files for the past several years, trying to organize and convert old hard-copy data to computer files. Ah, technology.

Janie had contacted her earlier, and she'd promised to put together all the information she could find concerning my grandfather's prison time, including his death as an inmate there back in 1916.

The pleasant, bespectacled lady at the front desk pushed a button notified Ms. Munson I had arrived, then politely directed me to a door around the corner of her desk.

Nola was in her office waiting when I arrived, dressed in a tailored beige jacket with a red blouse and matching beige skirt that showed off her legs very nicely...purely a professional observation on my part as a trained investigator.

"Mr. Wallace, so nice to meet you," she said smiling, reaching across her desk.

Her nails were immaculately done in a brilliant shade of red that reminded me of OU crimson.

I removed my wide-brimmed Stetson and nodded, nothing like a good cowboy hat to impress the ladies. I had on my favorite 501's, God's gift to man, broken-in and just a tad worn, a royal blue short-sleeved shirt, and my favorite pair of Tony Lama full quill ostrich boots, also broken-in just right. I was going for that modern-intellectual-progressive-cowboy-who-was-comfortable-yet-stylish-in-cowboy-country look...or something like that.

"Likewise, ma'am," I flashed my most spectacular smile, the one guaranteed to get me all the answers I required.

"Please have a seat," Nola smiled again. "I've got the official record for you right here, and I've made you a copy to take with you. I think you'll find it interesting. I know you'll want time to look the whole file over at your leisure."

I sat.

"Your grandfather's records were…were a little different," she began with a bit of hesitance.

I nodded.

"Different, how?"

"The original report concerning the death of John William Wallace was hand-written by Simpson Burnett in July 1916. Mr. Burnett was a seventy-four-year-old former Confederate soldier and head of work detail guards until his death in 1917. He was in charge of the work detail where your grandfather was outside the walls, and unfortunately, met his death. I've come across Mr. Burnett's reports several times while logging the old records."

I sat patiently, holding the manila folder, thinking she had really nice eyes.

"What's unusual is that I found several erasures and corrections in a slightly different handwriting. I've highlighted those in your copies, but it appears to me that someone wasn't satisfied with the original reports, and some of Mr. Burnett's conclusions may have been…uh…altered."

"Any idea why that would've happened, ma'am?"

She smiled.

"Please call me Nola, Mr. Wallace."

I maintained my manly, intellectual, progressive cowboy detective composure but just barely.

"Call me Mickey, Nola," I said. "And tell me more about the modifications in Mr. Burnett's report, if you can please."

"I'll tell you all I know, but I'm afraid I can't tell you much. I have no clue who made the changes or why, but they weren't terribly obvious, almost like they were meant to be a covert act rather than a later-day correction. Something seems off. I've never found as many changes in any of the other handwritten reports, especially Mr. Burnett's. He was always concise and exact but in this...."

"Erasures and changes aren't very commonplace in these old reports?"

"They're fairly common, really, but honestly it's the only time I've ever noticed it in this manner to this extent. I haven't a clue as to why it occurred in this document, way too much water under the bridge, Mr. Wallace, but I'd say it's definitely unusual."

"Mickey," I smiled.

"Mickey."

"Mickey Warren. My dad was a big Yankee fan. I'm named after Mickey Mantle, but he's an Okie, too, so I got Warren for a middle name after Warren Spahn."

"And you're a private investigator rather than a centerfielder?"

"Hard to imagine, huh?"

"Not really, you've got enough Tom Selleck about you to sell me on the whole Magnum P.I. thing."

I flashed the grade A aw shucks smile.

"The account of those prisoners missing after the riot in which your grandfather died appears to have been altered where it comes to listing the names of the missing," she continued.

"Originally Mr. Burnett cited a guard, Virgil Simms, as being out of place during the riot, but by the end of the report, Simms appears to be almost heroic."

"How's that happen?"

"Well, interestingly enough that's where some of the erasures seem to be most evident, and the narrative takes on a different tone, possibly even a different handwriting."

"Someone trying to cover up for Simms or maybe Burnett?" I wondered aloud.

"I really can't say, but Simms comes off better in this part of the report. He's credited with shooting an escaping inmate after another escapee has clubbed a guard and released six other prisoners. Two of the six got away, as did an Arcelus Monroe, who apparently released the other inmates after the fight in which your grandfather and six others were killed."

"So Simms is a hero?"

"It would appear he single-handedly prevented a full-scale break, but oddly Mr. Burnett has been a bit critical of him in the early parts of his report. Then in the altered portions, he lavishes praise on him and recommends a citation," Nola said.

"Can you see if Simms actually received any commendation for his actions during the riot?"

"I thought of that," she smiled. "It's in the report I prepared for you. No record of any such citation exists, and Simms is off the prison payroll by the end of the month in which the escapes occurred."

I nodded again.

"It sounds to me like Simms was not on Mr. Burnett's good list at first, maybe never was, until some mysterious unknown entity put him on it."

"It's certainly odd, but I can't say what happened, Mickey. Mr. Burnett died in a logging accident on another work detail three months later. This was one of the last reports he ever filed. I really don't know what else to say."

"Lot of years gone by, Nola, I couldn't say what happened either, but I may have a few guesses. I'll let you know if I figure it all out. Was there an investigation of any sort following the escapes and riot?"

"Not much of one," she said. "When Mr. Burnett died and all but two of the escapees were accounted for, it seems most of the interest faded away."

"Too bad, but I guess that's to be expected."

"Yes, state senators conducted a congressional review and concluded that Simpson Burnett, probably due to his age, made a series of errors in overseeing his work detail that allowed a riot and attempted escape."

"This investigation took place after Burnett's death, I'm guessing," I said.

"And I'm also guessing that one of the senators was Davis McBride."

"You are a detective after all, aren't you, Mick?"

She smiled widely.

"Well, I'm no Tom Selleck, but I try."

I picked up the manila folder, replaced the Stetson on my head, tipped the brim, smiled, and stretched my hand back across her desk.

"Better saddle up, I reckon, if I'm going to make Broken Bow by nightfall."

She took my hand and flashed her own Cameron Diaz smile back at me.

"If you find anything else on this, I'd really appreciate a call; you've got my cell number, right? I know a lot of these old files get lost," I said as I released her hand.

"Count on it, Mickey. There are a couple of huge gaps where reports should have been filed by other guards," Nola said, "but in almost a hundred years, who knows where they've gone."

"Just look for me, okay, and let me know if you find anything at all."

"I sure will, cowboy," she smiled, almost wickedly I thought.

"I'm easy to find," I smiled and touched the brim of my Stetson again with two fingers as I stepped out and closed the door.

9

"**WHAT DO YOU THINK** we're gonna get out of Mason McBride?" Brant asked as we unloaded the ice chests and duffle bags from the back of the Jeep.

I shrugged and set a cooler on the front porch of the little cabin just outside of Broken Bow that we'd taken for the night and next day. "Don't have a clue."

Brant reached in the ice chest, pulled out two cold *Rolling Rock Extra Pales*, and handed me one.

"As long as we have a plan," he laughed, unlocked the door, and stepped inside with his duffle.

Cold beer, great stuff, useful for deep introspection and crime solving, I finished another with the last of my peanut butter crackers that I'd picked up at the Easy Mart on our way out of Durant.

"If we had any gear, we could fish," Brant offered, looking out at the lake.

"Yep," I said.

"Yep," he came back.

He finished his beer and got another from the chest.

"This Wallace – McBride feud's been cool for quite a while," I said, "kinda hate to see it kick back up."

"Does Will really think the senator's involved in this somehow?"

"Hell if I know, Brant; he's not saying much right now. I think he's worried we can't figure the whole mess out before… You know…before he's gone."

"I can understand that. I mean we're talking about his dad maybe. We'd want to know if we were in his boots."

I nodded. "Yep."

"He's been a father to me, Mick, ever since Dad passed, treated me just like his own. So if he's gotta know, I'm with him and you all the way."

"Nothing me and you can't handle, bro. I got the brains; you got the…naw, hell, I got the body, too. You're just shit outta luck. Hand me another beer."

"Kiss my Osage ass, white boy."

"There you go with the reverse racism again. I am appalled," I said.

Brant twisted a lid off the *Rolling Rock* and handed it to me.

"I may have to speak with the senator tomorrow myself about your discriminatory behavior. Y'all can't keep kicking the Redman around."

I looked east toward Arkansas off the little porch. It was undoubtedly designed for catching sunrises, but I suspected we'd miss tomorrows. Brant wasn't an early riser any more than I was, and we still had beer.

"You know we're not that far from where your grandfather shot Franklin McBride and started the whole mess," Brant said.

"No, we're not, just a little north of here, somewhere outside of Eagletown," I said and took a long pull on the *Rolling Rock*.

It was quiet for a moment, just cicadas singing in the trees and a light breeze on the lake.

"You want me to go in with you to see McBride?" Brant said, breaking the silence.

"You hang around here, enjoy the lake. I think he'll be more relaxed with just me. It shouldn't take long; there's not much I need to say, and we can grab a bite to eat and head out for New Orleans the next day."

"Yeah, sure, keep the poor relatives out of sight."

"Cut a pole from a tree, find some string and fish; you people are supposed to be good at that."

"You people… I know I'm filing a complaint now. Your ass is mine."

"Okay, so you want a cheeseburger to soothe your wounded feelings?"

"Hell, I'm hurt. We Osage are a proud people. I want a steak and a damned big one."

"Well, we Choctaw are a poor people, and we're on a budget. Let's cruise into the Dairy Queen before it gets dark, come back, and eat here. There's bound to be a ball game on TV, don't want to waste cable."

"Damn, more employee abuse."

"At least you're back to acknowledging who the boss is. Do you want a burger now, or are we gonna open the Vienna sausages?"

Brant grinned.

"Cheeseburgers it is, but you gotta drive, make some amends to my people."

"Just shut up and get in the Jeep, Miss Daisy."

We picked up our Glocks, holstered them, locked the cabin door, and rolled toward the DQ.

10

ARKANSAS – OKLAHOMA BORDER, 1903

JOHN WILLIAM WALLACE'S HEAD *was on fire; the salve had soothed the pain a little at first, but he was hurting now. The wagons were just too slow, and he was beginning to realize they wouldn't make De Queen by nightfall.*

He wiped the sweat from around his wound and called out to Rena to pull the team over again.

She cleaned and redressed the burn on John's temple while he laid out his plan.

"Doll, Lucy's gonna have to fix the babe a place where she can reach him and still drive the horses. You take the mules and keep the wagons rolling east. Don't stop for anything. Y'all have to make Arkansas."

Lucy walked up holding Isaac. "What are you going to do, John William; what are you thinking? I can't drive those horses, not with Levi…gone. We need you with us."

"Lucy, I'm gonna take the rifle, plenty of shells, one of the pistols and fort up in those rocks right there on this curve. Those horses will bring someone looking for the riders, and that someone will come looking for us before we can reach the Musgrove place."

"Maybe the horses won't be found, John, and if they are, you don't know how many men will come…" Rena started to argue.

Lucy started to cry and plead, "No, Johnny, no, we can't… I can't. I just can't do it."

John looked at Rena and took Lucy gently by the arm and led her to the wagon.

"You can, Lucy; you have to. You have to do it for Isaac. You just guide the horses and follow Rena and the mules. You have to, or we're all in deep trouble. We'll fix little Isaac a nest right there behind you where you can see him, and if you really need to, stop and tend him for a minute, you can."

Rena knew her husband well. She realized the argument was over and turned to friend, "We'll do this, Lucy, and John William will meet us in De Queen. Won't you, Johnny?"

He nodded as he collected Aldean's Peacemaker from the wagon.

"I'm going to take Calavaras up that trail and hobble him. He'll be saddled and ready to run. No one can get up those rocks to get me. I can hold off an army from there. But, hell, I probably won't even need to."

"What if they get by you?" Lucy said in tears.

"They won't," he said. "Now fix that godson of mine up good and safe and get ready to roll."

He hugged Lucy for a minute, then came to Rena, hugged her tight, and gave her the final part of his plan.

The rocks tumbling off the foothills made a perfect fort. He'd take the topmost point behind the stones and hold off anyone who tried to come up or come past on the road below. He could delay anyone long enough to ensure that Rena and Lucy would make it to De Queen. If things got too hot, he promised that he'd scramble over the top, unhitch his buckskin stud, named for Mark Twain's short story about the jumping frog, and ride for Arkansas by a secondary route.

He kissed her. "Calavaras would never let me down, darlin', you know that."

"He loves that horse almost as much as he loves me," Rena thought, trying to smile.

If no one arrived by dark, he swore on all he held holy that he'd scoot out as fast as he could and ride hard to meet them at the Musgrove place in De Queen.

So Rena kissed him again, gently touched the bandage, and stroked his curly hair.

"You just get your skinny rear back to me as quick as possible, John William Wallace, or I'll come back after you, and I won't be gentle," she said.

In a matter of minutes, they had Isaac fixed in place and Lucy was sitting, ready to roll. Rena mounted the wagon in front of her. They both looked back once more as they moved slowly east down the road.

Once they made the bend in the road, John led his buckskin up the slope to a fairly clear spot just above and behind the rocks and tethered her to a tree. He took his saddle bags and the .44-40 and fixed a good place behind some boulders, piling a few decent-sized stones in just the right place to make a shooting hole. Content with his cover, he settled down to make sure he had a good field of fire at the road below where it curved around the tumbled rocks.

He checked the handgun, the ammunition, and some cold biscuits that he had put in the bags. Suddenly hungry he started a biscuit, but after only a bite or two, he decided he'd read a little of the book his father had given him before they left Arkansas, a leather-bound copy of Leaves of Grass by Walt Whitman.

He could read a poem or so and keep an eye on the road for approaching riders.

He hadn't covered but a few pages when a small stone hit the brim of his hat and bounced away.

He looked up…nothing but blue sky and green trees. He hadn't looked down good at the pages again when another pebble hit his hat again.

This time when he looked up, he saw a tall, powerfully-built man with a grey goatee and long greying hair braided back, standing above him holding a long rifle in the crook of his arm, a muzzle loader probably damn near as old as the man was.

"Good book you reading there, son?" the old man asked with a rough chuckle.

"I reckon so. Who the hell are you, and what's it to you?" was the best John could muster up at the time.

"Well, first, I'm Angus McDougald, and second this is my mountain you're on, so I reckon you need to tell me why you're all forted up here with that rifle watching that road down yonder, and while you're at it, you might introduce yourself, so I can decide whether I need to shoot you or not."

He had John William's attention.

"Yes, sir, my name is John William Wallace. I'm from Murphreesboro, and I'm afraid some men will be coming this way to do harm to my wife and our friends trying to get home. They want to take me back to Eagletown or kill me, one; I'm not sure which, maybe both."

"John William Wallace, good Scot's name, I reckon your wife and your friend's wife are the two womenfolk in the wagons carrying the dead fella?"

"My great-grandpa was a Scotsman, I think, but I was born in Arkansas, and how'd you know anyone was dead?" John William asked.

"Son, I'm over seventy, and I ain't stupid. I've smelt a lot a dead folk in my life. Even ones that ain't been gone long got a smell to 'em, and two women alone and you here, I jes' figured he was the man to the other woman. Pure guess on my part."

John explained who the dead man was and told McDougald how McBride had killed Levi for cutting grass near his cornfield in Eagletown and how they were trying to take him back home now to bury him proper.

"Just killed him for cutting grass…that's hard, even for Eagletown," the old man said.

John tilted the brim of his hat down to block the sun a bit more and to hide his eyes a little. "Thought he was stealing corn, or so he said."

"Still piss-poor reason to shoot a man, gotta be more to it than that for a fella to shoot your friend, then chase you all the way to Arkansas."

"He's not chasing us. I killed him. It's a long story."

"Well, John William Wallace, a very learned Scot once said, 'Nae man can tether time or tide.' So I reckon we ain't got time for a long story right now, 'specially if the fellows comin' for you, are them folks riding this way. I imagine I better take the ground t'other side a this road so they can't flank ya."

John William watched the four riders draw closer as the old man melted into the trees.

The riders were coming at a pretty good clip. As they neared the curve, he decided to fire a shot in front of the lead rider to find out just exactly who they were. He reckoned shooting someone for simply riding hard wasn't acceptable.

When the bullet hit the dirt, the rider drew up quick, dismounted, and took cover in the trees off the side of the road. The others did likewise, except for the one boy whose horse reared and threw him hard. John recognized him as the young boy who had been with the farmer, McBride, when he shot Levi. The boy left his rifle lying in the road and bailed behind some rocks with one of the other riders.

The lead horseman peered out from behind a big elm tree toward the rocks where John was hidden.

"That you up there, Wallace?" he yelled.

"Might be, who are you?"

"Davis McBride, that's who. You killed my pa, you low-life son of a bitch, and now I'm gonna kill you and them squaws with you."

"Well, he killed my best friend and set out to have me killed, so I'm not real sorry, and I don't see you killing me any too soon."

"Don't get too cocky, you bastard. There's more of us coming. Pa's horse came home; we found him and Constable Aldean and the other fellow you murdered, sent our cousin for a posse out of Eagletown. I think maybe we'll kill you."

"Come and do it then," came John Williams's voice echoing down out of the rocks.

McBride motioned over at the others, and they fired up at the sound, but John was about as safe as safe could be under the circumstances. When one of the other riders started to move out from behind his tree, John William fired, hitting him in the lower leg. He fell, and two more grabbed him and drug him back behind the trees.

"Andrew, you okay, brother?" Davis McBride called.

"I'm hit in the leg but not bad. Ben and Toby are here with me."

The man's voice came from behind the rocks and trees, where the men had taken cover just off the road.

"I coulda killed him, McBride, but I didn't," John called down. "Y'all need to leave. No way you're coming up these rocks. Just go home, and I'll go back to Arkansas."

"You go to hell," McBride raged back up at the rocks. "I'm killing you and your whole family. Count on it."

He started a flanking move around to the left. John fired at him and missed as he dove behind another tree. Then as Davis McBride was rising to return fire, John William heard what sounded like a small cannon blast from the trees south of him across the road.

McBride toppled backward.

"Davis, oh God, Davis," one of the McBride's yelled from behind the trees where John had them pinned down.

Davis staggered behind another large tree, holding what was left of his rifle. John William could have easily shot him as he took cover away from the direction of the shot that had struck his rifle and knocked him down, but he didn't, an act of kindness he would later come to deeply regret.

At the time, he honestly didn't know why he had held his fire, sick of death maybe, but for whatever reason, he didn't take the shot and allowed McBride to resume cover.

"I'm okay, boys," he heard Davis McBride yell back to his brothers. "My rifle is ruined though, and the son of a bitch has got someone with him, almost killed me."

"You're a lucky bastard, boy," McDougald"s voice came from the dense trees south of John William. "You hadn't a lifted that gun up when you did, I'd be spittin' on your worthless carcass right now."

"Just who in the hell are you anyway, mister?" McBride's voice rose from behind his cover.

"You mean, 'who the hell are we,' you sniveling little shit," the old man's reply came from a point further south. "We be the people gonna bury you and your brothers in these rocks, that's who we be."

There was a brief silence as the McBride's conferred in their cover before Davis yelled up.

"Wallace, we're riding outta here, but you'll get yours. Don't try to chase us. We'll meet the posse from Eagletown. We may not follow you right now any deeper into Arkansas, but someone will. I'll see you dead, you worthless bastard."

John William levered off a volley of shots into the trees McBride was behind, and the muzzle-loader roared again. The other three mounted up, one with the boy on back of his horse while another one brought Davis his horse. He mounted on the run, and they heard him cussing as they rode away.

Wallace sat back behind the stones, watching them ride, the acrid smell of gun smoke still hanging in the air. His knees were weak, and the sky was just beginning to go grey as the sun dropped behind the tall trees.

When he stood up, the old man was there above him again, tobacco stains on either side of the mustache into his beard, his dirty buckskins in need of cleaning, an almost sad look on his face.

"You shoulda kilt that fella, young Wallace," McDougald said. "He needed it. And I reckon he's gonna try you again when he gets a chance."

"Maybe," John said.

"No maybe to it, Buck. I tried to do it for ye, but I missed, and I'm damned sorry I did."

"I wouldn't call it a miss, Mr. McDougald. You just hit him in the rifle."

"He's still a breathing, ain't he? I wudn't aimin' at no rifle, laddie. That's a miss in my book."

"Well, anyway, I figure you saved my bacon, and I'm damn proud you did. If you ever get down to Murfreesboro, I reckon I owe you a beer."

"Too many bastards down there in Murphreesboro, John Wallace, pret' near as many as over there in Eagletown. Sorry, white sonsabitches ev'rywhere you look these days and not but one or two good honest Scots in a hundred of 'em. Can't let 'em go shooting a good Scots boy when I find one in these parts now can I?"

John smiled for the first time that day, "I'm not sure how much a Scotsman I am, but I reckon I'm glad I am what part I am, and I'm in your debt, sir."

"Keep your eyes peeled 'til you're back with your own, John Wallace. Go catch that pretty squaw of your'n and have babies. I'm gonna go find mine back up in these hills and have some more of my own."

John William started up the rocks to the clearing where his horse remained tied. "Yes, sir," he said as he climbed.

The big man touched the brim of his slouch hat. "As a good Scot once said, young Wallace, 'There's Liberty in every blow. Let us do or die.'"

He laughed as John William touched his wide brim and turned to unfasten Calavaras, but when Wallace turned back to look again, the old man was gone into the trees, and soon he could hear him singing off in the distance, "She is a winsome wee thing, She is a handsome wee thing, She is a bonny wee thing, This sweet wee wife o' mine."

John William Wallace shook his head and laughed at the kinder hand of fate that had sent him a savior as he swung a leg up on his pony's saddle to ride fast for Rena and Lucy.

He would never see Angus McDougald again.

11

JANIE HAD scheduled an appointment for me with Mason McBride at 2:00 P.M. in his family's law offices in downtown Broken Bow.

Needless to say, our families were familiar with one another. My grandfather had seen fit to dispatch his great-grandfather to another plane back in the infamous shootout of 1903, at least infamous according to our family lore.

After failing to kill John William Wallace back in the day, Davis McBride, Mason's grandfather, prospered with the family farm he had inherited and later served as an Oklahoma Congressman for over thirty years before finally stepping down not long after WWII. Mason's father had died a hero during WWII in 1942 the same year that his only son was born.

Following in his grandfather's footsteps, Mason served four terms in the Oklahoma Senate and was a possible Republican candidate for governor this coming fall.

I was not intimidated.

A middle-aged, very proper-looking lady greeted me with a professional, yet artificial smile as I entered. "You must be Mr. Wallace. I believe Mr. McBride is expecting you."

She rose and peered in my direction over the glasses balanced on her slender nose. "Let me check. I believe his guests are just leaving."

"Yes ma'am," I said, removing my hat. The name plate on her desk identified her as Stella Stevens.

I'd met Mason McBride before, once back in '91 when as a deputy U.S. Marshal, I had received a citation for shooting a Texan. Normally that's not a big deal in Oklahoma, but this Texan was running guns to a Mexican drug lord, and after all, I'd been wounded in the line of duty in this particular altercation.

As a state senator, he attended the ceremony, just to meet me, he said. Afterwards we talked briefly, and he mentioned he was well aware of our families' oddly linked histories. I'm fairly certain the accounts of the story vary widely from ours in his familial records of the incident.

I guess it was enough to merit a meeting with him on short notice during his preparation for what might be a busy last-minute campaign for governor. At least when Janie inquired, he told her that he had a few minutes before heading off to Tulsa if I wanted to drop by his Broken Bow office at two; he'd be leaving around three.

I reckoned time in Broken Bow must be spent wisely and well, so I had arrived at his offices right at two o'clock.

Miss Stevens returned to usher me back to his office as a couple of expensive suits were leaving. Both appeared to be in a hurry, and neither seemed very impressed with my Tony Lamas nor my Stetson.

He hadn't changed much in the decade since we last met. His hair had just the right amount of grey in the temples, and I figured the Ronald Regan haircut was a must in his party. His suit was tailored to perfection. I could practically see the snake oil dripping from him.

He did not appear intimidated.

He placed his left hand on my shoulder and clasped my right in his best attempt at a manly handshake.

I resisted the temptation to best his grip and shook hands in a normal manner.

He smiled and looked me in the eye. "How are you doing, Mick? Great to see you again."

I returned his gaze, "You, too, Senator."

"Call me Mason," he came back. "What can I help you with, Mick, if you don't mind me calling you Mick."

"Most folks do, Senator. That'll work fine. I'm looking for some information on my late grandfather, John William Wallace."

He looked puzzled.

"I don't know how I can help you there, Mick. All that bad blood between our families was…was all before my time," he stammered. "I'm sure you know as much about it as I do."

I nodded in agreement.

"I know it's all old hat, but if you could use your influence to help me find any information about his prison time and his death, I'd appreciate it," I said.

He regained the good-old-boy smile again. "Have you been to McAlester yet, Mick?"

"Yes, sir, but didn't get a lot of answers there. I just thought you might have contacts with access to some inside info that might help, just looking for old answers to some old questions, ya know."

I good-ol'-boyed it up right back at him as much as I could before I spoke more soberly. "Dad's been diagnosed with stage four cancer, and he's wanting to find out a few things before it's too late."

"I heard about William, really sorry about it, Mick. He's served our state and our nation well, but I just don't know what I can do. I will ask around some offices, see what I can find out. This is all private and just between us though, right, Mick?"

I was trying to count how many times he'd already called me Mick but was still able to answer, "Of course I don't see any need for anything of a public nature here, and I would really appreciate any help you can give me, Senator. It means a lot to Dad, and it would mean a lot to me as well."

"There were some ugly things going on way back then, Mick. I'm sure some bad things happened on both sides of our people. I just don't want to deal with any of that right now in the papers, Mickey. I know you understand."

At least he'd swapped in a 'Mickey' — to break the monotony I guess.

"I think I can speak for all of my folks, Senator. We're just looking at family history right now. I'm gonna be poking around in the past for the next couple of days at least, and I wanted to make you aware of it, ask for your help, and assure you this has nothing to do with your potential race for the governor's mansion. As far as I'm concerned, this would be just between us right now."

His smile was back at full power.

"Good. I'm not a hundred percent committed to running yet, just testing the water, thinking about a possible last-minute entry in the race to save the party. Your buddy, Daniel Letts is kicking our candidate's butt right now in all the polls."

"Yep," I said, smiling.

I wondered if he practiced the smile as he broke it out once more. "Still I really don't want to deal with a magazine or a newspaper article dragging out our old family history right now either, just in case I do step in and give it a run," he said.

I noticed he didn't ask for my vote if he ran, which was good. I was pretty sure he knew I would be voting for Daniel Letts anyway, since we'd been friends ever since way back in Durant Junior High School.

"I gotta run, Mick, big dinner in Tulsa tonight, babies to kiss, flesh to press, you know, but I'll get my staff on this right away, see if we can find any information at all for you."

He was pumping my hand again and reaching for his hat as he tactfully steered me toward the door to his office.

For a guy who hadn't committed a hundred percent, he sure struck me as candidate, if not this term then the next.

I tipped the brim of my Stetson to Miss Stevens as I went out the door. She barely glanced up. Some women are simply impervious to cowboy charm.

In a matter of minutes, I was headed back to the cabin to find Brant and pack our gear. I was pretty certain we wouldn't hear anything back from the good senator any too soon. He needed old news to remain old news right now.

I also knew there were only two Rolling Rocks left in the ice chest when I left. Those would have been consumed by my faithful Indian companion by now, and I wasn't about to journey into foreign lands without sufficient supplies, so a quick stop at the Broken Bow Easy Mart was in order.

I grabbed a couple of six packs of *Landshark* for a change of pace, a couple of bags of ice, some almonds, and a few more packs of peanut butter crackers, can't be too careful. A guy could break down on the road, and where would he be without the basic necessities?

Back at the cabin, Brant was watching the History Channel and waiting patiently, our leather duffle bags already stored in the back of the Jeep, the empty cooler sitting on the front porch.

"Red Sox and Blue Jays game on," he said.

"So no baseball, huh?" I said with dripping sarcasm.

He laughed. "You're as bad as Will."

"Come by it naturally," I said. "Got beer in the sacks, you about ready?"

"Reckon so, Civil War documentary is almost done. I heard the North wins anyway."

I laughed. "Wouldn't be mentioning that where we're heading. I hear it's still a hot topic for debate."

"You bring us supper?" he asked, "or am I to be deprived once again?"

"DQ cheeseburgers on our way outta town, man, your turn to buy." I laughed. "Be late when we get there. You can eat while you drive."

"I think I'll eat while you drive," he said, stowing our duffels in the back of the Jeep.

We iced down the *Landsharks*, opened one apiece for the road, and set the ice chest in the back seat..

"New Orleans, here we come," Brant said as we pulled out onto the road.

I shifted gears and we accelerated down the highway. We still had several hours of drive time before we reached or hotel in the Quarter.

"Put in some Buffett, bro," I said.

"*Changes in Latitudes, Changes in Attitudes* seems like a good way to go," he said and punched play.

12

MURPHREESBORO, ARKANSAS, 1904

THEY BURIED LEVI in the Carroll family cemetery, and Lucy moved in with his parents on the Carroll ranch. The family seemed to be adjusting as well as they possibly could, but Levi, the oldest of eight boys, had been the brightest spark in a huge family fire.

Christmas of 1903 came and went without its usual joyous celebration in the Carroll home. Only the presence of baby Isaac kept Lucy and her brood of in-laws sane.

John William was home again in Arkansas but with no house or land of his own. He and Rena were living with his brother James. John started working in the Wallace Blacksmith Shop after James broke a hand shoeing a surly mule shortly after their return.

It looked like their own land in the Territories was a distant dream for John and Rena as they started to build a small house on Wallace land.

Even John's father, William, was heading back home. Judge Parker had died, and William worked at another forge in Ft. Smith for a while, but Isaac Carroll had persuaded his good friend to return to Murphreesboro to become the police chief. He pulled all the political strings he could when the current chief announced he was retiring. William had served Judge Parker as a deputy and a blacksmith until Parker's death, and Mr. Carroll saw a chance to bring back an ally.

Unlike his father and brother, James Wallace had never left Murphreesboro and had kept the family forge running. Now he would act as police chief until his father returned in a month or so after tying up loose ends in Ft. Smith.

By spring things were returning to normal when a stranger came riding into town asking questions about a certain John William Wallace with whom he wished to speak.

The man wore a nice suit and a fancy set of pistols. He even had little cards printed with his name on them – Preston Edward Allen: Dallas Texas.

The fellow stopped by Isaac Carroll's feed store, the first building on the west end of Main Street, and asked if anyone knew John William Wallace. One of the men loading feed that day happened to be Rena's cousin, David Milner. He told the man that John William left town almost a year ago, then sent his boy running to tell Isaac someone was in town asking about John.

Iscac, still the strategist, had feared this day would come. He sent two of his boys over to the blacksmith shop before the gunman arrived at that end of town and instructed John William to ride out to the Carroll place, where Rena was visiting Lucy and little Isaac, and be on guard until they had determined if the stranger was a threat.

One of the Carroll boys, Jeremiah, hid in the loft of the blacksmith shop with a rifle. Jacob took John's place at the forge beside James, ready for whatever might happen.

John had barely cleared the shop when the stranger arrived. But James Wallace stuck with the preconceived story that John William had never returned to Murfreesboro but had headed for Fort Smith where their father was working.

Allen looked him in the eye and smiled. "Mr. Wallace, I believe your brother came back here, and I am willing to wager that he's still here. Mr. Davis McBride has employed me to find and return him to Indian Territory to stand trial for the killing of Mr. McBride's father. I have accepted 500 dollars already with five hundred more due on his return. I assure you I will return him. Should you happen to see him, tell him I will guarantee his safe return and ride with him to Eagletown, or I will hunt him down and take him back in chains, whichever he so chooses."

James smiled back at the man and said, "Mr. Allen, I'm the acting police here until my father arrives in a week or two, so I reckon you'd best not be taking anyone anywhere without going through the law. I told ya, Brother John's been gone a while now. Best you just go on your way now, sir."

"I'm not certain a brother is an unbiased agent of the law, Mr. Wallace, but I will keep that in mind, sir."

The man handed James one of his cards and left.

Allen continued asking folks there in town about John William. Most of the locals knew the deal, but not everyone loved the Carrolls, nor did everyone care for the Wallaces. So far Preston Allen just hadn't found the right person to sink John William's story and lead the gunman directly to him.

Although he'd never owned another human being in his life and found the institution of slavery personally repugnant, Isaac Carroll had served as a captain in Colonel Newton's cavalry for the Confederacy, where he learned the hard ways of combat. He knew sooner or later Allen would learn John was in Murphreesboro, and there'd be big trouble. He began to hatch a plan, putting the oldest three of his seven remaining sons to watching the gunman, separately at safe distances while he continued to weigh their options. One thing was certain: William Wallace, a former Union cavalry officer, was a good friend, and the Wallace boys had practically grown up on his ranch. They would come to no harm on his watch.

It wasn't but a couple of nights after the stranger arrived when Isaac's oldest remaining son, Jacob, rode up to the Carroll home place with news that Allen was camped on the Jenkins ranch bordering the far east side of their ranch.

Isaac gathered his five oldest boys, two Milner boys, first cousins to Rena, a full-blood Cherokee named Ben Ross who had grown up with Levi and John William, two or three other friends of the family, James, and John William. They all met at the Carroll feed store in town.

"James, you're an officer of the law, and this may not be lawful. Best you stayed here," Isaac Carroll said as the men were preparing to ride out to find Allen.

James pinned his badge on the hitching rail. "Reckon the badge can stay here, I'll just take a leave of absence, 'cause I'm going, sir. He's my brother."

Carroll nodded, and they started for where Preston Allen of Dallas, Texas was camped.

Twenty minutes later, as the sun was setting, they dismounted and proceeded on foot. Isaac deployed the men in a semi-circle with instructions to not shoot unless told and be aware of their friends' positions.

Allen had found a layout where he could fort up pretty well. He had a fire going near an enormous flat rock, maybe four feet thick. His horse was unsaddled and tied behind some other large rocks that rose up high behind him in a natural wall.

"Who goes there?" the gunfighter asked, lifting a pistol as Isaac Carroll stepped toward the camp.

"Don't fire," Isaac said, "I'm here to talk with you concerning John William Wallace."

Allen had been reading Under the Redwoods, Bret Harte's newest book. He marked his page with one of his cards and placed it near his other pistol on the rock. "Just reading Mr. Harte's latest work, I rather enjoy him, don't know why Mr. Twain finds him so offensive. Do you, Mr. Carroll? I presume you are Isaac Carroll."

"I am, sir, but I haven't come to discuss literature with you. I've come to save your life…or take it if you make that necessary."

Most of the men remained back at the edge of the firelight while Mr. Carroll talked with Allen, warning him that they would not allow him to take John William.

Allen placed the handgun down beside its mate and the book. Speaking calmly he said, "I'm afraid I must take him, Mr. Carroll. I have already accepted money, and you sound like an educated man, a man of breeding. You know I have to take him. I am obligated now."

Carroll motioned the others to step up where Allen could see them plainly. All were armed with rifles or shotguns, all pointing at the gunfighter.

He was sitting back against the rock; his handguns were lying on it, his rifle resting against it as well. He never flinched, nor showed any fear at the larger numbers in front of him.

"It is my duty, Mr. Carroll. I have no say in it now, but I would truly like to see the man who killed Little Red Ivers, just to ask him how he managed it."

Isaac motioned to John William, and he stepped forward.

"Why he's just a boy," the gunman said. "Tell me, son. How did you ever manage to kill that rattlesnake and two other armed men?"

"I guess I just got lucky, sir," John replied.

"Well, I'd like to hear the whole story, maybe on our way back to Eagletown. I have no choice but to take you back; however, I assure you I won't allow them to murder you. There will be a trial and…"

"Mr. Allen, you aren't listening, sir," Isaac Carroll broke in. "He's not going back. They would murder him with or without your permission. Any trial would be a sham there in the Territories. McBride's father killed my boy; now he's dead. Call it even, an eye for an eye."

No one moved or spoke for a second.

"Look around you, sir," Isaac continued. "This isn't a negotiation, nor is it an even fight. There are fifteen of us. We have the drop on you. Go home. Dying here won't earn you a thing. You have 500 dollars. You've done your best. The boy stays here. That's my final word on the matter." Isaac lifted his Winchester, cocked, and pointed it straight at the center of Allen's chest. Most of the others followed suit at that point.

"Perhaps you have not seen my best yet, Mr. Carroll," Allen replied and reached for his pistols.

They blew him to bits.

Isaac gave the horse to the two Milner boys and told them to take it north and sell it in Little Rock. Ross took the saddle. Mr. Carroll told one of his boys to collect the pistols. Jeremiah picked up the book by Harte, and one of the others picked up Allen's rifle.

His pockets and his saddlebags were emptied and the money split between the ones who wanted it. None of the Carrolls or Wallaces took any of it, but Isaac kept the fancy pistols saying they deserved proper treatment and shouldn't be lost in some poker game. Jeremiah Carroll kept the Harte book with one of Allen's calling cards, marking the page for the rest of his life.

"I never saw such elegant foolishness," was all that Mr. Carroll said before he told them to dig a grave and bury what was left of Allen.

They buried him deep, then used a couple of small trees as levers, and flipped the huge flat rock over onto the grave, forever entombing Preston Edward Allen.

"Give me a lever long enough and a fulcrum on which to place it, and I shall move the world," Carroll said as the men mounted their horses.

13

WE CHECKED IN at the Marriot on Canal Street where Janie had booked us rooms, cooled off for just a bit, then headed for Jaxon Moon's office at the U.S Marshals Services, just a couple of blocks away on Camp.

Decked out once again in a pair of Levi 501's, a tan collarless shirt under a cream-colored blazer and my full quill ostriches, I walked into Jaxon Moon's office with Brant in tow. Not to be outdone, he'd cowboyed up, too, and was just as well arrayed: charcoal grey short-sleeved shirt under a light grey blazer, new Levi's, and a pair of bison leather boots, really nice boots, but I loved my ostrich skins too much to covet his.

We'd left our Glocks locked in the Jeep outside rather than deal with the metal detectors in the federal building, but we presented our permits and licenses and informed the officer downstairs of our intent to carry concealed firearms as soon as we got into cooler clothes.

We looked damned good and oh so Oklahoman in our boots and jeans, but, holy hell, it was hot. I was ready to lose the jacket at least.

Up on the second floor, we found U.S. Marshal Moon's office and his secretary, a very petite, dark-haired beauty with striking green eyes and an absolutely dazzling smile.

Dressed in a tailored burgundy dress that fit her like a glove, she met us with a slight Cajun lilt to her voice and rose from her desk as we entered and moved toward us, extending her hand.

"Well, you two gentlemen must be the Oklahoma cowboys I've been hearing so much about lately. I'm Marshal Moon's assistant, Maggie Comeau. We've been expecting y'all."

Brant appeared transfixed. I was merely struck momentarily dumb. We stood with hats in hand in search of our voices. Fortunately Brant recovered quickly and smiled broadly.

"At least one of us is an Indian, ma'am," he said, stretching his hand toward her. "I'm Brant Bluesoldier, and this quiet fellow is my associate, Mickey Wallace. He thinks he's a cowboy. I just like the boots and hats."

"Pleased to meet you, ma'am," was about all I could muster as I reached for her hand after Brant.

She smiled and said, "Follow me. Marshal Moon and his father are waiting in his office right down the hall."

She pressed a button and said, "The boys from Oklahoma have arrived," before she came around the desk and was very, very easy to follow. She rapped gently on the office door and turned the knob.

"Thanks, Mags, come in, gentlemen," the younger man behind the desk said as he rose. "I see you met Miss Comeau. She's the glue that holds this office together. We'd be lost without her."

She smiled again as Tommy Moon, white-haired, a fit and handsome older gentleman wearing khakis and a dark gray, short-sleeved shirt, rose from his seat beside the desk.

"You boys pay attention to Mr. Moon, boys; he's the real brains in this outfit," she said with a smile.

"You know I love ya, darlin'," the older man winked as he moved forward.

"Right back atcha, my main man. You keep these cowboys in line while I get back to the grind," she said as we entered. "I'm sure I'll see you fellows again before you leave."

She stepped out and closed the door behind her.

"So you're Will's boy," Mr. Moon said, extending his hand. "I can see the resemblance."

"Yes, sir, and this is my faithful Indian companion, Brantley Bluesoldier."

"I'm just here to keep Mickey's butt off of Bourbon Street, on task, and out of jail, sir," Brant tossed in.

"I knew your dad pretty well, too, Brantley, helluva man, one of the best I ever had the pleasure of working with," Tommy said, firmly shaking Brant's hand.

The younger man, looking every bit the tan, out-doorsy federal officer, came around from behind the desk, extending his hand as well.

"As you probably know, this fine-looking young man with the U.S. Marshal's badge is my son Jaxon," Tommy said as Jaxon Moon shook both our hands with a friendly, sincere smile on his face. "He's not named for the beer; his momma just liked the romantic spelling. I don't think she ever took the inevitable shortening to Jax into account."

"It's all good. I just claim the old brewery down on the Square is mine," Jax said. "It's a pleasure to meet you, gentlemen. I've heard a lotta good things."

I elbowed Brant. "Hear that, Brant, I'm even famous in New Orleans."

Brant rolled his eyes. And did his best Jay Silverheels imitation, "You're famous everywhere, Kemo Sabe; you want me to just wait in clearing outside of town?"

"Good Lord, you are your father's son, Mickey," Tommy Moon said, "Sound just like him."

"Actually, sir, if I may disagree; I always found Mr. Wallace to be quite sane and very intelligent," Brant said in a flat serious tone, the stoic Red Man. "I suspect a beaning during Mickey's baseball career caused most of his confusion."

Tommy and Jaxon both laughed.

"You're sure you're not William's son, too, Brant?" Jaxon asked and laughed again.

"Adopted," Brant grinned.

"This is gonna be real interestin' I reckon," Jaxon said. "Where you fellas wanna start?"

"First, Dad wanted to say thanks for sending him the painting," I said. "He knows you went the extra mile for him, and he says he owes you for it."

"William Matthew Wallace will never owe me a thing. I'm way behind in that column. Learned most of what I know about the law and administering it from that man. The painting had his name on it, I reckoned it was his," Tommy said.

"Anyway he really appreciates it, but this is where it gets a little hairy," I continued. "Dad believes the painting may have actually been meant for his grandfather, also named 'William Matthew.' It was signed by John William Wallace and dated 1930, as I imagine y'all have already noted. He's pretty sure my son J.W. is not the 'John William' who sent it, a fine piece of detective work, I might add. I suspect Brant may have helped with that some."

"A boy gets a college degree, becomes a deputy marshal on his daddy's rep, and thinks he a friggin' genius," Brant said, shaking his head. "We think there's a chance the 'John William' in question may actually be Mr. Wallace's father… Mr. Wallace, being your former colleague, William Matthew."

"We previously believed his father, John William Wallace. to have been killed in Oklahoma in 1916," I added. "But this has raised a lot of doubt for Dad, and there's no way of knowing right now. We've got a million questions and very few answers as of yet."

"Well, maybe we can provide some clues to help find a few of those answers," Jax said, picking up a brown file folder from his desk. "We've had some luck in tying the old cars we found on the Fontenot place to several known crimes and a couple of disappearances in Texas and Arkansas as well."

"Let's hope you've got some stuff for us to work with," I said, looking at Tommy Moon. "We're gonna be pressed for time, but I'll let Dad fill you in on all the details, Mr. Moon; all I can say right now is that we're operating on borrowed time."

"That really doesn't sound too good, boys," the elder Moon said.

"No, sir, it's not, but I'll let him talk to you about it. He said he'd call you again this week. Now how about these clues?"

"Don't know that I want to take that call, Mickey, but I do want to talk to Will again. You wanna tell 'em about the cars, Jax?" Tommy Moon said to his son.

"You know the details better than me. I'll fill in anything you miss," Jax answered and winked.

Tommy nodded. "In that case, let's sit, men. Here's what we got."

We took our seats, and Tommy Moon started his narration like he was still the marshal in charge.

"The first car we discovered, a '49 Cadillac, belonged to a Texas fella who was found, very dead, back in 1951, in the trunk of a car belonging to one of Marcel Fontenot's associates, just a few miles from the Fontenot house in Lafayette. I remember the case. I had just been transferred here from the Oklahoma City office, and we were investigating Fontenot's connection to an Oklahoma, Texas, Arkansas, Louisiana syndicate with their fingers in a lot of pies. We figured Marcel whacked him or had him whacked and the little fish was in charge of disposal when he got stopped for running a stop sign. Marcel claimed the deceased fella never showed for their 'business meeting' at his place, said he had no clue what had happened to him.

The driver of the car with the body in it claimed this same departed soul was killed when he pulled a gun at a poker game. Being a good guy and not wanting his friends involved, he was just cleaning up the mess."

We were listening quietly, impressed by the strong narrative and recollection of detail.

"The guy did a few years in the state pen but never implicated Marcel. I'm sure he was well rewarded. Apparently Fontenot already had a nice place for storing and hiding cars out at the farm, so someone else had driven the dead fella's Caddy to the barn, and it disappeared until I found it the other day among several others."

"Wonder why he kept the car?" I mused aloud.

"Why he kept the cars and why the dead guy was in a different car, we don't have a clue. Good for us though. We found five more cars out there, all stored in a barn under tarps."

"The painting was in one of those?" Brant asked.

"Yep, pretty little Ford Model A Coupe, 1929, I think belonged to a painter here in New Orleans, lived over in the Quarter. He simply vanished off the face of the earth along with his wife back in '30."

"A painter," Brant said, looking over at me.

"Fella, name a Samuel Whitman," Jaxon cut in. "He was just getting some local attention as an artist when he and his wife Renee vanished without a trace. His work has gained more attention since his disappearance. His paintings command quite a nice price these days. Sorry to interrupt, Dad, just had to show I'm a part of this, I reckon. Please go on."

Tommy picked up the narrative where he'd left off, "We figure Marcel Fontenot killed 'em. Don't know why, how, or even where, but all five vehicles out there belonged to murder victims or missing people, so it doesn't look good, and Marcel was an evil little bastard, just starting to take over his father's dirty business around that time."

"Can we start with Whitman?" Brant asked. "It's just interesting the painting was in another painter's car, almost has to be some connection. Anyone around that we can talk to about Whitman and his wife? Maybe get a relative's name from the files somewhere?"

"So William's father, John William Wallace, was actually an artist, too?" Tommy Moon questioned. "I wasn't sure."

"Well, all Dad knows for sure is that he had an artistic bent, liked to draw, and had an interest in painting but never had a real access to the tools and supplies," I replied.

"I'll see if I can find some more info on the Whitmans for y'all, bound to be some cold case files still around. I still got some friends in the NOPD," Jax said. "I don't think Daddy has run 'em all off yet anyway."

Tommy grunted. "Hell, they love me. I am an icon."

Jax laughed. "I'll send whatever I can turn up over to y'all soon as I get names, addresses, or anything else that might be of interest. The Marriot on Canal, right?"

"Yep," I said.

"You boys heading back over there when you leave here?" Tommy asked.

"Yep, we're gonna see more of the Quarter, walk around Bourbon Street a bit, check out the artists down on Jackson Square, but we'll be back in our room before too long, or you can reach us on our cells."

I handed Jaxon one of our cards embossed with our cell numbers on it, very classy little items, money well spent, according to Janie.

"Well, enjoy yourselves, boys," Jaxon Moon said. "This is the Big Easy, good food and great music everywhere you turn. Call me later after you've done a bit of sight-seeing, and I'll hook you up with some of the best Cajun food you've ever come across."

Tommy Moon chuckled. "Don't forget to take some crawdads back to that old Okie when y'all head home. That ought to make him happy. He always called 'em bait, but he never failed to eat his fill."

Brant and I both grinned.

"We'll do that, Mr. Moon, along with a case or two of *Dixie* beer, but we better investigate Bourbon Street first. We haven't been up and down it in several years and, heck, we're staying almost right on it now so..." Brant said, giving my shoulder a nudge.

Jax smiled.

Tommy Moon chuckled more to himself than anyone else with sort of a far-off look, probably recalling past events in his and Dad's own checkered pasts.

"You men try to behave and not get too rowdy. The big man back in Oklahoma said to call him and he'd come down here and personally straighten y'all out if I needed him to," Jax said. "Just check at the desk when y'all get back in the room. With that kind of agenda ahead of you, I should have enough time to come up with plenty of good stuff you can use."

I nodded.

"We'll be looking for any help you can give us on this," Brant said. "The quicker we get this done, the better the boss will feel about it all."

"Yep," I said. "Just can't have him down here right now, we won't get to see any of the sights. Man's a slave driver."

The Moons grinned as we all rose and shook hands again.

"I'll try to keep Mick in check," Brant said as we headed out. "Later, gentlemen."

Maggie smiled as we passed her desk. "See you cowboys later. Be safe."

"Yes, ma'am," I said with my grade A smile.

Brant winked and said, "Remember, I'm the smart one. Then in what I thought was a poor Swarzenegger imitation, "We'll be bach."

Somehow it managed to get a laugh from Maggie as we closed the door.

14

COLD BEER AND New Orleans nightlife kept us entertained longer than we planned. It was after midnight when we rolled back into The Marriott, but the desk clerk met us with a fairly thick, large yellow envelope as soon as he saw us wander in. Jaxon Moon was a fast worker; it looked like we'd have plenty to look over in the morning.

Brant and I met in my side of our adjoining rooms the next morning and divided the copied pages from the cold case files. As I sipped on room service OJ, Brant was diving deep into reading his half of the files, which primarily focused on interviews with Samuel Whitman's young son, Mark, and his sister-in-law, Michelle Guidry.

I was reading the detective-in-charge's notes on Whitman and the details involving the beginning of the case.

"Says here Whitman's wife, Renee, was the secretary for a Dr. O'Dell at Tulane. She and Samuel lived in the Quarter with their son, who was around eight or so at the time," I said aloud. "They were supposed to be gone on a Friday-through-the-weekend trip and back in time for his wife to go to work on Monday."

"The boy and the sister-in-law were frantic enough to convince the detective something unusual was going on," Brant replied. "They immediately started looking on the roads leading out of New Orleans to the west."

"It says here that Samuel's work was gaining some notice in the local art world when he and Renee disappeared," I said, scanning my half of the documents, which were speculating on lack of motive for their disappearance. Other than possible theft of the auto and robbery, there seemed to be no ideas.

"Maybe the painting is actually a Whitman," I said with a grin. "His work is really starting to get expensive. We may be rich and not even realize it."

"Mick, the sister-in-law says Renee took off Friday from work, asked her to keep Mark, said they were gonna see 'a friend' in Oklahoma and that she'd explain more when they got back that coming Sunday."

"Going to Oklahoma, now that's interesting," I said. "But they didn't get back, did they?"

Brant leafed through more pages. "Nope, didn't leave much for the local guys to work with either. Michelle filed a missing-persons report on the Monday after they failed to return, but all they had was that the Whitmans were going to Oklahoma, driving a black 1929 Ford Model A Coupe with Louisiana plates. New Orleans called in the state police later, even had the feds involved for a little while, but nothing ever turned up. It was like they vanished without a trace. They never found any Oklahoma connection. No witnesses reported seeing them or the vehicle there or Texas either."

"Whitman at least must've known something about the Wallaces, must've had some connection to John William," I interjected. "I mean, he had the painting which was addressed to Dad's grandfather, and he was apparently bringing it with him to Oklahoma."

Brant finished his coffee. "Maybe Whitman was bringing it as a peace offering of a sort from John William Wallace in order to reconnect with his Oklahoma folks."

"Why wouldn't John William come himself?" I wondered aloud.

"Who knows?" Brant mused. "But seventy-plus years later, the Whitmans' Ford, with the painting still in the back seat, turns up in Lafayette, Louisiana without a clue as to where Whitman and his wife went or how they came by the painting. How do we explain that, Mick?"

I shrugged.

"We know Fontenot was a bad man," Brant continued. "And the car was found on his property between New Orleans and Oklahoma. I guess we have to assume there's a connection of some sort there."

"Do you suppose there's a chance the painting could have been placed in the Whitman car later while it was in storage?" I asked. "But, damn, the dates sure line up conveniently with what we know was going on. I guess I'd better call Dad, see if any of this makes sense to him. He's supposed to be in the office with Janie while we're on this."

Brant chuckled softly. "Ninety-six, and he's in the office. Reckon where we'll be when we're ninety-six, Mickey?"

"Hopefully I'll be on an island somewhere warm, and you'll be outta prison."

Brant rolled his eyes. "Okay, smartass, just call Will."

"Hell, he'll be watching baseball if there's a game on yet or reading if there's not. But you can bet your big old Randall knife that if any of this makes sense, he'll figure it out."

Janie answered on the second ring.

"It's about time you called home," she said. "You boys out carousing all night last night?"

No hello, no kiss my ass, no nothing, just bang, I was on the defensive side.

"Just investigating the crime scene, beautiful. You know us, all business," I said, dancing around the fear of soon-to-be-sharper chastising that was coming for our tardy check-in report.

"Yeah, right. My little angels. I can only imagine how down-to-business y'all were, first night back in New Orleans. Just try to stay out of trouble, okay?" she said.

"We're working hard on the case, doll. I won't let Brant go too far astray, promise. You know how he is. But I do need Dad for a second though."

"Yeah, I know how *Brant* is," she snarled. "Hang on. I'll try to get Will for you."

"He's not there?" I asked.

"Oh, he's here, but there's an afternoon Yankee game on, so good luck. I'll call him, and you better call me back tomorrow, Mickey. Don't make me come down there. Tell Brantley that goes for him, too."

She put me on hold.

"Three to one, Yankees, bottom of the sixth, Bernie Williams up and Jeter on second, this better be important, son," came Dad's voice over the phone. He sounded like a man of thirty, and for just one moment, I couldn't believe he was dying.

"Yanks are winning, Brant," I said over my shoulder. "We may have to wait a couple of innings."

"Don't be a wise ass, boy. What do you need?" The voice literally boomed through the receiver.

I laughed. "Okay, Dad, you ever hear of a fellow named Samuel Whitman?"

"Nope…double in the gap, all right, four to one, that's better now. What's the deal, bud?"

"The fella whose car the painting was found in was a local artist, a painter name of Samuel Whitman," I told him. "He and his wife disappeared apparently on their way to Oklahoma in 1931. Tommy Moon thinks Marcel Fontenot killed them or had them killed. That's why Fontenot had the car, looks like it was pulled into one of his barns, covered with a tarp and left untouched for all this time."

"Hmmm, coming to Oklahoma huh? Now that's interesting," Dad said, more interested now. "Well, what else have you found out about this Whitman fellow, Mick?"

"He was a painter, lived in the French Quarter, had a wife named Renee, who disappeared with him. They left their young son named Mark with Renee's sister when they left, then they just disappeared. That's about it right now, I'm afraid."

"And they were coming to Oklahoma with a painting that had Granddad's name on it?" he said softly.

"It looks that way, unless somehow the painting got put in the car later," I offered.

"Do you think that's much of a possibility, Mickey?"

"According to Tommy Moon, the package had been there for years apparently, and pretty much all the vehicles had their original contents still in them, but we still have to consider it for now," I said.

"Whitman and Dad were both artists…even though Dad wasn't a professional. He did love to sketch," he paused. "They musta been connected somehow, but I sure don't know the name, best y'all get busy detecting some clues, Mickey boy. We both know that nobody simply vanishes, just some folks don't get looked for hard enough."

"Reckon so. We're going to head..."

"Hold on, Mick..." Dad broke in. "This is a long shot, could be nothing, I don't know the name Samuel Whitman, but I do know the names."

"You're talking in riddles now, Dad," I said, glancing at Brant.

"I know, bud, but here's the deal. My dad's favorite poet was Walt Whitman. I remember him reading to us from *Leaves of Grass*. He loved that book, and your grandmother's cousin, who was also killed in the same attempted break from McAlester as Dad...his name was Samuel Musgrove. He and Dad were always pretty tight."

"What are you saying, Dad?" I asked. "You think Samuel Whitman could be an alias your dad was using?"

"Well, I reckon I'm saying maybe Daddy didn't die in that prison break, maybe he was Samuel Whitman, maybe he was trying to get back to us with that painting for some reason." Dad paused. "Or maybe I'm way off base. I don't know. You boys try to find some personal info on Whitman. If he was a legit guy, that shouldn't be hard."

"Those old family rumors are still dancing around in your head, huh?" I asked.

"Reckon so," he came back, sounding more far away now, lost in thoughts he was keeping to himself.

"Well, you're right about one thing: it shouldn't be tough to find something on Samuel Whitman. He was gaining some recognition for his work about the time he disappeared and has gained even more since. We're about to get all over it, have more for you real soon, maybe tonight even."

His voiced perked back up, "Mo's coming in to close this game out, bud. You and Brant see if you can do likewise way down yonder in New Orleans. Call Janie tomorrow. She worries about her boys when they're off on their own."

"Game's over, Brant; Mo's coming in," I called back over my shoulder again.

Brant laughed, still turning pages. "Tell Will we'll close this out just like Mariano always does and be home soon. And tell him I love him more than you do."

"You boys better bring me back a mess of crawdads," came Dad's voice in my other ear, distracting me from a witty retort to Brant's juvenile remark.

"We'll do that, Dad, and a case or two of *Dixie* beer, if I remember right," I laughed.

"That's my boy. Now go find out who this Whitman fella is and why he didn't get to Oklahoma with that painting. I need to know, buck."

"Will do, Dad, you know if it's important to you, it's important to me and Brant, too."

"I won't let him screw this up, Will," Brant called loudly from across the room.

Dad chuckled his familiar Okie chuckle. "Good Lord, boys, just try to stay out of trouble for a little while if that's possible. I shoulda known better than to send y'all both off together."

"Later, Dad," I said.

"You two just behave. I love both your worthless asses," he said. "I'll talk to y'all later."

"We love you, too, Dad," I said.

Brant nodded as I clicked the phone off.

15

MURPHREESBORO, ARKANSAS, MARCH 1908

THINGS HAD SETTLED *somewhat back to normal. John William and Rena had built their own place next to Brother James, and John had taken Angus McDougld's advice. He and Rena had two sons, William Matthew, almost five and dutifully named after John's father, and Robert Michael, who had just turned three. With Robert's birth, James gave John the family home and took their smaller house for himself.*

The family blacksmith shop was doing a booming business with both John and James working at the forge, and no new threat had appeared since the demise of Preston Edward Allen. A telegram had arrived a couple of months after the incident, addressed to the police chief inquiring as to his knowledge of Allen, but William had replied with the notification that the man had been there but departed for Little Rock at last sighting.

John's father, William Matthew, had been the city police chief now for almost five years. He and his wife Irene had a nice place in town, and he and Isaac Carroll played checkers regularly on the porch of Isaac's feed store.

"Did you know Bass Reeves is an officer with the Muskogee Police Department now that Oklahoma is a state?" William asked as he pondered taking one of Isaac's checkers.

"They hired a black man?" Carroll said, shaking his head in disbelief.

William made the jump and took the man from Isaac. "Yep, you were on the wrong side of that war, old friend."

Isaac eyed the board carefully. "Mighta been."

"Well, you were on the losing side for sure," William Wallace said with a grin.

Carroll touched a red checker but changed his mind on the move. "As I recall, you had to leave Georgia on account of your affiliations in that conflict, my old friend."

"You left, too, if I'm not mistaken," Wallace said. "And this match is starting to look like another stalemate."

"Could be a stalemate, isn't that how we always wind up, William Matthew?" Isaac said. "And the difference in my move to Arkansas was I didn't have to. I wanted to."

"Bass is a good man," William said, changing the topic. "Got to know him pretty well when I was working for Judge Parker, great fisherman."

Isaac moved a checker to protect another possible jump from William. "What's that got to do with the price of tea in China, William Matthew?"

William quickly moved a black checker up a space. "He's offered me a job on the force there, Isaac, and I'm thinking about taking it. Pays a lot more than being chief here, and I always had a hankering to go further west."

Isaac looked up from the board. "Bass Reeves or no Bass Reeves, you're too damned old to head off into the Territories, William. Look at all the shit John William and Levi got into there, and they were young men."

"It's a state now, Isaac."

"Yeah, I know it's a state, a brand new one still full of the same old outlaws." Carroll kept looking at William. "And you'd be working with an old black man, even older than you. I doubt Oklahoma has raised the cultural level of their 'state' high enough to offset the stigma attached to that particular aspect, even if he is a famous lawman."

"I know things are good here now, Isaac, and we owe a lot of that to you, but I am thinking about it. Are you gonna move today? My ass is getting numb."

"Well, shift it to the west," Carroll said and looked back down at the board. "Bass has got to be getting on toward seventy, and you're no spring chicken yourself. You got grandchildren here. I just think it's a bad idea."

"Might be," William said and shifted in his chair. "For Christ's sake, Isaac, this is a stalemate. Get us a drink, and I'll set the board up again."

"You're on duty," Carroll said as he stood up and moved toward the feed store's front door.

William began to reset the board. "Like that matters," he laughed. "We're not getting drunk, are we?"

"Anna doesn't even allow whiskey in the house," Isaac said as came out of the feed store with a glass of bourbon for each of them. "That's why I keep it here."

"Irene won't have it in ours either," William said with a mischievous grin. "That's why I play checkers with you."

Isaac looked at the reset board. "You head off into the Territories and..."

"The State of Oklahoma," William interrupted.

"The goddamned state of Oklahoma," Isaac growled. "And there won't be no more whiskey on the porch, no more unwinnable checker games. You won't get to watch those grandboys grow into men. You'll be out in the damned wilderness with a black man, too old to keep you out of harm's way. You will die out there, William Matthew."

William took a sip of the whiskey and thought, Isaac always keeps good bourbon on hand. "Maybe, but I'll die just as dead here in Arkansas, too, if I stay, Isaac."

"I doubt as soon though," Isaac Carroll countered, unsmiling.

William took another sip. "Well, you could load up and come with me, keep me safe from all them outlaws."

Isaac took a long sip of his own bourbon. "I reckon I could sell the business and the 200 acres and all the cattle and load up the boys I still got at home, along with Anna and Lucy and little Isaac, and chase off with you into the great state of Oklahoma."

There was a pause, and William was quiet for a change.

"If I was totally fucking insane," Isaac finished calmly. "Now give me your glass if you want one more."

William handed him his glass. "Hell, no reason to get your bowels in an uproar. I said I was thinking about it, didn't say I was actually going."

Isaac reemerged with the glasses filled again and handed one to William. "Let's put up the board. I'm tired of playing for the day."

Two men stacked the checkers and the board in silence.

"How long have I known you, William Matthew? Nigh on fifty years?" Isaac said. "You're going. You've already got the idea in that thick skull of yours, and there's no getting it out. I don't know when, but you're going."

William looked down at his boots and almost didn't notice when John William rode up on his buckskin.

"Mr. Carroll," John said, touching the brim of his hat.

"Get down and sit a spell, John William," Isaac said. "I need some intelligent conversation for a change."

"Wish I could, sir, but I just came to tell Dad that Jim said..." John started without dismounting.

"Don't let your momma hear you calling him Jim," William said with a grin.

"James said he needs us down at the stable," John said, correcting himself. "Old man Barlow is drunk again and blaming us for crippling his mule. He's got a shotgun."

William remained seated. "And you and James can't disarm one old drunk? You feel compelled to disrupt my checker game?"

"Sorry to break up the game, Mr. Carroll," John said.

"Checker game's over," Isaac said to John. "Your dad's just being an ass like usual."

John William laughed. "We can disarm him, Daddy, but we don't want to kill him, and besides, I'm not even on the force. That would be you and Jim... James I mean."

William Matthew stood and downed his drink in one swallow. "Well then, I reckon duty calls. Let's go, son. Isaac, same time tomorrow?"

Isaac rose with the board under his arm, the box of checkers in one hand and the empty glasses in the other. "If Old Man Barlow doesn't blow you to bits with that scattergun of his, I guess we'll try it again tomorrow."

"Reckon I'll see you later, Mr. Carroll," John William said as he turned the horse down the street and headed for the livery stable.

"Don't get in a hurry, Pops," John called to his father, who was already walking toward the stable several blocks down the street.

William waved his hand dismissively at John William. "Just ride, boy, I'll get there soon enough."

Isaac noticed William was checking the loads in his .44 pistol as he sauntered toward the stable and just shook his head. He knew William would be leaving before too long. There was something about staying in one place that just didn't sit well with William Matthew Wallace, but he had a really bad feeling deep in his gut about it this time.

16

AFTER OUR FIRST FULL DAY of looking, Brant and I found no one left in The Quarter who actually remembered Samuel Whitman personally. Plenty of the arts and antiques dealers knew who he was, and some folks remembered relatives that had known him and spoke of him, but it seemed no one remained who actually knew him back when he was living there. We even located two of his paintings for sale in French Quarter shops.

And through the magic of the internet, it didn't take us long to discover that Mark Whitman was killed in the Pacific during WW II and had been interred in Metairie Cemetery for almost six decades now.

"We've been there before," Brant said. "Remember Mel Ott and John Bell Hood are out there with Josie Arlington, the Storeyville madam and a host of other well-known characters and some unbelievably ornate tombs and monuments."

I closed the laptop. "Yeah, what's left of Gram Parsons after his buddies' attempt at the desert cremation is out there, too. If we had a little more free time, it'd be worth the drive through just to look."

"Reckon we oughtta call Will and let him know things aren't going so great. Apparently there's not a Whitman left that's any kin."

"We still got the Guidrys," I said.

"But I guess I need to tell him we're going to Tipitina's tonight and catching Bonnie Raitt's show?"

"We'll catch holy hell," grinned Brant. "But I don't see a way around it. He'd just find out, and it'd be worse. He always finds out about everything, ya know."

I laughed. "Yep, that he does."

"Call Jax first," Brant said. "We can see if he's found any of Renee's folks. Maybe it'll take some of the edge off if it looks like we're actually working."

I punched in Jaxon Moon's cell number.

"Mick, I was just about to call you fellas, got some good news maybe," Jax said before I got in a word.

Caller ID, where were you all my life? Gotta love it.

"Let's hear it, buddy; we're in need of good news right now. We haven't found a soul who actually knew the man Samuel Whitman."

"I was checking on Renee's sister, Michelle Guidry, and it turns out I actually know her granddaughter."

I gave Brant the wait-until-you-hear-this look. "Really?"

"Yep, her names not Guidry though, so it didn't register with me at first," he laughed. "Her name's Leslie Waldrum. I met her at a fundraising event of some nature a year or two back, had no idea about her connection to Whitman until we ran Michelle through our system."

"Can we set up a meeting with her, Jax," I asked. "As soon as possible."

"Sure," he answered quickly. "She's bright and willing to help if she can. I took the liberty of calling her but didn't tell her that much, just that I had some friends down from Oklahoma doing some research that I'd like her to meet. Thought I'd leave the sordid details of the formal introduction up to you."

I wanted to high-five him over the phone. "Jax, you are the man. When can we meet her? We're ready right now, if that's possible."

"I was pretty sure you'd want to see her quick as you could, didn't figure you were too tied up yet, but she's got a university thing of some sort at Tulane tonight. I fixed up a meeting tomorrow around 11:00 A.M. in her office."

I glanced at Brant who was waiting patiently for the whole story, just looking out the window at the madness down on Canal Street.

"Something at Tulane?" I said loud enough to catch Brant's attention.

"Oh, yeah, guess I didn't mention she's a professor of American Lit, *Dr.* Leslie Waldrum. She wants y'all to meet her on the campus."

"That works out even better for us anyway. We're going to Tipitina's to see Bonnie Raitt tonight, so all is well," I said. "We should be up and recuperated by eleven."

Jax laughed. "Sounds like you boys are just having yourselves a high old time."

"Hey, man," I said, "it's not often we Okies get to come to the Big Easy and then miraculously tickets appear. What could we do? We had to take 'em. We'd be fools not to."

He laughed again. "Get back to me tomorrow after the meeting, Mick, and you guys enjoy the show."

I relayed all Jax had told me to Brant.

"Damn, that's a break," he said as he pulled two *Dixies* out of our mini-fridge and handed me one. "Maybe Will won't kick your butt too hard now. Better call him, tell him we're finding a few clues anyway."

I started to dial Dad's number but paused. "Why I always gotta be the one to call Dad?"

"Cause you're the AIC," Brant said dryly. "Agent in Charge, the man with the plan."

Mercifully Dad answered before I had to endure more, and Brant walked into his room to start getting ready for our New Orleans night out. It would do him no good. I was simply, by nature, better looking than he was. The women throwing themselves at him were not sufficient markers.

"Hey, Dad."

"Hey, Buck, tell me something."

"Well, right now we haven't got a lot to tell," I started. "Haven't found a living soul who knew Samuel Whitman personally yet."

"You know someone in a city that size is still around," he said. "Damn it. Don't tell me you called me just to tell you haven't got a thing to go on. What happened to the boy?"

"More bad news, it turns out that Whitman's son, Mark, was killed in WWII but..."

"What about the wife's folks?" he cut in. "Guidrys, weren't they?"

"Well, there's a ray of light in that tunnel," I answered. "Jaxon Moon located a granddaughter of Samuel's wife's sister, and we're supposed to meet with her tomorrow morning."

"And you couldn't have led the conversation with that?" he said. "Thank God there's at least one real detective on the case. Tomorrow morning? Can't see her any sooner? It's not that late yet."

I laughed out loud, unable to resist twisting the blade just a bit. "Well, Dad, we're gonna catch Bonnie Raitt at Tipitina's tonight."

"Uh-huh. I figured you two were in full party mode. Jax and Tommy doing all yall's work I suppose."

Brant was snickering as he walked through from his room carrying his boots.

I grinned. "You really can't blame us for Bonnie Raitt, now can ya? Just so happened we noticed she was playing when we arrived."

"Figured as much, I ought to come down there and get the job done right. All you two are gonna do is soak up the local culture and drink beer."

Brant was sitting on the end of the bed, pulling on his boots and still grinning at me from across the room.

I could hear Dad's voice change. He'd figured out I was giving him the run around.

"So you boys just couldn't meet with this little lady that Jaxon found for you tonight, huh?"

"I tried to talk Brant out of going to see Bonnie, Dad, but he just wouldn't listen."

Brant threw one of my sweaty socks at my head.

I could practically hear Dad smile over the phone. "Yeah, I know how *Brant* is."

"You know I'm just kidding, Dad," I laughed. "Jax gave us her number. He called her just a little while ago, and she's got some event scheduled tonight at Tulane where she teaches, so we arranged a meeting in her office tomorrow."

"She teaches at Tulane? Now I know I'll have to come down. Neither one of you will be smart enough to understand what she's telling you."

"You're a million laughs, Dad, but we gotta get out of here. The show starts around nine."

"Just giving you a hard time, son." His familiar chuckle filled my ears for a brief second. "I know you boys are on it, and you know I like that Raitt girl, too. Request *Feeling of Falling* for me, boys."

"Brant said he'd pick up her new CD and get it signed personally to you."

The second sock narrowly missed my head.

17

MURPHREESBORO, ARKANSAS, OCTOBER 1908

IN MID-JULY, *about four months after William Wallace's great checker debate with Isaac Carrol, William resigned as police chief of Murphreesboro, Arkansas and took Bass Reeves' offer to join him on the Muskogee police force, just as Isaac had predicted he would.*

"I reckon you boys know your daddy is a damned old hard-headed fool, but I'm gonna miss him and Irene both," Isaac told John and James after William's departure. "Your momma cooked mighty fine chicken, and I'll never find another checker player as easy to defeat as William."

James was hired to replace him as the chief of police. John William reluctantly took over the blacksmith shop and livery stable. He still had big dreams of a new start in a new land, a chance to make it rich and raise his rapidly growing family.

In late August, a fellow from New Boston, Texas rode in to town and made John William and James what they considered an excellent offer on the livery stable and forge.

The gentleman had two grown sons, both blacksmiths like himself. He declared the automobile a passing fad and wanted to invest his money in a business that his family could depend on for years to come.

The Wallace brothers contacted William in Muskogee, since legally the property was still his, and he agreed that the offer was more than generous. He instructed them to make the deal and they'd split the money three ways if they felt that was fair and equitable.

The deal was done in a very short time.

John William had real money for the first time in his life, and he took it as an opportunity. He'd read about the growth of a new university in Oklahoma in the city of Norman, and it struck him as the place to be. He figured he'd open a livery stable and blacksmith forge and make a fortune. He'd put his children through school there and life would be good.

Meanwhile James had fell in love with the new smith's only daughter and had absolutely no intention of leaving, much to Isaac's relief. Good law enforcement was hard to come by, and Jim Wallace was most definitely good at his job.

With Rena sitting on the porch of their home, one night after supper, John William began to pace as she sewed a patch on one of the boys' pants.

"Just say it, Johnny," Rena said without looking up from her stitching. "By now I know when you've got something on your mind, so quit pacing before you wear your boot heels off."

He stopped and looked at her, then at the boys playing in the dirt at the end of the porch.

"I want to go back to Oklahoma."

She stopped sewing and looked up at him without a word, stunned by the words.

"It's a state now, Rena," he hesitated, then started again. "And they've built a new university in a town called Norman up by Oklahoma City."

Rena still sat there, shocked, in disbelief.

"We've got money now, and that city is about to boom. I can buy a small forge and start a livery stable. We'll put the boys through school there, darlin'."

"They'll put you in jail there, John William," she said, her voice quivering just a bit. "Have you already forgotten what happened before?"

John sat down beside her. "No, love, I haven't forgotten a thing, but it'll be in another part of the state. No one will know us there. It'll be a new start."

Rena sighed. There was the look she knew so well. He'd never be satisfied with a little piece of Arkansas, not even with her and the boys on it. She wanted to just smack him until he came to his senses, but she'd known he was a dreamer *when she married him, and she knew he wanted great things for the boys more than for himself, so she just sighed and gave in to the inevitable.*

The following Monday, John William picked up both boys in his arms and held them tightly. "Y'all mind your momma. I'll be back soon, and I don't want to hear about any trouble."

"I'm always good, Daddy," William said with his arms around John William's neck.

Shelby just looked confused and clung to his dad as they walked outside where John set them on the front porch and took Rena in his arms.

He could tell she wasn't completely on board with his idea yet, but he knew he'd win her over soon enough. "I love ya, darlin'," he whispered in her ear.

She kissed him deeply. "I know you do, but that won't be enough if you get your fool self killed out there, John William."

He smiled. "I'll ride north to Fort Smith and cross over at Sallisaw, won't be anywhere near McCurtain County."

She kissed him again but didn't say a word.

John tousled each of the boy's heads, stepped off the porch, and mounted his buckskin horse. "I'll send you a telegram when I reach Norman, babe," he said. "Just watch these two hoodlums, and I'll be back before you know it.

As soon as he was out of sight, she felt the tears welling in her eyes and wiped them with her apron before the boys, who were playing with the dog at the moment, even noticed.

18

BRANT PULLED the Jeep off St. Charles and onto Cowen Circle in front of Tulane. He parked in a spot in front of the limestone building where we could exit and take the first walking path to the north, which we had been assured would lead us past the Amistad Research Building to the Norman Mayer building where we'd find Leslie's office on the second floor in room 222.

I knocked lightly, and a soft southern voice came drifting out, "C'mon in, the door's open."

Her platinum blond hair, cut short, in striking contrast with her soft brown skin. Leslie Waldrum rose from behind her heavy mahogany desk in her office wearing blue jeans and an Aaron Neville tee shirt. Prints of Mark Twain, Walt Whitman, and James Dickey peered down from the wall to her right, and the live oak branches outside brushed lightly against the windows at her back.

At thirty-seven she was an absolute brown-eyed knockout, Halle Berry with her "Storm" hair cropped close.

Brant and I both, deeply and instantly, fell in love once again. I was growing worried that every woman in Louisiana was a goddess, and Brant and I would spend our entire time down here, struck dumb.

We seem to fall like that a lot in all fifty states though. I blame him. His people are supposed to be more disciplined and in control.

"Ms. Waldrum," I stammered, "we're down here from Oklahoma... and, uh...we were looking for someone who...uh...knew Samuel Whitman, the...um...artist."

I felt like a giddy schoolboy.

She smiled. "The artist? I believe he disappeared in the early 30's, Mr. Wallace, 1931 maybe."

"Before your time, we know, ma'am," I said, recovering from my swooning just a bit.

"But we were led to believe you might be kin to Mr. Whitman's wife, Renee, in some way."

Brant was silent, trying to appear suave and sophisticated, I'm sure, while enjoying my stumbling introduction.

Her teeth were so white and perfect, it was hard to concentrate. Even with him being a former Navy Seal, a trained investigator, and an Osage warrior, he was barely able to function, much less cover my ass.

"She was my grandmother's sister, as you already know of course. Most of everything my mom has today comes from her mom selling original Whitman artwork." She smiled again. "My grandmother, Michelle Ladd, raised Samuel and Renee's boy, Mark, after his parents disappeared back in the thirties. She was granted guardianship of Mark, and he inherited all the paintings in the Whitman studio. They even owned Samuel and Renee's home and studio in the Quarter for quite a while."

"Ma'am, you are most definitely who we've been looking for," Brant said, regaining the use of his tongue. "Do you have a few minutes to talk?"

"Have a seat, gentlemen," she said with a New Orleans lilt. "Jaxon Moon told me you Okie boys were coming. I've got time, plenty of it today anyway. As a matter of fact, let's take a break here and drive over to Momma's house. You can follow me. It's just a few blocks over on Audubon Street, right off St. Charles. I live there, too, most of the time. If anything personal is left of Samuel Whitman in this world, my momma will probably have it. She'll definitely have some family lore to pass on."

"Yes, ma'am," Brant said as we both rose.

After a couple of turns to get going the right way on a one-way street, we pulled into the drive right behind Leslie. The house was a slightly modernized Queen Anne with a double gallery painted a teal color. A wrought iron fence set it off from the sidewalk in front.

"Don' see that color much in Oklahoma, do ya, cowboys?" Leslie's voice sang as she moved up to the front porch. "Come on inside, and I'll warn Momma we've got company coming."

Brant glanced at me as I stood, gawking up at the second-floor gallery for just a moment.

"Nope, not very often," he said as we moved toward the front door that was standing open.

As we headed up the steps to the house where Leslie had already entered, a silver-grey Toyota Camry passed by on Audubon Street and continued down the road. It had followed us at a distance all the way from Tulane.

Brant and I glanced at each other, without giving any indication that we'd both seen the tail.

Marie Waldrum greeted us along with Leslie as we came through the door. She looked like Leslie's older sister. I thought no way she was over sixty, but according to math, she had to be. She had the same caramel colored skin and sparkling eyes as Leslie, but her hair was dark and pulled back in a ponytail behind her head.

Leslie made the proper introductions and motioned us to follow them into the dining room where we took seats at the table. She sat beside Marie across from Brant and me with a large collection of photographs of Samuel, Renee, and Mark Whitman that she had assembled for us.

Obviously Leslie had prepared her mother well for our pending arrival.

"My momma kept all these photos. Renee was her much-loved big sister, and she was crazy about Samuel, too," Marie smiled, pointing at the pictures, some in frames, others in piles of old smaller photos. "It broke her heart that they never even found any trace of them. They were just gone. Momma raised their boy, Mark, like he was her own. A few years later, it absolutely broke her heart again when we lost him, too."

"If you don't mind me asking, what exactly happened to Mark?" I asked. "We read he died overseas in the war."

"He died in the Pacific in 1944. I don't remember a whole lot about him of course. I wasn't quite six when he went overseas," Marie said in a soft southern voice. "He was eighteen when he joined the Marines and had just turned twenty-one when he died on Saipan. Many of these were taken of him in uniform before he left, and there is another album with group pictures that may not be as clear as these, if you'd like to see those as well."

"Of course," Brant said.

As Marie stood and retrieved a small album, I walked over and looked out the front window toward the silver-grey Toyota Camry that had circled and parked across the street and up the block a bit.

Marie brought out more pictures, and Leslie walked over to where I was standing.

"What are you looking at, Oklahoma?" she said, flashing that smile that could light up the world.

"Nothing, just admiring the neighborhood," I replied.

"It's a nice place to live, and it was a great place to grow up," She peeked out the window at the front yard. "And Samuel is responsible for all this. This house was paid for with the sale of his paintings and the studio-home he and Renee owned in the Quarter. He had twelve unsold paintings finished when he disappeared, plus one, almost completed, that he was working on when they disappeared."

I nodded, keeping the Camry in my peripheral vision, an old Indian trick.

"Grandma Ladd kept that unfinished one and two others for herself," she continued as Brant and Marie looked at pictures. "She sold the first one or two pretty cheap. Then demand increased. She held out and sold a few more for more money than she ever dreamed of. The last two went for six figures. Momma didn't ever have to work and put me through South Carolina University."

"South Carolina Gamecock, huh?" I grinned. "That's a long way from home."

"Yep, but James Dickey was one of my professors there. Ever hear of him?"

"Of course, *Deliverance*," I smiled.

She returned the smile. "I was more a fan of his poetry. That's where I met Lisa. We've sort of been together here with Momma ever since Tulane hired me in '96 on Dickey's recommendation."

Did I hear that right? I was trying really hard to focus. I guess maybe I looked a little surprised. She smiled again.

"Don't look so shocked, Oklahoma, occasionally I find a man worth my time, too, but I love Lisa. Can I get you a beer? We've got some *Dixies* in the fridge."

Apparently my vocal cords were paralyzed. I nodded and watched as she walked back to the kitchen, and I was thankful for my Choctaw stoicism and skin tone, otherwise the blush would've blinded her.

I left the Toyota sitting there and returned to the dining table, wondering what Lisa looked like.

As I returned, Brant looked up at me. He apparently had made a command decision to lay all our cards on the table. "Can I borrow a few of these to make some copies, Marie?" I heard him ask.

"Certainly, I'm sure Leslie can have them made at Tulane if you'd like, but may I please ask why? We've been puzzled ever since Agent Moon told Leslie you boys were in town looking into Samuel's past."

"Yes, ma'am, you sure may," Brant said, looking to see if I said hold on or not. "This may surprise you quite a bit, but we think there's a better than average chance that Samuel Whitman was born John William Wallace from Oklahoma by way of Arkansas, Mickey's grandfather."

"I've seen pictures of my grandfather from around 1910 or so, and there's really a great deal of resemblance," I added as I sat back down at the table. "Previously we believed he was killed in 1916, but recent events have started to make us wonder about that now, and that's part of the reason we're down here. I promise to explain more once we know more, but right now we're really not positive about much of anything,"

Leslie brought four ice cold *Dixie* beers.

"I guess that would make us some sort of kin, huh?" she laughed softly, handing Brant and me our beer.

I smiled. "I reckon it would in some odd Okie, Arkie, Cajun, weird sorta way."

"And these pictures of Mark, they sure look like the old pictures of Mickey's dad that I've seen," Brant said. "They'd easily pass for brothers."

"Maybe they were," Leslie picked up several of the best face shots of Samuel and Mark. "Let's scan these. I've got a good setup in my office. Can you send the scans to someone who might know for sure?"

"Yep," I said. "We can email them back to our offices in Durant, and Janie, our office manager, can show them to Dad. He's probably there right now. I'm certain he can make a good guess. After all he has several old photos of his father. He can put them together with these and have a great idea without even using facial recognition I bet. But we'll use the program anyway. We bought it, ought to get some use out of it."

"His father? Don't you mean his grandfather, Mickey?" Marie asked, visibly surprised.

Leslie stood with a look of more disbelief. "His father? You've got to be kidding."

Brant just grinned.

"Nope, Samuel could be his father and my grandfather. Dad is ninety-six," I said. "We Wallaces tend to last quite a while as long as folks don't shoot us."

Both ladies smiled and shook their heads.

"And I really am beginning to believe Samuel Whitman was very likely my grandfather, John William Wallace," I said, looking at one of the old photos of Samuel.

"I think your dad has been suspicious of that ever since we first made the connection of John William Wallace's name on the painting he received from Tommy Moon," Brant added.

"A painting?" Marie said, surprised once again.

"Yes, ma'am," I said with a grin. "That's what started this whole mess, a painting found in a stored vehicle from back in the early thirties."

"Was that vehicle a nice little 1929 Ford coup?" Marie asked with a quavering voice.

"Yes, ma'am, it was," I said.

"I've heard Momma talk about the new car Samuel and Renee had just bought the year before they disappeared. They were so proud of it. We even have a picture somewhere of them and Mark standing beside it just outside their studio in the Quarter," Marie said.

She shuffled through the pile and produced the black and white photo. "Tell me where the car is. Is there a chance that could lead us to whatever became of Samuel and Renee?"

"Well, Marie, what we know so far isn't much, but it's a pretty long story," Brant said, finishing off his beer.

"Then you better let me get you cowboys another round," Leslie laughed. "I do believe we need to hear the whole thing. Right, Momma? You want one more, too, Mom? I sure do."

"At least one more," Marie said, shaking her head.

"I'll have Janie send a photocopy of the painting Tommy Moon sent my dad," I said. "We may have a Samuel Whitman work that's signed 'John William Wallace.'"

"Yeah, now that you mention it, we probably need to get some experts to compare that painting with some of Whitman's work," Brant chipped in.

"This is getting a little spooky," Leslie said, returning with four more beers.

"To say the least," Marie said. "To say the very, very least. And I can't wait to meet William."

"We'll have to make that happen soon. I'm sure he'll be just as excited to meet y'all," I said.

"Well, you men have a seat and let the tale commence," Leslie said.

19

NORMAN, OKLAHOMA, LATE OCTOBER 1908 THROUGH MARCH 1910

RIDING CALAVARAS *down the streets of Muskogee, John William was thinking about his impending visit with his father before riding north to Norman.*

He'd brought his father's share of the money after selling their blacksmith shop in Murphreesboro, and he planned on convincing William to come to Norman with him and invest in a shop there.

Finally he found his father and Bass Reeves eating breakfast and couldn't help but notice the famous lawman's puffy eyes and back stiffness when he tried to rise. The man was looking old.

"Bass, this is my oldest boy, John William," William introduced him. "He dropped by to see me on his way up to Norman, thinks there's a pot a gold on the ground up there."

Bass extended his huge hand and nodded at John. "Hate to disappoint ya, son, but there ain't no gold up there neither."

"I reckon not, sir," John said, noticing again the man's obvious pain. "But I figure it's as good a place as anywhere to start a new life. I think Arkansas is played out. Anyway I plan on getting my boys set up for that university they've got there."

"That sounds like a plan, John," he said in a low voice. "Sit down and talk to yo daddy. William, I'm gonna walk back to the office, check them boys that think they be lawmen. You be along directly I reckon?"

"Yep," William said. "I'll be there in two shakes, Bass. The boy's ridin' out in just a bit. Aren't ya, son?"

Yep," John echoed his father. "It was an honor to meet you, Mr. Reeves."

Reeves just looked sort of puzzled and touched the brim of his big hat, turned, and walked toward the door.

After the big man had left the restaurant, William Wallace shook his head. "The man's sick, John William, real sick. He's pissing blood, and his back is a wreck, not many miles left in him I'm afraid."

"Well, what's that mean for you, Dad?" John asked as quietly as he could.

"You bring the money from selling the forge and stable?" William asked. "I'm gonna take that and head south to a place called Durant down near the Red, that is if Bass don't get to looking better by next spring."

"I brought it, Daddy, but why don't you come to Norman with me?" John William asked. "We'll pool our money and open the biggest livery stable and forge in the town."

William just sighed softly. "The money in smith work is leaving the faster growing towns, Johnny, I know you're all fired up about that college up there, but the little country towns are where forges and livery stables still have a little time left."

"There'll always be smith work left and..." John started to argue.

"Yep, but not like it was, Johnny. It's dying out. I like your idea of getting little Will and Shelby in college, but you need to study some about them automobiles, boy. They're gonna change everything."

John knew there was no use in arguing with his father. He would do what he would do. Rena would have told him it was simply obvious where John William came by his own streak of uncompromising bull-headedness.

It was time to head north if he was going. He handed William the cash out of his saddle bags. They shook hands and he mounted up.

The next day, he rode in to Norman and swung down out of the saddle at the Renfro Livery Stables on the east edge of the town of town. It was well-maintained and obviously successful. The future competition looked very stiff to say the least. He stabled his buckskin and headed for the hotel two blocks west that was recommended by the fellow at the stables.

Within a short time, he learned there was a much smaller forge and stable located a block north. He made himself at home and took a short nap before heading out to explore the little forge and stable on East Gray. It was run by a big Swede named Halvorsen according to the man at the desk when John checked into the hotel.

On his way down the street, he stopped in and sent Rena a telegram, telling her that he'd made it to Norman and would probably be heading back to Murphreesboro by the same route he'd left by in about a week, two at the most.

John William started his negotiations with the big Swede by asking for a job at the forge, explaining he was a smith by trade. However, the big man said he wasn't hiring. There just wasn't enough business with the Renfro Livery Stables and Forge taking in the lion's share.

He looked at the little shop and could easily see why it was struggling. At Renfro's where he'd stabled his horse, the livery stables were three to four times what Halvorsen had, and Renfro was running two forges, compared to Halvorsen's one. The little shop needed to expand.

All John William could see was opportunity. "Well then why don't you just sell me the place?" he said to the big blond who appeared to have enough muscles to lift a horse.

"Might not want to sell," the Halvorsen answered. "And I don't know you got enough money to buy."

"If you're reasonable, I got enough money," John William smiled at the smithy, who was skillfully hammering a horseshoe into shape. "I'd even hire you to stay on a week or two while I move my family up here from Arkansas."

The big blond quit hammering and looked at John.

"That is if you're reasonable," John William repeated.

In less than a month, John, Rena, and the boys rolled into Norman up to the small house he'd bought on South Crawford. He got them all settled in with their meager belongings before he returned to the forge on East Gray Street.

Maybe he should have taken it as an omen of things to come when he got down off Calavaras to find the stables empty and the forge locked up. The big blond Viking had left for parts unknown just a day or two after John headed back to Arkansas.

"At least he locked the place up," John thought to himself.

But nothing could shake his optimism. He set about cleaning the place. He'd be open for business tomorrow, and in no time, he was sure the world would be his.

Sure enough his reputation spread like wildfire. Through that winter and by spring, he had the shop and forge making a decent living for the family, which was growing as well. Rena gave birth to their third son, Robert Michael, less than a year after they completed the move to Norman.

He built another ten livery stalls and hired a boy to help stable horses and keep the place clean while he tended the forge and made new customers with his good nature.

Toward the end of the fall of 1909, a letter came from William, telling John that Bass's condition had worsened. He had something called Bright's Disease and was going to retire.

William was unwilling to stay on the force with a bunch of younger men and without Bass Reeves. He had been to Durant and found a building on the Market Square there for rent. He told John he'd bought a little house for him and Irene on South Fourth Street and would be there by the first of November to open up a new forge without any livery stalls.

"Mighty small business," John William thought as he closed the letter from his father.

Christmas of 1909 was a good one for the Wallaces, and the New Year brought more prosperity as well. His business was growing, so he wrote his father and asked him to join him in the Norman forge and livery stables.

William, however, was bent on opening his on shop in Durant and wrote back informing his son that he'd already started the paperwork to purchase the building there and start his own forge in the summer of 1910, a decision that would later prove beneficial to the whole Wallace clan.

By 1911 John William and William both were in business and doing well, even if William's shop was on its first legs. But the stars were already aligning again to bring John's world crashing down.

In October of 1912, John William and Rena were awakened by the frantic knocking of Micah Jamison, a twenty-year-old young man that John had taken as an apprentice.

The livery stables were on fire.

Micah had been at a bar a block or so away from the stables when he heard the noise of the firemen rushing to the blaze. He ran to the scene and started getting the three or four horses stabled there out of danger, but the building was a roaring inferno before he could do anything else.

John William and the young smith ran from the house to the forge and livery stable, leaving Rena to watch the children, but there was nothing that could be done. In a matter of hours, the thriving shop had been reduced to ash and embers.

Christmas of 1912 was not a good one for the Wallaces. They would sell the little house on Crawford and most everything else they had just to pay off loans, take what little they had left, and head for Durant, where William was waiting for his son and family to join him.

20

WE WERE STILL waiting on the final results of the facial recognition program, but according to Janie, after looking closely over the photos, Dad was already convinced that Samuel Whitman and John William Wallace were indeed one and the same man.

"He's taking it pretty well, says there's no doubt in his mind anymore," Janie said over the phone. "I think he may be planning to come down there himself."

"Brant's here, I'm putting you on speaker, so don't be saying any of that sexy stuff. You know how pouty he gets," I said. "But convince him to stay put for right now at least, please, doll."

"Yeah, beautiful, and give us fair warning before the boss comes down here," Brant called across the room to the phone.

"I'm staying in Oklahoma for now, Brantley Bluesoldier, but you better know who the boss is around here," Janie replied.

"Yes, ma'am, we'll be real good," Brant replied.

"After you finish with our program, send the photos over to Jerry Michaels at OSBI," I added, "just to be a hundred percent on this, see what their experts say. He owes me one, and send a photocopy of the painting down here too, please, darlin'."

"Leave no stone unturned, huh?" Janie said.

"Nope, no mistakes, and see if you can locate an art expert to compare the painting with some of Whitman's known work. Maybe that will keep him busy up there."

"Will do, Mick, y'all please just be careful, okay."

"Promise, beautiful, you just keep the big man grounded in Oklahoma for now."

"I may marry him while y'all are gone. He's the sweetest man I know, much unlike his offspring, both natural and adopted. You two behave and call us back with news sooner than later."

"Promise," I laughed.

"Later, girl, but don't marry no one 'til I get back," Brant spoke in the direction of the receiver. "You know you love this mighty Osage warrior the best."

"Well, you better hurry back then. Later, boys."

The phone clicked.

"Let's see the Quarter some more while we wait on further developments," I grinned.

"Beignets sound good?" Brant asked.

I pulled on my boots. "Sounds excellent."

Brant wanted to see the William Faulkner House in Pirates Alley. It was a bookstore now, and he'd been reading about it in one of the local guides. We decided it was on our way and set out afoot.

We had a few hours to kill before we were to meet with Jaxon and Tommy Moon again, and who knew when Janie would get the OSBI info back, or if it even mattered. We headed for Jackson Square. Café DuMonde's powdered sugar-coated treats were right across the street anyway.

A sudden shower coming in off the Mississippi moved us under the covered sidewalks across from Jackson as he tipped his hat toward us.

"Sorry bastard," Brant said, looking at the iconic statue.

I laughed. "You just say that 'cause you're an Indian."

He rolled his eyes, "He screwed your tribe a lot worse than mine. Damn, let's just get to the bookstore before I smack you around."

His Navy Seal ass was barely saved by the vibrating phone in my shirt pocket.

I glanced at the screen: *Leslie Waldrum*, it read, and I almost sprained my wrist hitting the button.

"Hey, Leslie."

"Mickey, got you some good news, I think. After you left, Mom and I went up to the attic where some of Mark's things are stored. I guess you got her thinking about Grandma. Anyway we went back up again this morning, and she found some things you are going to want to see," she said again in that beautiful New Orleans lilt.

"Such as?"

"Just come over to the house again tonight; you're not going to believe it. There's some of Mark's personal letters and…" she paused.

"And what? Quit teasing me, woman," I tried my cool voice on her.

"I would never tease my favorite Okies," she laughed. "Mickey, there are two journals written by Samuel. Looks like he's your grandfather alright, but you'll have to read it. I couldn't believe it myself."

"Hey, Mick, can you not walk and talk at the same time?" Brant said. "Let's roll."

I motioned for him to wait and tried not to faint, never looks good for a strapping macho detective to faint in public.

"Are you still there, cowboy?"

"Yeah…um, yeah, Brant's just in a rush. You've read them? And you think they're for real?"

"Oh, they're for real, Mick; they've been stored in our attic for over fifty years. I've read enough to know Samuel was John William Wallace. Grandma Chelle must've packed up Mark's personal stuff and stored it right after he was killed. I don't believe she read them, then just packed them up. I imagine she was so hurt after Mark's death, she simply put his things away without even going through them much, if any."

"God, Leslie, this is a lot to take in. We've got to meet Jaxon and his dad in less than an hour; he's got new info, too, says we have to hear it in person."

"Don't worry, darlin', I'll guard everything 'til you get here. You just see Jaxon, then call me, and we'll meet at Momma's house."

Being a trained investigator much like myself, Brant had quit champing at the bit and had already figured out big things were happening.

I dropped the gist of it on him, and we decided to put off the trip to the bookstore for later, walk back to Canal, and catch a cab to the federal building, maybe see the Moons early. It looked like we weren't going to need the facial recognition confirmation after all.

We met Tommy Moon, who was arriving just as we were, and Jaxon motioned us all into his office with his cell phone at his ear. He was wearing Wranglers and a short-sleeved white shirt with a pair of Caiman alligator skin boots that I immediately coveted.

"We're digging up bodies at the Fontenot place in Lafayette right this minute," Jaxon said, clicking off the phone. "Since Whitman's car was there, Mickey, your people may be there among the bodies, too, thought you'd want to know."

Holy crap, suddenly it was raining clues. Our reputation must have preceded us and now time and space, even fate itself, was giving up… or maybe we just got lucky. Nah, gotta be investigative genius.

"Bodies?" Brant asked.

"Six so far, all males," Jaxon said. "Still looking for more though. Apparently there's a whole cemetery out there behind the barns, said they'd be digging all day and maybe tomorrow. They're trying to find more with ground-penetrating radar right now."

"I'm sure they have the cadaver dogs out there, too, right, Jax?" Tommy said.

Jaxon laughed. "Yep, looks like you're gonna get your wish answered as far as the Fontenots go, Dad."

"Good Lord, Jaxon, it's all blowing up, huh?" I said. "But there's no sign or identification of Samuel Whitman or his wife?"

Jax Moon strapped on a Glock 40 caliber in a shoulder rig and pulled on a tan corduroy blazer. I admired his fashion sense and continued to covet the boots. A good pair of boots tells you a lot about the man.

"No positive ID's on anyone yet but no females at all; I'm headed out there in an hour or so. I can't really take you guys to an active crime scene, or I would, but I'll call you as soon as I know more."

Brant and I followed him and Tommy into the lobby and outside where a black SUV picked him up and sped away.

"Well, that was fast and furious," Tommy Moon said. "You guys want to catch a ball game? Kill some time, wait on Jax to call us back? The Zephyrs are home tonight."

"We'd love to, Mr. Moon," I said. "But we've gotta see Leslie in just a few minutes and then call Dad. We need to seem busy. He's a hard-ass you know."

"If he was a hard ass, you'd be working at Wal-Mart, and I'd be second in command of the agency," Brant said.

Tommy Moon roared.

21

TWELVE MILE PRAIRIE BETWEEN DURANT AND MADILL, OKLAHOMA, FALL 1915

Willie and Shelby Wallace were playing marbles in the side yard of the house they'd moved into a little over a year ago. Their baby brother, Robert, was watching, hoping to be included in the game while Rena sat outside on the porch sewing up a rip in a pair of John William's good work jeans.

A peddler's wagon was moving slowly up the road toward their yard.

"Momma, better come here quick, somethin's wrong," William called as Shelby and Robert stood up to watch the approaching wagon.

The old man sitting on the driver's seat was slumped over. He still had a loose hold on the reins, and the well-fed little matched paint ponies just kept heading toward the house pulling the peddler's cart, like they knew he was coming to make a sale.

The ponies obediently stopped at the house, waiting for their driver to make his pitch.

Rena stepped off the porch into a warm Oklahoma October day, moving toward the wagon, telling the gawking boys to step back.

The driver had on a well-worn brown suit with a faded string tie and a small Stetson hat, also well-worn. His white hair and beard looked a little ragged, his face was flushed, and he wasn't moving.

"Is he dead, Momma?" five-year-old Shelby asked, peering from behind her and his older brother, William.

"No, stupid, he's still breathing, can't you see anything?" William, almost ten, was of course an authority on almost everything.

"Don't call your brother stupid, William Matthew," Rena frowned.

She reached up to touch the old man's hand, and he bolted upright with a glazed look in his eyes.

"Indians, Indians, goddamnit, they're everywhere," the old man shouted as he rose bolt upright.

William and Shelby ran into each other, Robert ran for the house, and Rena jumped back as the peddler fell face-first off the wagon seat.

Her first impulse after her heart slowed just a bit was to kick the stuffing out of him. "Drunk," she muttered and knelt to see if the fall had killed him. He was breathing but in labored gasps. His eyes came open again, and she was afraid he was going to fight, but he couldn't seem to control his limbs.

Robert peeked out from the doorway almost in tears and called to her, "Momma, Momma, what's an Indian-goddamitt? Will it get me?"

"No, Robert, he said... Never mind what he said; it's all okay, baby."

"Indians, Indians," the old man slurred almost unintelligibly.

She felt his face. It was clammy and sweat-covered.

"You boys just stay back. He's sick, or he's had a stroke. I'm going to move him over into the shade. William, go get me a wet rag."

The two older boys took off together, headed for the water bucket with Robert, not quite five-years-old, remaining in the doorway peeking out.

"Think there's really Indians around here, Willie?" Shelby asked.

"Probably right behind him. They always scalp the young ones ya know and take the oldest one into the tribe; you and Bobby's goners."

He laughed at his little brother at first but then saw the true fear in Shelby's eyes and quickly had mercy.

"There aren't any wild Indians anymore, Shelby. I swear sometimes you really are stupid."

Rena had managed to drag the old man into the shade by the time the boys got back with the water bucket and a dish cloth.

Robert still refused to leave the house.

"I think he's had some kind of stroke, boys. He's not running a fever. William, you'll have to help me get him into the house. Shelby, tie the team until we get him fixed up, then you and William can stable the horses in the barn."

"I get to drive his wagon down to the barn," Shelby called.

"I don't think so," countered William.

Shelby stood his ground. "Just watch me."

"Mama just said to tie 'em up, not to drive 'em," William said with a snarl.

"Mama…"

"Hush, Shelby, both of you hush. William Matthew, come with me. I need you. Shelby Angus Wallace, you wait on your big brother, then you can drive the wagon down to the barn once he gets back outside."

"Mama…" William started.

"Son, help me. You drive your daddy's wagon enough. Let Shelby drive and you watch him."

Shelby stuck his tongue out at William.

"Once more, mister, and you can just sit in the wagon and William will drive," Rena said sharply.

"Yes, Mama," Shelby said and sat down to wait for his big brother.

22

AS OUR CAB pulled away from the federal building, the silver-grey Camry fell in behind us again at a respectful distance.

"Still trailing us?" Brant asked.

"Yeah, I'm betting on Mason McBride's boys, but let's just let 'em play right now."

Marie and Leslie Waldrum sat at the kitchen table once again with Brant and me across from them, still no sign of the Lisa yet. Marie wore a bright red blouse and a pair of jeans while Leslie had on a Jimmy Buffett Margaritaville tee shirt with a nice pair of shorts. Arranged between us on the table, several books were neatly stacked. Leslie held a cloth-bound book with no markings that I could see.

"These were in Mark's things. We've decided Grandma Chelle packed his books and a few other things in several trunks sometime after Mark was killed on Saipan, maybe even years later when the room was being converted into Mom's room."

Marie flashed a trace of a sad smile.

"Grandma Chelle was Michelle Guidry, Renee Whitman's sister, right?" Brant asked.

"That's right. She married Delmon Ladd, and I was born a year or so later," Marie confirmed. "But she kept Mark, raised him like my big brother. He was about twelve when I was born. Daddy died in a car accident when I was a baby and Mark was still a boy."

"After you boys left the other night, it put me to thinking of Mark, and I remembered these trunks up in the attic," Marie continued. "I'd prowled through the old trunks years ago when Momma was still alive but hadn't paid much attention, other than just recognizing some book titles. There were some shirts and jeans, a pair of boots, a couple of athletic trophies, a bundle of letters he'd written back home, but I didn't do much more than leaf through a few books before I closed the trunk back up. Momma never really got past Mark's death. He was a son to her, and she asked me to just leave the trunks closed unless I really needed something from them. That was in the early sixties; I was discovering boys and had other interests developing then, so I left the stuff mostly as I found it. It's sat in the attic now for over forty years unbothered until you boys set me to thinking about Mark again."

"Exactly what all do we have here?" Brant asked.

I knew, like me, he was dying to reach over and start examining the pile of books, but we were raised to be polite, respectful Oklahoma boys.

Leslie, however, was loving torturing us; she smiled that smile of hers, and again those beautiful white teeth lit the room when she spoke, making it hard to focus.

"We found nice early edition copies, *Drums along the Mohawk, The Yearling, The Rains Came, For Whom the Bell Tolls,* and *The Grapes of Wrath,*" she said, "and a number of books that must have been Samuel's. *A Connecticut Yankee in King Arthur's Court, The Adventures of Huckleberry Finn, Treasure Island, Ivanhoe, Leaves of Grass.*"

Her voice always seemed to be flirting with me. Brant said she was flirting with him. I knew better. It was me.

"It's good to know such a young man was reading well, but get to the big news, the journals." I tried my best sultry drawl back on her.

"The book I'm holding is one of two personal journals we found," she said.

"Mark's?" Brant asked.

"Not exactly," her Southern voice was soft. "There are two that were Samuel's. I've read them all now. Mark must've found them before he shipped out. He wrote several pages in the newer one only days before he left apparently."

She looked me right in the eye and flashed that beautiful smile again. "It's all there, Mickey, some of it laid out very plainly. John William is telling his son, Mark, all about his past, the whys and wherefores of his becoming the man known as Samuel Whitman."

She paused for just a second and extended the book to me. "Here you go, cousin."

I was unexpectedly stunned, suddenly uncertain of our next move. How do I tell Dad this is definitely real? He had a half-brother that he never got to meet? How does one explain to someone that his father had apparently lived more than a decade after the family presumed him dead? I knew Dad was already leaning toward this knowledge about his father, and now we have a brother to boot. Strong possibility and undeniable proof are very different things. I was stunned, so what would his reaction be?

Fortunately Brant was holding his end up pretty well and focused on the task at hand. "Can we make some copies of the journals as well, Marie?" he asked in a hushed tone.

She'd been sitting there quietly, taking our reactions all in. I guess, like me, she was trying to solve this sudden mystery in her head.

"Of course you can; you can take them with you and study them over, but I'd like to keep the original copies when you're through. I don't know why really. I never read them before. I never knew they even existed, but it just seems like they belong here with Mark's stuff. I want to read his notes in the journal and his letters again, too, maybe get to know the boy who became the man who became the ghost before I had the chance to really know him."

Leslie handed her Mark's letters.

Marie placed the bundle on the books, one cloth-bound, the other nicely bound in leather, and pushed them toward us across the table. "I'm sure you boys will want to see these first though, and that's fine."

"This all feels surreal," I finally managed to mumble.

"There's one hell of a story in those books, Oklahoma," Leslie said. "Remember I've already read them, both journals and the letters. You got some twists and turns coming. Samuel's last entry is apparently written only hours, maybe a day at the most, before he and Renee drive off the planet."

"Since you've read the journals already, Leslie, do you have any idea what actually happened to Samuel and Renee, any idea at all?" Brant asked.

"There's nothing concrete about that in there," she said, shaking her head. "When they left New Orleans, they were going to Durant, Oklahoma to find his dad with the painting. He'd first decided to mail it with a letter explaining it but then he changed his mind and decided it would be best to hand-deliver it. You boys are the detectives. I'm sure you two will figure it all out soon enough, though."

I looked at Brant. "Well, we'll be up reading late tonight, I reckon."

"You won't be bored," Leslie said. "I'll tell you this; he was as good a writer and storyteller as he was a painter, and that's a huge compliment."

"We'll guard these with our lives, Marie, and we'll get them back to you pronto," I said.

Less than a half hour later, we were back in our rooms at The Marriot, poring through the journals, me pondering the possible incestuous feelings I was experiencing, Brant, hungry as a bear.

Room service delivered our BLT's and *Dixies* as we spread the material out on the desk and dresser.

I opened a beer.

Brant took a bite of his sandwich first. "Should we call Will yet?" he asked. "This seems like it's going to break the case wide open."

Still a little dazed, I wasn't sure. I took a long pull off my beer and a bite of sandwich.

"Let's at least read the two journals before we do. Then we can give him more particular details," I suggested, coming to a command decision. "And try not to spill beer on the books."

"I never spill beer, bro. What's wrong with you?" He laughed and took another bite.

The two journals were apparently written by my grandfather, John William Wallace, while he was living in New Orleans under his assumed name of Samuel Whitman. Maybe he sensed some imminent danger since they were both addressed to his son, Mark, to be read in case of his unexpected demise.

He plainly states that if Mark or Michelle was reading them, he would be dead. He'd kept the older one in diary form, and he'd started the newer one likewise but had shifted to a confessional explanation to his son.

The cover of one was a dull olive-green canvas without any markings on it. It had a considerable amount of wear and fading, some stains, obviously a book handled many times. The second was a newer book bound in leather with a fancy script "*W*" stamped on its cover.

I turned the more worn volume over several times, then opened it to the neat, well-penned narrative of my grandfather.

"I'll take this one. Brant, you take the later one; then we'll scan through the boy's letters. Let's see if we can find anything to keep us here, or if we need to roll back to Durant after we break what news we've got to Dad."

Brant opened the cover. "Sounds good to me, but I'm betting Will's gonna say find out the hows and whys of the disappearance if we can."

"You're right," I said. "He's got his teeth set into this. We're gonna have to give him a lot more before he'll be satisfied."

"Yep. Better read fast in that case, and don't spill your beer, bro."

I took a bite of sandwich and tilted the bottle neck toward him.

23

TWELVE MILE PRAIRIE BETWEEN DURANT AND MADILL, OKLAHOMA, EARLY FALL 1915

JOHN WILLIAM WALLACE *and his cousin Harrison Wallace pulled the wagon into John's yard and were preparing to unload the wood they'd cut that day and stack it into ricks for sale beside the house when Shelby came running out.*

"Daddy, Daddy, there's an old man in the house. He's sick. He just fell off his wagon. He…"

"Boy, boy, slow down a minute; what in the world are you talking about?"

"I saw him first, Daddy. He's old, real old, older than Grampa. I thought he was gonna just fall outta the wagon, and he did…"

"Shelby, what are you talkin' about?" Harrison asked as he kept picking up the firewood.

"He yelled, 'Indians,' and fell right outta the wagon, scared William and Robert 'bout to death. Momma's got him in the house. Me and William put the horses in stalls and…"

"William and I," John corrected. "Okay, buckaroo, let's go in the house. Harrison, see what's going on in the barn, will ya? I'll talk to Rena and be right back."

John moved toward the front porch trailing in Shelby's wake as he bolted for the house.

No one knew it then, but fate was lining up a lot of different futures right there on that warm fall afternoon in southeastern Oklahoma out on the edge of the Plains.

The old man lay on the mattress that Rena had pulled off Shelby and Robert's bed, intermittently cursing Indians and mumbling incoherently.

"He's a peddler, John," Rena spoke softly. "The boys say his wagon has pots and pans and kitchen gadgets hanging all over it and boxes of several different patent medicines inside. I think he's had a stroke. One side of his face is drawn and his right arm and leg don't seem to work as well as the left."

"You have no idea who he is? Has he made any sense at all since he drove up?" John whispered.

Rena shook her head. "No idea at all, he's just a peddler I suppose. He yelled something about Indians, almost scared me and the boys to death. Then his words got more and more slurred, but his voice seems to be coming back. I can understand most of what he says now."

John William looked at Rena; she was a thing of beauty, black hair, dark skin, brown eyes, and she was good, really a good human being. She was smart, had schooled all three boys when there weren't nearby schools. What had she ever seen in him?

He glanced out the window at their three boys helping Harrison stack wood in the front yard and began to focus on their problem at hand.

"What are we going to do with him, darlin'?" he finally asked aloud.

"We better send into Madill for Dr. Baker," Rena answered. "I found almost fifteen dollars in his jacket pocket, and the boys brought in his till from the wagon with over fifty more dollars in it. If the doc thinks we're footin' the bill, maybe he won't rob the old man blind, so I reckon we don't need to tell anybody about the money just yet."

John nodded in agreement. "I'll have Harrison stop at Dr. Baker's place on his way home and send him this way as soon as he can come."

"Something else, John, he's talked about money buried by the Daltons somewhere north of Hartshorne. I haven't made it all out yet, but I know he's talking about burying the money with some of the Dalton gang. Could he have been part of that bunch? It worries me to think he's some kind of old outlaw."

"No need to worry, babe, the Daltons are a long time gone. But don't say anything to anyone. We'll keep him here in the boys' room; they can sleep in the front room on pallets. After Doc Baker comes, we'll figure out what to do next from there. Might as well send Harrison home now, I reckon."

They stood together arm in arm for a minute, looking at the old man who seemed to be resting more easily now. Then John walked outside and told Harrison most of what he needed to know.

Doc Baker showed up the next day, looked the old man over, and told Rena that it was in fact a stroke.

"Mostly it's up to God at this point," he said. "I've seen men unable to move or speak be up and going in a matter of hours. Then again I've seen 'em die even quicker."

He gave her some tonic that he thought might help some, then mounted his buggy to head back to Madill.

"Any changes, send somebody for me and I'll be here as quick as I can."

He touched the brim of his slouch hat and nodded to Rena as he left.

"If he makes it, Doc, we'll send him to settle the bill," Rena said. "If he doesn't, I guess we can sell some of his property and pay you then."

"Either way, Rena, either way, two dollars oughtta do it, I reckon. Unless I gotta traipse back out here again."

For the next few days, the old man showed very little change. Rena lifted his head and spoon-fed him soup and broth like a baby as he looked at her with an expression somewhere between fear and confusion. She changed him and bathed him and listened when he would start to speak in his sleep, but mostly it sounded like gibberish or rambling nonsense.

In the meantime, John William took to using the old man's paint ponies to pull a lighter load of wood in from the timber they were cutting while Harrison was driving the big mule team. In no time, they almost doubled the amount of wood brought in for sale.

Every night after coming in from cutting timber, John tried to help Rena with the old fellow as much as he could. He shaved the old peddler and watched him sleep, and he always kept a pencil and paper handy.

He'd heard the man mention the buried money now and then, and he intended to get any details down that might slip from the rambling. The lure of buried treasure excited him and reminded him of Robert Louis Stevenson's *Treasure Island* that he'd read as a boy.

Then one night as John stood in the doorway near the peddler, he heard him say plain as day, "I can't find it. Where is the rock? That big rock's got a star cut in it, a six-point star."

John William wanted to hear more, so he tried speaking to the delirious man, "Star cut in a rock where? What star?"

"Bob Dalton cut the star hisself. Me'n Grat lined up a big oak…due west… big oak, real big, bigger'n…" and again the voice trailed off.

John was so excited that he almost forgot to write, but really he didn't need to. The words were already burning into his brain. He saw gold everywhere.

"Big oak?" he repeated out loud to the old man.

"Twenty-five paces…twenty-five right straight at that oak…then…"

"Where? Where's the rock at?"

The old fellow was stone silent for a minute, then suddenly opened his eyes and looked right at John William.

"Who…who are…where am I?"

John William just looked at him for a second.

"Can I have some water please, just a sip? I'm mighty dry, real thirsty."

"Sure," was all John could manage, but the old man was either unconscious or asleep one before John could even move to get him a drink.

24

TWELVE MILE PRAIRIE BETWEEN DURANT AND MADILL, OKLAHOMA, FALL 1915

THE NEXT DAY, *John and Harrison drove the ponies and mules back into the front yard after a long day of cutting timber. The old man was sitting up and fully awake next to Rena in a rocker on the front porch.*

"Howdy," *he said and smiled weakly as John William walked up the steps.*

The old fellow was barefooted but had managed to rise on his own and walk out on the porch to enjoy a little sunshine.

"Well, howdy yourself," *John said and glanced over toward Rena.*

"This is Mr. Albert Britt, John. I've been tellin' Mr. Britt here that he's been our guest now for a little over ten days. He was able to sit up by himself this mornin' and walked to the privy this afternoon with my help. We've had us a good conversation, but I reckon he's just about tired out."

Rena smiled.

The old man extended a hand in John's direction and started to rise.

"You just stay seated there, sir; you've had a pretty rough go of it," *John said.*

"John, I'm beholden to you and your family, and I want to talk to you some, but I feel like I can't hardly keep my eyes open any longer, if'n you don't mind."

John was more than a little shocked to see the old fellow up and awake.

"No, sir, that's fine right now. Let's get you back to bed, Mr...uh?"

"Britt," *Rena said.*

The old man nodded. "Call me Albert."

John William helped the old man walk to the bedroom where he was sleeping. "Yes, sir, right now let's just get you some more rest and then we'll talk later." Rena followed close behind.

"Thank you, John, and thank you again, Rena. I reckon I owe you good folks my life," the old fellow said weakly.

"Don't concern yourself with that, Mr. Britt. We'll talk more when you're back on your feet and feeling your oats again," Rena said.

Albert Britt nodded feebly and said, "Yes, just a bit later, and please call me Albert."

John sat with Rena at the kitchen table, listening for a sound to come from the room where the peddler was sleeping, but none did.

Rena looked across the table and smiled. "I walked into the room to check on him this morning, and he was sitting on the edge of the bed. He was confused, didn't know the date, didn't know where he was, but he knew who he was," she said. "It was like someone just erased the last fifteen days or so. He told me his name and asked where he was, who I was, what day it was. Wasn't long before he'd told me all about where he was from and about peddling things out of his wagon for a living."

John simply nodded.

"He asked about his wagon and his team," she continued. "I told him about how he just showed up after he had a spell of some kind while driving his team and had been with us for almost two weeks. I told him we had his money, and his wagon and goods were in the barn. I told him you were using his ponies to haul wood. He's still pretty confused, but he's coming out of it, I think."

"Looks that way," John William smiled. "I guess this means finding the gold isn't going to happen; I'd sure like to have found where the Daltons buried that money, if they really did, but I'm glad the old man's going to be okay."

"I can't see him traveling for a week or so yet," she whispered and reached across to touch her husband's rough hand. "Maybe he'll keep talking in his sleep, and you'll figure it all out. But anyway it may all just be talk, John, just rambling, might not even be any gold, other than the gold in his mind. Right now let's just be glad for Mr. Britt's recovering."

"Yeah, I reckon so, but if he says anything while I'm not here, write it down, Momma, just in case, write it all down."

Rena smiled across the table. "I guess we better get Doc Baker back out here in the next day or so."

"Yep, let him know his tonic's already worked a miracle of some sort," John grinned.

She smiled again and squeezed John's hand.

The following day, Doc Baker arrived at the Wallace place again and pronounced Mr. Britt well enough to travel as soon as his strength returned.

Britt paid the doctor a couple of bucks once again, and Rena explained to Albert they'd previously paid the doctor out of the money in Mr. Britt's pocket earlier on the doc's first visit.

Britt grinned ear to ear. "Well, the man's gotta make a living, and he did ride all the way out here again."

It wasn't November yet, but the nights were finally starting to cool, and in a matter of days, Britt was walking around outside and helping Rena with some small chores, telling the boys stories about outlaws and Indians back in the Territories two decades past. The boys seemed to enjoy the old man's company, but they were still sleeping on pallets in the front room while Mr. Britt occupied their room.

He was getting stronger day by day, and he and John were getting along well, too. He was a likable sort. They sat out on the porch relaxing and smoking their pipes since the nights were still fairly mild.

"You've taken good care of my ponies, John," Britt said one night. "I appreciate that. I don't mind you usin' 'em one bit. That's the least I can do for what you and Rena done, and I aim to pay you some money before I leave here, too."

"They're mighty fine horses, Mr. Britt," John William said as he looked up at the stars. "They've been a big help to me. I'll make sure no harm comes to them before you're ready to go, and you don't owe us any money. We just did what was right."

Britt relit his pipe and drew in the smoke. "For the last time, John, please call me Albert; you make me feel plumb old with that Mr. Britt stuff."

John smiled. "Sorry, Albert."

"Them ponies are all I really got in this world, John. The wagon, my goods, money, that's all easy to replace, but them ponies can't be replaced, no two better matched paint horses on God's green earth. No, sir, none a'tall."

"Long as they're in my care, they'll be well-fed and well-tended, Mr… uh…sorry… Albert."

"I know, but it won't be long. I'd like to make it across the Red to Gainesville and then east to Denison before Christmas, got a niece in Denison where I can stay until spring," Britt said, blowing a smoke ring.

"You're welcome to stay here long as you want. The boys get a kick out of your stories, so do Rena and I, but when you're ready, just let me know, and we'll help you get all your stuff together and ready."

Lost in his thoughts, the old man just nodded and blew a couple more smoke rings skyward.

John watched him for a few seconds, then spoke. "Albert, when you were still about half out, you talked about Indians and the Daltons and some buried gold…"

John felt his way into the subject carefully, watching Mr. Britt's reaction to what he was saying.

The old peddler didn't flinch.

"Reckon I was outta my head pretty bad, John," the old man said evenly. "I seen plenty of Indians in my day, been all through West Texas and through Arizona and New Mexico Territories, had some close calls with Comanche and Apache, too, but I never crossed the Daltons before, heard about 'em plenty, though, guess that's where that come from."

"Just thought if you needed any help to get…" John William started.

The old peddler cut him off. "Johnny, if I knew where any gold was buried, I'd a dug it up a long time before now. I was just outta my head, boy."

John sighed, "Reckon so, I guess I was just dreaming some big dreams, thought you might be some long-lost outlaw, maybe Jesse James' kinfolks or somethin'."

Britt just chuckled softly.

John blew his own set of smoke rings toward the stars and rocked. "Well, Harrison and our cousin, Roy Mack Taylor, another fellow or two from town are comin' over to play a little cards tonight. You wanna play, you're more than welcome to join in, Albert."

"Stud poker?" the old man asked.

"Probably stud and five card draw, too, if there's enough cards, dealer's call," John answered.

"Friendly game, low stakes?" Britt asked.

"We ain't got enough amongst us to play but for table stakes, Albert." John tapped the ash out of his pipe. "Whatever a man puts up is what he's got to play with. Boys usually play for four or five dollars, ten at the most."

"Friendly enough," Albert smiled, "I'm in; I still got some cash after payin' the doc."

"Yep, and Rena's still got your till money hid, too; you might as well get it. She's got it put up safe for you."

Britt emptied his pipe, and both men moved inside for the night.

25

BRANT AND I had been up well into the early morning hours, each reading both journals. We'd learned the heart of John William's story since he had escaped from McAlester up until he and Renee loaded up the Ford and left for Oklahoma, but we had no clue what had happened to end the journey before they reached their destination.

Around ten I decided it was time to let Dad in on the story so far. I dialed the office.

"Mick, it's about time you called. I was starting to think y'all were in jail," Janie said.

"They haven't caught us yet, darlin', even though Brant's pretty slow," I tried to sound upbeat.

"You two better behave, or it won't be Will you need to worry about," Janie cooed in my ear.

"You know it, darlin'," I said. "Always."

"Any idea on how much longer y'all are going to be down there?" she asked.

"Well, I got plenty to tell you concerning that," I said, "but first how are Deb and Wayne Ray doing, and were there any problems with Daniel's security detail?"

"Everything's running smoothly here. Deb and Wayne Ray wrapped up the Benson case, and Daniel was in yesterday. He's fine, spent an hour or two with Will just shooting the breeze and making sure all was well. We barely notice you two are gone."

"That's hurtful but good, I guess. Big stuff is unraveling down here. We may have this wrapped up soon if all the pieces keep falling in place," I said. "We really do need to get back home."

I sighed.

I guess the journals had put me in mind of fathers and sons because JW was now on my mind, as well as my aging father. Strange how that goes, I thought.

"They haven't kicked Johnny outta OU yet, have they?" I asked as if I were being serious.

"No, darlin', they don't kick out straight A students on the golf team, even if their fathers are royal pains in the rear," she answered in just as serious a tone as I'd used. "He called yesterday and talked to Will for a long time. Your daddy caught him up on everything. He said he'd be in on break."

"Wonder where he got all those brains?" I laughed.

"His momma must've been one sharp lady, I reckon," she said. "I know she's where he got his good looks. Now what are you really calling about? I know it's not just to chitchat with me."

"I love to chitchat with you, babe," I laughed, "and you are right; his mom was a smart lady, not unlike some of the hired help around the shop."

There was a pause on her end of the line.

"I guess I'm trying to stall a bit, darlin'," I said, changing the subject. "I'm not sure how to give all the details to Dad. I know he's a big boy, and he wants to know everything, but he's my father, and we both know he's dying. I want to sit down with him and tell him face to face what all we've found so far but…"

Now the silence was on my end of the line. I guess I zoned out a bit; the silence from Janie's end of the call was begging for further response.

"Mickey, did I lose you, babe, you still there?"

"Still here, doll," I said. "Okay, here's the deal. Brant's going to have some copies made of Samuel Whitman's journals for us down here, but we're sending the originals to y'all, so Dad can hold them and read a bit of the story. It answers a lot but not all of our questions. Marie wants to keep the original journals, so after he's had some time with them, make more copies and send them back down here, please, darlin'."

"Don't worry about Will, Mickey," Janie said softly. "I'll be right there with him when the journals come. Is there anything else you can tell me ahead of time?"

"In them he's telling his son, Mark, that he is in fact, John William Wallace and explaining how he came to be Samuel Whitman, the whole story," I started. "He was apparently heading back to Oklahoma to tell his father and possibly the rest of the family as well what all had happened, but something happened. What? We don't know yet. He simply disappeared somehow and never made it back to Durant, where his parents, Rena and Robert, were living at the time. What happened on their way is the big mystery we haven't managed to solve just yet."

"I think Will will be glad to know that, Mickey," she said sweetly. "You know he will. Knowing is better than not knowing, and I promise I'll stay with him as long as he'll let me when I take the journals in. He'll be fine."

"I know," I said. "He's still strong as a bear. But it's gonna be a bit of a shock. Janie, he had a half-brother."

"One he never got to meet," she sighed. "But you know William Wallace even better than I do. He's been through the fire before, and he's a survivor. Have y'all learned anything more about Mark, other than he's gone now?"

"Mark had found out everything, too, before he shipped out. He had Samuel's journals in his possession for a little while. He even wrote his own entries in the later one just before he left. He mentioned finding his father's journals while going through some of his dad's things that had been in a safe deposit box. He was getting some deeds and titles settled for his Aunt Michelle, putting everything in her name before he went overseas. He never told anyone what he'd found, but he made a lot of plans for when he got home," I said as Janie listened quietly.

She was probably jotting down key notes to tell Dad once he was on the scene.

"I don't think anyone else, not even Michelle, had ever read Samuel's journals until Leslie and Marie dug them out of the trunks they'd been packed in up until yesterday," I said with a sigh. "Mark was planning on contacting the Oklahoma branch of the family. He also planned on looking into Samuel and Renee's disappearance but..."

"That never came to be," she finished for me.

"He's made his peace with most of this already, Mickey. I honestly believe seeing it in black and white can only help," she spoke softly. "Don't worry."

"I know you're right, babe, but it's all about to be 100 percent real. Some of it he's not prepared for. He lost three brothers in the war, not two. And John William talks about him, Robert, and Shelby, how much he missed them. He agonizes over decisions he made concerning the whole family. I just feel like I should be with him when it all hits the fan."

"You can't though," Janie said. "Besides he's in that self-assured boss mode of his where he wants to direct the traffic right now. Told me to get my sweet rear in gear and get you lazy, sorry excuses for detectives on the ball before he had to come down there himself and get it done."

"Good thing you're in charge of HR," I laughed.

"He knows I love him," she laughed back. "So you might as well send those journals on. You'll just piss him off if you delay telling him anything."

"Of course, as usual you are right," I laughed. "Where is he?"

"Been here since before eight when I got here," she chuckled quietly. "He's in your office asleep. I peeked in to see if the phone woke him. He was rereading Lonesome Dove again and nodded off. I'm supposed to bring him the Whitman photos again later, before we slip over to Naifeh's and eat, says he wants a steak."

She laughed lightly once more, and I fell in love all over again. I guess I do that a lot.

"I love it when you laugh," I said. "Don't wake him, doll, tell him I'll call him later. Brant and I are going to meet with Jaxon Moon again. He's still out at the Fontenot place, and we're just killing time, waiting until he calls. If the big man wants a steak, make sure he gets the best one available, and tell him if he behaves, I'll bring him back a case or two of Dixie Beer and a mess of crawdads."

"I'll keep him occupied and informed. You and Brant just figure out this whole puzzle and haul yourselves back to Oklahoma as fast as possible," she said. "This place doesn't simply take care of itself, you know?"

"I know that, and I know who keeps it running smoothly, too. I don't keep you on the payroll for your cute tush alone."

"Now who's lucky I'm in charge of HR?" she said with just the right hint of flirtation.

"Just don't forget that you're tending to the real boss back there, and I love you for it," I said, wondering what was taking Brant so long to get the journals copied. "And now whatta you want me to bring you back from the Big Easy?"

"You just bring yourself and that Osage warrior buddy of yours back in one piece, and all will be well and harmonious in my little corner of the world."

"Well, I guess the Bourbon Street bikini was a waste of good company money then," I laughed

"No, sweetie, I need something to gag you with," she said flatly. "But now that I think about it, you can just send me back down there after we get this all settled. A week in the French Quarter sounds like a fun time."

That's why I loved her. She could give as good as she got, or better.

"It's a date," I said.

"Who said you were going with me?" she laughed. "I think it'll just be me and Will. Now get to work."

"I adore you," I said, smiling from ear to ear.

"Love ya, Mick, now get to work." She hung up.

26

TWELVE MILE PRAIRIE BETWEEN DURANT AND MADILL, OKLAHOMA, EARLY FALL 1915

THE POKER GAME *at the Wallace place usually ran on a pretty even keel, family and friends, competitive but not cutthroat, and the boys seldom played past ten o'clock; eleven was a late night.*

They easily added Mr. Britt to the mix, turned out he knew how to play better than most.

"You always have to watch the old guys," John William kidded as Mr. Britt raked in another pot.

By ten o'clock that night, the money had all shifted in a couple of directions, and most of them were just trying to hang on to a couple of bucks.

It was getting late. Cousin Roy was already up the most and starting to get cocky when he caught the Queen of clubs down and the King of clubs up in a game of five card stud.

Harrison, John William, and Jeff Levins, a little fellow from Madill who helped John and Harrison cut wood every once in a while, were all treading water, but Mr. Britt still had a decent stack left to play with.

The old peddler looked at his down card, the King of spades, and his up card, the Queen of spades.

"That'll cost y'all five dollars, gentlemen, I'm feeling pretty lucky," Roy grinned. "And I reckon it's about time to end this little soiree anyhow."

Jeff and John immediately folded their cards and looked over at Albert Britt, the next to play. He peered at Roy first, then down at his remaining money for a second or two before he said, "I'll call, but I should know better; you're catchin' all the good cards tonight, Mr. Taylor."

Harrison was dealing and the last to call. He had the Ace of diamonds down and the Jack of clubs showing. He looked down at his dwindling stack; the bets had been mostly dollars for the big bets all night up until now. This was the first five dollar bet of the night.

"Damn, Roy Mack, five dollars… Damn it, you already paired the Kings, huh?"

"Five dollars to find out," Roy repeated.

Harrison counted his money; he'd lost six dollars already and only had six left.

"I oughtta just put it all in right now, but I'll just call." He cut a hard look at Roy and paused. "But I swear, if I get the opportunity, I'm gonna bust your balls, Roy Mack."

Roy grinned. "Deal, cousin, I ain't scared."

A nine of clubs fell on Roy's cards, giving him three clubs. The Queen of hearts followed on Albert's hand pairing his hole card. Then Harrison dealt himself the Jack of diamonds to pair up.

"Might as well take your last dollar, cousin," Roy said, seemingly unfazed by the pair of jacks, "and another five dollars for a side pot between me 'n the old fellow here, if he wants to try his luck."

Albert didn't like being called old, even if he was. He'd played enough poker in his life, and he was pretty sure Roy was just being a bully, bluffing with his bigger money, plus he thought he saw a glimmer of fear in his eyes when the Jack first paired Harrison.

"I'll call the dollar in the main pot and your five on the side, too," Albert said

"You're an asshole, Roy," Harrison whined. "I ain't folding a pair of Jacks. I call. You win, no soda pop for me while John William and I cut wood all week."

Harrison could have happily slapped his cousin out of his seat at that particular moment, but he just dealt out the next cards. The five of clubs went to Roy, a ten of hearts to Albert, and a three of spades to himself.

"Look at all them clubs," Roy whistled. "How much you got left there, Mr. Britt. We might just end this game right here with this hand."

"Whatever you think, sir," Albert said a bit too evenly for Roy's taste.

"Surely you ain't willin' to risk it all on filling that straight with Jacks up there in Harrison's hand and looking at my clubs?"

Albert Britt never made a sound.

"Your bet, cousin," John William prodded.

Roy looked at the seventeen one-dollar bills stacked neatly in front of him. "I'll take it easy on you, Mr. Britt, don't wanna see you head for Texas hurting for spending money. Make it an even ten bucks."

"Call," was all Albert said.

Levins, who had almost fell asleep, was suddenly awake and leaning forward with Harrison and Roy while John relaxed back in his chair.

"Nervous now, huh, Roy Mack?" Harrison goaded.

"Deal, peckerhead." Roy growled.

He paired Roy's nine, no flush. Then he threw down a deuce of clubs on Albert's hand and a four of hearts on his own.

"I'll check my nines out of respect for the older gentleman," Roy tried to put a cocky edge to his voice.

"Queens," was all Britt said as he turned up his hole card.

"That beats my jacks, and unless you got a surprise down under, Roy Mack, that beats you, too," Harrison said evenly, knowing the look on his cousin's face said it all.

"I can't believe you called a ten-dollar bet on a pair of queens. That's not a smart bet," Roy fumed.

"I'd say it was smart enough to win the pot, Roy," John William said, frowning at his cousin. "You know the rules, no bitching. Take it like a man and stay quiet."

Roy Mack had gone from big stack to loser in one fell swoop. He looked over at Harrison. "Oh well, it coulda been worse," he said. "I still got seven dollars left. I can have me a sodie pop this week while y'all cut wood."

"Very funny, Roy, very funny," Harrison said.

"Well, I'm ready to lick my wounds and quit," John William yawned. "Gotta be at work with Harrison early in the morning anyway."

"You gonna need me, John William?" Jeff asked as he put his last couple of dollars in his pocket.

"Not for a couple of days anyway," John said. "Looks like it'll be a little slower for a while."

Roy leaned back in his chair, still thoroughly pissed but getting over it. The game was done. He'd simply been out-played. "You can come have a sodie pop with me, Jeff," *he said.* "Somebody tol' me that Judge Murphy may need a couple of hands out on his place for a while."

Everyone started getting up and helping to move the table and chairs out of the way in John's barn.

"Reckon I'll get that money back next week, Mr. Britt," *Roy chuckled.* "I'll remember you ain't easy to fool next time."

"Leaving in the morning, boys, but next time I'm back this way, in the summer maybe, I'll be glad to give you another shot at it," *Albert said, smiling.*

"Damn the luck," *Roy Mack said as he Harrison and Jeff mounted up.* "Summer it'll have to be then."

The three rode out with Harrison and Jeff still ribbing Roy about his whipping as Mr. Britt and John William headed up to the house where Rena and the boys were fast asleep.

Albert looked over at John as they made their way back from the barn toward John's house. "John, I want to give you and Rena twenty dollars for the time y'all put me up, took care of me and…"

"I already said no to that once, Albert." *John cut in.*

Britt grinned. "I know ya did, but that was before I become a wealthy man."

"Albert, we didn't do it for money. A man's just supposed to…"

"Here's twenty, John. Don't argue with your elders," *Albert said firmly.* "I took it from your cousins and your friend anyway. I even got some from you, I reckon."

John took the bills and said, "Okay, Albert, but you got a stop on your route here with us any time, no charge."

"That's a deal," *the old man said, shaking John William's hand.* "I want to feel like I paid my share. You and Rena have been real kind towards an old peddler."

Early the next morning, Albert hugged Rena, scruffed each of the boys on the head, and handed them each a quarter despite John and Rena's protest.

"It's rent for the use of their room," *he smiled.*

"We're rich, William," *Shelby said. looking at the silver coin, thinking of candy and sodas.*

William shoved his deep in his pockets. "Momma, you better take Robert and Shelby's. They'll lose them sure as we're standing here."

Both younger boys shoved their money in their pockets, too, and immediately began shaking their heads no.

Mr. Britt laughed and walked, carrying his money box to the barn where John helped him hitch his ponies to the wagon with his goods still on it.

After a last handshake and his promise to return that summer, Albert Britt set out for the Texas border with Rena, John William, and the boys standing in their front yard, waving.

27

BRANT HAD ON a pair of Nike running shoes, beige Wrangler walking shorts, and a New Orleans Saints tee shirt pulled out to hang over the Glock 43 holstered in his waistband.

"Let's stroll down to Tujague's, see what's happening," he said. "Maybe see if our Toyota boys are better at tailing someone on foot than they are in a car."

It was hot outside. I was wearing a similar get-up, except for the Chris Wall tee shirt covering my Glock and a good pair of Pumas, far superior to Brant's Nikes.

"I could use a beer, some andouille sausage, maybe some red beans and rice," I said. "But tell you what, let's walk down to the lobby and split up. You go on down to Tujague's, get us a place at the bar. I'll walk back up and call JW for a minute or two, and let's see how they do with separate targets."

"Thought Janie said JW was okay?"

"He is, just got to thinking about him, thought I'd touch base," I said.

"I worry about you on the mean streets of N'awlins alone. You sure you won't get lost?" Brant needled.

I kept polishing my boots, might need 'em later. A dance can break out anywhere in New Orleans at just about any time. "I'll call you if I can't find Tujague's," I said.

We walked down to the lobby. It only took a second or so to pick up the two guys following us outside on Canal across the street looking at tee shirts.

"You know you civilized Indians don't have the native tracking skills we Osage do. You sure you want to chance the walk to Tujague's on your own?"

"Keep it up, genius," I said. "Besides, like I said, I've got your cell number where you can come rescue me if I get lost in the bad old city."

I headed back up to the room as Brant grinned and walked outside.

JW, Johnny, my only son, was a really good kid. I guess all the family confusion swirling around had made me miss him more than usual. I needed to hear his voice.

He picked up on the second ring, a miracle unto itself.

"Hey, Dad, how's New Orleans?" he said with a laugh. "Pappaw said you and Brant were goofing off down there, trying your best to bankrupt the agency."

I laughed back. "He would."

"Let me guess, you need my expertise," JW said. "I'll come right down and tie up all the loose ends for you and Brant. I can be there by tomorrow easy."

"You just keep your happy ass in Norman, boy. I just wanted to hear your voice for a bit, looks like we're tying things up here now anyway. Just waiting to hear from the big boss on the state of things."

"Aww, ya miss me," he chided.

"Yeah but then I miss M.A.S.H. on TV, too; just wanted to make sure they hadn't tossed you out of the university yet."

"Way to crush my self-esteem," he laughed. "And no, they haven't tossed me yet. I did change some stuff up; I'm going to take a shot at forensic chemistry, see if I can save the agency. Janie and Papaw both seem to think you and Brant are pretty hopeless."

I laughed.

"Okay, I think I'm over missing your voice now," I said. "We'll try not to bankrupt the place before you get your degree, but you may need a Master's degree at least before we can hire you, boy. A little more experience wouldn't hurt either."

"No way you can make it that long."

"Maybe with a little luck we can," I said. "But thanks for putting up with your old man."

"It's my job," he chuckled, still playing.

"And you do it well, but I gotta run now. Brant's leading one of the two yahoos that are tailing us around the Quarter, waiting on me to follow him to Tujague's with the other half of our entourage."

"Tujague's... I see," he said. "Pappaw and Janie were right. You two are just partying the family business away while I work my butt off in school."

"I love you, son; we'll try to hang on to a couple of bucks just for you."

He laughed. "Love you, too, Dad, just be careful, okay? I know you and Brant are a couple of bad boys, but you're not the only bad boys in New Orleans, you know?"

"Don't worry, buddy pal, these guys are no match for us. Anyway I think Mason McBride's just having us watched to alert him of any potential surprises."

"You know what Pappaw says, 'Take nothing for granted, keep both eyes open, and watch your back.' Just be safe. I love you, Dad, see you during the break."

"Love ya right back, Johnny. We'll play a few rounds when you're home."

"I hate beating up on an old man on the course, but whatever you want," he said tauntingly.

"Okay, sure. Just get to work and I'll talk to you soon. Love ya a ton, son."

I shut the phone down and walked back to the lobby where one of the two guys were still lingering inside the Marriot lobby now, reading a copy of *The Times Picayune* in a chair near the front exit.

Without a second glance, I went through the doors and started for Tujague's.

In less than a block, I noticed him behind me. He'd pulled on a Saints cap, obviously a master of disguise.

Brant was seated at the bar, drinking a *Dos Equis* lager when I entered. I didn't see a sign of the fellow who had left behind him.

"Where's your friend?" I asked.

"He's walking up and down Decatur, saw him go by the entrance just now. Where's yours?"

I shrugged.

"Aren't we tired of these guys yet?" Brant asked, sipping his beer.

Since his looked so damned good, with the water beading cold on that green bottle, I ordered a *Dos Equis* as well and took a seat beside him.

"They seem harmless enough for now." I smiled. "Let's just let 'em make a few bucks unless they become a couple of real nuisances."

"Whatever you say, boss. How's JW?"

"He's just being JW. You know that's a full-time job. He's changed majors, so he can take a degree in forensic chemistry."

Brant nodded as one of the two guys passed the open door.

"He still thinks he can beat me at golf."

"He can beat you at golf. So can I," Brant said.

"Keep dreaming, big guy. I can handle the both of you. Don't matter how far you hit 'em. It's that next shot that wins the match."

"You just keep telling yourself that, and JW and I will keep picking your pocket."

The guy who'd tailed me came in and sat down at the far end of the bar. He ordered a draft and sipped it.

"Guess his buddy drew the short straw and has to wait out in the heat," I spoke in a low voice, trying not to laugh out loud.

Another *Dos Equis* went down well, and foolishly Brant refused to acknowledge my superior athleticism on the links. It was getting late, and the two guys were probably getting tired of watching Tujague's door.

"Wanna walk back to the hotel together, make it easier on the boys?" I said.

He shrugged. "Yeah, we gotta see Jax again tomorrow early anyway, but what do you say to one more nice cold beer?"

"Well, okay, I guess, but you know how firewater affects you people."

Brant waved at the waitress. "Your treat, white-eyes. I am going to take all your money when we play again. You'll be too poor to play with JW."

28

AFTER LEADING our little tag-alongs back to The Marriot, we spent the rest of the night rereading the journals again, eating room-service sandwiches, and drinking *Dixie* beer before hitting the hay around 1 A.M.

I'd risen and showered a little earlier than Brant and was watching *Sports Center* on ESPN when I heard his shower kick on in the adjoining room.

I was thinking about flushing the john a couple of times, see if it had any effect on his water, when my cell rang. It was Jaxon Moon's call we'd been waiting on.

"Mickey, don't know if it's good news or bad, but we've found five more bodies, including a female this time, a man and a woman in the same grave, no positive ID of course, but you know how it looks."

"Uh-huh," I said. "Looks like things may be coming to a head; when do you think you'll have a positive ID? We're still at the hotel. We got big news of our own last night, thanks to the Waldrums. I'll fill you in later, but you'll let us know more for certain as you find out, right?"

"I'll get back with ya soon, real soon, just thought you oughtta know at least that much right now. And here's an extra twist for you, Mick; one of these new bodies is literally that, new, probably not much more than a few years in the ground."

"Really?" I said. "Now that is interesting. When do you want to meet up?"

"Meet me at *Mulate's* on the corner of Julia Street and Covention Center Boulevard. I'll be there in about two hours. Cajun food's on me."

Brant was already buttoning up a collarless short-sleeved black shirt and tucking it into his Levis, such a fancy Dan.

"Cajun food," I said. "And bigger news, looks like they may have found Samuel or John William…my grandfather or whatever I should call him. A couple, man and woman, in the same grave at the Fontenot place."

"I think it's safe to go with 'grandfather' now," Brant said solemnly.

I just nodded and pulled on my new Tony Lamas again, grabbed a tan short-sleeved shirt of my own to show off the muscle tone, and decided I looked much more striking than Brant.

"You ought to put on a long-sleeved shirt, bro, don't want to go toe to toe with these guns," Brant grinned and flexed his biceps.

Unshaken I decided I was much better looking; after all muscles can be ugly if they're too big.

The cab dropped us at *Mulate's*, and we were promptly escorted to Jaxon Moon's table near the back.

"So what's your big news, boys?" he asked as we were seated.

"You won't believe this, but there's a *Margaritaville* in the Quarter," I said.

Jax cut his eyes over at Brant.

"He ain't lyin', Jax, right down by the French Market," Brant grinned.

"You guys are funny. Now spill it, or I may forget the news I've got for y'all."

I grinned and ordered us a round of *Dos Equis*, since Jax's was almost empty.

"You want to tell him, or me?" I said, looking at Brant.

"We native people are stoic men of few words, noble savages, vocabularily challenged. Perhaps it would be best if you disseminated the information, arrived at due to our difficult detective work or…"

Jax almost choked. "For Crissakes, somebody tell me something. I've got big news, too, you know."

"The gist of it is: we've found John William Wallace/Samuel Whitman's journals and have established they are one and the same and he is, indeed, my grandfather. Now the case turns to finding out what happened."

The waitress returned.

Brant ordered the blackened catfish. I concurred with his choice. Jax ordered a crab dish of some sort and another round of beer for us all.

"I'm pretty sure I can tell you where he wound up," Jax said. "I just can't tell you how or why, and of course, and until we have a positive DNA match, I could be wrong about the whole shooting match."

"I called Dad back again before we left the room, told him we thought you may have found his father's body but no positive ID yet, we'd have to make sure."

"How'd he take it?" Jax inquired.

"Pretty well, said we weren't as worthless as he'd feared, but we had a lot more questions to answer before we even thought about coming home."

"So your big breaking news is what?" Brant asked as he sipped the cold beer.

"We've ID'd the fresh corpse, and he has past ties to Marcel Fontenot and to Samuel Whitman," Jax said between bites of his crab.

Brant looked up from his catfish and back over at Jax. "Really? Who is it?"

"An old student of Whitman's who parlayed his study with him into a career as an art teacher and ran a studio and a gallery in the Quarter until around six years ago when he disappeared."

"Delbert Jones?" I asked.

Jax stopped in mid-bite. "Damn, you boys are good. How'd you possibly know that?"

"A lucky guess," Brant said, "a name from the journals, maybe the last person outside of the family to see Samuel Whitman or John Wallace, whichever we're going to call him, before he disappeared. We were gonna start looking for him today."

"Oh, faithful Indian companion speaks now," I said.

"Well, you won't have to look far. I know right where he is," Jax chipped in.

The cold *Dos Equis* was delicious, I thought.

"I guess it's on to Plan B now," Brant said between bites.

"While you contemplate Plan B, here's what I know," Jax started.

"Jones disappeared without a trace not quite six years ago. And now suddenly his is the freshest corpse in the Fontenot burying grounds so far, by at least sixty years. He was in his eighties when he went off the grid in '96, no prior criminal record."

"And if he's the right Delbert Jones, according to Mark's notes, he was right there when Samuel or John William or whoever left for Oklahoma and fell off the planet," I said.

"I'm calling him Whitman for now. This 'whoever' thing is giving me a headache," Brant said. "Besides anyone we interview down here is gonna recognize that name, not your grandfather's name."

"We know anything for sure about Jones?" I asked. "Any next of kin? An address? Anything?"

"I'm waiting to hear from NOPD now. They handled the missing person's case back in '96, should have all we need to know," Jax said as he finished off his meal. "By noon tomorrow, you two will have plenty of leads to follow up on." He grinned and turned up his beer.

"I reckon," I said, grinning back.

Jaxon handed the waitress his card and smiled.

As we moved toward the door, Brant and I each left a ten on the table for the little dark-haired girl who had served our meals and kept the cold beer flowing.

"Generous and smart," Jax grinned. "I knew I liked you men. I'll call you with names if I get 'em and anything else I learn. Gotta run for now though. Later, men."

"We'll be waiting, big guy," I said.

Brant touched the brim of his Yankee cap as Jax walked up Julia Street toward his car.

29

"**NOW THAT** Johnny Law's gone, I say we shake up the two yahoos that are following us around and see what their deal is," Brant said.

"So you saw 'em, too. I was worried your detective skills had grown lax. I say we walk them around on a string just a little longer, see if we learn anything. Whatta you think?"

Brant adjusted his cap bill. "You're the boss."

I laughed. "Yeah, right."

"Okay then, if we're gonna remain non-confrontational, let's walk down to *Margaritaville* since you mentioned it at lunch," Brant said. "See if they start to sweat."

"It is nice and toasty," I grinned. "And I got my Hushpuppies on."

"Yeah, I know. Never was meant for glitter rock and roll," Brant said. "But they look more like Tony Lamas to me. Still, even in our best cowboy boots, I say we can outwalk 'em. Let's stroll."

We set out for Buffett's place at a nice pace with our watchers in tow.

Sitting at the bar, we watched the two guys following us come in and be seated at a table a safe distance away.

"C'mon, let's send 'em a beer," Brant said. "They look thirsty after the walk."

"Not just yet. Let's ignore them for now. They don't seem to pose a threat. They're just like our shadows, and we may want the element of surprise later."

Brant sighed without ever looking at the guys at the table; however, I knew that he knew exactly where they were and was well aware of their every movement in the bar mirror.

"Sometimes you are just no fun, Mick, no damn fun at all."

"I know, but I promise you get first move on 'em when the time comes."

"Dibs on the taller guy," he said.

We named our top ten favorite Buffett songs, agreed the Yankees were becoming a dynasty again, decided we'd both become Saint fans when the NFL season started again, even though they'd missed the playoffs last year, and hatched a very clever plan to split up on our way back to the room.

The beer was good and cold, but when "A Pirate Looks at Forty" played for the second time, we decided it was time to break camp and get back to business, time to split again. We left our bartender a five on top of our tab and I stood.

"I'll head back to the room. You have one more," I said quietly. "One of our friends should take the street behind me. Let him, then you follow me and my shadow, see what happens. The other should follow you, of course."

"Of course, or shoot me in the back."

"Well, don't let him do that," I grinned.

"I'll try, but you know sometimes I freeze up without you covering me," he said without looking up.

"Just pretend I'm still here," I grinned wider. "Let them think they're still free and clear, see if they tell us anything with just their simple ineptness for the time being. Maybe they have a contact here somewhere."

"Once you've had time to get back to the room, I'll have one more beer at one of the little joints on Decatur before I get back to Canal Street, and if they're still just in follow-the-leader mode, I'll call you," Brant said.

"Be careful, sweetie, don't lose the nice man."

He discreetly flipped me off.

I grinned again. I liked grinning.

"I don't think they want to do anything but see where we're going right now anyway," I said. "Let's just dazzle them with our ability to walk and drink beer."

Brant nodded and signaled the bartender for one more.

I finished my *Landshark*, shook Brant's hand, and started to the door out on Decatur Street.

Sure enough one of the duo eased toward the bathroom and exited behind me. He watched as I crossed over to the little park near the golden equestrian statue of Joan of Arc, the Maid of Orleans, giving me enough time to move ahead, then moved in behind a couple walking hand in hand between us.

A few minutes later, I reached the hotel, and he peeled off across Canal Street and into a tourist shop on the other side of the street again. I paused in the lobby and watched him through the front door for a second or two, wondering how many tee shirts he'd bought so far, then hopped on the elevator.

Fifteen minutes later, Brant called. He said masked man number two had waited for him to leave the *Margaritaville* bar, then followed him out. He was still wearing his tail as he spoke over the phone and had turned back north on Jackson Square, then east on Chartres.

"I think you're right, he said. "They just seem to want to follow us and keep tabs on our whereabouts. I haven't seen another soul make any contact with the dude behind me."

"Of course I'm right. When was the last time I wasn't," I gloated. "My guy simply trailed me like a lost pup back to the hotel and is likely talking to yours on their cells right now."

"I'd tell you that mine is leaning up against a building talking on his now, but you'd take it as more evidence of your uncanny intuition," Brant said.

"Of course, but you're right about one thing, yourself," I spoke into the phone. "We've about led them around enough. They've seen Leslie and Marie's place. They know we're talking to Tommy and Jax Moon. I'm okay with it all as long as they're on us, but pretty soon we gotta make sure they belong to McBride, just to be on the safe side."

"Good," he said.

I knew he was smiling that wicked little smile of his right then.

Alone in my room, I shook my head in mock sadness. "Not just this minute, killer, and promise you'll try not to break them beyond repair when we do get around to 'talking' with the nice men, okay?"

"Always the spoilsport," he chuckled softly.

"Yep, you come on back up to the rooms, and we'll figure out how to kill the rest of the night, maybe take a stroll later and lose the chumps out on the spookier edge of the Quarter."

Brant laughed and hung up. He walked a couple of more blocks into the heart of the Quarter and lost the guy easily enough, just for practice he said.

30

TWELVE MILE PRAIRIE BETWEEN DURANT AND MADILL, OKLAHOMA, LATE OCTOBER 1915

JOHN WILLIAM LOOKED OUT *the window from the breakfast table and saw Roy Mack and Harrison coming into the yard leading Mr. Britt's paint horses.*

"Oh, Lord no, damn it all to hell, Rena, something's gone bad wrong," he said, grabbing his hat hanging by the door to meet the two of them outside.

Unsure what was going on, Rena rose and looked out the door where she saw Roy wave to John as he walked in their direction. Then she began to clear the dishes as the boys started out the back door in mass.

"Looky what we got, John William," Roy Mack said with a grin. "How'd you like to buy a fine pair of paint ponies?"

"Those are Mr. Britt's horses, Roy," John said. "How did you and Harrison get them?"

Roy Mack started a long and rambling tale, explaining how they'd won the horses from Mr. Britt in a card game. He told John that after Britt left the Wallace place the other morning, he and Harrison decided to catch him and get the old fellow into another card game, maybe get some of their money back before next summer.

"Turns out he wasn't such a great poker player after all," Roy said. "He's sittin' over north of Gainesville right now without a team to pull his wagon."

"So that why you missed work Monday?" John William asked Harrison directly.

Harrison, usually playful and smiling, was quiet and looked like he could cry. He just sat in his saddle and wouldn't even look John William in the eye.

"Yep," he finally mumbled.

John knew they were lying.

"That's bullshit, boys, and you know it," John started in. "Those paints were Albert's everything. They were his living. He might gamble his money but not those horses."

"I don't reckon you know everything, John William," Roy said. "He bet 'em, and he lost."

Harrison sat silent in his saddle.

"He left here with nearly seventy-five dollars, boys," John glared hard at Harrison. "Y'all win that, too, at three-handed poker?"

Neither cousin spoke a word.

"How did you boys really get the ponies, Harrison?" *John asked, certain they'd stolen them.*

Harrison looked away without a word, and Roy started in again, "John, I'm not gonna say it again. We won them ponies, fair and square, and we come to sell 'em to you."

John just looked hard at the two men, both his blood kin.

"Harrison said you made good money while you tended to 'em. We just thought you'd like to have 'em again, cheap," Roy said. "Hell, you can even pay 'em off as you haul more wood."

John wasn't having any part of it though. He knew they'd not come by the horses honestly. He just didn't know right then how bad it really was.

"I can't believe you two worthless bastards stole Mr. Britt's horses," John William started in. "He's gonna figure out it was y'all, and you're going to jail, the both of ya."

Roy Mack just looked at John without speaking, but Harrison cracked and started to cry like a little boy. "We didn't plan to kill him, John William. We just wanted to get our money back," Harrison said through his tears. "We didn't mean to. I swear we didn't."

John was stunned. He couldn't believe the words that had just poured out of Harrison's mouth.

Then Roy Mack exploded in anger. "Harrison, you dimwitted idiot, quit sniveling, you worthless sonuvabitch."

John William stared at Roy, still in disbelief. "Oh, Lord, oh, Lord, what were you two fools thinking? Good Lord, what were y'all thinking."

He pulled off his hat and began to massage the bullet scar on his temple.

"If the old man would have just done as he was told, we'd have gotten his money and been gone," Roy said, finally showing a little remorse for their actions. "I never meant to harm the old fella."

They confessed to catching the peddler camped just the Oklahoma side of Red River. They had worn masks and planning to rob the old fellow and run back to Madill.

The whole event was fueled by moonshine and stupidity. They didn't even have a gun, didn't think they needed one to strong-arm one old peddler.

They were wrong.

"He pulled a knife on me, John; the old fool pulled a knife, a big Bowie. What was I supposed to do? He was swinging it at me, like some old knife fighter, threatening to cut my liver out, so I swung the blunt side of an axe I picked up near his fire," Roy said.

"We were drunk, John William," Harrison blubbered. "I liked Mr. Britt. We thought he'd be too scared to do anything but hand over his cashbox. Then it all just went to Hell."

Roy Mack finally broke down. "I didn't mean to kill him. I just swung the ax, and I caught him over the eye. Terrible, terrible sound, and he just sank down, dead... I'm sorry, John. I am so sorry. So help me God, I never meant to kill that old man."

He and Harrison both just stood there crying like two lost children, wishing desperately they had never followed the old man after he left John's place.

John felt sick at his stomach. He could not believe what he was hearing. He was simply stunned and spoke to the earth beneath his feet.

"What have you boys done? You've made a mess of things now."

"We were drunk, John," Harrison said weakly.

John felt his head begin to throb again. He reached up and massaged his forehead through his brows, trying to make some sense of it all. "My God, what did y'all do with the body?" he finally asked.

Harrison looked at him through his tears. "We were right there on the river, so we found a wash off the banks and rolled him into it and buried him deep, piled junk and brush on top of him. Then we got more drunk on a bottle of whiskey from his wagon."

"We took all the cash off of him, and we took a bunch of the stuff we thought we could sell at a little store I knew about across the river in Texas," Roy Mack said. "Then we drove the wagon down a ways to a little bluff and rolled it into a deep part of the river and threw the ax in behind it."

Tears were streaming down Harrion's cheeks. "It was the worstest thing ever, John. I can't get the sound of that blunt side of the ax hitting Mr. Britt's head and the look on his face as he fell."

John just stood there in his yard with Rena looking out the window again and the boys running in the backyard down toward the barn. This had to be just a bad dream was all he could think.

"Y'all should turn yourselves in, boys," John William said. "You know they'll catch on to ya sooner or later. What did you do with the other stuff you took?"

"We rode on across the river to a little store I knew about and sold the fella there some of the medicines that were still in their cases and..."

"Christ a mighty, Roy Mack," John practically wailed. "How can two grown men be so damned stupid. You're as good as caught now. Just go to Sheriff Sheffield and turn your selves in. Maybe they'll have mercy if you say you're sorry and surrender."

"We brung you the horses, John William," Harrison sobbed. "I didn't know what else to do."

"They'll hang us both, John," Roy said, wiping his eyes with his sleeve. "You know they ain't gonna have no mercy on us."

Right then John knew, in his heart, that he should turn them in to the law himself, but they were blood, and he couldn't bring himself to do it. They both were sorry, really sorry, crying and begging him to help, so he drove the final nail into his own coffin and sent them off as he took the horses to the barn.

Later, after Rena learned everything that had happened, she was distraught and angry. In a fury, she forbade Roy and Harrison from ever entering her home again. She was unhappy with John for weeks and would have turned in both cousins if John would have allowed her to have her way, but he begged her, said they couldn't bring Albert back no matter what they did. It was best to do what they could without bringing anymore tragedy down on the family.

He used the team of paint ponies all winter and doubled his normal wood supply while Harrison missed more and more time, staying home drunk. He finally had to hire Jeff Levins full-time, and of course, the first thing Jeff asked was how he'd gotten Mr. Britt to give up those fine paint horses.

John delivered the lines just as he'd practiced them, Albert had retired somewhere over around Sherman, Texas, living with kinfolks there now. He sold John the ponies and had Harrison and Roy bring 'em to him not long after he left their place.

He told himself he needed the ponies and that Mr. Britt would have wanted him to take care of them, but that didn't ease the guilt much.

Every time he hitched the horses up, he saw Albert's face and heard him telling one of his tall tales to the boys and the guilt would set in.

It was an odd kind of guilt he felt. The old man was gone. He had the horses. Harrison appeared to be ruined by it all, and Roy had taken off for Texas to work one of the big ranches during the coming winter.

He couldn't find a way to put it all back together, couldn't figure out how to help Harrison either. He was making more money than ever, but things weren't right, and he knew it all too well.

Someone would have to pay sooner or later.

31

BRANT AND I were headed back to Jaxon's office in the Federal Building on the corner of Camp Street and Poydras, where Jax had summoned us with all the info he'd found on Delbert Jones.

Maggie Comeau wore a forest green dress that pulled Brant immediately toward her desk, where she sat at the computer, as we came through the door.

"How are my two favorite cowboys this fine day?" she said as she rose and moved to meet us.

"Well, one of us, the good-looking one, is hoping to find a green-eyed date to have dinner with him tonight," Brant smiled. "The other one's just wanting to cry to your boss about how everyone mistreats him."

"Mickey, I'd love to have dinner with you, darlin'," Maggie laughed out loud.

I laughed right along with her.

"He's spoken for, Maggie, and you know I'm the good-looking one, darlin'," Brant flashed his best smile.

"Well, you're a little tall for me, but I might be talked into a meal and a drink or two," she smiled back at him and winked at me. "That is if you play your cards right. Mickey, how do you put up with him?"

"It ain't easy, Maggie," I said. "It ain't easy.

She laughed again. "Jax is back in his office. Y'all know the way. I'll tell him y'all are headed that way."

I headed down the hall.

Brant winked at Maggie and said, "I'm a good card player, Maggie, and I like a woman who can put me in my place, so I'm gonna be calling you real soon, soon as I can lose this dead weight that I'm taking care of right now."

He followed me into Jaxon's office where Jax was leafing through a manila folder.

"Have a seat, boys. I've got you fellas a few things to work with as far as Delbert Jones is concerned. It looks like we've found all the graves at the Fontenot place, so we'll be waiting on some forensics. Possibly we'll know more later, but right now, let's go over what we have."

Maggie buzzed Jax on the speaker. "Clay is here, Jaxon. I'll send him right in if that's okay."

"Good deal," he said back to her.

To us he said, "You men need to meet Clay. He's probably gonna come into play if y'all stay on this case much longer. He's one of, if not *the* best, investigators that we have."

An athletic-looking African-American gentleman about the size of Brant walked in wearing boots and jeans with a Marshal's badge clipped on the right side of his belt and a forty caliber Glock on the left side. He looked like Michelangelo had carved him out of black marble.

"Gentlemen, this is Deputy Marshal Clay Sanders from Lafayette. He's as good as they get," Jax said.

We both stood.

"Clay, these two reprobates are the Okies I was telling you about," Jax smiled as we shook hands.

"Anybody ever tell you that you look like Frank Thomas, man?" Brant asked.

Sanders grinned, and Jax laughed. "We call him The Big Hurt, guys."

"I can see why," I said as Sanders handed Jax a folder and grinned even more.

"This is everything we have from the Fontenot place right now," Sanders said. "Maybe some stuff in there y'all can use. I don't know, but it's pretty much what we've got. And I don't see much new stuff turning up. I think we're close to calling it a wrap out there."

"Clay will be working with us more here in New Orleans along with Dani Hebert, who you'll get to meet as soon as she's back in town," Jax smiled. "Maybe between the two of them, they can keep you two out of NOPD's way."

"Be looking forward to seeing you cowboys later," Clay grinned. "I'm headed back out to the Fontenot barns to tie that part up, but I imagine we'll see each other again if you're staying around a little longer."

"We'll make it a point to catch you, Clay, and at least have a beer," I said as he left the office.

"Super agent and one helluva man," Jax said. "Dad said he put him in mind of Ira, Brant. Coming from my father, that's a huge compliment."

Brant and I both nodded.

We all took a seat again.

"Okay," I said, "down to new business, let's rock and roll."

Jax flipped the folder he was looking at when we came in back open and started his summation.

"Mr. Delbert Jones owned and operated an art school and gallery in the Quarter for over fifty years. He made somewhat of a name for himself here in the arts community primarily as a student of…you got it, Samuel Whitman."

"So I reckon we're pretty sure this is the same Delbert Jones we read about in the journals and from Mark Whitman's notes," I said.

"Certainly looks like it," Jax said. "Graduated Tulane in the mid-thirties with a degree in art. He never attained the respect he wanted as an artist, had some shadowy connections to the Fontenots and the New Orleans underworld, mostly as his benefactors. He was reported missing by his 'significant other,' Rickey Dale, in December of '96. Much like Samuel and Renee, he simply vanished without a trace."

"But maybe most importantly, according to Mark's notes in the journals, he recalled Delbert Jones, a student of Samuel's from Tulane, was actually there at the Whitman place when Samuel and Renee set out for Oklahoma," Brant added.

"Now half a century later, the guy winds up in the same hidden burial ground used by Anton and Marcel Fontenot," I said, "along with Samuel and Renee Whitman and a handful of other corpses all buried over fifty years before him. Sound suspicious to you, Jax?"

"Plenty, but there's still a hell of a lot of missing pieces," he replied.

"How about this Rickey Dale character, he still with us?" Brant asked.

"He's about forty-five now, was Mr. Jones' legal heir, took over his place in the Quarter when they declared Jones legally deceased last year," Jax answered. "And according to friends of mine, he mostly promotes the school as a gay and lesbian art studio now."

"Good place to start as any, I reckon," I said.

Jaxon handed us copies of about everything he had and could get from NOPD. "Okay, but you cowboys have to play nice. This isn't Oklahoma now."

"Hey, we happen to be very culturally sensitive men," Brant said. "Yeah, we just look like Neanderthals," I smiled.

Jax just shook his head.

A half hour later, we found Rickey Dale at his studio. He looked up from his easel where he was working on a very Picassoesque work with a lot of bright reds in it as we entered the front door.

"Mr. Dale, I'm Mickey Wallace, and this is my associate, Brantley Bluesoldier," I said, extending my hand as we walked toward him. "We're looking into the disappearance of my grandfather who may have been an acquaintance of Delbert Jones. Jaxon Moon sent us here. Do you mind if we ask you a few questions?"

He nodded, smiled broadly, and shook mine and Brant's hands like we were paying customers.

"Not at all, gentlemen. If Jax Moon sent you, I'll be happy to help anyway I can."

"It seems Mr. Jones was the last man to see my grandfather alive back in 1930," I started.

"Oh, sweet Lord, I wouldn't know anything about anyone back then," he said. "I first met Delbert in 1988. He was teaching art classes right here, and I enrolled in one and fell madly in love with the man."

Brant loosed his most charming smile. "That's understandable; art will do that to a body. How about a gentleman named Marcel Fontenot? Did you ever hear Mr. Jones mention him?"

"Sure, I met Mr. Fontenot on several occasions. He was a true patron of the arts," Rickey volunteered. "He purchased several of Delbert's best paintings, and I believe he and Delbert were working on a business deal of some sort when Delbert disappeared. I really don't know much about the business end of things though. Delbert always tended to it. I hire that part out now."

I smiled and nodded as Brant made notes that he'd most likely never look at.

"Did he and Mr. Fontenot ever have any problems with each other that you know of?" Brant continued.

"Oh, no, everyone loved Delbert," Rickey replied.

I could tell this was good to know. I saw Brant jot down, "Everyone loved Delbert."

"After Mr. Jones disappeared, did anyone with the investigation ask about his dealings with Mr. Fontenot during your time together or earlier?" I asked.

"Not to my knowledge, but I was simply distraught with Delbert's disappearance. I do know, however, that they contacted Riley Postier," Rickey frowned. "But personally I was always certain Riley had something to do with Delbert's disappearance."

"And Mr. Postier would be…?" Brant asked.

"The old bitch was with Delbert for years before he met me," Dale practically hissed. "He never really cared for Delbert though, just used him for his money. Delbert bought him a place over on Esplanade. The old devil still lives there. He thinks he's an artist, but he couldn't paint houses for a living."

"Just how old a fellow is Mr. Postier?" Brant continued.

"He must be in his eighties by now. He looks like a dried-up old boot," Dale answered.

"You say Mr. Postier and Delbert were no longer together when you met Mr. Jones?" I asked.

"Delbert had finally gotten fed up with Riley's constant whining and bitching," Rickey said. "When I first met Delbert, he told me that he bought Riley the place on Esplanade where he lives now just to shut him up. I believe they'd been together over thirty years, although I don't know how. I don't mean to sound petty, but he was unbearable and always very rude when we met at an event or such."

"And you say the police spoke with him about Delbert's disappearance?" Brant came back in.

"Yes, but supposedly he had an ironclad alibi, or at least so I heard. I still feel like he was involved somehow," Dale insisted. "He's a horrible little toad."

Brant nodded. "Mr. Dale, you've been a great help. I think we need to check this Postier fellow out. Maybe the detectives missed something. Thanks so much."

We made a helluva team. Rickey Dale loved us.

I handed him one of our cards; they were nifty little things, an obviously Native American tracker and a traditional cowboy figure with *Cowboys and Indians Investigations* emboldened in black between the two with all our appropriate contact numbers.

He seemed appropriately impressed.

"Call us if you think of anything else that might help. We'll appreciate your time and any assistance you give us," I said as we shook hands.

"I do hope you find something new, concerning Delbert's disappearance, and I hope you find out about your grandfather, too, Mr. Wallace," Rickey said. "It was good to meet you, too, Mr. Bluesoldier. I love that name."

Brant and I both smiled and eased out the front door, leaving him to his painting once again.

Outside on the sidewalk, Brant looked over at me and said, "Sounds like true love to me. What do you think?"

I grinned. "I'd say we need to find Riley Postier."

32

TWELVE MILE PRAIRIE BETWEEN DURANT AND MADILL, OKLAHOMA, APRIL 1916

MONTHS PASSED, *Christmas came and went, but the guilt hung on. John William had seen his business prosper and tried to console himself with better than usual gifts for the boys and Rena.*

A few months later when spring came, bringing with it heavy rain, it wasn't long after that Mr. Britt's body washed out of its burial spot, and very soon after that, John William's world spiraled forever out of control.

Two boys skipping school for a little fishing trip on the Red found the old man's decomposed body. The damaged skull left little doubt to the cause of death. Roy and Harrison had buried enough evidence, along with Mr. Britt, and he was identified quickly.

In less than a month after finding the body in his county, Marshall County Sheriff Floyd Sheffield was on to Roy Mack first and then Harrison as well.

As soon as the news began to circulate about the gruesome discovery, a store owner across the river in Texas recalled Roy, selling him two cases of patent medicine back in late October or early November.

He knew Roy Mack from the year before when Roy worked on a nearby cattle ranch. He told Sheffield that Roy and another fellow brought two cases of Dr. Kilmer's Swamp Root Kidney Cure into his store that Roy claimed he won from a peddler in a poker game.

Never considering the ease of later identification, Roy had actually chosen the store because he was familiar with it and the owner. Harrison, more sober then but still shaken by the killing, agreed this was an excellent idea. Neither Roy Mack nor Harrison ever was much of a thinker.

It didn't take Sheffield long to locate Roy Mack working on a ranch in Cooke County, Texas. He contacted Pete Maxwell, the local sheriff over there, and they arrested Roy in mid-April. In short order, Roy was back in Oklahoma, and he soon identified his cousin, Harrison Wallace, as his accomplice.

Of course John William still had the horses when they arrested Roy and Harrison, and he, too, was quickly implicated in the crime. He knew it looked bad on him, but he never doubted that Harrison and Roy Mack would tell the truth since they were caught red-handed.

And at first, they did.

They told Judge Murphy that they gave John the ponies as payment for a debt they owed him, and John was released for a time, pending possible minor charges.

Then came the bad luck.

A young U.S. Senator running for re-election made a campaign stop in Madill. While there, simply by chance, he saw John William Wallace's name in the local paper.

Senator Davis McBride smiled. The wheels were placed in motion, and in short order, he confirmed that John William was the same John William Wallace that he'd lost to Arkansas over a decade ago, before Oklahoma was even a state.

He'd waited a long time for revenge, had almost given up on it, and then fate simply handed it to him, so with great fervor, Davis McBride arranged a few more days layover in Marshall County where he began to plot John's ultimate destruction. He was damn near giddy.

Judge Arnold Murphy, apparently McBride's good friend and campaign contributor, upped the ante. He told Harrison and Roy Mack that he knew John was in on the killing. He reckoned they were just trying to protect their cousin since he had a family and all. But John was the oldest, he was the one who wound up with the horses and who was probably the ring leader.

Murphy swore he'd see them both charged with capital murder and hanged if they didn't testify against John William. However, if they did the right thing, he'd see that they all went to Big Mac with a life sentence and a chance for parole in a few years of good behavior.

Without Harrison and Roy's testimony implicating him in the murder, all they could pin on John was possession of the stolen horses, but the boys were scared; they lied, and all three men were charged, and a month or so later, sentenced to life in prison at McAlester State Penitentiary.

Again John William knew they regretted it, but that didn't soften the blow and it didn't help a whole hell of a lot. He was going to McAlester for a crime he didn't commit, and he was angry. He had a wife and three children. He couldn't forgive his cousins, even knowing the dirty deal they'd been handed, nor could his family.

John's father, William, was already sending telegrams to men he'd met through Judge Parker and some he'd met working with Bass Reeves in Muskogee, but Parker had been dead twenty years now, and Bass nearly five years. Things didn't look good.

Davis McBride, unable to resist a chance to gloat, paid John William a visit in the Marshall County jail, after he'd been sentenced, before they took him away to McAlester.

John didn't recognize him when he walked into the jail dressed in his expensive suit and spoke with the deputy sheriff for just a few minutes before the deputy stepped out the front door.

McBride walked back to where John was the only prisoner. Roy and Harrison hadn't fought the sentencing and had already been transferred. Only John had appealed the sentence.

Looking into the cell, McBride smiled and said, "Nice scar you got there, Wallace."

John looked up at the stranger, confused. Where had the deputy gone?

"Do I know you, mister?" he asked.

"You murdered my father and two lawmen over ten years ago and got away with it. You tried to kill me and my brothers, but I told you I'd get you, Wallace. It took me a while. Hell, I thought you were still hidden somewhere in Arkansas, but thank God you're a stupid bastard."

"McBride?" John said, shaking his head in disbelief.

"Senator McBride, Wallace, Senator McBride, and you can forget that parole shit. You're going to pay and pay hard. I intend to crush you like a bug."

John decided silence was his best response. He suddenly feared what might happen to Rena and the boys without him and what hardships McBride might decide to inflict upon them as part of his retaliation.

He knew his father would take care of Rena and the boys as best he could, but John was still worried sick, and he didn't feel any better when McBride finally grew bored with his refusal to speak and decided to leave.

"You'll be dead in less than a year unless I can get you lynched before they take you outta here," McBride said as he turned and started to walk away. "I just wanted you to know it was me that got you, you son of a bitch."

He refused to give McBride the benefit of a response, just picked up a newspaper that Rena had brought him earlier, and did his best to ignore the man. What else could he do? The bastard had him, for the time being anyway, he reckoned.

"Go ahead, read your paper, you piece of shit. I'll be reading about the end of your miserable life pretty soon. If any rag of a newspaper finds that print worthy."

With that McBride smiled and walked out the door, leaving him alone in the cell.

Later that day, his father came to see him, this time without Rena, to tell him there was drunk talk of lynching John William going on in some of the local bars. He warned John to keep his eyes open.

The elder Wallace had already spoken to Sheriff Sheffield and made it plain there'd be no vigilante actions taking place as long as he could fire a weapon.

Sheffield respected William Matthew Wallace and knew well he had been good friends with Bass Reeves before Wallace had moved to Durant. William's name still carried enough weight to put a little fear into men, and Sheriff Sheffield would take the necessary steps to protect John in his jail.

John told his father everything McBride had said. William just nodded and assured him there'd be no lynching, and he'd have him out before long.

"Just watch anyone they try to put in here with you, boy," his dad said. "The sorry coward may not be able to get you lynched, but I wouldn't put it past him trying to have you killed by some fool, and that goes for later on at Mac, too."

"I'll keep both eyes open, Poppa, but get me out and bring Rena back later as soon as you can before they take me."

His father nodded and walked out.

Rena and William came back later that afternoon, both looking tired and worried.

"*Tell the boys I'm okay. I'll be free soon, and we'll be back together,*" John told them through the bars.

"*Oh, Johnny, this just isn't right. How can this happen?*" Rena said through tears.

"*No, it's not right,*" William said, "*I ought ride down to San Marcos and whip my brother Andrew for letting that worthless boy of his come up here. If Harrison wasn't up here, Roy wouldn't be here either. Roy Mack's never been worth a tinker's damn. His daddy was nothing but trash, John. I told you they were no good.*"

John didn't argue. His dad was definitely not in the humor. Besides that he was undoubtedly right.

"*We'll get past this. Y'all don't worry,*" John pleaded.

They left with Rena still crying, like she knew he wouldn't ever be back, and his father clenching and unclenching his fist.

Several deputies took him to Big Mac the next day without another meeting.

33

BRANT AND I made a call to Jax, caught a taxi, and in a matter of minutes, were knocking on Riley Postier's door on Esplanade, where Jaxon had alerted him to our arrival.

Postier did in fact look a good deal like an old boot. He was leathered and well-aged, but he still seemed plenty aware and in good health.

We introduced ourselves and once again explained why we had come to his fair city.

"I was with Delbert for almost forty years," Postier said, "there's nothing I don't know about him. He told me everything. I know all about his learning to paint with Samuel Whitman, and I know how he got the money to start his art studio. I know a lot of things about Delbert, but, gentlemen, I don't know where he went. I've already told the police that."

"We understand that, sir; we're not accusing you of anything," Brant said.

"We would like to hear though, what you know about Samuel Whitman, Mr. Postier," I added.

There was a significant pause as the old man looked me straight in the eyes.

"Oh well," he sighed and then smiled. "I guess it's time. I'm eighty-four, Mr. Wallace. I have terminal liver cancer, and I know for a fact that Samuel Whitman was really John William Wallace, most likely your relative and I figure you do, too, or at least you suspect it; otherwise you wouldn't be here talking to an old queen now, would you?"

The old man smiled once again at his own quip.

I instantly liked him.

"And how do you know all this about Samuel Whitman for certain?" I asked.

"Delbert told me," he stated matter-of-factly. "We didn't have any secrets from one another. I suppose once Delbert disappeared, I believed this day might never come. But once upon a time, I feared it would have come long, long ago."

"Why didn't you tell any of this to the police, Mr. Postier?" Brant asked.

"They didn't ask when they were speaking with me about Delbert's disappearance, and before that, it could have only hurt Delbert. I loved him."

"So you know what actually happened to my grandfather?" I asked.

"Yes, Mr. Wallace. I'm afraid I do," he answered. "But I'm afraid it's a sad story, one you might not want to hear. And I know Delbert was responsible and never forgave himself. He didn't kill anyone, but he *was* responsible for Samuel and Renee's deaths. He told me everything that happened."

"Would you mind telling us what you know, sir? It would mean a lot to the family," Brant added.

"Of course I will. Like I said, I suppose I've been waiting forever to tell someone who mattered. I imagine you've already surmised they were no longer alive. I'm terribly sorry for your loss. It troubled Delbert as long as I knew him. You boys better have a seat. This isn't really a short story."

We sat on the antique divan as he took his place in an equally expensive-looking chair.

"It all started several years before I met Delbert," he began. "Delbert was taking lessons from Mr. Whitman when one day he overheard a conversation between Samuel and Renee concerning the details of Samuel's true identity. I suppose he was eavesdropping. Delbert was a gossip and a snoop, even if I did love him. He could be a manipulative, devious shit when it came to getting ahead in the art world. I'm sure he was planning on using any information to his personal gain somewhere."

Brant pulled out his handy notepad.

"But I digress," Mr. Postier said. "Delbert was seeing this really nasty fellow named Pierre Toussaint, who worked for Marcel Fontenot at the time. He overheard Samuel explaining to Renee that an Oklahoma Senator, named McBride I believe, wanted to find him for earlier transgressions, and as fate would have it, Delbert had actually met Senator McBride at one of Marcel and Anton Fontenot's parties. Once again Delbert was snooping and conniving."

Postier paused and asked if we'd like a beverage.

We both passed and waited for him to resume.

He continued, "Delbert thought he saw an opportunity to make a little money, so he used Pierre to have Fontenot contact the senator with an offer to sell him information as to Wallace's whereabouts. He never dreamed the seriousness of the situation and always claimed that he believed Whitman probably just owed McBride money."

I sat listening intently and nodding occasionally while Brant was making notes like a real detective.

"McBride had Mr. Fontenot pay Delbert 500 dollars for identifying Whitman as Wallace. There was some sort of very unique scar that convinced the senator that Whitman truly was Wallace. Anyway Marcel saw the opportunity to get his hands-on Whitman and perhaps gain a good deal of leverage with McBride. He told Delbert to watch Whitman or Wallace, as he was known to the senator, and keep him apprised. Later he told Marcel about Samuel's planned excursion back to Oklahoma, and Fontenot decided to seize the chance to take him. It wasn't until then that Delbert learned they were going to kill Whitman. He knew his wife Renee was going, too, so he told Pierre he couldn't be a part of the kidnapping. Pierre explained rather painfully that it wasn't optional."

Brant continued writing in his note pad. I think for real this time.

"To make a very long story a little shorter, Delbert was scared of Marcel. He was scared of Pierre." Postier coughed a dry cough. "Again, I loved Delbert, but he was not a brave man. He did as he was told. He pretended to have problems with his own vehicle and asked Samuel to drop him off at his apartment as they were leaving the Quarter. Toussaint and some other men were already lying in ambush at Delbert's place. Delbert pretended to be ill and have trouble opening his door and signaled Samuel to help him, but when Samuel helped Delbert into his apartment, Toussaint and one of the other men were waiting. Others pulled guns and took Renee. They put Samuel and Renee into their vehicle while another man took the Whitman car and followed them to Marcel's place outside of Lafayette."

"Whitman… Wallace…my grandfather, just got in the car with armed men and without a fight?" I asked.

"They had Renee. He surrendered his own pistol and tried to negotiate her release. Delbert claimed he pled with Pierre not to hurt them and got slapped around for his trouble. Toussaint told your grandfather they were going to see Fontenot, and he'd let them know why they were being taken. They drove to Fontenot's place near Lafayette, and I guess your grandfather figured out what was up and realized there would be no negotiating."

Riley Postier stood and walked to a polished mahogany liquor cabinet that fit with the rest of the expensive interior of his home. "Are you gentlemen sure I can't fix you a drink?"

We both nodded and said no thanks again.

He poured himself a drink, a fine single-malt Scotch, before continuing, "As they got out of the car, your grandfather somehow managed to wrestle a gun from one of the thugs and shot him, then shot and wounded Pierre, but a third man shot Samuel. In the gun battle that ensued, Pierre shot and killed Renee while she was fighting one of the attackers."

I must have looked surprised or sad or something. Postier paused and looked at me. "I know this must be hard to hear, Mr. Wallace. I am so sorry."

I nodded. "It's okay, sir. I need to know everything you know. Please go on."

He nodded and drank. "Pierre made Delbert help bury them together in a single grave that had already been dug. Then two of the guys your grandfather shot actually died while he was burying Renee and Samuel, so Pierre made Delbert dig a shallow grave and bury them, too, but this final act of sadism proved to be his downfall."

"How so?" Brant said, looking up from his scribbling.

"First it was a miracle they didn't kill Delbert then and there, but as soon as Delbert got back to New Orleans, he made a map and a set of notes, copied them several times, and put them in several different safety deposit boxes, mostly because he feared for his own life, but later he blackmailed Fontenot and McBride, convincing them he had the goods on them."

"He played the big boys?" I asked.

"They 'bought' his paintings and promoted his work, paid to get his studio started, and he stayed quiet for years, but I heard he'd fallen on hard times with his new young piece of ass spending all that he had. I know that little jerk got Delbert's life insurance and his art studio. Delbert was getting older, becoming less and less relevant in the art community. When I heard he had disappeared, I was certain that he had tried something stupid with Marcel Fontenot," Postier said. "Maybe Fontenot just got tired of him; I don't know for sure, but you can bet he had a hand in Delbert's disappearance."

"But what about the safety deposit boxes?" Brant asked.

"I believe they may have been all a bluff," Postier said, finishing his scotch. "He never told me where they were or showed me a key, but he convinced Marcel they were real though and that there were five or six of them to be opened in event of his early or suspicious demise. Maybe Marcel finally called that bluff."

"You don't think Mr. Jones just didn't tell you where they were?" I asked the old fellow.

He poured another scotch and sat back down. "He would have told me at that time anyway. I know Marcel Fontenot had Delbert killed. I can say that now that Marcel's dead, too. Maybe he figured the bluff was in, or maybe he just got tired of paying Delbert and decided it was safe to end it after so much time. Anyway I imagine Delbert will be like so many others and just never be seen again, but he's dead, boys. I'd bet all I've got on it, and I'm not telling this tale to another soul, young Wallace. I'll be gone in less than a year most likely. It was for you and your friend's ears alone. I hope you can help put your remaining family's minds to rest."

"My father will appreciate that, Mr. Postier," I said. "You've brought a lot of closure to a great many questions, sir."

"Are you sure we can't change your mind on taking this whole story public?" Brant asked.

He smiled and shook his head. "No, boys; I just want to pass in peace."

Brant shot me the "we-owe-him-one" look.

I nodded. "I suppose we might as well tell you something, Mr. Postier. It'll be all over the news soon anyway. They've found Mr. Jones' body along with my grandfather's, Renee's and several others on Marcel Fontenot's place outside of Lafayette. He's probably been there since he disappeared. All the other bodies were at least half a century old."

Postier sat down on his little brocaded divan as tears welled up in his eyes. "I loved him you know."

"We know that, sir," Brant said, placing a hand on the old man's sagging shoulder. "I'm sorry we are the bearers of such bad news."

I placed one of our cards on the mahogany coffee table in front of him. "Call us if you need us or think of anything else, Mr. Postier. We're sorry for your loss."

He started to rise.

"That's fine, Mr. Postier, just rest," I said. "We can show ourselves out."

"And don't hesitate to call us if anyone gives you a problem about any of this. We owe you, sir," Brant added as we stepped outside and closed the door behind us.

34

AS BRANT AND I were standing on the front porch of Mr. Postier's little house, we noticed the nice, quiet neighborhood looked like it was once a refined part of an elegant city. There were a number of similar Bracket Shotgun Single-style homes on the street, but now most were showing their age just a bit. Fences needed a little work; some houses could stand a touch of paint.

I was calling a cab to pick us up when Brant noticed the Toyota parked a few yards down the street in front of a neighbor's house. Our guys were sitting inside the Camry wearing fashionable sunglasses, very Secret Service-looking. I couldn't help but wonder if they had matching earpieces as well.

Brant nudged me with an elbow as I was in the process of summoning the taxi. "Have the cab come from the west and pull up nose to nose with the Toyota. You take the passenger. I got the driver," he said.

"Are we sure we want to do this right now?" I asked.

"Good a time as any," he said, "and we need to make certain they don't plan to cause any problem here for the old guy, or anyone else for that matter. Besides I want to know who's been watching my ass all week long."

We leaned against the railing, discussed the strength of the American League East, and debated the most attractive actresses of all time, occasionally pointing in arbitrary directions as we waited on our cab.

Then I nodded toward the taxi, which was pulling up in front of the Toyota as Brant and I started walking their direction, simply chatting, paying the two men in the Camry no mind.

I discreetly pulled the Glock from my waistband and stepped quickly to the passenger window, allowing the man seated there to see the muzzle pointing at him. Brant had already stepped around the front of the car, yanked the front door open, and pulled the driver out with what seemed like one effortless motion. The Osage are a quick people.

He slammed him into the front end of the cab, which suddenly shifted into reverse and was beginning to haul out of there, rudely abandoning his fares.

Brant swung his victim from the hood of the fleeing cab onto the hood of the Toyota with relative ease.

"I'm tired of seeing your sorry excuse for a tail peering through those lousy sunglasses every time I turn around," he said, sounding a tad unhappy.

My guy kept his hands on the dash, just as he had been told, while I rested my left arm on the top of the car just above his door, and gave him my most charming smile.

The other guy made a grab for his weapon, not a smart move. Brant wrenched his arm up behind his back with one hand, removed the .38 with the other, and kneed him in the groin, undoubtedly another old Indian trick used to exploit the naïve and unprepared white man.

"First, you're going to tell me who you're working for," Brant growled. "Or I'm really gonna hurt you. Second, if we find out you even slightly disturb the old man in that house or anyone else you've seen us with, I'm going to kill you and make it very slow and very, very painful."

The guy was down on one knee bracing himself with his left hand as Brant maintained the right wrenched up behind his back.

"Fuck you," the guy rasped.

"Have it your way," Brant said as he stepped on the fingers of his left hand, palm down, on the street and wrenched the right arm up higher.

"Okay, okay," he moaned. "Get off my damn fingers and let me up. Senator McBride just wanted you watched. That's all. He just wanted eyes on you, nothing else. I swear. We don't give a shit about that old man or anybody else."

I caught the sudden turn of a speeding car onto our street out of the corner of my eye.

"Brant! The car, look out!" I yelled as I saw a smaller machinegun pistol extend from the driver's window of a black Camaro coming toward us from the east down Esplanade.

He dove behind the Toyota with me, dragging the guy he'd been pummeling with him as bullets ripped the hood and driver's side front tire.

I rose up, elevated the Glock above the Toyota's roof, rested the gun on the car, aimed very carefully, and fired twice, striking the Camaro as it raced down the block. When I looked down, the passenger still had both hands on the dash and both eyes closed.

Brant grabbed his victim by the throat.

"Just eyes on us, huh, asshole?" he growled. "That's what you call 'just eyes on us/' I oughtta kill you right now." He pulled the man to his feet by his shirt front.

The man was obviously shaken and stunned.

"We had nothing to do with that. I promise. We don't know who that was," the guy sitting in the passenger seat, happy to be alive, finally spoke.

I saw Postier and several other neighbors peering out their windows, but no one ventured outside.

In minutes police cars were screaming to a halt all around us. I gently laid my Glock on the Toyota's roof and slowly raised my hands.

"Show us your hands and do not move, not a muscle, anyone," the first officer out of his car yelled.

"We're private detectives," I said, my hands raised, nodding my head at Brant, who was standing now with the other guy, both with their hands raised.

"Us, too," Brant's prey mumbled to the officer.

"Keep your hands in full view and exit the vehicle, sir," another officer instructed sunglasses guy in the passenger seat as he picked my Glock up.

"I have a gun in an ankle holster and another in my waistband," Brant said. He nodded at the tall guy standing beside him now. "That's his .38 on the ground."

"I have a fully-loaded pistol in a shoulder holster, officer," passenger guy said as he stepped out of the car and raised his hands.

"And I suppose we've all got the proper licenses for these?" said another uniformed officer, pointing his weapon at all of us in general, along with a couple of other uniformed officers from New Orleans Finest.

We all nodded in affirmation.

"Jaxon Moon can vouch for us," I said to the Sergeant who was collecting the weaponry as the others trained their weapons on all of us.

They were cuffing Brant and the guy beside him.

"I don't know about these guys," I said as they were cuffing me and my buddy. "A black seventy-something Camaro drove by, fired an automatic weapon at us, and disappeared down the street that way, very cool car, really tricked out. I shot it twice, hated to."

"We'll get everyone's story at the station," the sergeant said as they loaded us all into backseats and transported us to the Royal Street station.

Our concealed carry permits and licenses were all gathered, checked, and returned to us. Our statements were taken, and in a few minutes, we were ushered into a room where Jaxon was waiting for us.

"I thought I told you boys to play nice," he grinned.

I grinned back. "Sorry, Marshal, it was reflex. When someone shoots at me, I return fire. I hit his car twice. The only other shots fired came from the Camaro while we and the other gentlemen were discussing the pennant races."

"The other guys were Red Sox fans," Brant said. "So I guess it could've been anyone shooting at them. We were probably just caught in the crossfire."

Jaxon just shook his head.

After another round of preliminary questions, Jax drove us back to his office in the federal building and returned our pistols and licenses, leaving McBride's boys to fend for themselves.

We told him everything that Postier had told us.

"You're okay here, but you may have a little flak coming from home," Jax said. "I was talking to your dad earlier, Mickey, when you called from NOPD. He said use of excessive force was permissible if we needed to keep you two in line."

Brant and I both just shook our heads.

Jax laughed. "You gotta love dads who were former officers."

"You gotta," I said.

Maggie, knocked on his door, winked at us, and said, "I'm glad they missed you boys." She laughed. "William Wallace is back on line one and would like to speak with Mickey."

I winced as Jax punched a button on his phone system.

Brant gave Maggie a playful wave as she ducked back out the door.

Jax punched a button on his phone system. "This is Jaxon Moon, Mr. Wallace. I'll put you on speaker. Mick and Brant are right here."

"Thanks, Jaxon. Okay, boys, who'd want to shoot you two down there besides me," Dad said over the speaker phone. "Y'all haven't been there that damn long."

Jax laughed and spoke in a friendly tone, "You're not giving them enough credit, Mr. Wallace."

"I don't have a clue, Dad," I jumped in. "Brant was bustin' one of McBride's boy's balls and, boom, this black Camaro comes right at us, automatic pistol blazing."

"I was busting no one's balls," Brant said. "I was conferring with a fellow investigator as to his intended purpose in being at Mr. Postier's home."

"Regardless," I said, "McBride's boys swear they were just a tail and have no clue as to who the shooter was, and whoever the shooter was, he could've hit them as easily as us. I believe they're telling the truth."

"But why shoot any of you?" Dad asked. "What's the point? What does any shooter gain from any of it?"

Brant and I looked at each other and shrugged.

"Let me toss a theory at you, Mr. Wallace," Jax popped in. "Brant and Mickey have been chasing down leads on Delbert Jones, whose corpse we recently found in a rather antique burying ground on the Fontenot property, along with your father's body, as well as several other folks, some identified now and some not."

Brant and I focused on Jaxon Moon sitting behind his desk.

"Delbert was shot once in the back of the head, execution style," he continued. "Let's say Marcel Fontenot had that done, and let's say the shooter's not the brightest bulb on the tree. At the time of Mr. Jones' dispatching, Marcel had been semi-out of the life, so let's say he has gotten old and sort of inconsequential. Maybe he can't secure the cream-of-the-crop hitter anymore. He takes a cut-rate guy, then Marcel dies, leaving his hitman to function on his own, and the fellow gets word someone's asking questions about a guy he popped. He gets nervous with no Fontenot to protect and guide him, so he decides to take out whoever the problem is and make it look like a gang thing."

Dad was quiet on his end, considering everything Jax had just said, I was sure.

"Or maybe it was a gang thing and we were just a mistaken target," I said.

Brant smiled at Jax. "But you know something else, don't you, something you're not telling us yet."

Jax was smiling like he'd stolen something. "Word hasn't gotten out on the street yet that we've found Jones' body, or any details on the other bodies for that matter, so a shooter might think silencing y'all would put an end to all of it."

"Seems to me something is still missing, men," Dad's voice emanated from the phone.

"Yes, sir, Mr Wallace, but a couple of names have recently surfaced with connections to both Mr. Jones and Marcel Fontenot just prior to Mr. Fontenot's rather sad demise," Jax added.

"I could tell you had something new for us," Brant said. "Reckon a fellow might get those names if he had connections in the right places?"

"He might," Jax said with a grin. "Once we've learned just a bit more, but for the time being, he'd probably have to wait, at least until after supper."

"Well, I reckon, you boys may have earned a couple of more days down there," came Dad's Okie drawl from the plastic box. "So if you see fit to cut 'em loose, Marshal Moon, I personally promise they'll ride straight for a while, or I'll be down there to kick somebody's rear."

"Dad would like that even if these two wouldn't, Mr. Wallace," Jaxon answered. "I do hope you can set aside some time to have a beer with him soon, sir."

"I wouldn't think of missing him if I can get down there," Dad said. "Your father's been a good friend for a long time, and I want to be on his good side; you don't ever want to cross Tommy Moon."

"No, sir, at least that never worked well for Jeff and me, and we tried it a time or two." Jax laughed. "I'll get these boys fixed up, Mr. Wallace, and I'm sure they'll call you with more details later. It was good to talk with you again, sir."

"We'll call you later tonight, Will," Brant said. "I'll make sure Mickey doesn't forget."

"I'm holding you both accountable," Dad said. "Later, boys. Jax, keep an eye on 'em for me."

Jax punched the button again, nodded, and winked over at Brant and me.

"I'll get back to you fellas with a name or two soon as possible tomorrow, if you'll promise not to shoot 'em unless it's absolutely necessary.

"Absolutely," Brant said.

"We promise," I said as he called us another cab.

35

NEAR HARTSHORNE, OKLAHOMA, JUNE 1916

THE DAY WAS incredibly humid and muggy. *John William Wallace sat on a large rock in the shade of a massive oak tree just outside of the town of Hartshorne, Oklahoma. He was the farrier for a prison work crew, working outside the walls of McAlester. The crew was logging the heavy timber in Pittsburg County for a local lumber company.*

John mopped his forehead with a bright red bandana as he waited on Samuel Musgrove to bring the big bay horse into the shed where they worked on the logging-crew animals. Sam was Rena's cousin, a full-blood Choctaw, John William had picked him to be his assistant. He believed he could trust him, at least he'd known him a long time, and he couldn't say that about very many others in that hellhole.

Still angry he'd gone out of his way to avoid Harrison or Roy Mack. Both of them had avoided the work detail anyway, choosing to remain behind the walls, possibly to avoid John. But John William and Sam had volunteered for the first work detail that came open, figuring work outside would sure as hell beat being behind those damned walls.

The man in charge outside was an older fellow, Simpson Burnett, a big man with an even bigger mean streak, probably how he got the job. He'd been a guard at McAlester since the penitentiary opened in 1908, and now he was the boss guard on their work detail.

Burnett, almost seventy, still cut an imposing figure. He didn't carry a weapon, not even a sidearm, said he didn't need one to handle the likes of the reprobates he was watching over.

During the Civil War, he had enlisted in the Georgia infantry in 1862 at the age of sixteen to fight "Yankee sonsabitches" and had seen his share of death and combat before coming to Indian Territory for the Land Rush of '89. It turned out he wasn't much a farmer, so he served as a Guthrie police officer after the land run until the prison job opened in McAlester after statehood.

Burnett was watching the logging crew prepare for the day's work. Two riflemen stood next to him. Another guard with a shotgun was walking about fifty yards away to the east, and several others were on duty throughout the camp. He might not be armed, but his henchmen damn sure were well armed.

He drew a heavy puff off of his cherrywood pipe and nodded toward Sam as he was unhitching the bay horse from the remuda string.

"Keep yer eyes on that Choctaw bastard, Musgrove," he said to one of the riflemen. "He'll run first shot he gits."

Vernon Daniels, the older of the two riflemen, nodded and spit in the dirt.

Burnett walked over to where John William had started working with a rasp file on the front hoof of a powerfully built grey mule.

"Where'd you get that there bullet burn above your ear, Wallace?" he drawled.

John looked up from his work. "What makes you think it's from a bullet, Mr. Burnett…if you don't mind me asking?"

"Seen enough bullets flyin' round to know the kind a marks they make, boy. Somebody damn near kilt ya."

John looked at the big man's grinning face. "Huntin' accident a few years back."

"Huntin' accident, my ass," Burnett smirked. "And I'm watchin' that goddamned Indian you call a cousin, Wallace. I don't trust him a bit."

The old man practically growled the word "Indian" when he spoke.

This time John William didn't look back up from the mule's hoof he was working on. "He's my wife's first cousin, boss."

"If'n I's you, that wouldn't be close enough for me, by God, just givin' ya fair warnin'. If you had a damned brain in your head, you'd gitchoo a white boy to help with these animals."

Simpson Burnett was pure Georgia hard case through and through.

John kept the rasp moving smoothly. "I'd have to teach 'em, boss. Sam knows the trade already and handles the stock better than most men could."

"And he's your wife's cousin," Simpson said.

"And he's my wife's cousin," John William agreed.

"He's just one notch above a nigger, Wallace, cousin or no cousin; you can't trust his ass any futher'n you can pick him up and throw him."

John William just kept working. It was white men that had given him the most grief in this world. No black man or no red man had ever caused him the misery that the McBrides had, but he was smart enough to keep his thoughts to himself.

He looked the old man square in the eye. "You may be right, Mr. Burnett, but I'm gonna keep him as my assistant if you'll let me."

"Your ass, Wallace, it's your ass," Simpson Burnett said and walked back toward the riflemen as Sam Musgrove approached leading the bay.

"That man don't like me much, John," Sam grinned.

"He'd like you fine if you were white…or dead," John replied. "And it wouldn't really matter much to him either way."

"I don't think I'd like him if he was full-blood Chahta," Sam said, looking over at the group of men watching them for just a second, then back at John holding the mule's foot. "This, bay needs a new shoe. You want me to do it while you finish that on'ry mule?"

John William grunted. "Burnett says I can't trust your worthless ass, cousin or no cousin, so you can't fault his ability to assess character."

"You real funny, John; where's the damn hammer?"

"Two of 'em over in the box. Try hard not to cripple the horse, Sam; I'm tryin' hard to convince Burnett you're the best man for this job."

"Yup, you plumb hysterical," Sam said without breaking stride as he went for the tools.

"Just keep your eyes open and don't screw up," John William said sincerely. "He can't make you white, but he can damn sure make you dead and not mind it one bit."

Sam looked back at John and grinned "I'll be the politest savage he ever saw, John William. I promise."

36

STILL NEAR HARTSHORNE, OKLAHOMA, JUNE 1916

MCALESTER PENITENTIARY *had released forty-eight men to work the lumber detail in the camp where John and Samuel were. It was hard, hot, physically demanding work, but many of the prisoners still found some respite from the hell inside the walls of the prison they called "Big Mac," and the state made a nice profit leasing out the convict labor to boot.*

The men cut the big trees, hooked them to teams of mules or big draft horses, and dragged them into camp, where they were loaded onto wagons and carried into the Hartshorne lumber mill and sawed into planks.

There were two prisoners serving as cooks. Their jobs were coveted due to the fact they weren't subjected to the hard labor of the men cutting timber.

But John William and Samuel's jobs were the second most desired because they at least caught breaks from the miserable work in the hot sun from time to time, as they worked on the mules, horses, and equipment.

The other forty-four men were worked hard with little rest, but most were happy to be there. They tried to behave since a slight infraction could cost them the privilege of being outside the walls, where they could breathe clean air, feel a breeze on their skin, and hear birds singing, for a brief time at least.

Most nights you could hear owls calling and foxes barking, along with the night sounds of crickets and tree frogs beginning to sing out in the woods as summer was heating up, and most mornings began with birds before the logging started. Hawks soared. Raccoons ambled through the trees. It gave a man hope to know some things lived free and unchained.

Every night before lights out, two guards moved among the groups of prisoners, attaching hobbles to the men, then to the heavy iron balls. They were shackled in pairs, twelve men per tent in four tents with one guard per tent in shifts of two.

Their fourth or fifth night out, an older, very thin man asked the guard chaining him to the ball, "Can we sleep outta the tent tonight, Mr. Daniels? Some of these boys smell mighty ripe. We can't get nowhere with these balls chained on."

"Nope," Vernon Daniels growled.

"Just be happy you can't get loose, Bob," the second guard said. "There's bears and panthers out there in them trees. You wouldn't even make a good snack. They'd make short work of your dried-up old ass."

"I ain't sure, but bein' et by a bear might be better than smelling these critters in our tent, boss," the old man grinned as the chain was snapped shut.

His partner, already chained on the ball, said, "Just shut the hell up, Bob, and let's get to the back of the tent."

Inside the tents was a cacophony of men snoring and clinking metal as they rolled over trying to sleep with chains on their chafed ankles, but still nothing seemed as bad to most of the men as going back behind the walls of Big Mac until they were forced to.

Every night for the first two weeks, John William had lain at the back of their tent shackled to Sam. He was certain his father was trying to call in any favors still owed him from his days with Judge Parker and Bass Reeves, but he wasn't allowed any visitors while the men were on the outside, leaving him in a sort of limbo.

That was his only regret about taking the outside work detail, but he simply couldn't stand the high walls and metal bars. He'd wait until the detail was back inside for a couple of weeks to hear news, plus he was sure if William Wallace was able to call in enough favors to free him, they'd manage to find him even way out here in the woods and release him right there.

Like John William, Samuel hated the penitentiary. The smells, the walls, the abusive guards, just being so closed in made him want to scream, so he was grateful John had managed to get him as his assistant.

"I appreciate you getting me outta that place, John William. You know I hated being locked in that cell worse than anything," Sam said one night.

"Hell, Sam, it was no big deal," John whispered. "I need someone to talk poetry with. Who else you figure in this snake pit even knows who Walt Whitman is?"

"I just read your book, cousin, not like I know what that damned old white man was even talking about," Sam chuckled in the dark.

"I reckon you know enough to not sound too stupid," John laughed.

"Well, maybe my people do know all about that 'barbaric yawp' pretty good though."

"Yeah, sure, you're a regular Geronimo," John said in hushed tones. "Just get your red rear end to sleep. We won't be in a shade tomorrow. We got plenty timber to haul outta these hills tomorrow, be workin' on those mules and hosses all day long. You'll be yawping plenty enough then."

In an adjacent tent, Arcelus Monroe and Andy Burks, two lifetime criminals, lay awake, talking low.

"A hundred bucks a piece and we get our happy asses outta here," whispered Monroe, a dark man with a scar running through his left eyebrow. "And that's cash money and no more time in this shit hole, Andy,"

Burks, his counterpart, a big red-complexioned fellow with thinning, curly hair, lay with his ankle chained to the same iron weight as Monroe.

"I ain't a fuckin' idiot, Monroe," Burks growled in a low voice. "We can't just kill the sonuvabitch, collect our money, and tip our hats as they unchain us and show us the gate."

"It won't be hard, Andy, trust me," Monroe said.

Burks glanced around at the men he believed to be sleeping soundly.

One wasn't.

Burks rolled onto his back and listened to the rattling snores. "I don't trust nobody, and I sure as hell don't see how this shit'll work."

Their voices were soft and almost inaudible as the feigned sleeper strained to catch the conversation.

"A United States senator wants him dead, Andy, ain't that good enough for you?" Monroe retorted. "We're not talking about some hayseed farmer here.

This is a man with power who will be beholden to us for all time if we do this for him."

"You ain't got shit for brains, Arch," Burks whispered. "Think about it. We kill the bastard. They have a murder charge on us, don't have to pay us a goddamned dime, hang us, and their problem is solved, and we're fuckin' dead, too."

"I'm smarter than that; give me some credit, Burks," the darker man said as he shifted his weight, trying to find a comfortable position. "One of my old lady's brothers has worked for Senator McBride on his ranch for years now. He's been trying to get me an early release, talking to the senator every time he's back on his ranch in McCurtain County."

"And cause your brother-in-law is a ranch hand for the good senator, he won't screw us," Burks grumbled. "I say we still wind up hanging. He saves 200 dollars, and Wallace is as dead as the senator wants him to be."

"Look, Andy, the only reason I'm out here sweating my ass off is because of this chance," Monroe said. "I thought you'd want out as bad as I do, and we're not getting out for years without someone like Senator McBride pulling some strings."

Burks was silent for a moment. He was in McAlester for killing a guy in a barroom brawl. He wasn't a short-timer, and he was starting to warm to the idea of anything that got him out early.

"Look, Andy," Monroe said as quietly as he could. "The good senator come up with the plan hisself. He come to my brother-in-law and asked him if he still wanted me out, then he gave him the plan to kill Wallace."

"Just don't see how he can get two of us out at once," Burks said. "I feel like the senator is trying to pull one over on us."

"One gets out one month, the other, the next," Burks whispered, tiring of begging Burks. "Senator McBride wouldn't want the story getting out. He'll stick to his bargain, Andy."

Again Burks fell silent for a moment. "I get out first, Arch," he finally said. "I get out first, and I'm in on the deal. Not that I don't trust ya, but I don't trust ya."

"That hurts my feelings, Andy," Arcelus Monroe snickered quietly. "But it's a deal. You get out first."

"How do we go about killin' the fella, Arch?" the dark man said, rubbing his scar in the dark of the tent.

"All we do is wait and watch," Monroe said low and confidently. *"We'll get a chance to make it look like an accident. Loggin's a dangerous business,"*

"Okay, I'm in," Burks said, *"but why's a United States senator want a nobody like Wallace dead in the first place, huh? Tell me that."*

"Don't know, don't give a damn," Monroe answered. *"I just want out of this stink hole, and I'll take the hundred bucks to boot."*

Andy Burks rolled over the best he could and tried to sleep. *"If I get screwed in this deal, there'll be hell to pay, Arch, and I'll be looking to you to collect."*

"Nobody's getting screwed," Monroe sighed deeply. *"Just get some sleep, and we'll start looking for our chance first thing in the morning."*

The sleeping man, who wasn't sleeping, made a mental note to tell his buddy and fellow Choctaw, Sam Musgrove, everything that he had heard that night.

37

AFTER SURVIVING our little shooting scrape, Brant and I agreed Marie and Leslie deserved to hear, at least some of the details of Samuel and Renee's final hours that Riley Postier had revealed to us.

I'd called Leslie with a rudimentary summary, mostly saying we were close to a positive ID, and we had heard a trustworthy account of what happened.

She immediately suggested we meet at their home again and tell them as much as we could.

"I make a pretty mean French onion dip, cowboy," she said. "And there will be beer of course."

"Some of it's pretty rough, Les," I said hesitantly.

"Momma deserves to know," she replied. "Don't worry. She's stronger than you think."

So now I was sitting in the passenger seat, rolling down a tree-lined stretch of St. Charles Avenue, praying that Brant would manage to not get us hit by the street car and wondering how much of the tale to break at once.

Brant eased the Jeep up to the curb in front of the familiar teal colored Queen Anne house, where Leslie and Marie were sitting outside in wicker chairs on the lower gallery. We hadn't seen our Toyota boys all day.

"Two Southern belles sipping sweet tea on the front porch," Brant said as we came through the wrought iron gate and past the crepe myrtle bushes.

"Well, I do declare, Momma," Leslie said with a huge grin. "I do believe we have some fine-looking gentlemen callers coming up the walkway."

Marie smiled as she rose. "You boys come inside. I believe the heat is getting to this child of mine."

Brant and I followed them inside.

"We heard you boys had a little excitement," Marie said. "We are so glad you're both safe."

Brant and I both smiled.

"Takes more than a couple of thugs shooting automatic weapons at us to scare an Okie," Brant chuckled.

"I told Momma that y'all believe they've found the remains of Samuel and Renee," Leslie said. "That's about as far as I got. I figured it would be easier to understand coming straight from you men."

I took a deep breath and looked at Brant. "They're conducting DNA tests right now to prove Samuel was in fact my grandfather, John William Wallace, and that the female body is truly Renee."

"That's pretty much a formality though," Brant helped me out a bit. "I believe we've all come to the same conclusion. The two bodies, one male, one female, buried in the same grave on the Fontenot place are most likely Samuel and Renee."

Leslie gently touched her mother's back. "Maybe there's some form of peace that Grandma Chelle's spirit will sense now that they're found, Momma."

"The not knowing has been hard for me," Marie said. "It had to have been a thousand times more terrible for my poor momma."

"I know, Marie," I said softly. "I can't even imagine what my father is going through right now."

Brant and I just looked down and sort of shuffled our feet, not knowing exactly what to do or say next.

"Both of you cowboys have a seat. We'd like to hear the as much of the story as you have time to tell us," Leslie said. "I'll get us all a beer. Y'all want to snack on anything?"

"Some of your world-famous French onion dip that I've heard so much about might be nice," I smiled.

"I knew you were a sharp cat the first time I laid eyes on you, Oklahoma," Leslie said as we moved toward the dining room and took our seats at the now familiar kitchen table.

"We learned most of the details today, who was involved and why," I said. "We'll give you as much of what we know as you want us to."

"Tell me everything," Marie said.

We drank a couple of beers and related Riley Postier's account of Renee and Samuel's last day as they were leaving New Orleans, just as he had told us.

"It's sad," Marie said. "And practically everyone involved is gone now. It's almost like Marcel Fontenot got away with what he did."

"Yep," Brant nodded. "There are still a few McBrides left back in Oklahoma, but even they are of a different generation. I don't think they're as bad a dude as Davis McBride was."

"Time can be the most formidable enemy of all," I smiled. "There may be no one left to punish for the wrongs of the past."

Brant collected the empties and placed them in the waste can under the sink, and there was that awkward silence again for just a second or two before Marie spoke again.

"What will we do about a reburial?" she asked.

Brant cut his eyes over at me.

I was so fixed on finding answers for Dad that I really hadn't stopped long enough to even consider the inevitable aftermath of the case.

"I think we'd like to keep Samuel here with Renee, Michelle, and Mark if that's possible," Marie said quietly. "How do you think William will feel about the situation?"

"I honestly don't know, Marie. Let me talk to Dad," I said. "But I'm sure we can work something out. Seems we're going to be here for another day or two, tying up some loose ends. We just wanted to come over and tell y'all in person that we were pretty sure we'd found Samuel and Renee."

"That's really all I can ask, Mickey," Marie said.

"I suppose you Okies will be heading back home pretty quick after those loose ends are tended to," Leslie said. "But if William can't travel down here, Mom and I'd love to come up there."

"He told me he wants to come down for a day or two, see Tommy Moon again, and meet y'all after we put a lid on the whole deal," I said.

"I don't think we don't have many questions left to answer...that can be answered. We'd probably be ready to head back to Oklahoma right now if those guys hadn't shot at us," Brant smiled broadly. "I'd kinda personally like to tie up that little mess before we go."

"Yeah, kinda hard to leave that unaddressed," I said. "But I really don't see any alternative right now. We do have a business to run."

"Well, y'all just better not try slipping out of our fair city without saying goodbye," Leslie smiled. "Or there will be hell to pay."

"No, ma'am," Brant chuckled. "We wouldn't dream of it. And Janie said she'd mail the journals back here to Marie's address in a few more days."

"Ther's no rush on that," Marie smiled. "Maybe William will get to deliver them himself."

"Wouldn't that be a treat," Leslie smiled. "Who wants another beer?"

"I'm sure we both do, but we really need to get going," I said as we both rose. "We're supposed to meet Jax and Tommy Moon."

"They're good folks, but they're sure not as easy on the eyes as you ladies," Brant laughed.

"You boys are just awful," Marie laughed. "Tell William his Cajun side of the family will be headed up to Oklahoma to meet him before too long if he doesn't get down here soon."

Leslie winked. "Uncle William…got a nice ring to it, doesn't it?"

"We'll be back before we leave, ladies. Y'all stay out of trouble," I said.

Marie stepped toward us as we started out.

"Again, please, Mickey, talk to William for us, see what he thinks about Samuel and Renee's bodies and burial," she said, touching my forearm. "Have him call us if he doesn't mind."

I nodded.

"I'm sure he'll be tickled to talk to both of you. We'll be back before we go. Promise."

We stepped out the door and headed for the Jeep.

38

TOMMY, JAX, AND JEFF MOON were sitting at a table in Pat O'Brien's when we arrived. Jeff looked like a younger, slenderer version of Jax.

"This is my younger brother, Jeff," Jax said as they rose to meet us at their table.

"He meant his smarter brother, Jeff. Already heard a lot about you men," Jeff grinned.

We shook Jeff's hand and took our appointed seats.

"Thought y'all ought to get the full tourist experience," Tommy Moon said. "Hurricanes all around?"

"Better stick with beer, too much Indian in Brant, give him firewater and he starts looking for a wagon to burn and white people to scalp."

"You real funny, Mickey," Brant said. "Probably related to Custer somewhere down the line."

"Damn, one little semi-racist joke among friends and you get all personal. Custer, really? Custer?"

Jeff Moon smiled. "You men like this all the time?"

"He's always an asshole, if that's what you mean," Brant grinned. "But you get kinda get used to it after a while."

The Moons seemed to find that funny, only encouraging Brant at more weak attempts at low-brow humor, I'm sure.

"Just for a little change of pace, how's your dad doing, Mickey? I haven't talked to him in a day or so," Tommy said.

"Ornery as ever," I laughed. "He's finally over the Yankees losing the Series last year, since they're off to such a good start this year."

"Yeah, but it was a little touch and go when O'Neill retired," Brant said. "We were afraid the strain on his heart might be too much for him."

"I doubt anything would be too much for William Matthew Wallace," Tommy said. "Toughest SOB I ever met in my life, and I've come across some real hosses in my day."

"I find him to be a gentle soul with a great heart," Brant smiled again. "He treats his Native American friends with great respect, unlike his son."

Tommy laughed. "I imagine he does. He's about half Choctaw."

"There are rumors of Indian blood," I said.

Tommy leaned back in his chair and took a long pull on his Budweiser. "Boys, I can tell you a hundred stories about that man. I watched him clean out a redneck bar in Texarkana, Arkansas when some yahoo called Mickey Mantle a draft dodger. Me and another agent were trying to convince him not to over-react among the locals, and then the next thing we knew, they were all unconscious."

"Sounds like him all right," I chuckled.

"No kidding, badmouthing Mantle, he'd probably have gone easier on 'em if they'd spit on the flag," Brant said.

"He slapped a fifty down on the bar, told the bartender we were U.S. Marshals, and he was in charge of the whole investigation. If the offensive, unconscious loudmouths had a problem when they woke up, to send them to us at the motel, and he'd explain the intricate workings of law enforcement to them once again. The other marshal and I didn't even know we were investigating anything. We just thought we'd stopped in for a beer on our way back to Oklahoma."

Tommy ordered another round as we all laughed and shook our heads.

"We were young and figured we'd all be fired," Tommy continued. "But Will just said, 'Don't worry, boys; they need you too bad to fire you.' Reckon he was right. We didn't get fired."

"I'm surprised Uncle Ira wasn't with him," I said.

"Brant's daddy was in Mississippi trying to convince the Klan that wanton disregard for the rights of the minority was unkind. Will got himself assigned down there with Ira as fast as he could. He never did care for anyone too afraid to speak out in the open."

I lifted my Dixie bottle.

"Here's to crime fighters everywhere; long may they follow the teachings of Batman."

"And Red Cloud," Brant added.

The Moons all lifted their bottles to meet with ours above the table.

"Lord, you two act just like them at times, full of bullshit and sharp as razors," Tommy said.

Brant handed a card across the table to Tommy. "Here's the office 800 number. We figured you might want to talk to the old bear again. He's in the office regularly for a while. We called just a few minutes ago."

"Janie says he's getting a haircut, but he'll be back in just a bit, looking all pretty, in about an hour, as soon as the girl finishes and brings him back," I added.

Tommy Moon took the card and smiled like he had a secret we couldn't be told. "Valet barbering, only your father can get a pretty little hairdresser to come get him, cut his hair, then deliver him back home again."

"I think he may try to make the trip down here before fall," I said. "I know he'd like to see you again, Mr. Moon. He wants to see Marie and Leslie as well and to visit New Orleans one more time if he can."

Jax elbowed Jeff. "Reckon he's got any Dad stories?"

"He's a helluva a man and was a real hoss, but you simply can't believe a word the old man says," Tommy said. "He's an incorrigible liar."

Jaxon almost spit his beer everywhere; the rest of us were fortunate enough to have not taken another sip yet.

After a quick recovery, Jeff lifted his beer again in a toast. "Well, as a famous fictional cowboy once said, 'Here's to the sunny slopes of long ago.'"

"And to the Crescent City and good friends," Brant added. "I reckon we'll be heading home soon."

"Well, boys, I'm not sure you're gonna want to leave just yet," Jax smiled. "Here's the other reason besides the tourist experience, I called you guys to meet us here."

"I told you it wasn't just our sparkling smiles, Brant," I said as seriously as I could.

"Nope, not by a long shot," Jax grinned. "NOPD found your black Camaro in a Wal-Mart parking lot over on Jefferson Highway this morning, back glass shot out, blood on the passenger seat."

"Well, now that is interesting," Brant said, looking over at me as I sipped my *Dixie*.

"Maybe you boys can hang out down here a while longer," Tommy Moon chuckled.

"Y'all did say you wanted to find out who was shooting at you," Jeff added. "And I can offer free legal counsel should you decide to pummel the offenders."

"That we did," I chuckled. "And we may need a good litigator. What all do we know as of right now?"

Jax grinned. "They ran the security cameras from the parking lot. A white Chevy Tahoe pulled into the lot a few minutes behind the Camaro, and a taller white guy got out and helped the driver, a black male of medium height, get the passenger, a much heavier built black guy, into the Tahoe. They exited the back of the lot and drove away. The Camaro was stolen of course, Tahoe was, too, but, hey, it's a start."

"Damn, I was aiming at the driver," I said.

Brant took a big swig of his *Dos Equis*. "Pure luck you even hit the car."

Jeff and Tommy smiled. I just shook my head.

"We couldn't pull up enough resolution on the cameras to recognize anyone," Jax said. "But we know one of them's hurt fairly badly. At least he needed considerable help in switching vehicles."

The phone in Jaxon's pocket buzzed, and he picked up the receiver, asking us to hold on a second.

We all held on.

"Really," Jax spoke into the phone. "That's interesting. What can you tell me about this guy, Dave? Uh –huh, uh-huh, sounds like it could be our guy. Where was he hit? Uh-huh. Nobody with him? Uh-huh. We got him on file I suppose. Good deal, Man. Uh-huh… Thanks, buddy. I owe you one."

"Guys, you're gonna like this. Just give me a second more." Jax hung up and pushed another button on the phone.

"Maggie, can you give Deputy Marshal Hebert a file NOPD will be dropping off there in just a minute on a Malcom Morgan please? Ask her to bring it to Pat O'Briens. We're showing the Okies I want her to meet the tourism aspect of the Big Easy."

"Tell Maggie, she's welcome to come down here, too," Brant said. "What's good for the boss is good for the secretary, I believe."

"Okay," Jax spoke into the phone. "She said to tell Mr. Bluesoldier someone had to fight crime, but she was off at six and she'd love a Hurricane after work."

I thought Brant was going to faint.

"Okay, Mr. Matchmaker, who's Malcolm Morgan?" I asked as Jax pocketed the phone again.

"Liquor store owner just off Jefferson Highway shot and killed him last night."

"And...?" Brant said.

"And there's a pretty good chance it was the passenger in the black Camaro that Mickey shot day before yesterday," Jax said. "The store owner fired three rounds through the counter and struck the guy three times in the chest with a Browning .40 caliber semi-automatic."

Jeff leaned forward. Tommy sat back and sipped his beer.

"That will usually kill a guy fairly dead," I said. "But what makes you think he's our guy?"

"During the autopsy, they found a fourth untreated gunshot wound on the back of his left shoulder, covered by a big adhesive store-bought bandage. Had everyone wondering for a little bit. Then one of the detectives on the case remembered we were looking for missing gunshot victims. They pulled the slug. We'll see if we can match it to Mickey's Glock."

"So the liquor store dude, Malcom Morgan, I'm guessing he's not an upwardly mobile young college student in the wrong place at the wrong time," Brant popped in.

"That would be correct," Jax said. "Got a rap sheet going back to about the third grade according to Dave Brubaker, the New Orleans detective working the case."

"Wounded and takes time to pull a liquor store heist," Brant said. "Stupid or desperate?"

"Maybe both," Tommy Moon interjected.

"Good chance," I said.

After a brief pause to let it all sink in, I said, "So maybe we can do a little checking around with some of the late Mr. Morgan's known associates? I mean, of course as long as we're very sensitive and inoffensive."

"The ballistics test will likely connect Morgan to the black Camaro shooting, and that will put NOPD on it, too, but they'll have plenty more to keep them busy," Jax said. "I don't need to tell you, no interference with their investigating the Morgan shooting or the liquor store robbery attempt."

"Of course not," Brant said. "My God, man, we are the consummate professionals."

The table was a mixture of grins and shaking heads.

"I don't suppose we can get a list of those known associates?" I said. "Save us a lot of professional, time-consuming investigating."

"Deputy Marshal Hebert will have all we've got here in a bit," Jax grinned. "We can catch her up on the whole deal. She just got back in the office today, think you guys'll like her well enough. I'm trusting you guys a ton on this. Do not screw up, or Mickey's dad will have your asses, and my dad will have mine."

A very petite, dark-haired beauty wearing jeans and a beige jacket entered Pat O'Brien's carrying a manila folder and strolled over to our table.

We stood with Jeff, Jaxon, and Tommy to meet our new arrival, who couldn't have been more than five-four. She had classic high cheek bones and her hair pulled back in a ponytail. She strode toward us like with the grace of an athlete or a Greek goddess, depending on how you looked at things.

"Dani, beautiful as ever," Tommy Moon said as she leaned over and kissed him on the cheek.

"Tommy Moon, I love you," she smiled, then turned her grey eyes on Brant and me. "So I assume these are the wild Okie cowboys I've been hearing so much about lately."

Brant smiled and took her extended hand. "At least one of us is an Indian, ma'am."

"Pleased to meet you, Dani," I said. "How did you ever fall in with the likes of these fellows?"

She smiled.

"Gentlemen, this is Deputy Marshal Dani Hebert; proud to say she's one of our best agents," Jaxon said. "And, no, you may not call her while you're in town. She doesn't hang around with troublemakers."

"What would you like to drink, Dani?" Jeff asked.

"Nothing, sweetie, I've got to get back and preserve your brother's job." Her eyes twinkled when she smiled. "I didn't want anyone else sneaking files out of the office, and I had to have a look at these rugged Oklahoma fellows that Maggie said were so handsome."

Jaxon grinned like he'd stolen something and gotten away with it. "I told you they were ugly."

"You lied," she smiled. "Ignore Jaxon, you boys, call me later. I'll show you the real N'awlins, not the tourist traps."

She smiled, turned, and sauntered back out onto Bourbon Street, leaving us spellbound, holding our beers.

"I'm in love," Brant stammered. "She's just about the prettiest thing I've ever seen and no bigger than a minute."

"Like you have a chance," I said. "Try to keep your mind clear and stay focused. Do you see me drooling and stuttering like an eight-year-old?"

"To be honest, I thought you passed out," Brant said.

Jax handed me the folder.

"Reel your tongues back in, gentlemen. You've got work to do if you're gonna keep on this. Looking at this guy's record, I'm afraid you're about to venture into some of the seedier sides of our fair city," Jaxon said. "So once again, let me remind you to keep your head up and be on your best behavior."

"We are guests in your home, my man," I said. "We'll act with the utmost civility."

"Just try not to shoot anyone else, and don't get yourselves shot either, and I'll be a happy Cajun."

"Count on it," I said.

"I'm calling Dani first," Brant said.

"I thought you were calling Maggie first," I laughed. "So I reckon I'll call Dani."

"You can both just forget all about her. She's in love with Dad," Jax smiled.

"What can I say? The lady has refined and discriminating taste," Tommy said straight-faced.

39

NEAR HARTSHORNE, OKLAHOMA, JUNE 1916

SINCE NO ANIMALS *were in need of their farrier services the morning after Monroe and Burks had made their pact, Sam and John William were put to hauling logs out of the timber. Now they would be forced to avoid "accidents" out in the wilderness for the time being.*

"That Roberts boy told me they was laying to kill you, John," Sam said as they were hooking the chains to drag out one of the big trees they'd cut. "He wouldn't lie about it, John; said some senator was payin' 'em and getting' 'em both outta here once you was dead."

"I figured he'd try something like this sooner or later," John William said as he hooked the massive chains on his side of the drag.

"You reckon McBride has got the clout to pull that off and get away with it, John?" Sam asked.

"I reckon," John William said. "Keep both eyes open, Sam. I don't want you getting hurt on account of me."

"Hell, John William, I am a mighty Chahta warrior," Sam said. "I can smell danger before it gets here. I got your back, besides Rena is blood kin. She'd have my ass if I let anything happen to her man."

"Sure, Pushmataha," John said. "Just keep your eyes peeled for Burks and Monroe while trees are falling."

The chains on one side of the drag released as they were negotiating a turn with the trees.

"Damn it," Sam muttered, making sure no one was around as he and John William moved to re-hook the drag.

John glanced up from the chains they were fastening again, and there on a rock face of a sloped hill about ten feet above him was a six-point star, interlocking triangles with the initials BD carved in the right-hand star point.

"Holy shit," he breathed.

Sam kept locking the chain around the trunk without looking up or reacting.

"What?" he whispered.

John looked south to his right, where the inmates had just cut another huge tree and tried to remember the number of paces needed to be stepped off from the star.

"Later," he said. "There's no threat. Just keep hooking that chain up, and don't act out of the ordinary. I'll explain it all later. Monroe's coming this way now."

Arcelus Monroe came walking toward the two men.

"Reckon we're gonna get this tree drug outta here this week, boys? Mr. Simpson's puffin' mighty heavy on that pipe of his. I think he's getting' a little pissed that y'all ain't moving quick enough, might have a stroke if y'all keep dawdling."

John William met Monroe's gaze. "Arcelus, you tend to your own knittin'. You and Burks just go around us. Me and Sam will be ready once y'all get around us. Boss looks okay to me."

Monroe grinned, almost friendly-like, John thought.

"These boys are 'bout ready, Andy; let's push the goddamned mules back to camp," he yelled at Burks, standing a few yards away with their team.

Burks cracked the reins, and they started toward Simpson and the riflemen waiting up ahead.

John popped his lines as well, and he and Sam brought their team up behind the two convicts.

Sam glanced over at John. "You looked like you saw a ghost back there, John. What was it?"

"Sorta was a ghost, it's a long story. I'll explain it all tonight. Right now I'm just not sure where to start."

"Long as it weren't no real ghost. You know us savages spook easy when it comes to that shit."

"Naw, no ghosts," John grinned at Sam. "I think it was a vampire, Dracula maybe."

"You're probably the most well-read bastard in the pen, John," Sam said flatly. "You're an asshole but a well-read asshole all the same."

John William grinned at Sam again and popped the reins on the outside mule.

That star was exactly like the one he'd heard Albert Britt rambling about back what seemed a lifetime ago, and he was trying to figure the best way to get word to his dad or Rena, someone who might benefit from the value of this new-found knowledge, if it was the right star, which he knew it had to be.

By the time they had driven the mule team into the camp, the day had grown unbearably hot, a stifling, humid Oklahoma heat that would cook you in your clothes, but the main body of prisoners was heading back out into the timber again to cut more trees to be dragged into camp later.

Burnett saw John and Sam unhooking their team from the logs they had pulled in and motioned for John to walk over to where he was standing.

"Got a couple of the mules and two big draft horses need re-shoeing," he said. "I thought you was supposed to be a blacksmith, Wallace."

"Am, boss, this is just awful rough ground on these animals," John said. "We'll have to re-shoe plenty."

Burnett re-lit his pipe. "Well, get yer damned Indian and get busy. I need you back out in the timber."

"Sure thing, boss."

John walked back over with the news to where Sam was waiting patiently.

Sam smiled. "He sure picked a good time to re-shoe the stock, cousin. Bet them boys burn up out there in the woods."

How the man remained always cheerful puzzled John. He lifted the big roan's front leg and glanced at the guard Burnett had left to watch him and Sam while they worked.

"Yep, but it won't exactly be cool here either."

"You gonna tell me about that vampire now?" Sam asked under his breath.

"Yep," John answered through the nails he held in his teeth as he hammered the shoe in place while Sam dressed one of the mule's hooves down with a rasp. "I think maybe I found Bob Dalton's buried treasure."

John spoke in low, soft tones without giving any indication Sam was even there.

Sam laughed quietly. "Really? All of it?"

John walked over to look at the mule's foot that Sam was working on. "Probably just a part."

"And Dracula showed ya where it was buried, did he?" Sam asked. "Did he tell ya how we was gonna dig it up?"

John looked around to see if the rifleman assigned to watch them was paying any attention. He was sitting on a stump rolling a cigarette, his Winchester across his lap. He nodded at them when he caught John's glance.

John nodded back.

"Nope. I need Dad to figure that out," he said to Sam. "The old man that Roy Mack and Harrison killed and got me put in this stink hole, he was talking out of his head while Rena and I were takin' care of him. I think maybe he rode with Dalton once. He kept talking about finding a six-point star carved in a rock up around Hartshorne."

Not looking up, Sam continued to rasp at the hoof, but he was listening intently now. "That's sure nuff where we are now all right. And you seen this star?"

"Yep. Initials BD cut right in the right wing of the star. I saw it while you were staring up that mule's ass when our drag chain come off."

"Holy shit," Sam muttered.

"That's what I said," John grinned.

"Well, what you gonna do, John William?"

"Hell if I know, I can't just go up ask Simpson for some time off to dig for treasure," John answered. "Maybe we can get word back to Rena and Dad somehow. After we've cleared this area, there may be some way they can sneak back in and find it. Who knows if there's anything really even there?"

"You think it's there though, doncha?" Sam said.

"Yep. I do," John answered matter-of-factly.

Sam continued to work the rasp lightly on the mule's hoof. "You know William's gonna get you outta here, John, just a matter of time. He's your daddy, and he's still got some pull left. You can come back then."

John nodded.

"Just don't do nothin' stupid, John William," Sam continued. "I can see them wheels turning in that tiny little brain of yours right now."

"Aww hell, Sam, don't worry," John said as he dropped the roan's newly shod hoof. "I couldn't leave you here with Simpson. You're out in eight months anyway. I'll escape then."

Sam just shook his head and nodded toward a mule team pulling a huge log in with two more teams right behind it. "Looks like the boys are comin' back for the night. They'll be plenty pissed that we been here in the shade."

"They shoulda learned a trade instead of leading lives of crime, the hell with 'em."

John William started to nail the new shoe on the mule Sam had finished with.

40

"**MAGGIE AND I** are gonna eat at Clancy's, Mick," Brant said. "She says it's a great place. You think you'll be okay without me for a bit?"

I laughed. "Be tough, but I'll try."

"Bring ya back a doggie bag if ya want," he grinned. "I figure since we're gonna get at least a couple more days down here, I better get in good with Maggie before I go."

"I gotta call Dad," I said. "Bring him up to speed. You go ahead and have a blast without me. Maggie's cool. You just got lucky that I didn't ask her out first."

"Yeah, you just keep tellin' yourself that," he said. "I'm gonna hit the shower and change. I'll stop back in if your light's still on when I get back."

"Try to make it back at a decent hour," I said with a grin. "We're gonna hit the Malcom Morgan neighborhood tomorrow, see what shakes out. That'll probably determine how much longer we stay down here."

"I'll be ready, bro," Brant laughed. "I don't tire out and need as much rest as you do in your twilight years."

I picked up the phone to call Dad. "Just go before I decide to fire you."

Dad answered his phone on the second or third ring. "Don't tell me y'all are in trouble with the law again," he said without even a "Hello, son."

"Not me," I said, "but Brant's heading out to play, so keep bail money at hand."

His deep chuckle came through the ear piece.

"Just thought I'd call and see where you want to go from here, Dad," I said. "We've just about exhausted any further leads to the specific details. Mr. Postier filled in most of the gaps, maybe all that can be filled in."

There was a short pause followed by a sigh. "I guess that I'm satisfied we've found out where the painting came from," Dad said. "My father painted it, and he was preparing to return to Oklahoma with it when his world went all to hell somehow. Postier says Marcel Fontenot had him killed as a favor to Davis McBride. I'd sure like to know exactly what happened, but that's most likely impossible to know now."

"Postier's about the only living soul we've found who had some contact with people who actually knew your father," I said. "And honestly we've looked pretty hard."

"A lot of water has passed under the bridge, son," Dad said. "Assuming Mr. Postier is being honest, and he has no reason not to be that we know, and putting that with what we know from the journals, we can guess he planned to tell his folks, and maybe Mom, about that six-point star he'd found in Pittsburg County in some sort of attempt to reconnect with his Oklahoma family to some extent."

"Evidently he hadn't figured how to resolve his marital status; he was bringing his current wife with him," I interjected. "Granny had remarried after his presumed death and was a widow for, what she believed, a second time."

"I know," Dad said. "And the journals suggest that he intended to maintain the Samuel Whitman persona, but who really knows what he was thinking."

"Most likely we'll never really know his full intentions," I said. "I'm sorry, Dad."

"Of course you're right, Mick," Dad bounced back a little more upbeat than I expected. "Whatever your grandfather was planning to do once he arrived back in Oklahoma is most likely lost to time now, but the subject matter of the painting makes me think he was hoping to lead them to the buried money."

"Yep," I agreed. "I reckon he'd put two and two together and figured out they were cash-strapped with the depression not over at the time."

"Remember, son, at that particular time, he still perceived Davis McBride to be a major threat to him and to us, his family," Dad continued. "I believe he just wanted someone to know he was still alive, maybe test the waters with us and feel out some sort of possible reunion. We, his boys, were pretty much grown by then. Maybe he hoped to find some sort of peace between his two families again, who knows?"

There was another long pause as we fumbled around for the words to take us forward.

Then Dad said, "You said he mentioned Frederick Buchanan's death in his journals, Mick."

I wondered where he was heading with this. "Yep, he was well aware that Granny had married him and taken you boys to New York."

"I wonder if Daddy had never learned of Buchanan's suicide after the stock market crash of '29, would he have just continued on with his life in New Orleans as Samuel Whitman and never looked back, just remained 'dead' to us?"

"I don't know, Dad," I said softly. "But I do know that he was already writing a journal for Mark before Buchanan died, so the thought of some kind of redemption must have entered his mind, and I believe he hoped a time would come when he could unite all four of his sons as brothers but..."

"But the best laid plans..." Dad finished for me.

There was another pause, and I figured now was a good a time as any to change the subject for a break. "So...how's the office running without Brant and me?" I asked, knowing the answer that was coming.

"Janie said it was always smoother with you two yahoos out from underfoot," he laughed.

"Good because we'd like to stick it out just a little longer and see why we were being shot at. It could have a tie to Mason McBride or the case we're on somehow. I don't think so, but I'd like to be sure."

"I figured as much," he said. I swear I could hear him smirk. "Well, anyway, you can tell our new kinfolks that I've decided, in a very Solomon-like fashion, if it's okay with them, to have Dad's remains cremated and half placed with Renee alongside Michelle and Mark down there and the other half divided again. We'll bring part of him back to lie with your granny and his parents here in Durant. Then we'll scatter the rest of him in Arkansas where he grew up. He led at least two different lives, traveled the world, he might as well travel in the afterlife, too."

"Leslie and Marie will like that I think," I said. "Once you're through reading the original journals for yourself, maybe I'll drive you back down here to deliver them to Marie and let you hang out with our new relatives and visit with Mr. Moon for a few days."

"Give them my deepest thanks, Mickey. Tell them I'll protect the journals, and we'll be down there to personally deliver them real soon," Dad said. "And tell Tommy I owe him a beer or two."

"They say they're coming to Oklahoma for a visit before Leslie's classes restart in the fall," I said.

"Good, I want to meet them," Dad said. "But I still want to go back to New Orleans myself this fall, the good Lord willing and the creeks don't rise. But right now, I need to go have Arcelus Monroe's sorry hide disinterred from my father's grave and reburied elsewhere. I really don't care where. They can toss it in the local garbage dump for my part."

I smiled. "Yeah, best he's gone from there."

"By the way, before I let you go, Mick, Janie, said that Mason McBride stopped by the offices yesterday…to 'bury the hatchet' and talk about hiring us to work security on his potential run for the governor in the near future of our native state."

"That's sort of odd, don't you think?" I said. "I mean considering we're already working Daniel Letts' security, not to mention our discovery and rough handling of his two boys tailing us down here. I wonder just where he wants to bury that hatchet."

"Maybe he's planning on running after Daniel's term is up this go round. I don't know," Dad laughed. "But I'm sure he has something up his sleeve."

"I wondered how he'd react to the likely unveiling of his grandfather's criminal activities, but offering us a job wasn't what I expected," I laughed out loud. "The news of the Fontenot/McBride connection should be hitting the wires at any time, and I was pretty sure he wouldn't appreciate the bad press, no matter how distant in the past it was, with his probable run for the governor looming this term or next."

"I'll bet his boys have sent him advanced warning," Dad said cheerfully. "I hate that we may have hurt the senator in any way, form, or fashion. I'll tell him we're too busy right now if you want me to."

"That's okay. I'll talk to him after we get back," I said. "Reckon the bad press may put a damper on his push to get a statue dedicated to Davis McBride."

"I heard that was in the works as part of the Oklahoma Centennial a few years up the line," Dad chuckled. "You gotta hate that, but what can you do when a state icon turns out to be a lowlife criminal sonuvabitch?"

I laughed again. "Well, we're gonna push over a few more rocks and see what crawls out from under 'em. There may be more answers yet. You know what you always say about leaving no stone unturned."

"Okay, but you and Brant be safe and get back here before Christmas if you can, for God's sake. You're bankrupting the business."

"Remind me again who sent us down here," I needled back.

"I didn't intend for y'all to move down there," he said flatly. "I figured a day or two like it would have taken me and Ira, and y'all would be back."

Of course there was no winning against him. I laughed and said, "Do what you want if Mason McBride comes back, but we gotta get hunting leases in Pittsburg County. Somewhere out there, not too far from Hartshorne, Grandpa saw a six-point star that he believed marked a treasure. We may make something off this case yet."

"Another excuse to miss work," he said.

I laughed. "Y'all just hang on. We'll be back before the Series starts. Love ya, Dad."

"Love you, too, Mick," he said. "Now you and Brant watch each other's back. There's no telling what might crawl out from under those rocks y'all kick over."

"Will do, Dad, and I'll tell Brant you fired him for leaving me alone."

"Sweet Lord," he said and hung up.

In just a matter of minutes, Brant knocked on my door. He was decked out, ready to go all cowboyed-up on New Orleans.

"How's Will?" he asked

"Thought you'd already rolled," I said. "He's really doing fine. I told him we were gonna take a couple more days and see if we could find out why we were shot at, make sure McBride had nothing to do with it."

"Good man," he said. "You got us another couple of days in the Big Easy. You need anything before I go?"

"No, I'm going to stroll through the Quarter a bit and lay out our game plan for tomorrow," I answered. "And oh, yeah, Dad said you're fired."

He laughed. "Will knows you couldn't even find your way back to Oklahoma without me. See ya early in the morning, bro, beignets for breakfast."

He left, and I slipped on my Pumas to see the sights on Bourbon for a bit, maybe grab a "big ass" beer.

Tomorrow would be a busy day, most likely spent in some darker corners of The Big Easy.

41

NEAR HARTSHORNE, OKLAHOMA, JUNE 1916

THERE WAS NO REST *for the wicked or the weary on the work detail it seemed. Only a day after catching a break from the logging to re-shoe a couple of draft horses, Sam and John William were right back out in the trees with the other men.*

On this day, they were the last ones in. They had put in a long day with all the logging crews, had just stabled their team, and were carrying their equipment back to the camp when they saw one of the guards walking toward them carrying his rifle in the crook of his arm. It was Virgil Simms, a mean, little beady-eyed piece of crap that the men all hated with a passion.

"Wallace, you and Musgrove come with me, got a couple of mules throwed shoes," Simms ordered.

"But it's getting late, boss, almost supper time, can't we get them early in the mornin'?" John William asked, feeling something was out of the ordinary.

"You can get 'em right now, boy," Simms snickered. "I'll have 'em bring you some beans out from the camp. Now you and the Indian there get your worthless asses movin'."

Sam cut his eyes over at John.

This was odd. They were well over a hundred yards from the main camp, and Mr. Burnett was nowhere to be seen.

"Just leave the saws and the chains here?" Sam asked, looking around the trail.

"You gonna need 'em to shoe them mules?" Simms snarled. "I'll send Reynolds and Whitaker to pick 'em up. Just git on down to the shed."

John and Sam laid the saws and chains down, turned, and moved up the trail toward the stable, ten or twenty feet ahead of Simms, who was following after them with his rifle.

Sam looked over at John William and spoke low enough only John William could hear. "What's goin' on here, John?"

"Hell if I know," John spoke equally low. "Just keep walkin'; you know Virgil's a prick."

Simms spit tobacco in the dirt as he walked. "What're you two mutterin' about up there? You boys wouldn't give me an excuse to make the world a better place, would ya?"

"Reckon that means he's gonna shoot hisself, cousin?" Sam said, low again and grinned.

John William glanced back. "Not us, Mr. Simms, we're just discussin' the mules, boss, hopin' that damned on'ry black one's not up there when we get there."

"Guess you boys heard they found some fella's whiskey still up in the trees?" Simms spoke, taunting them. "Musta been twenty pints of good corn liquor. How long's it been since you had a good shot a whiskey, Wallace?"

"Quite a while, boss, quite a while."

"Smith and Bodine carried it into camp, gonna lock it up. You boys behave and you might get a taste, Wallace, none for the Indian of course."

"Of course," John said.

"Of course," Sam mouthed without sound.

A young guard named Billy Burns was still at the stables when they reached them, and the big black mule was indeed standing there with a sorrel and a bay horse that John had just shoed the day before.

"Get back to camp, boy," Simms growled at the young guard with a dismissive wave of his hand.

"Mr. Burnett told me to make sure everything down here was locked up and all the animals were..." Burns started.

"Do as your told, boy," Simms glared at him. "Captain done changed his mind, gonna shoe these critters before supper. You go straight on to eat though. I'll watch these fellas."

"But..." Burns started, then thought better of making Simms angrier. "Yes, sir," he said and headed up the trail.

Simms slipped a small pouch out of his shirt pocket and moved back to a stump, set his rifle against a small tree, and started rolling a cigarette.

"Get after it, boys," he said with a grin.

Sam lifted the bay's hoof. "Look here, John."

There was an ugly mark where it looked like someone had pried on the shoe with something.

John lifted the back foot of the sorrel and found the same mark. He glanced at Sam, then quickly back down and spoke to the ground. "Something not right going on here, Sam."

Sam quickly checked the area, both left and right. "Yeah, I know. Whadda we do?"

"Keep your eyes on Simms, and fix the bay's shoe while I check that big black sonuvabitch."

Simms stood up and stepped on the butt of his smoke. He cradled the rifle in the crook of his arms and kept looking up the trail as he paced.

"John..." Sam nodded toward the trail.

Four prisoners appeared, leading another mule toward where Simms was standing. Andy Burks and Arcelus Monroe were about twenty yards behind them with what looked like plates of food.

Virgil nodded toward where Sam and John were working and then started walking toward Burks and Monroe coming down the trail.

John laid the black mule's lead rope across a rail. "Get ready, Sam. Something's going on."

"It's the Jarvis brothers, Reynolds and Crazy Fred," Sam said, working the loose shoe off the bay.

"Don't take four men to bring us a mule, and they ain't shackled," John said. "And our boys, Monroe and Burks, are back behind 'em."

"Shit, cousin, Simms is leavin' and Burks and Monroe are comin' this way, too." Sam's voice rose slightly, "This is it."

John William picked up the hook-bladed horseshoe knife with his left hand, still holding the big hammer in his right. "I'd say we're in trouble, Sam; arm yourself."

Rufus Jarvis was leading the grey mule by a rope halter, his brother, Alvin, the larger of the two, and the other two prisoners right behind him.

"Boss says for you two to look at this mule's foot and fix it for us," Rufus grunted.

"Hold him right there for a minute, boys, don't want to spook these we got here." John tried to sound natural as he could, slipping the knife in his pocket and stepping out with Sam toward the men.

"That supper?" Sam called up the trail to Burks and Monroe, who had stopped several yards back.

Simms looked back once, then began to trot up the trail faster and farther out of sight.

"Yup," Monroe said as he turned the plate up and dumped it.

Burks tossed his plate on the ground too and said, "Sorry, boys."

Then without any warning, Crazy Fred let out a blood-curdling scream, rushed around the grey mule's backside, running straight at John and Sam.

Sam dropped Fred, crushing his skull with a single swing of the horseshoe hammer.

The Jarvis boys and Reynolds froze.

John looked down at the bleeding heap. "What the hell are you fools thinkin'?"

"Goddamn Indian sonuvabitch killed Fred," Reynolds shrieked in a high-pitched voice.

"Don't just stand there, you drunk bastards," Monroe growled. "You know the deal. You want to piss me off? I'll have all your asses. Kill 'em, like I said."

Rufus Jarvis and Reynolds were already moving at Sam, who was swinging the hammer again. Alvin charged John, who side-stepped the rush and caught him on the shoulder blade with a hammer blow.

Reynolds' arm snapped as Sam landed another blow. Then Rufus tackled Sam and Reynolds, still holding his broken arm and screaming, started kicking Sam in the head.

John William swung the hammer again and took Reynolds' lower jaw almost off.

The horribly injured prisoner made a gurgling sound and fell as Burks rushed in with Sam's hammer that he'd picked up and hit John a glancing blow in the ribs.

John fell backward onto Rufus, who was still trying to strangle Sam. He pulled the horseshoe knife out of his pocket and drew it across Rufus's neck and back, cutting a wicked gash.

Howling like an injured animal, the burley convict turned Sam's throat loose to reach for his attacker, but John had rolled away again.

Burks swung again and missed as John kept rolling, but Alvin was back up and kicking him now. All he could do was slash wildly with the wicked little blade to keep the men back as he rose up off the ground.

Out of the corner of one eye, John William saw Sam slashing at Rufus's face with his own hooked blade. Burks tried to move in to help again, but John stomped hard, taking his knee out just before the larger Jarvis brother kicked John down from behind.

But Sam had a free shot, and he cut Rufus's throat ear to ear before jabbing the blade into the soft spot below his breast bone and ripping it down past his navel.

As the smaller Jarvis brother fell, Sam grabbed John's hammer up off the ground and crushed the back of Alvin's skull, where he stood kicking John William in the ribs.

Unable to avoid the fight, Monroe finally joined in and caught Sam across the arm with a length of chain he'd picked up. Until now he'd hoped that he wouldn't have to enter the lopsided battle.

"Get up and run, John William, run," Sam yelled just before Burks' hammer swing ended his voice forever.

John rose with another hammer and swung for Burks head but caught him between the shoulder blades. Monroe, still swinging the chain, struck John's arm, and he felt the chain wrap. He held on and yanked Arcelus to the ground with him.

Reynolds, somehow still alive, tried to rise up with his mangled jaw, but John kicked him square in the face, rolling him again with inhuman groans as Monroe tried to tear the chain free.

Burks was up again and advancing with his hammer drawn back. John released the chain and gutted Andy Burks like a fish, but not before Burks landed a blow on his shoulder, knocking him under the bay horse, who immediately kicked him several time before tearing loose.

Monroe was on John swinging the chain again, and Burks was still coming despite his gaping abdominal wound until the chain struck a glancing blow on John's forehead, taking him to his knees. Burks swung the hammer forcefully with both hands but missed, falling with a scream as his stomach tore open, spilling his insides into the dirt. He didn't move again.

Down on his knees and almost out, John William weakly threw the knife at Monroe and missed. The chain caught him across the back again, driving pain throughout his body.

Arcelus Monroe swung once more, but John lifted his arm, catching the heavy chain again as it wrapped around his forearm.

But it was over. Monroe knew it was. John could see the look in his eyes. Still holding his end of the chain, Arcelus reached for a bloody horseshoe hammer, thinking maybe McBride would give him Burks' share as well.

John William was struggling to remain conscious but would have already fallen if not for Monroe holding him up with the chain wrapped around his wrist and forearm.

Monroe spoke through his bleeding lips, "Senator McBride says to tell you it was him had this done, Wallace. Didn't want you to think it was random, said to be sure you knew, said he told you he'd get ya."

Monroe drew back the heavy hammer to swing it at John's skull just as the big black mule's kick drove the iron mule shoe into the back of Arcelus's brain, turning his whole world dark.

Likely already dead, the hammer falling from his hand, he spun, taking another kick directly in the face, dragging John William down to the ground with him.

The big mule kicked at empty air a couple more times and moved away from the body.

John William struggled to his knees and began untangling the chain from his arm, trying to focus on its other end. It was still wrapped around Monroe's lifeless hand and arm.

The only sound in his world was the ringing in John's ears. The animals had all settled down, and not a human was moving, except for him as he tried to unwrap the chain from his arm. He sat up, but he fell face first and was out again.

When John regained consciousness a few minutes later, he was confused. How long had he been out? He blinked, then blinked again, staring into Arcelus Monroe's smashed and lifeless face with its open-eyed stare looking back at him.

He recoiled and came back to a sitting position. Nothing moved. He was alone in the dark of night.

42

NEAR HARTSHORNE, OKLAHAOMA, JUNE 1916

STANDING WAS *almost impossible. John realized he was hurt bad. There was still an unnatural ringing in his ears, breathing was unholy pain, and he could taste his own blood in his mouth, but he made it to his feet and surveyed his surroundings. Thinking was difficult.*

He checked Sam for any sign of life. His heart broke to see his faithful friend was gone. Twice now he'd lost men he could depend on, trust, and the feeling of being totally alone came back even worse this time.

All the others were dead, and he didn't give a damn. He kicked Burks' lifeless corpse several times, despite the pain that hit him with each kick, then looked around at the horrific scene. Inexplicably there was no one anywhere in sight, and suddenly he knew he had to move while he still had the chance.

Slowly the ringing in his ears was starting to subside, and he noticed the quiet that was gathering in the twilight, along with a plan.

He and Monroe were a similar size with similar builds. The con's face was pretty rough from the mule kick but still not rough enough to serve John's intended purpose.

Using his less injured hand and arm, he dragged Arcelus Monroe to the hay piled in the corner of the shed and managed to get Monroe's upper torso pretty well into the loose straw. He piled more kindling around the corpse.

John's right hand touched the silver ring that Rena had given him ten years ago. He hesitated for the briefest time but finally slipped it off and put it on Monroe's left hand, which was extending from the straw.

Breathing was labored and painful. He assumed he had at least cracked several ribs in the skirmish, but he knew he was operating on borrowed time. He found a lamp near the forge and poured kerosene onto the dead man's broken face and upper body. He carefully soaked the back walls and wooden posts before sloshing the remainder all about the body and the straw. Methodically he lit the wooden wall and another lamp. As the posts started to burn, he tossed the second lamp into the hay near Monroe's head and shoulders and watched as the stable shed ignited with a flash.

Rifle shots were ringing out from the direction of the main camp. Something was happening up there, but he had no idea what. All he knew was that his time was running out. John looked toward the sound of the shots, slapped the grey mule's sturdy butt, sending him off in a run with the two horses that had already fled, and then pulled himself up onto the back of the big, black monster that he now considered an ally.

Still more shots rang out. He was certain that whatever was happening in the camp couldn't be good. He remembered Simms saying liquor was in the camp after the discovery of a whiskey still in the woods, and he'd smelled the booze on the prisoners as they struggled. That had to be a big factor in whatever was happening at the moment, but he had no intention of hanging around to find out.

He figured the "accident" that was supposed to kill him was probably a riot in the midst of a drunken melee during an attempted prison break. More than likely, Crazy Fred had a bit too much juice and pulled the trigger too quickly on their attack, but who knew?

For all he knew, McBride had even arranged for the whiskey to be planted and discovered by the prisoners. One thing he knew beyond a shadow of a doubt was that Simms was definitely in on the plot, and Arcelus Monroe sure seemed to be the ringleader, but none of that mattered anymore. This was his chance to run.

Right now the hay was catching fire. A bright blaze was flickering, hot in the hay pile, and Monroe was beginning to burn as well. The smell was godawful, horrible, one that John would never be able to forget.

It was time to ride if he was going to.

He looked over at Sam, as dead as a man could be, his last words still echoing in John's ears, "Run, John William, run," and he felt the need to kill Davis

McBride. It was the same burning for revenge that had originally put his life in jeopardy, what seemed so many years ago, when he'd loaded Levi's body in the back of the wagon before heading out of Oklahoma.

It was then he made himself a promise: if he lived and got away from here tonight, he'd be smarter this time. He wouldn't blindly follow impulse. He'd be careful and precise and get retribution without endangering everyone he ever cared for, but he would get his revenge.

The moon was high in the western sky, and the stars were peeking through the branches as the little stable shed broke into full flames, bathing him and the mule in the eerie firelight.

He sat on the unsaddled back of the black mule and spoke aloud but softly to the woods surrounding them. "I'm sorry, Sam. This is truly all my fault. Oh, God, how I wish I could fix it. You were my friend, and I hate to leave you lying here, bud, but I just don't know what else to do."

John William felt the tears begin to roll down his cheeks as he looked up at the moon and stars. He wiped them with his sleeve, glanced back at the fire burning, Sam's lifeless body a safe distance from the flames, then started the mule down the trail toward the heavy woods. He was bleeding and beaten, but he was alive, and no one was there to stop him.

43

ARMED WITH THE INFO that Jax had supplied us on Malcom Morgan, his known associates, and the neighborhood where he once lived, Brant and I drove the Jeep into a seedier part of New Orleans. It's tough to get cabs to go into some parts of this town.

We parked and walked into a little bar just off Chef Menteur Highway, a dive in every sense of the word, but it was the first one we'd seen in this part of the city. A beat-up Chevy pickup from the eighties at best and a nice-looking older Cadillac sat side by side outside. There were no windows and a not-so-well-made hand-painted sign near the door that read, "Big Mike's Place."

We walked into the dimly lit room and waited a second for our eyes to adjust. There was one older, white-bearded, black gentleman sitting at the far end of the bar, where the bartender was leaning against the bar across from him under a small television mounted on a shelf. Both appeared to be watching a fuzzy screen showing a baseball game. Possibly the Braves were playing someone, but the picture was so bad, I wasn't sure.

The bartender looked up as we entered the door and rose to his full height. He must've been six seven and muscled like an old athlete. Had to be Big Mike I figured. As he moved toward us, I noticed the eye patch over his left eye and the well-defined biceps straining his white tee shirt.

I considered retreat, but Brant stepped forward and said, "Howdy, boss, can we get two *Rolling Rocks*?"

He stopped and eyed us both cautiously. "Don't got no *Rollin' Rocks* in yeah," the big man said. "Bud, Bud Lite, Miller Genwine Draft, Miller Lite, three bucks a piece."

"Two Miller Lites," I said.

He pulled the beers out of a cooler behind the bar and set them in front of us. "Be six dollahs."

"Mind if we wait on another round," Brant asked. "We'd like to catch a score on that game, drink a couple more maybe."

"You boys be outta da tourist ditrict," he said. "Watchoo needin' down yeah?"

"Just looking for some fellows we met recently," Brant said. "Heard they lived in this neighborhood."

"Not a good neighborhood to be prowlin' 'round in," the big man said. "People 'round yeah kinda keep to deyselves."

The older man at the end of the bar kept his gaze on the pitiful television reception.

"Danarius Brown, Jacoby Anderson, Malcom Morgan, you recognize any of these guys?" I asked, laying out the mug shots Jax had given us.

The old man kept his eyes glued on the ball game, never looking our direction.

"I know all of um," the presumptive Big Mike said. "Nothing but trouble they whole lives. Dat Morgan boy got killed yestiday robbing a liquor sto... Dis about dat?"

"Nope," Brant said. "Just want to talk with Mr. Brown or Mr. Anderson, either one, that's all, find out why they might want to shoot a couple of Okies."

He looked up with his one good eye without smiling. "Din't think you boys was cops."

"You were right," I smiled. "We really do just want to talk with these gentlemen."

He laughed. "Dos boys don't do nuttin' less they's sumpin in it fo demselfs. If they be shootin' atchoo, they be some cash in it fo dem somewheah."

Brant looked at me.

I shrugged.

"All the same, sir," I said. "We'd like a few minutes of their time. Would you happen to know where we could find either of them?"

"Nope," the big man said flatly. "But if'n I did, what makes you think I'd tell you two white boys?"

"Who you calling white?" Brant said

The big man big man looked at Brant, squinting his one eye, and laughed again. "They don't be runnin' des streets no mo' lately. They got um a skinny little white boy keepin' um in some serious cash. He maybe paid um to shoot yo asses whatever cullah you happen to be."

"By any chance this white kid got a name you know of?" I asked, hoping he were finally bonding.

He slung a towel he'd been holding up over his shoulder. "You fellas ask too many questions," he said as he leaned forward on the bar. "But y'all got balls. Ain't neither one of ya scared. I know a scared white boy when I see one."

He laughed to himself as Brant and I took long swigs of our beers.

"They call him Larry. Don't know da boy much but don't care for him much neither; he got sneaky white boy eyes. Das 'bout all I can tell ya."

"Braves leading Cubs 2-1 bottom of the sixth," the white-bearded gentleman said out of nowhere. "Best you boys head on outta here now. Like Lucius say, them boys ain't been 'round here in months."

As he turned toward us slightly for the first time, I noticed he was carrying a pistol in a shoulder holster under his linen jacket.

"Yes, sir," Brant said. "We were just leaving. Appreciate your time, gentlemen."

The older fellow turned back to his ball game as the big man stood, looking solemn and serious.

We finished the beers, and I laid one of our cards on the bar with a ten as we walked out. "If you see 'em, tell 'em the fellows they shot at over on Esplanade the other day want to talk with 'em about Delbert Jones...that is if you don't mind, sir."

"Don't mind a'tall," he said as he picked up the ten and the card both.

"So...reckon Big Mike was the one packing heat and not Lucius behind the bar?" I smiled at Brant as we re-entered the sunshine. "I'd have bet the Jeep the big man was Big Mike."

Brant just rolled his eyes.

"I don't reckon it matters in the grand scheme of things," he said. "But I figure if someone paid those fellows to shoot at us, it had to have something to do with Delbert Jones. The rest of this stuff all happened over half a century ago."

"Yeah, I reckon it's got to be something with Delbert, but damned if that makes much sense," I said as we walked out to our Jeep Cherokee.

"I think we're wasting our time in this neighborhood," Brant said. "If the Lucius says they're not running around here anymore, I believe him."

"Agreed, especially if the little fellow with the big gun under his jacket says so, too," I grinned.

"Let's try Rickey Dale again, see if he ever saw Morgan, Brown, or Anderson hanging around before Delbert disappeared," Brant said. "If Delbert's the key, Rickey was most likely among the last to see him."

"Worth a shot," I tossed Brant the keys. "You're driving back into the Quarter."

Brant shook his head and looked down. "Always the indigenous people have to suffer at the hands of their unjust oppressors."

44

RICKEY DALE was once again in his studio working on a strikingly similar painting to the other one when last we saw him, except this one featured multi-shades of green.

He paused when we came through the door and turned our way, "My Oklahoma friends, good to see you gentlemen again," he beamed. "Have you any news for me? Tell me they'll be locking up that bitch Postier soon."

"Good to see you again, Mr. Dale," Brant said. "I'm afraid we haven't found anything on Mr. Postier, but our search for Mr. Wallace's grandfather has led us to take a further interest in Mr. Jones's murder."

"Really?" he said. "I'd be happy to have Delbert's case solved. I don't believe it's being pursued actively anymore."

"Would you mind looking at some photos for us?" I asked. "We may have new info."

"Of course, Mr. Wallace, Mr. Bluesoldier, I'll be happy to," Rickey said. "But I just don't see how I can help. I've already looked at pictures and told everything I know to those police detective gentlemen."

Brant placed the three photos on the counter in front of Dale and spread them for him to see.

He studied all three, shaking his head. "I don't believe I've ever seen any of these faces with Delbert," he said at first, but then he pulled Danarius Brown's photo out a little and tapped it with a finger. "Wait a minute. I may have seen this fellow somewhere else before though."

"Can you remember where, Mr. Dale?" I asked.

"Call me Rickey. Yes, I think he was with Larry Pearson at the memorial showing of Delbert's work to mark three years after Delbert disappeared. Mr. Fontenot, himself, sponsored the show here at the gallery."

"And you say this man attended?" Brant asked.

"Yes, yes, I remember him now. I've never been shown a picture of him before though. Do you think he had anything to do with Delbert's death?"

"Who is Larry Pearson?" I asked.

"He was Mr. Fontenot's driver, sort of a jack-of-all-trades assistant type, and I believe this person may have been a bodyguard," Dale said, tapping his finger on the photo of Danarius Brown. "I don't know for sure, but he was here with Larry. I remember him now."

"You've never seen the other two though?" Brant questioned.

"No, I just remember this man," Dale said, tapping Danarius Brown's photo. "When Larry helped Mr. Fontenot out of his car, he stood around outside the studio, smoking a cigarette until Mr. Fontenot left the showing. He never came inside during the showing."

"Thank you, Mr. Dale, that could be important," I said. "You wouldn't happen to know how we could contact Mr. Pearson nowadays by any chance, would you?"

"Call me Rickey," he smiled. "He was staying with Mr. Fontenot then, I think, but I don't know where he lives now. I haven't seen him in over a year, maybe two."

"That's still a great deal of help to us, Rickey," Brant said as he gathered the photos back up.

"Just glad to be of service to such fine gentlemen," Rickey Dale said, shaking our hands as we were leaving. "Please keep me in the loop if you find out anything at all on Delbert's disappearance."

"Will do," I said as we headed for the front door onto Dauphine Street.

"I notice you didn't break the news to him about Jones' body being found," Brant grinned. "You're not playing favorites, are you?"

I shrugged and was already dialing Jaxon Moon.

"A new player in the game," Brant said. "Are you seeing what Jax knows about Pearson?"

"Yep,"

Jaxon picked up on his end. "Mick, glad to hear from you; I was worried someone might have shot you both by now."

"Never, I told you, people love us once they get to know us. We've even turned up a person of interest. You ever hear of a fellow by the name of Larry Pearson?"

"Yep, I recall the name. He was working for Marcel Fontenot when Mr. Fontenot passed from this plane, sort of a step-and-fetch-it flunky, small-time punk really. What have you got on him?"

"Nothing solid yet; he may or may not have ties to a friend of Malcom Morgan, Danarius Brown," I answered. "Rickey Dale seems to recall an association of some sort while Pearson was driving for Mr. Fontenot, and another gentleman in Morgan's old neighborhood recalled the boys working with or for a 'white boy' named Larry, so it has possibility."

"Now wouldn't that be interesting?" Jax said. "Could connect up some loose ends."

"You've got nothing on Brown working for Fontenot?" I probed gently.

"Mickey, Marcel kept meticulous books," Jax answered. "I gave you all I got. We've got Marcel tied to half the politicians in Oklahoma, Texas, Arkansas, and Louisiana in the forties and fifties. We know who he did business with for the last sixty years of his life, and I haven't seen a single reference to Denarius Brown. Now Larry Pearson's a different story. But regardless let's just say Denarius is not the proper shade of skin tone to be working for Marcel Fontenot."

I decided to tell him everything Dale had told us concerning Pearson and Danarius Brown and a possible connection to Marcel Fontenot. It seemed only fair.

"Maybe Pearson led him into the fold or, more likely, Marcel allowed Pearson to hire Brown if he was desperate for some muscle," Jax said. "But if he was acting as a bodyguard or anything else, Fontenot kept him off all the books we have access to, and we believe we have all of them. Still I'll see if I can find out anything else for you, buddy. Sounds like something's up."

"Locating Larry Pearson would be a big help. Brant says he thinks the dude's a figment of someone's imagination."

"I think we can find Mr. Pearson. We've got him on our radar with the Fontenot investigation. Let me talk to some people and see what we can do. Maybe then we can convince Mr. Bluesoldier that Pearson is real."

"We're headed back to the hotel to change now," I said. "If my driver doesn't get us lost that is."

Brant flipped me off as he navigated through the narrow French Quarter streets.

I shrugged at Brant.

"Think we're gonna grab a burger at Ernst Café first, yell at us soon as you find something. We're gonna see Steve Earle with Leslie later tonight," I said to Jax.

"Good burgers at Ernst's, you guys will love it," Jax said. "Tell me what you think of their rather unique floor design later."

"I'm sure that has some significant meaning, but you're not gonna tell me right now, correct?"

He laughed again. "Right, y'all just let me know what you think, and don't cheat and Google it."

"I can't even spell Google," I laughed.

"Okay, let's just say it's often misunderstood, and a lot of folks feel a little perplexed about it. We'll discuss it in detail later if you have any questions."

"I'm already intrigued," I said as Brant seemed intent on not hitting a bicyclist on the narrow streets.

"Anyway you guys will be in a good part of town, and they make great burgers. You'll be fat and happy," Jax said sounding as happy as if he had good sense.

"Later," I said

"Call you back real soon with everything I can get for you on Mr. Pearson. Just remember NOPD is looking at him in the Delbert Jones shooting."

"We're always the souls of discretion," I laughed.

He hung up with a chuckle.

I hung up as Brant wound the Jeep around the blocks on one-way streets.

"Are you lost again? My God, man, you're supposed to be a tracker, an unparalleled guide of Native ancestry, a..."

"Would you just shut up for a change?" Brant said as he skillfully maneuvered our vehicle into a difficult parking space very near The Ernst Cafe.

45

ON THE RUN – PITTSBURG COUNTY, OKLAHOMA TO ANTLERS, OKLAHOMA, JULY 1916

RIDING AWAY *from the burning shed, John William's first impulse was to head back home to Durant, but even through the fog clouding his brain, he was worried someone would figure out that wasn't him dead in the fire, and the law would be laying for him there.*

His head hurt, his ribs hurt. Hell, he hurt all over, but he had to go somewhere before they found him just wandering aimlessly in the woods. Finally through the fog in his brain, he recalled that Rena and Sam had kinfolks in Tuskahoma. Surely they would shelter him for a while and get word back to his father and Rena if he could just make it there.

He looked into the night sky and located the Big Dipper, then the North Star, and pulled gently on the rope halter heading the mule southeastward toward Tuskahoma and friends.

He never made it.

About twelve miles out of the logging camp, bleeding and almost unconscious, he looked up for guidance again and simply fell off the mule.

Not long after sunup, John opened his eyes to see an old Indian fellow peering down at him, lying on the ground.

"I saw the mule," the old fellow smiled. "Then I saw you, thought you was dead."

John tried to rise and passed out again.

"Guess that means I don't get a new mule," the old man said to himself and began to haul John up and get him on the tall beast's back once again.

It was no easy chore, but a short time later, he managed to transport John William back to his little shack where he and his wife lived deep in the woods.

Two days later, John William came back far enough from the dead to decide he might as well go ahead and live.

"Hailito," his savior said as John opened his eyes again and sat up on the edge of his cot.

"Looks like he may live, Maw," he called to a tiny woman in a calico cloth dress standing at a wood burning stove.

The little brown-skinned woman spoke something to her husband in Choctaw and smiled a toothless smile at John.

John William's ribs still hurt when he took a breath, but his wounds had been poulticed and bound in cloth. "Where am I?" he asked weakly.

"Nowhere," the old fellow laughed.

The old man told John William that he had just started out to hunt squirrels two days ago when he came across John and the mule.

"Like to have never got you back up on that mule," he laughed. "Lucky for you, I'm a patient man."

John tried to smile.

As the old Choctaw sat cleaning his ancient rifle, he told him about the escape of four prisoners from a convict logging crew and how he'd been in the front yard skinning squirrels when a search party had come to his shack the day after he'd brought John to their home.

The men told him the escapees were very dangerous men and asked if he or his wife had seen any strangers. He told the posse they'd seen no one out here this deep in the woods, as his wife stood in the doorway looking out, but watching John, covered by a quilt, lying on a bunk behind her in the corner.

The men eyed the house and the woman. He told them there was only one room. They were welcome to look inside, but they didn't. Probably didn't want to get down from their horses, he reckoned.

"Why?" John asked as he ate squirrel, fry bread, and wild onions at the old couple's table.

"You don't look too dangerous," the old man said.

The old woman put more squirrel in front of John and nodded at him to eat.

"Thank you, ma'am," John said, looking at the woman. "You know I'm one of the convicts though, right?"

"Yep," the old man said.

"Well, I appreciate your help."

The old man lit his pipe.

"Mule's safe, hid in the woods, no tracks for them prison men to find nowhere."

John finished eating.

The old woman picked up his tin plate and smiled without speaking. No love lost between the old Choctaw and the prison system in Oklahoma, John figured.

Although the manhunt was still in progress the next day, John felt like he was strong enough to travel again.

"Still a lot of people looking for those prison boys," the old Choctaw said. "Where you reckon them convicts went?"

John just smiled. A new plan was forming in his brain. He'd head for Antlers, catch a train for Denison, Texas, and work back to Oklahoma from there. No one would expect him to come up from the south.

"Can you tell me how get me to Antlers from here without being seen much?" John asked.

"Yep. I'll show you how if you can keep up," he answered. "We leave right after dark, take us a day or so if we go fast."

John realized he'd never even told the old fellow his name, nor had he been asked, but the man was willing to risk trouble with the law to help him. He looked at the couple. "I think I can keep up," he said smiling

At twilight John and the old man walked out of the little shack to where the mule and a small pony were already tied.

As he mounted the mule, the old Choctaw handed John a big-brimmed slouch hat to hide his scar.

"Don't wear it much anymore," he said. "Might help you hide that ugly white face of yours."

John pulled the hat on. It wasn't a bad fit. "Might take more'n a hat to hide that scar," he grinned. "But I reckon it's better than nothin'."

The tiny woman handed them squirrel and more fry bread wrapped in brown paper and patted her heart with her right hand as she smiled up at them.

"I can't thank you enough, ma'am," John said to the tiny woman looking up at them.

"I'll be back directly, Maw," the Choctaw said as they wheeled their animals.

He led John south over thirty miles through the woods to Antlers where John sold the mule, got a train ticket for Denison, Texas, kept two dollars, and offered the old man the rest.

"No money, boy," the Choctaw said as John tried to hand him some bills. "You were a guest in our home."

"Someday, I hope you'll be one in mine," John said. "I appreciate the courtesy, but I need to give you this money to deliver a note for me to, Andrew Musgrove, in Tuskahoma. I know that's out of your way, and I wish to pay you for the trouble. Even if you can't do it for a day or so."

The old man reluctantly took the money and the note, in which John explained as much as he could to Andrew and asked him to have Rena meet him in Denison, Texas outside the First Baptist Church on a Sunday at noon as soon as she could. He'd be there every Sunday until she showed up.

The Choctaw shook John's hand and promised he would deliver the message as he went back home. He knew Andrew personally and would make sure the note was placed in his hand.

John was moved by the old man's selfless nature and tried to give him the other two dollars, but the old man just shook his head.

"I do not think things will be free in Texas," the Choctaw said as he turned to leave.

"Wait a minute, sir," John said. "My name is John William Wallace, but I'd ask you not to tell that to anyone, and I'd like to know you and your wife's names if you don't mind."

"I am Anderson Hooser. My wife is Cheyenne. Her name is Ayasha, and only we will know John William Wallace's name. Go now."

The ancient little brown man swung up into his pony's saddle like a young warrior and rode north.

Like other men John had met lately, he would never see or hear of Anderson Hooser again.

46

FATE INTERVENES – TUSKAHOMA, OKLAHOMA TO ATOKA, OKLAHOMA, JULY 1916

SAM AND RENA'S UNCLE, *Andrew Musgrove, was sitting on his front porch in Tuskahoma, Oklahoma waiting on his wife, Annie, to call him inside and serve the rabbit stew she'd made from Andrew's little hunting trek when he spied the rider coming up the path to his cabin at an easy pace*

"Howdy, Andrew," Anderson Hooser said as he slipped down from little pony. "Long time, no see."

"Anderson Hooser, you old horse thief," Andrew said with a laugh. "What are you doing down here without Ayasha?"

"Bringing your mail," Anderson Hooser said flatly.

"Well, come in and eat a bowl of stew," Musgrove said with a puzzled look as Hooser handed him John William's carefully folded note.

"Annie, that old horse thief Hooser's here to eat our food," Andrew called through the doorway. "Hide the good silver."

Anderson just shook his head and followed Musgrove through the door where Annie met him with a warm embrace and a smile.

An hour later, he was riding for Ayasha and his own cozy shack in the woods southeast of Hartshorne, leaving the Musgroves to read John William's plea for help.

Andrew and Annie Musgrove were already aware of the whole story of Rena's man, John William Wallace, but the recent events concerning Sam's death and the prison break came as a shock.

Andrew took the news hard; Sam had been a special nephew, almost a son to him. He was determined to do all he could to help John though. He knew Samuel and John William had grown close after John and Rena's marriage.

He read John's hastily scribbled note, which held only limited information of Samuel's death and John's escape. Mostly it concerned John William's urgent message for Rena to meet him in Denison, Texas. He loves Rena as much as he loved Samuel and recalled them playing around his home with his children when they were all little. He would do what he could do.

The next morning, he saddled his blue roan, kissed Annie, and started for Durant to find Rena, who was living there with her in-laws. It would be a good three-day ride if he traveled easy and stayed on good roads and then another three days back home.

"Get Amos and Eli to help if you need it, my little flower," he smiled at Annie. "We raised them well. They can feed a few animals, I reckon."

Annie leaned off the porch and kissed him. "Just get word to Rena, whatever this secret message is," she said, a back-handed scolding for not letting her in on the secret.

He swore he'd explain everything later. Better not to know right now, he promised her. Mostly, however, he simply did not wish to leave her there alone to grieve the loss of Samuel.

But fate can be a cruel trickster, a sorry bastard with no sense of justice, and somewhere between Daisy and Atoka, Oklahoma, Andrew, a man of almost seventy-five years, began to feel light-headed and was sweating profusely just before he fell from the saddle onto the side of the road.

It was six days before Andrew's younger brother Abraham set out to find him. Annie was insistent that something was wrong and had convinced Abraham not to wait a couple of more days before following him.

No one knew who the old Indian gentleman was. He'd lingered in the hospital at Atoka for three days without regaining consciousness before he passed quietly from this world.

The funeral home in Atoka had prepared the body and was about to give him a pauper's burial after failing to locate anyone to claim the body.

"Some old Indian, no telling where he's from," the county official said. "Give him three days, then sell the horse and saddle to pay for burying expense."

Abraham found him on the day before he was to be buried, negotiated payment, and promised to return with wagon for his brother's body.

"Just leave the horse and saddle 'til you get back here, and don't dawdle," the undertaker told him.

Andrew had told no one of his mission. Not even Annie knew the details of the message, and he'd burned the letter after reading it. He told her it was better if no one knew what was in the note. She only knew he had to tell his niece, Rena, something very personal and very important concerning her husband, John, so Abraham never even considered continuing the trip into Durant.

He agreed to leave the horse and saddle as collateral until he could return to Tuskahoma to fetch a wagon and come back with cash for his brother's body.

The time was given reluctantly. The undertaker knew a good horse and saddle when he saw one. Abraham headed back home, and thus John William's plea would never be given to Rena or his father or anyone else in this world.

In Denison John William had found work at a livery stable the day he arrived. He slept in the hay loft of the stable and was saving all the money he could.

He allowed for a week at least before Rena or his dad would get the message from the Musgroves, Rena's uncles living in Tuskahoma and then possibly even another week before one of them could safely make it to Durant with instructions for Rena to come south and meet him in Denison.

John spent his Sundays walking around the two Baptist churches in Denison, but after a couple of weeks, he knew something was wrong. He couldn't just sit and wait much longer. He'd need a new plan.

He may have never known the cruel trick fate had played, but he was dead certain that his family had not gotten the message, or someone would've found a way to Denison by now. That much he knew as the days turned into weeks, and July disappeared.

47

STEVE EARLE had rocked the House of Blues; Leslie, Marie, Brant and I had a blast, but now it was back to work. We met Jaxon at Johnny's Po-Boys on Magazine Street.

"So how was the concert last night?" Jax smiled.

"It was Steve Earle, dude... 'Copperhead Road,'" I said. "It was awesome. What else could it have been?"

"*The Devil's Right Hand; nothing touched the pistol but the Devil's right hand, the Devil's right hand,*" Brant kicked in, almost carrying a tune.

"I guess it was a stupid question," Jax laughed. "And how did the ladies like it? Equally enthralled I assume."

"Of course, great company, great music, cold beer; it was perfect. Marie and Leslie had a blast, I think," I said. "Lisa's apparently still out in California on a movie. I'm starting to think she's not real."

Jax smiled. "Oh, she's real, quite an actress. I met her same time I met Leslie at that Tulane fundraiser."

"That's basically what Leslie told us," I said. "Seems Lisa has a role in a new movie being filmed in southern California and northern Mexico, might not be back in New Orleans until sometime this fall."

Brant grinned, "You bring us talking paper, White Eyes?"

Jax laughed again and handed us a manila folder with Pearson's photo and file. "Larry Pearson lives at the Gravier Place Apartments, nice digs, works for Marlon Landry now that his old employer, Marcel Fontenot, has passed."

"What's Landry do that requires the services of Mr. Pearson?" I asked.

"Officially he's in real estate," Jax said between bites of his shrimp po boy. "In reality he's the main honcho in smuggling anything and everything but drugs into the Port of New Orleans, guns, jewels, humans, stolen goods, you name it - except drugs. He hates drugs."

Brant finished a wolf-sized bite of his catfish po boy. "A criminal with some scruples. You kinda gotta admire that, I reckon. But how does Pearson fit in?"

"Pearson's uncle was legitimately employed in Marcel's construction business. He likely got Fontenot to hire the lad. We figure young Pearson just sort of wormed his way into Marcel's favor after that as a driver and an assistant once Marcel got old, sort of a jack-of-all-trades," Jax said. "After that Marcel probably got him in with Landry as a lower-level gopher before he died, must've owed Pearson's uncle or something. Fontenot even left Larry a little cash in his will to boot."

"Could've been payment for whacking Delbert Jones, you reckon?" I offered.

"Wouldn't doubt it, Mick, but at least Fontenot made it look legit, put it legally in his last will and testament and everything."

Brant finished his sandwich and was eying mine. "We know he keeps some pretty shady company," he said. "Bet there might be drugs involved."

He swiped one of my fries, the little crunchy ones that he knows I like best.

I gave him my most menacing glare.

"That sort of thing shouldn't sit well with the big guy if Landry is really anti-dope, right, Jax?" I asked.

Jax signaled the waitress for one more round of beer after our meals. "Nope, not well at all. We think good old Larry may be trying to climb the ladder and become a bigger and better player in the world of crime. We also figure that will not sit well with Marlon Landry."

I guarded my last couple of remaining fries. "So we're guessing that Landry has no idea about innocent tourists being fired upon?"

"Count on that," Jax answered.

"You think Pearson wants to pop us over a few Samuel Whitman/Delbert Jones questions?" Brant asked. "He must be dirty in regard to Delbert's death."

Jax shrugged. "He's not real bright. Smart money is he lined up the disposal site and had some of his thug buddies take out Delbert Jones, probably as a contract for Marcel Fontenot. Things cooled off, then he got nervous when you two started digging around."

He couldn't have known y'all had found Jones. Probably, like we guessed earlier, he thought he could hit us and make it look like a drive-by gang-related shooting, just some good old boys from Oklahoma visiting the Big Easy in the wrong place at the wrong time," I said and took a deep drink of my *Dixie*. "I say we catch the young entrepreneur outside his apartment tomorrow and get his take on all this."

"One on one though," Brant said. "I'll stay out of sight and watch admiringly from afar as you skillfully interrogate the lad using all your detective wiles."

"Yes, faithful companion," I said. "You wait in clearing outside of town."

Jax took a pull on his beer and smiled broadly.

Brant finally gave up on stealing another French fry as I popped the last one in my mouth. "If you think I'm calling you, Kimo sabe, now you're wrong," he said.

I lifted my beer and tilted the neck forward. "Here's to good friends, good food, beautiful women, and a few more days in the Crescent City."

Jax and Brant tipped their beer bottles forward to meet mine with the beautiful music of clinks.

"And to making Larry Pearson cry," Jax said.

I smiled. "We can do that."

"Love these po-boys and loved Ernst Café yesterday, too, by the way," Brant said. "The floor design didn't shake me up; the Navajo and Lakota people used it as well as a number of others long before Hitler did. You folks have a great city with great food down here. We may never leave."

Jax laughed out loud. "Heaven help us. One more round, then you fellows need to get some rest, big day tomorrow."

The beer came round again while I called Dad to let him in on what we'd learned and tomorrow's plans.

"So I imagine I'll find a charge for two tickets for a Steve Earle on the expenses, huh?" Dad said.

"Actually four tickets. I mean we couldn't ask Leslie and Marie to pay. Good thing you're semi-retired, huh?" I replied.

"Right, but I can't vouch for Janie's reaction when she sees all the beer you're charging on the company dime down there, and it's a good thing Leslie is kinfolks. That might not fly well either."

I laughed. "We're covering a lot of the beer out of pocket, maybe she'll take pity."

"Good move, boy, sometimes you'd think that money was coming right out of her own pockets."

"Besides I promised her I'd bring her back for a weekend at least, once we're closer to fall," I said.

"I'll say it again, boy: You really ought to marry that girl," Dad said. "If you don't, someone else might, you know. I mean it. Hell, I might. She's pretty as a picture and sharp as a whip."

"Dad, don't start," I moaned. "Just give us some more time. It's complicated."

"Complicated my ass," he grunted. "Where's Brant?"

I laughed out loud.

"He's visiting the little gentlemen's room with Jax, they can't hold their beer. I just thought I'd catch you up on things, see how you were doing," I said in an attempt at transition.

"I'm fine, Bud. It's really a relief to know what I know now," he replied. "I called the cemetery today and told them I wanted the pile of crap buried in my father's grave unloaded pronto, or I'd take a shovel and tend to it myself. Janie's been in high gear getting paper work all fixed up to dispose of said trash."

"Figured as much, I see the boys coming back. You need to talk with Brant?"

"Naw, just keep me in the loop. If nothing comes out of this Pearson fellow, I think it's time to wrap it up."

"Agreed," I said. "And you tell Janie we'll try not to break the bank. We'll talk again tomorrow."

"Y'all get your asses in bed tonight at a reasonable hour," he ordered in boss-like fashion. "And be ready for anything tomorrow, nothing stupid, watch each other's backs. Love ya both. I'll be waiting to hear something."

"Later, Dad, love ya."

I hung up as Brant and Jax returned.

We contemplated the possibility of one more round, but Jaxon said he had to work, thus ending the party, a concept neither Brant nor I could grasp.

We left Jaxon on Magazine Street waiting on a cab and started walking back to the Quarter to cruise up and down Bourbon Street a few more times just to watch the craziness that cohabits that street, but this time no one was tailing us, just me, Brant, and a few hundred drunks mingling with tourists come to see the show.

I couldn't help thinking about John William Wallace's metamorphosis into Samuel Whitman. I'd read through the journals again before sending them on to Dad, and I could picture him walking these same streets after coming back from the insanity of the first World War and the heartbreak of losing everyone he'd ever loved.

What would things have been like if he'd made it back to Oklahoma? How would my grandmother have reacted to his return? How would Dad have taken it?

I remembered a science fiction story I'd read in high school about a guy who traveled back in time and accidentally stepped on a butterfly and completely changed his own time.

"You ever read *A Sound of Thunder* by Ray Bradbury?" I asked Brant, who was watching a group of church folk handing out pamphlets, trying to save the sinners covering the most-wicked street in the Quarter.

"Yeah," he said. "What the hell brought that on? I knew you were too quiet. I think you need another beer, my brother."

"Probably," I grinned. "I was just thinking Samuel Whitman's return from the past as John William Wallace would have been a hell of a lot bigger than a fellow stepping on a butterfly. What changes would that have brought?"

He looked at me and shook his head. "Oh, yeah, you definitely need another beer."

He was right of course. The philosophical pondering was giving me a headache. But just in the nick of time, Brant pointed out two attractive young women flashing us from the iron-railed balcony above the street.

"Now those appear to be very friendly ladies," I said, feeling much better already.

"Yeah, that's a medical achievement worthy of grants and studies," Brant said. "Reminds me, we need to get back to the hotel and flesh out some plans for the morning."

"That won't take long," I said. "Maybe we should step into one of these little tourist traps and pick up some beads, maybe make a couple of new friends first."

Brant's gaze remained undiverted. "Well, they're certainly not shy."

We stepped into the little shop across the street.

48

THE NEXT MORNING, I was waiting outside the Gravier Place Apartments in the Central Business District when Larry Pearson exited and started down Gravier Street toward Baronne.

I was attired in boots and Levis with a short-sleeved chambray shirt and a New York Yankees cap with a light cream-colored summer blazer to cover the Glock 26 reverse holstered on my left hip. I'd heard Wild Bill Hickok preferred the crossover draw.

"Larry, Larry Pearson," I called to him as he exited his building and was walking a few feet ahead of me.

He glanced back over his right shoulder and kept going toward Baronne Street as if I didn't exist.

"Larry," I said louder this time. "Hey, Larry, it's me. Don't you recognize me? I need to talk with you if you've got just a second."

He stopped in a bit of shade and waited nervously as I caught up to him.

"Do...do I know you, man?" he stammered.

"Sure you do. I'm Mickey Wallace," I smiled my most engaging smile. "You remember me, you had Denarius Brown and Malcom Morgan try to kill me and my buddy a couple of days ago over in front of Mr. Postier's house on Esplanade."

He glanced all around to see who had heard me, then turned quickly and started again just a bit faster this time down Baronne Street toward Canal.

"You must have mistaken me for someone else, or you're crazy. I don't know what you're talking about," he said back over his shoulder as I came right up behind him.

I easily caught up with him and walking right beside him said, "Aren't you Larry Pearson, used to work for Marcel Fontenot? You had Delbert Jones killed for him a few years back? That's you, right?"

He tried to speed up. I could see the panic in his eyes. "Dude, you're fucking crazy," he said without stopping.

I stayed right with him. "Maybe a little, but hey, I'm from Oklahoma."

He walked faster. I thought he actually might break into a trot any second. "I don't know who the hell you are, mister, and I've got to get to work," he whined and kept walking. "Just leave me alone, or I'll call the cops."

"Mr. Landry probably doesn't like it when you're late, and I'll bet he wouldn't be too thrilled with you calling the cops either. Why don't you let me call 'em?" I pulled out my cell phone.

He came to a stop. "Just leave me alone, or I'll make you wish you had," he said, trying hard to sound threatening, but the crack in his voice gave him away.

I tried not to laugh. "Tell you what, here's my number," I said, handing him a card. Suddenly I was running out. "Call me, we'll meet, or I will call Mr. Landry and get an appointment to speak with…"

"No, please," he grimaced. "I'll call you at lunch. I promise." He tucked the card into his jacket pocket as quickly as he could.

I smiled my brightest smile and flicked imaginary dust off his jacket shoulder. "Nice suit."

Without another word, he turned and walked on toward Canal. Kind of rude, I thought as I turned and headed back toward Gravier Street.

Across the street, I saw Brant dressed in camo cargo shorts, a Waylon Jennings tee shirt, and Nike running shoes. He jaywalked across Baronne Street and continued walking behind Pearson toward Canal.

I guess the camo-colored walking shorts helped him blend in unnoticed as he pursued his prey without being seen.

Fifteen to twenty minutes later, Brant crossed over from Jackson Square, dropped a five in the saxophone player's case, and sat down at a table with me at Cafe du Monde, where I had the beignets and coffee waiting.

He pulled out a chair and sat down. "He went right on up Baronne, turned on Common Street, and went into the building where Landry's offices are located," Brant said sipping coffee. "I assumed he was safely at work and came to protect you from his possible wrath."

"Yeah, I was pretty scared there for a bit," I said and smoothed powdered sugar from my mustache. "How are you supposed to eat these things without making a mess?"

"Some good things are just messy, bro," he grinned and started on his second one with sugar going everywhere.

"I reckon so," I said.

"Now we wait," he said, polishing off another beignet.

"Ease up on those," I said. "I may need you to help me catch criminals in a little while."

Brant dusted powdered sugar off Waylon on his tee shirt.

"I can eat a dozen of these and fight crime all day."

I sipped my Coke. "I guess we've got time to kill anyway. Have another batch."

"Naw, I'm good," he grinned again. "Let's walk back up to Faulkner House Books. I still haven't seen that place yet, and I need to pick up some reading material for Janie, bet they have Komunyakaa's books there."

"Brown-noser," I said flatly.

49

DENISON, TEXAS, AUGUST 1916

IT WAS AUGUST. *John William was sure by now the state had shipped "his" body back to Durant, and "he'd" been properly buried, but he was clinging to the hope Rena or his folks had realized he wasn't the one in the box and they were awaiting news from him.*

He was well aware that he'd soon have to make an attempt to sneak across the Red and back into Durant without being seen.

The Denison Herald newspaper reported that two of the escaped prisoners had been captured, but two others remained at large. The search was ongoing, and a nice reward had been offered for the capture of the two remaining escapees, Arcelus Monroe from Hugo, Oklahoma, and Jackson Phillips from the north Texas area.

More bad luck for John William, thanks to Phillips, the pair was being actively hunted in Sherman, Denison and the surrounding areas.

John could almost feel the noose tighten. If he was caught, the whole thing would come apart. Arcelus Monroe, escaped prisoner, would become John William Wallace, and he would never see the light of day, family or friends again.

He recognized Phillips' name but didn't remember the man very well. Ironically he recalled him being a quiet guy who never caused him or Sam any grief. He guessed he couldn't blame him for what was happening now and actually hoped he was running free somewhere far away from here. He knew where Monroe was.

Regardless of the crap luck that brought the bounty hunters into North Texas, John decided Denison wasn't any safer than the next place. He'd head back to Oklahoma and see if he could reach his father or Rena. Maybe his father would know what to do. It wasn't like John had planned the escape. Maybe there was a way out that he hadn't considered yet.

He got his things together, gathered the cash he'd saved while working at the livery stable, and started the short walk down to the Katy Depot on Main Street.

Money was tight. There were strangers everywhere John looked, and he imagined a bounty hunter on every corner as he took a place in line.

He had decided to purchase a ticket at the depot and ride the train into Calera, Oklahoma, exit the train there, and then hike the last few miles into Durant under cover of darkness. But as luck would have it, he never got the chance. Fate raised his bastard head once again.

A tall, skinny fellow he'd never seen before approached him in the Denison rail depot and struck up a friendly conversation. He asked John about Antlers, Oklahoma, said someone told him John had arrived in town back in July from Antlers, said he had kinfolks there and just wondered how long John had been in Antlers before coming to Denison.

The mention of Antlers caused John William some anxiety, so he opted to lie.

"Someone must've been mistaken," he told the fellow. "I came here in July all right, but I came from Mt. Pleasant, Texas, where my folks are from, got a job at the livery stable, just gonna visit my uncle in Oklahoma."

"Now that is odd," the man said. "That fella was positive you'd come from Antlers."

John wished the train would get there. "Nope, not me, never been to Antlers in my life."

"That's real strange, ain't it?" the man smiled. "I found this black mule in Antlers, and the fella there described the man who sold it to him fitting you to a T."

John was trying to remain cool. "All I can say is it wasn't me. Reckon a lot of folks kinda fit my description."

"This fella said he bought the mule in July, and he thought the man who sold it got on a train there for Texas," the man said. "And you know what? That mule used to belong to McAlester penitentiary."

"Really?" John William said as he rose, needing to move around a bit, trying to figure out his next move. "What's that got to do with the price of tea in China?"

"Not much, but I think it has a lot to do with you," the man said, discretely pulling a small .32 pistol from his pocket and pushing it into John's ribs. "I believe you are an escaped prisoner, sir, from McAlester, aren't you? Arcelus Moore, I'd say, by the description."

"My name's Sam Whitman. I'm from Mt. Pleasant, Texas," John said in a low voice, not wanting to draw attention to them. "Now put that gun away, mister, before you get yourself in some real trouble."

"Let's just walk up to the police station and see if I'm not right," the stranger grinned.

"Look, I can't miss my train," John tried to argue.

"I reckon you may have to, Mr. Monroe," the man chuckled. "When I found that mule, I knew I was getting close, and now I gotcha. Walk." He pushed the gun at John.

"Okay," John relented, "But you're gonna be sorry once they tell you I'm not that convict."

As they exited the depot and started up the street, John made a desperate move. He whirled, grabbed the man's gun arm, and hit him as hard as he could square right between the eyes. The man went out like a light.

No one was close by, so John reached down, picked up the .32, and ran like hell back toward town as a few people started to come out of the depot to where the stranger lay unconscious on the street.

A few blocks away, he turned a corner, and there it was. Fate, chance, luck, whatever you want to call it, once again had intervened. A big recruitment drive was going on for the Texas National Guard. The United States was pondering war in Europe, and it seemed Texas was ready to get in the fight.

At the time, it suddenly seemed like a great place to hide, so he, Samuel Whitman, proud native-born son of Texas, signed up, then slipped over to the Palace Hotel and took a room for the next two days under the name of Arthur Doyle.

He claimed he'd ridden in from looking at some land he was buying outside of town. His wife would arrive by train tomorrow with their luggage. For now he just wanted a bath to clean up and relax for a bit before she arrived.

The clerk welcomed him to town and took his cash.

He knew the law and the bounty hunter would be looking all over Denison for him, but he doubted they'd check one of the nicer hotels, so he stayed put in the room without leaving, even for meals. He had his passage arranged. He could board his train with other troops to Brownwood, Texas and Camp Bowie the next day. All he had to do was make it back to the depot and blend in with the crowd of new recruits.

John was still worried about McBride though. After all Monroe hadn't reported in to claim any payment due him, and John doubted a man with that much hate in him would quit easy. But he had a brand-new plan now.

Something had gone wrong with his message to Andrew Musgrove, but Rena had another uncle there in Tuskahoma named Abraham and his own brother, James, back in Murphreesboro.

John figured he'd get a letter to both of them as soon as he landed at Camp Bowie and have someone deliver the news of where he was and what had happened, just in case Rena and his dad were being watched.

He'd try the Musgroves first since he felt they'd be less likely to fall under the scrutiny of Senator Davis McBride, and if that failed, he'd be forced to gamble on James, whom he was certain McBride had probably been watching ever since the prison break.

50

OUR OKIE CUISINE had taken over. Brant and I were sitting in *Daisy Duke's Restaurant* having cheeseburgers and *Dixie* beers when Pearson called.

"What do you want with me?" he asked without a hello or a how-do-you do, just plain rude.

"We need to talk in person, Larry," I said. "Today after you get free from Mr. Landry's employment will work fine. Meet me at the Spanish Fountain near the Riverwalk at 5:30."

"I don't know if I can..." he started.

"You can," I cut in. "Just you and me, and don't be late. I hate it when people aren't punctual."

I hung up.

At a couple of minutes past two, Brant and I were at the fountain to survey the layout one more time.

He glanced over at Poppy's Crazy Lobster and pointed. "I'll be sitting at an outside table over there enjoying a cold beer, just another tourist looking at the Mighty Mississippi while you two are chatting here at the fountain. Just stay up top on the river side where I can see you without drawing any undue attention."

"I'll be fine with Pearson," I said. "You keep an eye out for his boys. I'm sure he'll have backup, just in case I try something nefarious that he doesn't like."

"Nefarious? Really...nefarious? You gotta stop watching the old black-and-white movies, dude."

I laughed. "You started it with 'undue.' Besides what would Robert Mitchum do?"

"Yeah, yeah, I like Chris Wall, too. 'Pistol whip this surly waiter and turn this into *Thunder Road*, right,'" Brant said. "Just stay where I can have eyes on you, okay?"

"Will do, boss," I grinned. "We've got well over two hours; let's walk over to Jax Brewery, have a beer, and I can make my entrance here at the fountain."

"Okay, you trail me by five minutes when we start back over. I'll stop at the *Crazy Lobster* and get myself in position. If there's not a table, I'll take a seat on the low wall there."

"Sounds like a plan," I said.

We started under the Algiers Ferry entrance to the aquarium and the Riverwalk.

"You know, Mick, we pretty much got all we can get with your grandfather's murder. Remind me one more time why we want to screw with this Pearson cat."

I tugged on the bill of my Oklahoma Redhawks cap. "One, we don't like being shot at, right? Two, I'm thinking Mason McBride's still got a hand in this mess, and three, uh…we don't like getting shot at, right?"

"Oh yeah, that," Brant replied.

As we sat outside the food court in Jax Brewery at a terrace table, the Steamboat Natchez blew its whistle long and loud. We discussed the sad state of country music, debated the designated hitter rule, and finished our *Dixies* and hot dogs, getting ready for our walk back along the Mississippi.

I'd swapped out my Tony Lamas earlier for a pair of Pumas, always cooler than Brant's Nikes, and ditched the chambray shirt and jacket for a Yankees tee shirt that hung well over my Glock, but I still had my Levis on and cut quite a dashing figure I thought.

We walked down the stairs together with Brant going over the positions and rules again. He was a stickler for detail, and I could see him touch the Glock under his Waylon shirt tail, just for comfort I suppose.

As we crossed the railroad tracks and walked toward the Natchez, he said, "After we reach the aquarium, you have a seat, give me five or six minutes. If I see anything odd after I sit down with my beer, I'll signal when you come from under the ferry entrance; otherwise you walk on over and sit down above the fountain."

I winked. "Gotcha."

We stopped at the aquarium. I looked out across the muddy river for a few minutes without speaking.

"Mighty big, ain't it?" I said, breaking the few seconds of silence.

"Just don't do anything stupid, Mick," he said. "This should go down nice and easy."

He gave me a fist bump and started toward the ferry.

One thing for sure, I was as safe as I could be safe with that big Indian watching my back. There weren't many people on the planet more dangerous than Brantley Bluesoldier, both my dad and his once, but now Brant was probably the baddest man I knew.

Five minutes later, as I crossed under the ferry terminal, I saw him sitting peacefully sipping a *Dixie*, and I wondered if the Yankees were playing on television tonight. Maybe we'd stop by Harrah's on the way back to the hotel, and I could get twenty down on them.

I passed the *Crazy Lobster*, and there was Pearson down by the water of the fountain. I stopped up above him and motioned him to come up with me. Brant, sitting twenty or thirty yards north, just another lonely guy watching the river roll by.

Pearson walked up to where I was sitting on the fountain's raised surrounding wall and gave me that adolescent "what" shrug. I instantly didn't like him.

"Let's not play," I said. "I have undeniable proof that you're up to your neck in the killing of Delbert Jones, and I know you're trying to get your fingers in as many pies as possible with dope and prostitution."

"That's just ridiculous..." he started.

"Shut up," I said. "Lying to me only pisses me off. I know you tried to have me and my buddy hit over on Esplanade with two other guys outside Postier's house. I'm the one that put the bullet in your buddy, Malcom."

"Dude, I didn't…" he was whining.

I hate whining.

"Shut up, punk. I told you that just pisses me off."

"Okay, just tell me what you want me to do," he whined again. I let it go, but I noticed him looking over my shoulder to where two black gentlemen with sagging jeans were sitting on a bench on the other side of the fountain plaza.

I'd seen them when I first walked up, both wearing do-rags and black tee shirts, not a problem since I'd spotted them, no doubt Brant had seen them as well.

Brant remained calm at his table sipping his *Dixie*. "I want half of everything you've got going on," I said flatly. "Dope, girls, contraband, half of all of it."

He appeared stunned into silence, his mouth open without a sound coming out.

"What's half of that worth?" I asked. "You can lie to me, but I'll find out, and that won't be good. I'm talking a one-time payout. I'll even take the dope in product and 50,000 cash. You've got thirty-six hours to collect it all. Otherwise I go to my buddy on the force, and you go down hard."

I could see him looking over my shoulder again, probably trying to figure his next move with his henchmen. Then he focused and looked at me as hard as he could, which wasn't very. I managed to remain upright.

"And don't think I came alone. I'm not stupid. There's even a badge in on this with me right now, watching every move we make."

"Listen, dude, I've got over thirty pounds of meth, over fifty-one kilo bricks of cocaine and…"

"Don't call me dude, and don't lie to me. I've told you for the last time that pisses me off. That's not a drop in the bucket of what you've got. You think I haven't done a little homework? Do you want me to take it all? I'm trying to cut you a deal here, you little shit."

He looked like he wanted to cry. Maybe I shouldn't have called him a little shit. Even bad-guy dorks have feelings.

"Let me put it all together and give you a total. I know I can get you 20,000 in cash, too…" he whined.

"Fifty-thousand in cash," I cut in again, "A U-Haul with half, and I mean half of your meth, coke, weed, and pills tomorrow night, and I'm out of this cesspool of a city and headed back to God's country. I ought to take some of your girls, too, but, hey, I'm starting to feel sorry for you. Cross me and the law gets the goods on you and your pals. Killing that old man, shame on you, Larry."

He began to shift his weight nervously from one foot to the other. "That's way too fast to get all that together," he whined. "I can't..."

I couldn't remember if I'd officially warned him about whining, but he was really getting on my nerves with it. At least he didn't call me dude this time.

"Listen, Larry, you're a big boy; pull some strings, but remember I got bigger guys in my corner, and the more we keep out of the deal, the more I make and the less you pay, so be smart. We do this tomorrow night."

"I just don't see how..." he started.

I removed all humanity from my voice, narrowed my eyes, and fixed them right on his. "Don't fuck with me, shit-for-brains, tomorrow night, that's it."

He looked totally lost, but he nodded yes.

I returned to my smiling friendly self and gave him a little tap on the shoulder with my knuckles.

"Now I'm gonna walk back over to the aquarium and visit the sharks, and no one is going to follow me. You've got my card, call me by seven this afternoon, or at 7:15, everything I've got, and that's plenty, goes over to the U.S. Marshals working this Fontenot thing they've got going. Capeesh, Larry?"

He nodded yes again.

I smiled again and touched the bill of my Redhawks cap, turned, and walked back toward the West Bank Ferry entrance and the Aquarium.

Brant waited long enough to make sure neither Pearson nor his badly dressed friends were going to attempt following me, finished his beer, and came after me.

51

BROWNWOOD, TEXAS, EARLY AUGUST 1916

JOHN WILLIAM, *now officially known as Samuel Whitman - private, 71st Infantry, Texas National Guard, rolled into Brownwood, Texas, two days after slipping out of Denison and disembarked from the troop train.*

Now all he had to do was decide what his next move might be. He knew Rena, his boys, and his parents had to be grieving terribly believing he was dead. They had probably already buried that piece of shit Arcelus Monroe in his place somewhere. He knew he had to get word to someone he could trust that he was still alive and without McBride somehow finding out. That wouldn't be easy. The good senator had gone to extreme measures to hurt him already and wouldn't take any pity on anyone associated with John William Wallace. He'd make their lives a living hell if he could. If he learned for sure that John was still alive and running free, he'd turn up the heat even more.

Before he could do anything though, he needed to find his men and not be counted AWOL right off the bat. The arrival had been sheer chaos, and more trains were still arriving. All he had found out so far since they'd landed was that he wasn't in the cavalry as he'd been promised. Instead somehow he'd been assigned to the infantry in Company K.

As he walked around a corner in search of a Sergeant Young, he turned right into a bunch of Okies coming in from Fort Sill in Lawton. The young captain, with whom he almost collided, met John William face-to-face and looked like he'd seen a ghost. His jaw dropped, and he grabbed John's wrist.

"Wallace? John Wallace…oh, hell no, that's not possible," the young captain said, still looking him right in the eye with a look of disbelief.

John didn't recognize Toby McBride, all grown up and in uniform with a captain's rank. He was definitely stunned, but he recovered quickly. "Sorry, Captain, you must be mistaken. My name's Samuel Whitman and…"

"Hush," the officer said in a low tone, still holding John's wrist. "I know exactly who you are."

He released John and looked around to see who might be watching them, but the soldiers simply poured around them, moving to their own destinations.

John was stunned. He looked at the young officer and tried to deny his identification a second time. "No, sir, you must be mistaken. My name is…"

"John William Wallace," the captain said in a whisper. "I'm not your enemy. Step in here with me. I have news that you most definitely need to hear."

He suddenly piqued John's interest.

The young officer ushered John into a little café and sat him down at a table. "I met you near Eagletown, Oklahoma thirteen years ago. My brother is responsible for you being sent to prison," he said. "But trust me. I am not your enemy. I'm Toby McBride. I know all about you. I recognize that scar all too well."

John finally saw it. The boy had filled out into a man, but he was indeed Toby McBride without a doubt. He looked at the captain without saying a word. For just a second, he even considered pulling the .32 in his pocket that he'd taken from the bounty hunter, but he refrained. Maybe this was a good time to listen, he thought.

The waitress brought the men coffee.

"I know what my brother did, Wallace," Toby began. "I know he tried to have you killed after he managed to put you in prison. I know he's still worried that you may be alive instead of that Moore character the law is looking for."

John sat quietly, stunned, still trying not to react.

"Just give me a minute before you say or do anything," McBride continued. "I don't know the exact circumstances of my father's death, Wallace, but I imagine you killed him in that shootout back there in McCurtain County when I was a boy. But Father was wrong for trying to have you killed after he killed your friend. He was just afraid, and Davis was wrong for setting you up on the murder charges and hiring Moore to kill you there in McAlester."

John stayed quiet, looking mostly into his coffee cup. He wondered how young McBride would feel if he really did know how he had killed his father, and for the ten thousandth time, he regretted his actions of that day back in 1903.

"Seems like my whole family, especially Davis, just sort of went off the deep end after Father's death. All us brothers plotted against you then, but I've changed. I'm older now, and I just can't see destroying you and your whole family as an act of revenge. Ever since that day when Father shot your friend, I've lived with the regret of being a boy and not being able to make things right somehow."

Finally John William worked up the nerve to speak. "If, by some quirk of fate, I was this Wallace fellow, why should I trust you, Captain?"

"Because I'm your best hope, Wallace, I remember you and I've seen your picture several times now, not to mention that scar above your ear is pretty unique. And I wish to unburden some of my own guilt in all of this. I know who you are and much of what's happened to you, and besides that, you have to trust me, don't you?"

John didn't reply. His mind was racing. He had absolutely no idea what to do.

"Listen, Mr. Wallace. Davis is suspicious," Toby McBride looked John right in the eye. "That Moore character he hired to kill you in the pen never appeared to collect his money after the prison break. He thinks Moore is dead. He's hoping you are, too, but pretty sure you're not. He thinks you're on the run, and he's closely watching your family in Durant. He's a powerful man now, Wallace. I suspect he's even watching their mail. Make no attempt to contact them."

John looked up from his untouched coffee. "You know I don't know this Wallace fellow, Captain, but if I did, I'd bet he wanted the whole thing over and done. I imagine he'd want his family safe, no matter the cost, no matter what he had to do."

Toby McBride finished his coffee off.

"Just go about your business, Wallace," he said. "Fulfill your duty, and I'll help you get word back to your family. I promise. Maybe I can make some small part of this right."

"We'll have to see, sir." John finally sipped his coffee. "But I believe you're a good man, Captain McBride. I think I'm gonna have to trust you."

"My family owes you that much," McBride replied. "My brother has done enough damage to one family in the name of our family. I assume you haven't been able to contact your family to let them know you're still alive, have you?"

John shook his head no.

McBride picked his cap up from the table and stood. "Where are you assigned?"

"I put in for the cavalry, but they assigned me to the infantry, 71st Brigade, Company K."

"You're in the new 36th then, a Panther. I know some of the fellows in your bunch, good men. We'll all be at Camp Bowie for a while. Stay ready. I'll contact you as soon as possible. On my word, we will find a way to get word to your people."

John William stood as several of McBride's men came into the café. "Private Samuel Whitman, Captain, pleased to make your acquaintance,"

John saluted.

McBride returned his salute. "Good to meet you, Private, I'm sure I'll see you later."

John William turned and set out in search of his own company, hoping that fate had finally dealt him a lucky break.

52

CAMP BOWIE, TEXAS BEFORE SAILING FOR FRANCE, AUGUST 1916 TO JULY 1917

AS SOON AS HE WAS in place, John wrote his first letter asking for help. Unfortunately he picked Andrew Musgrove, unaware he had been the one to receive Mr. Hooser's delivery of John's original message.

Andrew's widow, Annie, had moved in with relatives by then, and where the letter wound up is anyone's guess. Suffice to say, John missed on his first swing, but except for no contact so far with his family in Oklahoma, John William thought the first month at Camp Bowie had gone well. Everyone had cots and mattresses and two blankets each, but new recruits just kept piling in with each new train.

He started to pen a second letter to his brother James but remembered Toby McBride's warning about contacting his family.

After a couple of weeks went by with no reply from Andrew, he opted to send James a letter using the name Preston Allen and identifying himself using only pronouns within the body of the letter, hoping James would recognize the hired gun's name and put two and two together to figure it was John William writing him.

Late in August, John sent the second letter to his brother, James, in Broken Bow, not knowing James had moved to Tyler, Texas to take a job with the police force there. Like the Musgroves, James never received John's message. Strike two.

To make matters worse, in early September, the first norther of the year hit early for central Texas, and the Army's winter gear had still not arrived. Most of the men gave up one of their blankets to the new guys still arriving daily since everything was suddenly in short supply. They had heaters for their tents, but there were ten men to a tent, and soon enough wood was scarce as well.

Men were getting sick in droves.

John was heartened though when Captain Toby McBride sent him word that he had scheduled a visit back to Oklahoma the second week of October. He promised he'd personally get word to Rena or William Wallace, informing them where John was and explaining what was going on.

After no replies to his first two letters home, John Wallace finally felt hope. It was short-lived though.

In early October, he developed a nagging cough, and by mid-October, he found himself in a crowded camp hospital with pneumonia and a raging fever. He rallied and relapsed and rallied again, but there were men were dying all around him. All in all, he felt pretty lucky when he finally started to recover.

Over 2,000 men had been confined with measles, meningitis, and pneumonia. More than fifty had died while he was sick and quarantined.

In early November, John William asked to be released and to see Captain McBride. He wanted to find out what his young ally had learned on his trip back home. Release was denied; General Blakely had ordered a full quarantine. Worse yet McBride was hospitalized as well. He'd become ill not long after Wallace and never made his scheduled trip back to Oklahoma. According to a friendly nurse, Captain McBride was unconscious, seriously ill, and not allowed any visitors.

John recovered strength daily but was still held in quarantine. Escape began to weigh heavy on his mind, but he wanted to talk with McBride first. Desertion carried a very stiff penalty.

Finally just before General Grebel returned and lifted Blakely's quarantine, John William was allowed to talk with the young captain, who had regained some of his strength.

Still very sick and weak, McBride was going to be sent home for Christmas. He assured John William that while there, he'd get word to someone, somehow. He asked John once again to hang on.

Not for the first time, John considered going AWOL, but instead he decided to put his trust in Captain McBride and write letters to James and the Musgroves again, one more mistake in a series he'd already made.

He went back to training, recalling Christmases past and wanting his family, his boys, and Rena, but in his "Whitman" world, he had no family, and those who had no one to return home to stayed and got busy learning warfare and the art of destruction.

During this time, he became close with two cowboys Montana Wall from Denison, Texas and Jimmy Ray Wright from Coalgate, Oklahoma. Both had been cowboying on the King Ranch when they decided to become patriots like Sam Whitman and enlisted in the cavalry.

Of course they all wound up at Camp Bowie in the infantry feeling like they'd been lied to, but by mid-January, things were looking up once more. Winter uniforms had arrived with more blankets, shiny new Enfield rifles, and more importantly, a letter from Captain Toby McBride saying he was bedfast and struggling but had convinced a trusted friend to take a letter asking John's father to meet with him. He'd write back in a week to let him know the message had been delivered and hopefully have word for John from his family.

But the cards being dealt to John William seemed to continue putting him deeper and deeper in a dark hole with little chance of winning.

February came with another letter from Toby, saying Davis had intercepted the letter somehow. He warned John William to be alert. Davis was more suspicious than ever, but the young captain had been wise enough to keep specific details out of the letter. Sadly security surrounding John's family would now be even tighter.

He promised though he would personally deliver a message before March as soon as he could, but he was still very weak. So John resigned himself to hope and settled in with Montana and Jimmy Ray learning the finer points of trench warfare and the evil power of machine guns. Sailing for Europe was beginning to look unavoidable.

The ides of March came with no letter, and John was way past worried. He wrote McBride again near the end of the month, pretending to be a soldier in Toby's company concerned with his captain's health.

The reply came in mid-April from McBride's sister saying her brother was still very ill and very weak but had asked her to write back to his troops assuring them all was well, and he hoped to return in late May.

June 1st John William wrote again.

By July no reply had come. Worried that the letter had been lost and with rumors flying that they would ship out in August, he wrote McBride once more, using Jimmy's name, this time and again claiming to be a man in McBride's company.

John William Wallace had been "dead" for almost a year now.

July 10th, an almost identical letter to the one he'd received previously arrived for Jimmy Ray from Toby McBride's sister again, saying her brother was up and attending to matters and would be there in August hopefully to ship out.

Strike three he was out. He just didn't know it at the time, even though he was suspicious of the letter instantly. Why hadn't McBride written him with news if he was "up and attending to matters?" The letter's intent, of course, was meant to keep the young captain's men in good morale. He was not up and attending to matters. But John wanted to believe it, so he did.

Later that same day, the Panthers loaded a train for Memphis, Tennessee without horses or motor transportation almost a month early from the rumored date. John William was trapped if he didn't run when the train stopped, but Montana and Jimmy Ray convinced him not to bolt. Several others had taken flight, had been caught quickly, and punished severely.

They knew he wasn't a coward, but he couldn't tell them the truth. He led them to believe he had a "girl" emergency that he needed to attend to back in Texas, but somehow they convinced him that ten to twenty years in Leavenworth would make a longer wait than the excursion overseas would.

The last half of July was spent on a ship crossing the Atlantic Ocean with thousands of guys, including John William of course, who'd never seen an ocean. He'd never seen that many men throwing up at once either. They were literally hanging over the sides, puking their guts up on a daily basis.

The second day out at sea, he happened upon some of the Oklahoma boys from Fort Sill and asked them if they knew how Captain McBride was doing.

A lieutenant by the name of Feller looked puzzled and asked, "You haven't heard?"

John William's heart stopped. He knew without a doubt what words were coming next.

"He passed late in June... I'm sorry," the officer said. "They didn't tell us until after we'd shipped out. Did you know him well? You look kinda rough."

"Yeah," John said, still stunned. "Pretty well. Thanks for telling me, sir. He was a good guy."

He realized he was addressing an officer, saluted, and walked away as the young officer returned his salute.

His first impulse was to jump off and swim for the east coast. He cursed his own stupidity. Why had he ever sailed without hearing from McBride first?

They docked at Brest, France on July 30th, and John was trapped without knowing for sure if McBride had ever gotten any word to Rena or John's father. He was certain McBride had tried, but he was terrified the young officer had failed again.

There was nothing left but war and, oh, God, he was pissed. He wanted to scream, but instead he swore then and there to himself he was going to get back home if he had to kill every German on the planet. And then when he got back to Oklahoma, he swore he was going to kill Davis McBride for good measure.

53

"**SO, GOOD BUDDY,** what kind of relationship do you have with Marlon Landry?" I asked Jaxon over the phone.

"Not much of one," he chuckled. "He's often a person of interest in my work, ya know, but Dad actually gets along pretty well with him. Landry was a pup, an up and comer in the world of criminality when Dad was a stud with the Marshals and cut him some sort of a break. So as long as certain business particulars are left out of the mix, they still mingle socially."

"Reckon he'd set up a meeting for us on short notice? We're pretty sure we have some information Mr. Landry might be interested in."

"Call him, you've got his number, don't you?" Jax laughed. "The less I know about it, the better."

I laughed along with him. "Well, for right now anyway."

Tommy Moon walked into Brennan's with Brant and me in tow to where Marlon Landry was waiting at his favorite table.

"You wouldn't want to eat here if Marlon wasn't picking up the check," Tommy said quietly.

Landry stood and extended his hand. "Mr. Moon, you're looking good; it's always a pleasure to see you. And these are the young Oklahomans you've been telling me about?"

Tommy shook Landry's hand and smiled pleasantly. "Yep, John William Wallace and Brantley Bluesoldier, meet Marlon Landry."

We shook his hand respectfully and nodded politely.

"I believe these boys have some questions regarding real estate, Marlon," Tommy smiled. "I assured them you were the best and told them to trust you implicitly."

Landry returned the smile. "Well, let's enjoy our meal first, then we'll see what we can do. You do have time to eat with us, don't you, sir? I know you said you had other business, but surely you wouldn't pass up a meal at Brennan's on me."

Tommy smiled pleasantly and directed Brant and me to sit at the table across from Landry.

"You know me better than that, Marlon," Mr. Moon chuckled. "I can always use a good meal."

Several hundred dollars and much discussion of the hope for an improved Saints team later, Mr. Moon rose. "I really do have to run, Marlon, but I'll see you at the Saints home opener, if not sooner."

"Sooner I hope," Landry said, rising to shake Tommy's hand again.

"Treat these boys right; they have my full blessing. I'd trust them with my life," Tommy said. "And you can trust them as well. They're very smart boys."

Brant and I stood with Landry to shake Tommy's hand and then re-seated ourselves.

Landry smiled, and I suddenly wanted to vote for him. "Well, gentlemen, if Tommy Moon gives you his blessing…how can I not offer my help. What exactly is it that you need?"

"Actually, sir, it's a little bit delicate, and it concerns an employee of yours," I started. "Larry Pearson."

I noticed Mr. Landry's forehead tighten just a little above his dark brown eyes.

"I don't know Mr. Pearson very well," he said. "I hired him as a favor to an old friend. That often proves to be unwise, but I owed the gentleman a debt. What about the young man? You can speak freely here."

I glanced at Brant, who was quiet but intent on our conversation and started, "As I'm sure Mr. Moon told you, we've come down here from Oklahoma to investigate my grandfather's disappearance over six decades ago. In the process, we stumbled across some things involving Mr. Pearson that we were told you'd disapprove of and that you might even feel to be embarrassing for you."

"Really?" Landry said very calmly.

"Mr. Moon said you…uh, that you took a very anti-drugs stance, sir," Brant started.

Landry frowned and interlaced his fingers on the table in front of him. "Downfall of mankind, my employees know my feelings on the matter. I have them sign permission for random testing and a pledge to abstain from all illicit drugs."

"Yes, sir," Brant continued. "That's as we were told, so we were somewhat surprised by Larry's behavior."

"You see, sir, prior to his employment with you, Mr. Pearson played a part in the murder of Delbert Jones," I added. "For some reason, he feared our investigation might lead to implicating him. He hired a couple of his street thug friends to shoot us, and we took unkindly to that understandably I believe."

"Understandably," Landry frowned. "I assume you are certain of Mr. Pearson's involvement in all this."

"Of course there was a possibility that Mick and I were targeted for other reasons," Brant said, looking from me to Mr. Landry. "So we began to investigate Mr. Pearson. To get him to incriminate himself, we made a couple of threats and negotiated a phony deal for 50,000 dollars cash and a U-Haul truck full of illegal drugs. We suspect he's violated your drug policy, sir, majorly violated it."

Landry simply nodded.

I took up the story, "We plan on busting him and his boys tonight when they show up to pay off or kill us, whichever it is. We're guessing that he'll have at least a token payment and try to settle with us, but that should be enough to put him away."

Landry looked across the table at both of us. "And you're telling me this because…"

"We didn't want to cause you any personal offense," I said. "But we do want to take him down, and we don't have any reason to cause you any problems. We just felt you should know Pearson has been working behind your back in areas you strongly oppose and might be an embarrassment for your company."

Landry remained calm. "I see."

"Plus there's a possibility a current Oklahoma senator may have paid him to have us shot," Brant continued. "We'd really like to know if that's true, and Mr. Moon seemed to think that if a certain senator was involved, it might have come across your radar."

"Mr. Moon said you were very knowledgeable to the real estate dealings of out-of-state bigwigs in your neck of the woods," I added quickly, trying not to offend.

"I've dealt with politicians from Texas and Oklahoma," Landry smiled. "And it sounds like I would have needed to deal with Pearson myself soon anyway. I've had an eye on him ever since I did Marcel the favor of hiring him. He's a natural born fuck-up, if you'll pardon my profanity. Tommy said you boys were solid. You're just saving me the chore of ridding myself of the boy. I appreciate your concern for my business reputation."

"Thank you, Mr. Landry, sir, we really just hate it when guys shoot at us for no reason. We're pretty big believers in simple retribution," I said.

"Understandable, gentlemen, I don't imagine I'd appreciate it much myself," Landry smiled. "And as for your friend, the senator… McBride I suppose. I met him at a fundraiser a few years back. If I were an Oklahoman, I doubt that I'd vote for him, but I also doubt he had a clue about Mr. Pearson's activities. However, his campaign manager, his son Benjamin I believe, may have had some dealings with Marcel Fontenot before Mr. Fontenot passed. That's about all I know concerning the good senator."

Brant glanced at me again and back to Landry again. "I reckon that's more than good enough for us, sir."

Landry motioned to the waitress for the bill. "Is there anything else I can do for you young men?"

I handed him the last of our cards I had in my pocket. "No, sir, but if you ever need detectives for any righteous reason, we owe you. Don't hesitate to call us. We work pretty reasonably, and I have to say, we're pretty good at what we do."

He tucked it in his jacket pocket. "I have no doubt about that, Mr. Wallace… Mr. Bluesoldier, very nice to meet you both. If you gentlemen will excuse me now, I have some business that needs tending to."

I nodded.

Brant smiled and returned an easy "Yes, sir" before we walked out to the street as the waitress approached.

Outside on Royal Street, Brant said, "Benjamin McBride was doing business with Marcel Fontenot; that's kind of interesting. Don't you think?"

"Yep, but what the hell does that tell us? We knew the McBrides were in this for generations. Let's walk back up to Bourbon and watch the show some more while we wait on good old Larry."

"Might as well, maybe the girls will be out and about again," Brant said.

I grinned. "It's a little early, but we've got some time to kill, at least enough time for a Huge-Ass beer."

"Yep," he said. "You reckon Pearson will call?"

"What do you think?" I said.

"He'll call," Brant grinned. "Then he'll try to set a trap and kill us."

"Don't know, I was pretty scary," I smiled. "Maybe he'll just show up with the U-Haul full of goodies."

"Either way we need Jax in on this with a few badges to clean up the mess," Brant said, looking at a kid playing saxophone with the case open for tips.

I pointed at the Huge-Ass beer sign being waved among the tourist traffic by a small black man. "Yep, but at the very least, we get to shake Pearson and his minions down before the marshals barge in and steal all the credit."

"Dani will be in on the bust. She can have all my credit," he smiled and tossed a five in the case as we headed toward the beer vendor.

"You're hopeless, bud. Couldn't you see how she looked at me there in Pat O'Brien's?" I said as we navigated the street covered with panhandlers, drunks, and tourists from Iowa.

"All I saw was her obvious affection for the brave and noble Native American."

We made it to the beer vendor's window. "You guys serve Indians here?" I asked and grinned at Brant.

The young man, wearing an Aaron Neville tee shirt and a coral choker necklace, flashed a big smile. "We serve people of all faiths, races, creeds, and denominations as long as they have good old American cash or credit cards."

Brant looked hard at me. "Racist asshole."

"Two Miller Lites please," I said as I handed the bartender in the window a twenty.

The young man drew us each a "Huge-Ass" Miller Lite in plastic cups, and I handed Brant his beer.

I grinned. "Let's drink these and go change into our super heroes' costumes."

Brant smiled.

"Sure thing, Kimo sabe, just be glad you bought the beer. I'm more forgiving after a few firewaters."

"Let's hope Jaxon is forgiving when we tell him what all we got planned for tomorrow night," I laughed.

"Well, we sorta dropped him a hint here and there that with any luck, it was all going down very soon anyway," Brant said. "He's just gotta get on board with the Okie way."

"That's right," I affected a most serious tone. "I mean it's not like we're not doing him a huge favor. Obviously Pearson is a threat to his fair city."

Brant took a big drink of his beer. "Yeah, I think he should be okay with playing Commissioner Gordon to my Batman and your Robin."

"Your Batman?" I said. "I think not, Boy Wonder."

Brant took another drink. "Know your role, boss," he laughed. "You could never pull off the cowl."

I polished off my beer. "Well, in all fairness to Jaxon, I don't think he's actually lit up the bat signal over the Mississippi just yet."

"We can call him once we get back in the hotel," Brant smiled. "Our plan may not sound as solid with a Bourbon Street sound track in the background."

"Still a few blocks back to the hotel, we need one more beer for the road, then I'll call him. You call Dad."

"Some Batman you'd be," Brant laughed.

54

FRANCE, WORLD WAR I, OCTOBER 1917

JOHN WILLIAM WALLACE *spent August and September watching the equipment come in bit by bit, still without draft horses to carry it. He drilled, he practiced, he grew impatient.*

Finally in early October, they received orders to move out for the village of Somme-Py, crossing the defunct Hindenburg Line. Partially-obliterated trenches, gun emplacements, and barbed wire entanglements were silent. Smashed and shattered equipment, abandoned guns, jagged tree stumps, and fresh graves gave the landscape a sense of desolation and destruction. A ruined village named Souain lay in the middle of it all. A little beyond this place, they saw the first bodies of men and horses lying where they had fallen. This was most definitely not a drill; this was very real.

To the north, the Panthers could hear the shelling begin and saw clouds of rising smoke, airplanes skimming the horizon, and observation balloons floating in the sky in what seemed like some sort of surrealist painting.

They trudged onward as the shelling grew heavier, but the maps were badly marked and soon they were lost within the woods. The Germans had the higher ground and snipers and machine gun fire was ripping them apart as they wandered around lost in the shattered pines.

At daylight they found another guide and finally their assigned position on the lines where they moved into the trenches as the artillery shells began to hoot again and fall all around.

A slow rain began to pelt the men as they took their ground. Jimmy Ray, Montana, and John were next to two boys named Jeff and Joe from Gainesville, Texas and a big old boy called Bull from Whitesboro, Texas.

The German artillery fire, emanating from the hills northeast of a town called St. Etienne, had caved in a section of trench separating the two groups.

Through the drizzling rain, German planes were out in force dropping bombs, strafing, and spotting for the artillery, an oddly fascinating sight for these poor country boys.

Toward late afternoon, Jimmy had nodded off while Montana and John were talking about the wonders of machined flight when a French plane suddenly engaged two German aircraft directly over them.

Seconds later a machine gunner opened up on the Gainesville boys and Bull, who had all turned in their section of the trench to watch the air battle. While the Americans had been distracted, the enemy had worked around a bit and got an angle on them.

Montana rose up just above the earth works and took careful aim. His Enfield popped once, and the machine gun fell silent for a second as another man moved behind it. The rifle popped again, and only silence remained. John William looked over at the boys, one was still moving. Bull and one of the Texas boys were stone still. Montana called the boy's name and edged toward him while John took aim in the general direction of the enemy machine gun nest.

Nothing moved.

"I'm going in with them, cover me," Montana said.

Jimmy Ray and John William took aim at the smoking machine gun, but no one moved there either.

In one quick athletic move, Montana rolled over the top of the dirt, dividing their trench and into their section.

"Jeff is still alive," he called back, "but he's bleeding bad. I'm gonna carry him to the back trenches with the medic. Just keep me covered."

"No," Jimmy yelled. "Bandage him up best you can and stay low. Wait for dark."

"Can't, he's hurt too bad. Just cover me," Montana said. "He don't amount to much more than sack of feed. I can run with him on my back."

He rolled the boy out of the trench and came out behind him as John and Jimmy Ray scanned the quiet lines lying in front of them.

Quick as a cat, Montana had the wounded boy over his shoulder and was running for the trenches behind them when a rifle shot echoed, and he went down in a heap. John and Jimmy were straining to see where the shot had come from and yelling back to Montana when another pop sounded and dirt kicked up near where their friend and the Gainesville boy lay unmoving. Another shot echoed, and a spray of dirt right beside them kicked up again.

Jimmy was still trying to get Montana to answer his calls when John saw the sniper shift positions to get another shot. The enemy sniper was so intent on putting another shot into his target that he failed to notice the young American rifleman lining him up in his sights.

John William drew a bead and fired before the German did. His target fell sideways without a sound.

Unable to get a reply from Montana, Jimmy slipped over the back of their foxhole and ran for their friend. Another sniper shot rang out, but Wright made it to where the two men lay, grabbed each by the collar and dragged while John fired as many rounds as he could in the direction of a German sniper he couldn't see.

A few minutes later, Jimmy Ray plopped back into the trench with Wallace.

"Montana's dead," he said. "The other boy's hurt bad, but he might make it. No Jerry better try to surrender to me tomorrow when we charge. I'm killing every last sonuvabitch I see wearing that little spiked helmet of theirs."

Tears were rolling down his face. John was quiet. He knew exactly how Jimmy Ray felt, and he knew there was no fixing it and no words that would ease the pain.

Neither of them slept that night as the lines filled up with more Panthers on both sides.

Around full dark, two Osage Indians, Billy Twohatchet and Alex Horse, pulled off their shirts, smeared their faces and chests with mud, and rolled over the top; each had a really large knife and wore a pistol, but neither carried a rifle.

Less than an hour later, they both dropped back in right beside John William and Jimmy, carrying three scalps a piece.

"A few less machine guns we'll face in the morning. These are for Montana and them other boys," Billy said, tossing the scalps to one side.

"We left a little calling card for the bastards over there, too. Maybe it'll help them run quicker after they see what their buddies look like when the sun rises," Alex laughed and put his shirt back on.

A couple of hours later, the whistles began to blow. The Americans rose up out of their lines and charged with rebel yells, war whoops, or fierce screams. It was an impressive sound, one no one who heard it would ever forget. In a matter of minutes, the German machine guns opened up.

Jimmy and John William were trying to keep up with Billy and Alex. The other Panthers were all around them trying to shout down the guns. As they neared the enemy trenches, several of the German machine gun nests sat silent and offered no fire. Panicked the German lines broke in spots.

John and Jimmy dropped into the trenches right behind the two Osage as they bayonetted Germans trying to stand their ground. One rose back up aiming at Billy's back, but Jimmy Ray put his bayonet through the center of the German's back, stepped on his shoulder, and twisted his rifle before pulling it out and kicking the body to one side.

More Germans came running from one end of the trench, and John William fired his last bullet. The front man pitched forward, dropping his rifle.

There was blood and gore with men screaming everywhere, mixed with the incessant chatter of machine guns setting back up in their fallback positions and opening up toward the American troops still charging other parts of the German trenches. Billy and Alex had their big knives out, hacking and cutting. Dozens of other Panthers were using bayonets fixed on Enfields or grappling hand to hand.

In a matter of minutes though, the position was secured and gunfire was dying down. John William could see American machine gunners setting up. A French plane was on fire above them and going down. His ears were still ringing. *So this is Hell,* he thought to himself.

Jimmy Ray settled in beside him and lit a cigarette from a case he carried. "Want one?" he offered John.

"No, thanks," John William said. "And you better not let Sergeant Drummond see you smoking that thing either. He'll have a shit-fit."

"Screw him," Jimmy said.

This would be their place for the next few days. The Germans had dug in in defensive positions, and the Panthers continued to throw themselves at the enemy lines in furious charge after furious charge to no avail.

By October 10th, the fighting was finally drawing to a standstill. The Germans retreated back across the river, and the Americans took their positions, pretty much convinced their foes would run all the way back to Berlin at the mere sight of Billy Twohatchet and Alex Horse.

It appeared the worst of the ground combat had subsided with the river separating the two forces and the Germans clearly struggling to resist the American advance. The men were finally starting to relax a bit.

Around noon a British plane locked in a dogfight with two Germans, and the Panthers started rooting like they were at a baseball game. The British plane took down both Germans, and the Americans let out a whoop. A "barbaric yawp," as old Walt would have said, John William thought.

But in the midst of the celebration, a lone sniper had gained a position and fired a single round.

Jimmy Ray Wright, standing right beside John Wallace, laughing and lighting up a cigarette fell stone dead with a bullet through his heart. He just looked over at John with a shocked look on his face and sank to the ground.

The sniper was cut to pieces by a volley of American gunfire in an instant, but John William, once again, was back all on his own and far, far away from home.

55

COMING HOME, FRANCE TO OKLAHOMA, 1917-1918

THEY HELD THE POSITION *until mid-November and then were relieved. They set the Americans up in Tonnerre on the Armancon River, and the 36th Division now officially became the Arrow Heads, with a new insignia and clean uniforms, finally receiving long-overdue supplies.*

Again they drilled, they built road, they played football, they played baseball, and they grew more restless. It was all one big athletic carnival, and John played to avoid sheer boredom, counting down the days to their impending departure.

Thanksgiving and Christmas passed. He wrote James again, knowing full well it was a futile exercise, but he was miserable, wanting to see his boys, his wife, his folks. The fighting was over, and he wanted to go home.

It was March before they even started to hear rumors they would soon be shipping out for home.

John had been "dead" for almost two years now, and he feared Toby McBride had failed to get word to anyone that John Wallace was really still among the living. He couldn't even start to imagine how Rena and the kids were dealing with everything. He knew his dad would take care of them, but despite this, John was more than just a little worried.

In May they were deloused and put on ships again at Brest, France, where they'd first arrived. They returned to America as heroes. There were parades everywhere as they landed back on native soil and slowly dispersed back toward Texas.

War Department policy dictated the men be discharged in the demobilization camps nearest their homes. John's final point of demobilization was back at Camp Bowie, and once there, he was mustered out of the Arrow Heads in forty-eight hours, a free man for the time being.

He started growing a beard and decided to risk heading back for Oklahoma, regardless of the danger. Two days later, he boarded the "Texas Special" for Antlers, Oklahoma again. There he used some of his military pay and bought a nice buckskin stud that reminded him of his old pony, Calavaras, a good saddle, and a brand-new Winchester.44-40.

He planned to simply ride into Durant and remain out of sight until he learned what all had taken place while he had been overseas, maybe even make contact with Rena or his dad if he thought it was safe enough. Whatever he did, he realized he had to do something.

When he rode into town, the first place he headed was his father's blacksmith shop on the Market Square. He could see, from across the street, it was busy with William Wallace working hard, and the place full of folks that John William did not know, so he decided to head on over to his father's home on South Fourth Street, only to find it occupied by a lady he'd never seen before.

He felt the panic grab his gut, but still he walked over to the fence where the older woman was kneeling on the other side, looking at some flowers she'd just planted. She was a stout woman, very plain, with her grey hair pulled back in a bun in typical Okie fashion. She was carefully weeding her flower bed.

John dismounted the buckskin and walked over to the fence where the woman had noticed him and was rising to meet him at the fence.

"My name is Samuel Whitman. I was looking for the folks who lived here a few years back," John said. "They were old friends of mine back before I went overseas in the war."

The lady wiped her hands on her apron and seemed pleased to meet him. "How do, young fella," she said warmly. "We bought this place from William Wallace right after Christmas last year."

Her voice was strong and her smile was genuine as she moved up to the fence. "Mr. Wallace still has his blacksmith shop on the square. He and his wife, Irene, live out east of town now I think."

John William realized his face must have betrayed his shock. He told her that he'd been gone for almost three years, first to Texas, then off to the war in

Europe, but he never expected William Wallace would sell this place and asked if something had happened.

Seizing an opportunity to gossip, she started. "Yep, plenty bad happened to those good folks. Mr. Wallace's son got killed in prison, where he was serving life for a murder. But he always denied his boy had any part of it. Did you know him?"

John nodded. "Grew up with him."

"Oh, I'm sorry," she said earnestly, "The boy's wife, Mr. Wallace's daughter-in-law, and grandsons moved back in with the Wallacees for almost two years until she met a very wealthy, very successful fellow, name of Amos Buchanan from Oklahoma City who was down here on bank business. He got transferred back east, New York City, I'm pretty sure."

John listened quietly, trying to remain calm but feeling his heart break with every detail of gossip the lady uttered to him.

"The Yankee fellow married the daughter-in-law just last month or so and paid off all his father-in-law's debts. Mr. Wallace had mortgaged everything trying to prove his son's innocence, so he sold this house and bought a nice new place just east of town near Blue."

Still stunned John just nodded.

"I heard the new husband was planning on putting the boys through some big fancy college as soon as they were old enough."

The woman sure liked to talk, and in true country fashion, knew everything that was going on in her small town. John just kept listening to the whole story with his world coming apart at every word.

"Mr. Wallace still does a good business at his forge. You should stop in and see him, Mr. Whitman. He'd probably like to see you since you was friends with his son. They say he's doing real good now, finally getting over the loss of his boy."

"Well, ma'am," John said, "I don't know Mr. Wallace as well as I did John, but I'll try to stop by his shop before I leave. I'm heading back to Texas tomorrow I think."

"My husband is the preacher on South Sixth Street," she smiled. "You'll have to come in and visit the Lord with us this Sunday, Mr. Whitman. I assume you are a Christian."

"Yes, ma'am," he replied. "I reckon I'll be there if I'm still in town. Thank you kindly for your time and all your help."

"Are you sure you're okay, son?" she asked, probably sensing his shock and grief.

"Be fine, ma'am, just a little sad about John being gone." He felt the irony in his voice as he swung back up into the saddle with a Ford Model T heading down the road toward them.

"Things sure do change fast these days," he said as it passed. He waved goodbye and rode away toward the east end of Main Street, where he went back to his hotel, sat down, and cried like a baby before he walked up the street to a bar and got a bottle. John William was never much a drinker, but now seemed like as good a time as any to start.

There were no answers, nothing could be done. Telling his father seemed like it would only add to the burden and bring back the grief he had just gotten past, and Rena and the boys… that was all too easy to see what was best there. They were in New York City, a million miles away. They'd have things he could never give them, a fine home, expensive educations, futures.

The next morning when he woke up, he declared John William Wallace dead, mounted his horse, and rode out of Durant, never to return.

56

EARLY, AND I DO MEAN EARLY, the morning after our meeting with Marlon Landry, Brant and I headed for Jaxon Moon's office. He had not been overly thrilled when I called him the night before.

"Who the hell sets up a strategy meeting at 7:30 in the morning?" Brant moaned.

Brant rubbed his forehead just above the eyebrows. "At least I put off calling Will until later today."

"Coward, that's why I'm Batman," I said as we entered the presence of Maggie Comeau.

"You men are looking a little rough this fine morning," she said way too cheerfully for the hour.

"Long day of detective work," Brant said. "But I'd sure like to see Steven Soderbergh's new movie tomorrow night after a meal at Galatoire's, if I could only find a lovely federal employee to go with me."

She smiled. "Well, if you're still alive after Jax is through with you and Mickey, I may not be as lovely as Jaxon Moon, but I love Galatoire's and Soderbergh, too."

I thought Brant was going to break out in dance. "It's a date," he smiled.

"Right now he's got Clay Sanders and Dani Hebert in his office waiting on y'all and Chief Boyer from NOPD, so good luck on the survival thing," she smiled back.

"You have a reason to live," I said to Brant as Maggie picked up the phone.

"Chief Boyer's here now, too," she said as a forty-something-looking gentleman with greying temples and a really nice suit walked into the office.

Maggie rose from behind her desk, a picture of efficiency and grace rolled into perfect legs. "Morning, Chief, this is Mickey Wallace and Brantley Bluesoldier. I'll let Jax do the full introductions. Y'all follow me please."

"I've already heard a lot about you fellows," Boyer smiled as we followed Maggie down the short hall and entered Jax's office again.

"Later, gentlemen." She winked at Brant, the last one in.

Dani, Clay, and Jax were all standing around a large layout of a street map when we walked in.

"Well, troops, it looks like it's about to get real cowboy around here," Jax said more in the spirit of things today than he had been last night when I broke it to him what we'd already set in motion without his knowledge or permission.

"Cowgirls can kick butt, too, ya know," Dani smiled.

Jaxon smiled back. "Yep."

"Let's rodeo then," Jax laughed. "Mickey, you and Brant will have Pearson and his boys meet you in this vacant lot at the corner of Franklin Street and North Peters. It's surrounded by warehouses. I'll have riflemen with me in the upper windows here on the west side of Franklin."

He pointed at the map. He'd obviously been up early setting the wheels in motion. "We should be able to see pretty much everything from up there."

"I imagine Larry will lay a trap somewhere there, don't you think, Jax?" I said. "I mean as soon as we give him the location this afternoon."

"Yep, we'll be in place by noon waiting," he replied. "And Dani will be in position with five men of her choice on the ground level below us." He pointed again at the map and some satellite photos. "They'll be ready to swarm the lot if anything goes haywire."

Dani winked. "Don't you boys worry. I'll have all the backup you need, and if things get too western, you cowboys will see what it's like when a Cajun goes off on ya."

Brant and I both smiled.

"That's real good, ma'am," I grinned. "I do wanna survive this 'cause I do believe I've been promised a night on the town, dancing the heels off my boots before we leave."

Brant was eyeing the map. "What about the railyard there on the river?"

Boyer leaned in to have a better look at the satellite photos. "We'll shut off the surrounding streets once we see the U-Haul and Pearson's vehicle enter the lot, but those trains across North Peters could be a problem."

"I'll be over there with five men," Clay Sanders spoke up. "Three of us hidden in the box cars on the south side of Franklin, and three more hidden on the north side, a rifleman with each group. No one's going to get away in that direction."

"My officers will hang well back, but we'll have cars that come in quick if needed," Chief Boyer said to Jaxon. "I know this is a federal deal, but we'll seal the block and have your backs."

"Some of it may be local," Jax said. "I'd like you to put a SWAT team on the ground across the other side of Franklin, that way we'll have 'em boxed in and you can get any new-found gangsters that might show up."

I looked at Brant. "What do ya think, brother?"

He smiled like he'd stolen something. "I say we got one helluva band, and it's time to rock and roll."

Jaxon clapped his hands one time. "Good enough. Clay, Dani, Chief, let's get started. Mick, Brant, hang on, I want to talk it over a little more with my loose cannons before you two escape back into The Big Easy."

The office emptied quickly with Clay and Boyer heading out and Dani pausing just long enough.

"I will dance your boot heels off, cowboy, so try not to get shot," she smiled.

I smiled back as she closed the door behind her.

"And there's your reason to live," Brant grinned broadly at me.

Jax took a seat on the edge of his desk. "I know you guys have been in the belly of the beast plenty of times, but I can't afford for either one of y'all to get your silly selves shot on my watch."

"Why, Jax, that's awful nice of ya, bud," I said. "We didn't know you cared that much."

"I don't, but my dad, your dad, and apparently most of my marshals would have my ass," he laughed. "So nothing over the top, no Superman routines, okay?"

"No way," Brant said. "We're strictly Batman kinda guys. Of course he's more the Boy Wonder, but you get my drift."

"Sweet Christ," Jax shook his head. "I'm still not over being left out of the early planning phase of this yet. Just get Pearson on the phone by three o'clock this afternoon, if he hasn't got back with you by then, and confirm the meeting place. Don't let him try to set up a different spot. We'll be in place and on the lookout for his early arrivals."

"Why, Jax, you don't think he'll try something unfair, like hiding gunmen to shoot us poor hard-working Okies just trying to make a living, do ya?" Brant said.

"No sweat, boss, he loves me," I grinned. "I could have him meet us naked in Hell if I wanted to."

Jax shook his head sadly once again. "Just get him there with the goods and stay out of the line of fire should he prove untrustworthy."

57

WE CAUGHT A CAB back to the hotel, switched into our classic tourist attire, loose-fitting Hawaiian-themed shirts from Margaritaville that draped classically over our Glocks, and walked the Quarter down to Huck Finn's, a sport's bar and restaurant on Decatur.

Missing our Okie roots again, we opted for cheeseburgers and cold beer and were watching a Mets - Cardinals game on the big screen. Sadly the Yankees were in Kansas City for a night game, but at least we had something resembling baseball.

My phone rang as David Wright led off the fourth inning with a homer. It was Larry Pearson in all his whining glory.

"I've got the money and as much…uh…product as I can get but…" he stammered.

I cut in, "Don't bullshit me, Larry. You're not about to say you can't get all the money, are you?"

"No, no, I got it," he whined, by nature I suspected. "Just meet us tonight at…"

"Shut up, Larry, I say when and where we meet. You just show up with the cash and the stuff loaded up nicely in a U-Haul."

"But…" he started again.

"No buts, Larry, in case you haven't figured it out yet, I'm running this show. Do as you're told. Don't try to screw me, or you'll regret it terribly, mi amigo."

Brant made a goofy face at me like he was scared and took a bite of our fried alligator appetizers.

"How do I know I can trust you?" Pearson whined.

"You can't trust me, dumbass," I laughed. "I'm strong-arming you for your money and your goodies. Bring backup if you need, but do we really want to have a shoot-em-up? Let's just do this, and me and my men will roll outta your life."

Brant continued his face-making routine while wolfing down the gator.

"Okay, just tell me where and when. But you better not fuck with me, Wallace," he said in his pseudo-tough-guy voice. "We will be ready for any shit you try to pull."

"I reckon you will, Larry," I grinned at Brant. "We're not pulling any shit though. We just want to get our cut and get outta here. Nine o'clock tonight at a vacant lot on the corner next to the warehouses on Franklin and North Peters. Be there and do not be late. I really hate tardiness, so unprofessional."

I hung up.

He immediately dialed me back. "Nine is too early. We'll be seen. We need…"

I swallowed my first bite of gator finally. "Shut up, Larry, it's non-negotiable. Everyone will be gone from that neighborhood, and it'll be early enough not to draw any unnecessary policemen to question your presence. Nine o'clock, Franklin and North Peters. Don't make me come looking for you."

I hung up again and grabbed another piece of gator before Brant could eat it all.

We finished our burgers and beer.

Brant rubbed his stomach. "Let's walk some of this off; I'm stuffed," he grinned.

"You should be," I said. "I barely got any of the alligator. You were eating like it was your last meal."

"Eat more. Talk less," he laughed. "You were too busy doing your best Bogie routine and scaring poor little Larry Pearson to death."

"Now we need to call Jax, tell him the time and place are confirmed, get his RSVP, and then call Dad." I said. "I'll call Jax. You call Dad."

"What do you mean 'we,' white man?" Brant grinned. "I'll call Jax. You call Will, or be prepared to be eternally regarded as my pasty-faced sidekick."

"Let's be fair," I said as we ordered a pre-departure beer. "Let's flip for it."

"I flip the coin," Brant reached into his pocket. Heads, you call Will; tails, I call Will."

I know he cheated, I'm just not sure how. I was watching as closely as I could. He leaned over and dialed Jaxon's number, refusing to recognize my official protest.

Janie answered the phone. "Mickey Wallace, it's about damned time."

"Hello, darlin'," I went for the sweet trick.

"Don't hello-darlin' me," she growled. "When are y'all coming back?"

"Soon, boss, very, very soon," I soothed as best I could. "I shoulda called sooner. I know, but we may well bring this to a close tonight and start back this weekend. Other than hearing your sweet voice, that's why I'm calling right now."

She softened just a little bit. "I'll make you think 'my sweet voice' if y'all don't get back here soon, Mickey. I'll get Will for you, but you and Brant are both still on my short list, sweet cakes, pick up the pace."

She must've simply handed Dad the phone. "Reckon that put you boys in your places," he laughed. "You better give me what you've got."

"Damn, she's a touch hot," I said.

"Don't say I didn't warn you about all the spending you two yahoos were doing," he laughed again. "Now what have you boys learned lately?"

"To start with, we've got Pearson on the hook," I answered. "Brant's on the line with Jax right now setting up a sting, and Marlon Landry doesn't think Mason McBride is involved with any of the modern shenanigans related to this; however, he did hint that he thought McBride's son, Benjamin, might have had some kind of ties to Marcel Fontenot before he passed."

"There's one of those damned coincidences we both don't like," Dad said.

"Yep," I answered, "but right now we know a little about a lot, and once we bust Pearson, I think he'll have a sweeter song to sing."

"And I suppose you and Brant are going to be right in the middle of all the crap?"

"There'll be more Marshals than you can shake a stick at, Dad, a whole herd of badges," I said. "We'll be fine, and I think we can squeeze any McBride connection out of Pearson. He's such a little weasel."

"I don't care if you think he's weak and worthless or not, Mickey," Dad said calmly. "He's not going to fork over big money like that without a fight of some sort."

"Don't worry, Pops," I laughed. "We're covering all the angles. Brant and I figure Pearson'll try to screw us over with a partial payment, but it'll be enough to put him away for quite a while, and maybe during the negotiating phase, we'll find out exactly what part Benjamin McBride has to play in all this."

He sighed deeply. "Still you and Brant are gonna be right in the center of the fire if the shit hits the fan, son, might as well tell me not to breathe as tell me not to worry."

"We know, Dad," I tried to sound even and solid for a second anyway. "Just trust us. You and Uncle Ira taught us pretty well. We've got really good pedigrees when it comes to dealing with the shit hitting the fan."

"Everything is easy on paper, son," he said. "Just remember even little weasel-dicks like Pearson can snap and blow up if you twist 'em too tight."

"Have a little faith, Dad. We got this."

"I know," he finally relented. "I'd just feel better if I was still fifty and down there with y'all. Stick close to Brant, son, have each other's backs. Remember what I told you, sometimes things happen fast, really fast. Be ready for anything, absolutely anything, expect the unexpected, and take nothing for granted."

"Count on it. I love ya, Dad,"

"I love ya, too, boss," Brant said across the table in our back booth. Apparently he'd finished with Jax. "You know I got his sorry ass covered. Janie would have me hung from a limb somewhere if I let him get a scratch."

"You and me both, Brant," Dad said. "You and me both. I expect both of you here in a couple of days max."

"Hey, guys, I'm right here, and I'm not six," I said. "Both of y'all probably would already be broke or in jail if I wasn't taking care of your sorry asses."

Brant finished his beer. "Now, now, Mick, don't get your knickers in a knot. We know you're a big ol' rough-and-tumble cowboy."

"Oh, for the love of Pete," Dad took up Janie's growl. "I trust you both, son. Like I said, I just wish I could be down there, too."

"We know, Dad," I said seriously this time.

"I'll talk to you both later," he replied. "Call me the second this whole mess is finished."

I extended the phone over the center of the table. "Will do, Dad," I said.

"Later, boss," Brant spoke to the phone before I hit the end button.

Brant signaled our waiter for more beer. "Jax said no more beer and for us to get some rest. He wants us on our best game for tonight."

"He's right," I grinned. "We need to be sharp, so let's have a couple more here and then get our butts back to the hotel."

"And maybe one more on our way back to the room," he smiled, and we touched the bottle necks in a salute.

"It is a long way back to Canal," I smiled. "We might need one more just to take the heat out of the long march."

We watched the Mets blow the lead in the ninth, shook our heads, finished our beer, ordered one more for the road, and started up Decatur Street toward the Marriott.

Brant took a long draught of beer. "I'm going with the plain black cape and grey tights. I think you should consider toning down the Captain America outfit."

I sipped my beer and said, "It may be too loud for this operation, but I'm still taking the shield, damn it."

"You're the boss," he grinned as we walked into the hotel right on schedule.

I tossed my empty in the trash. "Yep, let's get ready to rock and roll, brother."

He opened his door as I was opening mine. "See you in an hour for final game plans."

I laughed and went inside.

58

NEW ORLEANS, LOUISIANA, APRIL 18TH, 1921

NEAR THE CORNER of Decatur and St. Peter, an artist stood sketching the scene in front of him. From the back of his rearing horse, Andrew Jackson was tipping his hat in the direction of the Pontalba apartments, St. Louis Cathedral pressing against the blue sky in the background. Lost in his work, he didn't notice the dark-skinned girl who came up behind him.

In fact he smelled her before he saw her; the fresh lilac scent wavering on the spring breeze off the river distracted his pencil's scratching.

"I always wanted to be able to draw like that," she said as he turned to see who was watching.

She was standing, holding her purse, wearing a hat with a purple ribbon hanging down. He noticed the cut of her long beige skirt and a soft blue blouse but mostly he saw her dark green eyes sparkling above a sincere, kind smile.

It had been a long time since he'd carried on a conversation with an attractive, pleasant woman. He suddenly felt awkward and unsure of what to say. Smiling shyly he simply allowed his pencil to return to its work.

She noticed his blush. "Do you paint as well?"

Almost unable to speak, he cut his eyes down to the street below his boots. He'd always sketched scenery and landscapes, sometimes people and animals, but the painting efforts had only come recently with his arrival in New Orleans.

"Yes, ma'am, a little," he mumbled softly.

She smiled again. "I know most of the artists here in the Quarter, but I don't recall seeing you before."

"No, ma'am, I just got here a few weeks back. I'm from east Texas."

"Well, that explains the adorable cowboy accent," she laughed. "Now quit calling me ma'am. My name is Renee Guidry. Please call me Renee."

Suddenly aware of his worn jeans and scuffed boots, he shuffled from foot to foot.

She motioned toward the drawing. "Will you paint this when you finish the sketch?"

He blushed again. "I suppose I'll try. I'm not really much an artist...but...but I do want to be. I'm... I'm tryin' to learn," he stammered.

"I simply love your Texas accent, mister. ..." she paused.

"Whitman, ma'am, Samuel Whitman," he smiled. "I'm sorry my manners just slipped away for a second there."

She loved his shy nervousness. "What brings you here to New Orlee-ans, Mr. Whitman? Have you come to our fair city to study art?"

He loved the way she said "New Orlee-ans."

"Just fate, ma'am, I just wanted out of Texas I suppose."

"Renee, Samuel, Renee please; if you're going to be in this neighborhood, I'm sure we'll meet again. I love to come down to the Quarter. Life is different here," she said. "I work at Tulane, but I ride the streetcar over here and walk frequently when I have the time. Do you live here now?"

"Yes, ma'am."

She cocked her lovely head to one side. "Once more, Samuel, please call me Renee. Ma'am makes me feel old," She laughed her sweet laugh again. "I better get back over to Canal. I'm supposed to meet someone there at three."

"Renee," He touched the brim of his well-worn cowboy hat, one of the few he'd seen being worn in New Orleans.

Even the name sounded pretty, he thought, pretending to sketch again as he watched her out of the corner of his eye, walking down Decatur toward Canal.

He found himself smiling. That had been the closest thing he'd had to a conversation with a pretty young woman in years. It felt pretty good. He liked her green eyes. He liked her dark skin, and he loved her soft southern voice. But just as unexpectedly as the smile came, he felt the tears well up. He missed Rena and the boys.

He looked across the Square at Jackson as pompous as ever, and put his pencil back to the pad directing his thoughts far away from Oklahoma, family, and home.

"John William Wallace is dead," he said to himself. "Rena is remarried and the boys are well off, not needing anything, being educated in good schools."

The pencil danced across the paper. *I have to get past that old life, his life. I have to build a new life, my life. I'm Samuel Whitman now*, he thought to himself. "I am going to live and work here in New Orleans. I will paint, and I am going to let Rena and the boys live their lives without me causing them grief and danger at every turn."

Of course he'd made this or a similar commitment before. After he'd first learned of Rena's marriage to Amos Buchanan and their move to New York City, he'd left Durant immediately, rode east with no particular place in mind, only to wind up in Broken Bow, Oklahoma.

Still heart-broken and alone, a week or two after working odd jobs around McCurtain County, he decided he needed an even bigger change, so he headed south and somehow landed in Port Arthur, Texas. He sold his buckskin stud down there, took a job working on a freighter out of the Carolinas. Almost three years later, here he was in New Orleans.

The day he left Oklahoma, he made the decision to "stay dead," allowing his family to keep the peace they seemed to have found. To insure their safety, he knew the separation had to be total and a distance kept between him and the McBrides. New Orleans seemed a good enough place to start, and if he required more distance, there were ships leaving every day.

Not long after his arrival in port, he found a job at Martin's Warehouse unloading freight. And as luck would have it, one day during his lunch break, while he sat drawing a big ship on the Mississippi, Robert Adams was painting the same river scene. Adams, a respected artist in the Quarter, noticed the quiet fellow in the broad-brimmed hat, worn blue jeans, and western-styled boots sketching the water, and for no real reason, he took an interest in him almost instantly.

He asked about his previous training and introduced himself to the man who said he was Samuel Whitman from Mt. Pleasant, Texas.

Ever since John William had been a boy, he'd possessed a natural talent. Given a pencil, he could sketch almost anything.

"I just like to draw, never had any training, sir," John said. "It relaxes my nerves I reckon."

And Adams saw something in this cowboy fellow with his hat, boots, and jeans. He convinced "Whitman" to let him work with him, mentor him as an artist, a painter. Thus a new career was born on the banks of the Mississippi.

And now this southern beauty had appeared from out of nowhere and spoken to him kindly without looking down on him. Maybe these were signs that New Orleans was indeed the place for Samuel Whitman to bury the ghost of John William Wallace.

His mind considered the endless possibilities that lay before him. He didn't know if he should be happy or sad. He wasn't certain if he should feel relief or guilt. He feared his past would never relinquish its grip on his heart, and to make matters worse, he was suddenly unsure he wanted it to.

Renee Guidry had disappeared around the block, and it looked like a little rain shower was about to blow in off the river, but he wanted to finish the sketch and have something to show Mr. Adams before it was time for his shift in Martin's Warehouses down on the docks.

He looked again at the statue of Jackson, at the cathedral, at his drawing. He couldn't stare the work on to the page. He put the pencil in motion once again.

"John William Wallace is dead," he whispered to no one but himself.

59

THE FRENCH QUARTER – NEW ORLEANS, APRIL 1923

TWO YEARS PASSED *in a matter of minutes it seemed, and Sam Whitman sat looking out the window from the upstairs apartment where he was living on Tchopitoulas Street. The little restaurant on the corner was bustling, and he was considering walking over for a bite to eat. He'd recently grown a goatee and was positive he looked more like a real artist. His hair was streaked with a premature grey and longer now, but when he took his Stetson off, anyone who paid close attention could still see the scar that Constable Aldean's bullet had left on his temple two decades back.*

He had become accustomed to being Samuel Whitman. Only when he absent-mindedly touched the scar did Oklahoma come flooding back.

He'd worked up the nerve to speak more with Renee when she'd come to watch him work on the Square. He'd realized that she liked the cowboy hat and the accent, so he decided to keep the look. He bought a new John B. Stetson western style hat with his new-found money from his hard labor.

He and Renee had grown close. In fact he felt he'd fallen in love with her, a confusing state to say the least since he'd never quit loving Rena.

He still worked in the warehouse, but he was a painter now, and according to Robert Adams, a damned good one. Adams assured him he had the talent to make a living as an artist. He'd even sold a couple of paintings, thanks to Mr. Adams promoting his work, but he was still uncertain of how artists made a living. For him work was a physical activity.

All in all though, things were the best they'd been in quite some time. And now he was afraid he was about to bring his world crashing down. He was wrestling with a major quandary. He had to tell Renee everything, to lay his cards on the table and come clean if he was going to invite her into his life.

They had been pretty much together for over a year now. He knew every sweet curve on her brown body, had painted her, kissed her, traced his fingertips and lips over every square inch of that same body. It was simply time to let her know the whole story, a terrifying idea but a necessary one, he thought, if he planned to ever take the next step.

He couldn't stay in a relationship with her built on a lie, and he was terrified the truth would bring it all down around him. Had he waited too long already?

Sunday before last, he'd come within a heartbeat of telling her as they were walking down by the river, but, hell, it's hard to tell a woman you've been with for over a year, "Oh yeah, my name's not really Sam; I'm married with three kids, but they think I was killed in a prison break seven years ago back in Oklahoma, where I was serving life in prison for murder. She remarried and they went to New York while I was overseas in the war under an assumed name because a crazy, very powerful man wants to kill me because I killed his father twenty years ago."

Nope, it just didn't trickle off the tongue.

He knew she loved him. He knew he loved her, but still it was a scary thing he had to do. And even if she didn't throw him out on the spot, her sister and her momma had to be factored in. Would they need to know as well? Most likely, he reckoned.

He wondered, "How does a man get himself in such a complicated mess?" And if he found the words and the nerve to tell everything, he couldn't possibly blame her if she put him so far out of her life that he'd never be allowed back in.

What if it was all simply too much? No normal woman would stay with a man like him. Maybe he needed to just shut the hell up. But Renee wasn't just any woman. There was something real between them. He could feel it.

Lies and deceit had already cost him one family, one lifetime. He decided it wouldn't happen again. He'd come clean and hope love would keep Renee on his side.

His decision was made, and if she'd have him after he told her, they'd be married soon.

60

BRANT TURNED OUR rented Toyota off North Peters onto Franklin Street, and there was the U-Haul sitting on the vacant lot back toward an older warehouse. As he maneuvered our vehicle onto the lot, the headlights lit up Pearson, standing at the back of it wearing what appeared to be an expensive blue silk shirt and a stylish little fedora. He was accompanied by a young black man in baggy jeans and a bright purple LSU basketball jersey with a Tupac do-rag tied on his head.

From the photos we'd seen, I was relatively certain it was Jacoby Anderson with him, making me wonder where Danarius Brown was currently concealed from view.

I touched the Glock strapped on my left hip under the light tan sports coat. I had on Levis and my Puma running shoes. Remember, junior detectives, dressing for a possible arrest is critical, and Tony Lamas, while masculine and cowboy cool, do not make for great mobility.

Sitting behind the wheel, Brant, who had undergone a similar wardrobe change to my own, looked over at me and asked, "You see more than just those two?"

"Nope," I replied. "But I can't see the cab of the U-Haul very well, and you know Brown is somewhere close."

Not a fan of the crossover draw, Brant wore his Glock on the right. On his left hip, he wore a large handmade Randall knife, sharper than a razor. He wore no jacket to openly expose his weapons. I knew he especially loved the intimidation factor of the big knife.

"Just like the Guy Clark song," he had said back at the hotel as he was strapping it on. "If a finer blade was ever made, it was probably forged in hell."

An unbuttoned chambray shirt over his black tee shirt with a painted buffalo skull on the chest gave him the modern-Native-badass look as he exited the driver's side of the Toyota. I stepped out of the passenger side, glancing around the lot in search of hidden shooters.

Except for us, the place appeared deserted and dark to the naked eye, but I knew Jaxon Moon was in place somewhere with a host of U.S. Marshals and an NOPD - SWAT team. Nonetheless, we still found the absence of Danarius Brown somewhat disconcerting.

Pearson stepped forward and extended a hand.

Brant and I both ignored it.

"Everything I asked for in the truck?" I asked.

He looked pissed. "Yes, and Jacoby has a briefcase containing the $50,000 you asked for. This gets us all square, right? I don't want to ever see you again."

"Likewise," I said. "And of course, I want to look in the truck, not that I don't trust you, Larry, but…oh, the hell with it. I don't trust you."

I could see him squinch his forehead up, even in the dark. "You're an asshole, Wallace, a real asshole." It was almost a whine. Maybe I should whack him, I thought. "It's all there, but go ahead and look."

"Brant, have a peek," I said.

We walked over to where Jacoby stood with the briefcase at the back of the truck. I noticed he had an Uzi strapped and hanging from his right shoulder.

"Step back while I open up the back of the truck," Brant said to him.

He stepped toward Brant and thrust out his chest. "Or what?" he said.

The knife had appeared in Brant's hand without warning or even movement it seemed; it was under the Uzi strap and cutting before Anderson could flinch.

"Or I'll cut your goddamned head off and shit down your ugly neck, Tupac."

Brant smiled and held the blade for him to see as the Uzi hit the ground.

"Step back, Jacoby, hell, let him look. We don't give a damn," Pearson said quickly.

Anderson reached down to pick up the Uzi from where it had fallen.

"Let's just let it lay for now," Brant growled. "Back away from it and stand over by your boss there." He pointed at Pearson.

"Play nice, Jacoby, and you may get it back," I said. "We'll be outta here before you know it."

Brant hopped up on the back of the U-Haul and cut the first box, exposing the plastic bags of white powder. He stuck a finger in and smelled, then tasted the powder. There were several dozen stacked in neat rows.

"Cocaine," he said.

He cut another box and another; all were filled with white powder and pills. A pile of feed bags lay against the other wall of the truck. Brant kept the knife working. Inside each feed sack were plastic bundled bricks. He cut and smelled.

"Weed," came the verdict. "I doubt this is half though."

"It damn sure is half," Pearson whined. "I got all I could on such short notice. Aren't you satisfied yet?"

"Almost," I grinned and patted his cheek. "We still need to count the money and then there's the matter of you apologizing for trying to kill us earlier."

Anderson stepped toward me. "I ain't 'pologizin' to no motherfucker like..." he started.

I struck him with my pistol over his left eye, and he went down at Pearson's feet. "I hated to do that, Jacoby," I smiled. "But I was afraid you were gonna say 'like him.'" I pointed at Brant standing in the back of the U-Haul. "And he'd a killed you on the spot, and that would've probably upset Larry."

Anderson looked like he was thinking about standing up, but Pearson put a hand on his shoulder.

I pointed the Glock at Jacoby's face. "You can thank me later. Now sit while I count the cash."

I swear I could see Pearson turn pale right there in the dark.

"There's only $37,000 in the briefcase,"

Pearson started to whine again. "It was all I could get this quick. I swear I tried. I needed more time."

"Our agreement was $50,000, I believe, Larry. If you're trying to screw us on the money, what else are you trying to short us on?"

He looked worried. "Nothing, dude, I got all the cash I could lay my hands on. I swear... I..."

I smacked him with an open hand. "I told you, don't call me dude."

His eyes flashed, but that was about it.

"Larry, Larry, Larry, I am so disappointed," I said. "But I tell you what…apologize for attempting to murder us and tell me what you know about Benjamin or Mason McBride's involvement with your old boss Marcel Fontenot, and we might just settle for the cash on hand."

Jacoby remained seated. A Glock pointed your direction will keep you pretty still, but I could tell Pearson was nervous and wanting to move around a bit. "I don't know nothing about anybody named McBride…" Larry started.

"Don't lie to me, Larry; it hurts my feelings, makes me feel like you don't trust me. We know the McBrides were involved. We just want to know when and how," I growled. "We can use it against him back home. He'll never know where it came from."

Pearson hesitated. I could see the wheels turning in his mind as the hamster ran furiously.

Brant hopped down off the back of the truck and closed the back end of it. He picked up the Uzi and dropped it into the center of some old tires stacked near the front of the U-Haul.

"Can I stan' up now?" Jacoby asked pitifully.

Brant holstered the big blade and pulled his Glock out, pointing it at him. "Sure," he grinned.

Pearson stepped nervously to the side, a little out of the shadow being cast by the streetlights on the truck. "What do you care about Benjamin McBride?" he smiled as he took off his fedora and wiped his brow.

I saw him cut his eyes ever so slightly up at the warehouse windows, trying to catch a glimpse of something in his periphery I suppose.

"So Benjamin McBride *was* in on your shit?" I chuckled.

There was a pause. Then finally he just looked directly up at the row of windows in the top of the old warehouse.

"Was that the signal to shoot?" Brant asked, leaning on the truck's backend. "Reckon maybe something coulda happened to your shooter, huh?"

I could see the want-to-run in Pearson's eyes as he turned his head and shoulders.

"Don't even consider it," I said. "Talk to me about McBride. He pay you to have us shot?"

"Don't flatter yourself," he sneered. "Old man McBride wouldn't even kick in any cash for Marcel to get rid of Delbert Jones, said he'd paid all he was gonna pay to that old bastard."

"So you killed the old man for Marcel," I shook my head. "And you tried to kill us, too, all on your own."

"Look, you got all I can rake up," he said. "We just wanted you to quit snoopin' around. Marcel paid for Jones. McBride had nothin' to do with it, but his son promised…"

A rifle shot rang out, and Pearson dropped. There was another burst of gunfire from the train cars across the street, and Jacoby dove for the tires that held his Uzi.

Brant stepped away from the truck, kicked him in the face, and rolled him away from the gun as we both dove for cover.

I was behind the Toyota, looking for any sign of movement Brant was behind another couple of piles of stacked tires. Jacoby was moving slightly, moaning at the back end of the U-Haul. Larry Pearson lay stone-still just a few feet away from where I crouched, deader than hell.

61

THE FRENCH QUARTER - NEW ORLEANS, APRIL 1930

Life had been good for Samuel and Renee Whitman. His painting career was blossoming. They had married only months after he'd revealed his secrets, but she'd thought it best to tell no one else, not even her family. A year later, their son was born.

But now times were hard for the country. Samuel read the paper daily, and he was well aware of the hell, Oklahoma, in particular, was suffering through. He worried about his parents often, but he assumed Rena and the boys were probably doing well. William and Shelby would be almost grown now.

As he thought about them, he was working on a painting. A smallish boy peeked around his shoulder at the newest work on which he was putting the finishing touches. There were two men with a team of horses in a wooded landscape, one pointing at a six-point star carved in a rock on a stone outcropping nearby them.

"Who are those men, Daddy?" he asked. "What are they doing with those horses?"

Whitman turned and tousled the boy's hair.

"They're just some fellows I used to know a long time ago, buckaroo," he smiled. "And they're fixing the horse's foot."

The boy started toward the kitchen but stopped and called back, "I like the horses best, Daddy. You should paint a lot more horses."

Samuel Whitman smiled and made a mental note to paint his young son, Mark, a picture of a fine well-muscled buckskin stud named Calavaras.

Yes, all in all, life was good. He was a successful painter, and his work was gaining recognition and critical acclaim. He had sold a fair number of paintings before the stock market crashed, and he was sure he'd sell more. Things would get better. The market would return.

In the meantime, he was bringing in a steady income by teaching. He had three, sometimes more, students from families who were weathering the economic crash, and Renee had her job as a secretary at Tulane. Luckily she'd gone back to work there a few years after Mark was born when money was a little tight. Relatively speaking they were in good shape compared to the rest of the country.

Michelle, Renee's only sibling, was still living in the Guidry family home after the girls' mother passed in '28, and she loved taking care of Mark, the light of Samuel and Renee's lives, while they worked their relatively short hours.

Less than three weeks ago, it appeared that John William Wallace was dead, forgotten and laid to rest, until an odd turn of events had put Sam to thinking about resurrecting that ghost again, a ghost that might be better left in his grave.

It was that damned note, the note that had come with a cancelation of a commissioned work for a New York City banking firm.

At first it wasn't anything to him. Not long after the crash, several cancelations of commissioned works started coming in. A good number of once affluent patrons of the arts suddenly found themselves penniless or very near it.

The painting had been ordered by the Southern Boulevard branch of the Bank of the United States in the Bronx. It was a commission for two New Orleans street scenes. Samuel had done little work on the piece since he'd read of the likely failure of the bank among several others, so only by mere chance did he see the note: cancellation of two (2) - 20"x24" oil on canvas N.O. St. scenes for the personal offices of Amos Buchanan and Charles Perkins.

He, of course, recalled the name with great clarity, and he began to correspond with the bank officials, agreeing to cancel but inquiring as to why. It wasn't long before he learned that Mr. Perkins and Mr. Buchanan were Louisiana natives. Mr. Perkins regretted the cancelation, but the bank was failing, even as he was writing, and Mr. Buchanan was now deceased. Through further amiable correspondence with Perkins, Sam learned that Rena's second husband had taken his own life after the stock market crash, a single pistol shot to the head rather than face the poverty he saw coming.

Within days Samuel had begun to discuss the possible plight of his children and his "widow" with Renee. He was worried Rena would have little or nothing and would return to his father's house. She had nowhere else to go, and William Wallace would send for her, even if she didn't return on her own.

Simple math told him that his oldest son William would be twenty-five, and Shelby would be twenty-two. With good schooling, both were probably on their own by now, but Robert wouldn't be out of college yet. He thought about all three every time he looked at Mark and wondered what they were doing, what kind of men they had grown into or were becoming at that moment.

He was worried about them and Rena, and amazingly Renee understood and encouraged him to somehow offer support, anonymously or openly, whichever he felt best. It was then he knew how lucky he had been in his "second" life. He remembered the six-point star he'd seen and decided to go the anonymous route.

A day or so later, a plan began to form in his mind, one that might, with some luck, alleviate any money problems his original family might be facing while keeping him a ghost, a memory from a decade's past. And maybe with a little luck, his father could find the buried money, and it would help if they needed funds now that Buchanan was gone. He finished the painting, packaged it for mailing, and then plans changed.

Since he was certain McBride had grown even more powerful now, Samuel figured it was best if the family still believed John William was dead. He'd send the painting, a map to as near the area as he could recall, and a letter from "a friend of John William's from prison" to his father. But after more talking it over with Renee, they decided to make contact personally, and she'd go with him. Still he almost called it off out of concern for Renee, Rena, and all his Oklahoma people, but in the end, Renee actually convinced him that the trip was for the best. They could do it. It appeared the ghost of John William Wallace was going to rise from the grave.

Samuel and Renee discussed the plan late into the night. He was torn, but at Renee's prodding, he finally decided to face his father first and see what he thought, no letter, no phone call. Hell, William Wallace most likely didn't even have a telephone. He was still shoeing horses for a living. They'd make the trip and face William.

Now it became a matter of how to do it while inflicting the least possible damage to everyone involved. If William Wallace thought it best that John didn't re-introduce himself into the family, they'd give him as much info as they could concerning the location of the star and head back to New Orleans. If he felt there was hope of any possible reunion, they'd work out the details later, but either way, they'd present him with the painting and a map drawn to the best of John's recollection.

Mark was six. John hadn't even considered trying to explain any of past life to him yet. They'd make arrangements for Michelle to keep him with her as she often did when they were working. Renee would accompany Samuel, once again John William Wallace, suddenly alive again, back to Oklahoma. No matter what the outcome, she was with him all the way now.

If things went well, he'd bring Mark to meet his brothers and grandparents later. But for now, until final outcomes were much clearer, they both agreed the fewer people who knew any of this, most likely the better. They'd wait to tell Michelle, too, no use bringing her in if things didn't go well back in Oklahoma.

He had even signed the painting "John William Wallace." It soon became simply a matter of finding the right time. Thus they began to prepare for a trip back to Oklahoma and letting the chips fall.

Long before the planned excursion back to Oklahoma, his student, Delbert Jones, had gained some knowledge of Samuel's true identity and through gossip had unwittingly put Samuel's life in danger.

Now the week after they had made their decision to return home, Samuel had private lessons scheduled with Delbert on Thursday and Friday.

Another of the dozens of tiny circumstances that constantly alter the events of human lives occurred. Delbert, the perpetual snoop, eavesdropped on a conversation between Renee and Samuel during his Thursday lesson, and as it concluded, Whitman called him aside and postponed their Friday meeting.

Jones in turn put two and two together and saw an opportunity to make a buck with news for Marcel Fontenot. For the rest of his life, he told himself that he never dreamed of the plans Fontenot had made, nor the deal he had arranged with Davis McBride.

62

IN THE SILENCE immediately following the series of gunshots, no one moved, peering into the darkness from behind cover. Then to my left, I saw movement; it was Dani Hebert in black jeans and a black shirt under an armored vest. Her hair was pulled back and she wore a black New Orleans Saints baseball cap as she and another agent moved up beside me, where I was crouched behind the Toyota.

"May I have this dance?" I whispered.

"Shut up, wise ass," she whispered back. "This gentleman is Deputy Marshal Ron Nettles. We're here to save your ass."

Nettles nodded, and I saw several others take up defensive positions around Brant's tire stacks and the U-Haul truck.

Jaxon Moon's voice came into Dani's earpiece from the warehouse windows two stories above. "Dani, what the hell's going on? Are Mickey and Brant okay? Where did those shots come from?"

"They're fine," she spoke into the mic connected to her headset. "Only one shot hit here. Pearson's dead. Other shots were fired in the train yard."

I heard Jax's voice through Dani's headset. "Clay's over there in the boxcars across from the south side of Franklin. Josh Jones, from the DEA, is across from the north side. Each of them have two-man teams, but they're silent on the radio, must be some trouble over there."

"Yep," she spoke into the mic again and looked at me. "Can y'all see anything from up there? Should we advance across Peters Street?"

"Negative, my gunner sees movement in his night vision scope, but we can't distinguish who's who," Jax's voice came through her headset. "We've got Danarius Brown up here in cuffs, though. It's definitely not him."

Anderson tried to rise. I saw Brant reach out and crack him upside the head. "Lie still, dumb ass," he growled.

Seconds later Brant and another marshal, dressed in black much like Dani but not nearly as appealing, scampered over to join us behind the Toyota.

"Howdy, boys," Dani smiled. "Mickey Wallace, this is Mike Billings; I believe you know the other gentleman."

"Yeah, he's probably who they were shooting at," I said.

"Not hardly," Brant said. "One shot, a high-powered rifle, most likely a trained sniper with night vision from the train yard, then several more rounds from over there that sounded like pistols, maybe a semi-automatic rifle as well."

"It's been quiet for a bit now," Dani spoke into her mic. "Jax, still nothing from Clay or Jones. What do we need to do?"

Two more shots sounded from across the tracks. I saw the muzzle flashes between the box cars. Then another single shot.

"Okay, Dani, we've got to move. You take your team across Peters Street. Mike, take your guys further east down the tracks and cross there. Tell Mickey and Brant to stay put or their asses are mine. We're coming down."

"Tell him we're going with y'all," I said.

She shook her head. "No, you're not, cowboy. You and the big man wait right here on Jaxon. Clay's team is supposed to be on one end of the trains nearest the street, and Jonesy should be on the other end. Neither one is answering Jax right now, and shots are being fired. Don't give the big guy any grief."

Jax's voice came through the receiver again, "Make sure those two yahoos wait for me, and proceed with extreme caution. Let's not shoot each other."

Dani winked at me. Billings tapped Brant on the shoulder, and both signaled their teams before running in crouches in opposite directions toward the line of railroad cars across the street.

In a matter of seconds, Jaxon and a small army emerged from the rusted metal door in the warehouse behind us. Jacoby Anderson quickly joined Danarius Brown in cuffs and was hustled behind the U-Haul truck. Larry Pearson was dead before he hit the ground from the look of the hole where the bullet exited his chest.

Jax's headset popped, "Dani here, Jax, we need EMT's and a medevac copter quick. Clay's been hit. It looks pretty bad, but he's conscious. Jonesy looks even worse."

"Oh, shit," Jax said. "Do we know what the hell went down over there?"

"We have an unidentified white male, dead, looks like he was our shooter," Dani said. "And Jax… Jamison and Stevens are both dead."

"Goddamn it," Jaxon said as he massaged his temples. "How? Who the hell was in that train yard? This should never have happened, Dani."

Brant and I stood quietly beside the stunned marshal, listening to the report as it came across his receiver.

"I know it, Jax," she said. "You can't blame yourself. Something over here came flying out of leftfield, but we'll figure it out. You know we will."

"Any other sign of life?" Jax asked, rubbing his temples with his left hand once again.

Dani's voice carried the sadness even through the headphones. "Josh's team is sweeping the cars to the west but nothing yet. I sent Burns and Mullens down the line east, but Clay said they only saw the one shooter on top of a box car near the center of the string of cars."

"We're coming across. Everyone, hold your fire," Jax spoke into the mic and motioned four of his men, Brant and me with him across Peters Street toward the train cars along the wharf.

"This won't be over until we know what happened, Jax," I said as we moved toward the railyard.

"Count on it," Brant echoed.

Jax nodded and spoke into the mic again, "Chief, keep the block secure please. Your SWAT team has the lot secure, one dead and two in cuffs. We've got men down and a chopper coming. Go ahead and bring the troops in."

"He was on top of one of the cars in the second row of trains, Jax," Clay said as Dani applied pressure to a gunshot wound on the right side of the marshal's chest. His armored vest had been removed and lay on the ground beside him. "He fired over the first row. The extra distance didn't seem to faze him."

Jax appeared stunned. "From the second row of cars?"

"He fired once and was already down when I heard Jamison call out for him to stop. He dropped and rolled under the car I guess. He shot Jamison in the knee, and when he went down, the bastard shot him again. I fired as he was getting up and hit him, but he went back between the cars. We lost him."

"What happened to Jones and Stevens?" Jaxon asked as the EMT arrived and began to dress the wounds.

"They found the shooter's motorcycle hidden in a box car a few cars down. I was trailing the blood and moving toward them when I heard more shots," Clay Sanders said through his gritted teeth. "He came up behind Stevens and stabbed him just as I got there, but Jones came around a car and shot him again. He went down hard."

We all looked up to see the first helicopter sitting down in an open area near the tracks just a few yards away.

"Save your breath, Clay," Dani said. "We'll get the details later, big man."

"As I moved toward him, he just rolled over with a pistol in each hand outta nowhere," Clay continued. "He shot me two or three times; my vest saved me, but he must've had armor-piercing rounds. Then I heard Jonesy firing. I know Josh hit him, but he just rolled over, returning fire. I took aim and put a shot right in the back of the bastard's head, but Josh was already down."

"Just take it easy, Clay, you saved Jones. We'll clean it up from here, man," Jax said to Sanders as they loaded Jones into the waiting copter and it lifted off.

Almost immediately a second medevac was landing in the train yard.

"More like Josh saved my life," Sanders said. "Jax, that son of a bitch was a pro, no gang-banger thug. He was good, Jax, and he had to be wearing high-grade body armor."

They loaded Sanders on the second chopper, and it was gone in seconds.

Jax looked at me, "What the hell happened here, Mickey. Who was this guy?"

"Someone who really, really, really didn't want us taking Pearson in," I said. "Someone who knew where and what we were doing here tonight."

"This was a lot more than a drug bust gone wrong," Dani said as the ambulances arrived and loaded the bodies of the two marshals who had been killed in the firefight, leaving the bad guy for the time being.

NOPD was putting up crime scene tape from one end of both rows of the train cars to the other. The lot had already been taped off. Barricades were being placed across Peters Street on each side of Franklin and just east of the lot on Franklin.

Jax nodded as we walked over to where Brant was standing over the dead shooter. "Make no mistake. I will find out who did this," he said as we approached Brant sitting on his heels, looking the shooter's body over.

"Recognize him?" Jax asked Brant.

"Never saw him before," Brant spoke, rising but still looking down at the corpse.

I moved over beside him to get a better look at the shooter. He was dressed in black with expensive body armor and blacking on his face. He wore good leather gloves, also black, and black military-style boots.

"Me either," I said, "but he was obviously a heavy hitter. Somebody laid out big bucks for the hit on Larry Pearson, Jax."

"But who gave a damn enough to take out that trash?" Brant asked. "We put this together almost on the fly. Who the hell even had opportunity?"

"Not many," Jax answered, obviously angry. "But I guarantee that if it is at all possible, I will goddamned sure find out and make them regret it."

63

THE FRENCH QUARTER, NEW ORLEANS TO LAFAYETTE, LOUISIANA, SEPTEMBER 1930

DELBERT JONES *was standing at the corner of St. Louis and Dauphine Streets, watching the Whitman home from just over a block away when he saw Samuel and Renee exit the apartment with Renee's sister, Michelle, and the Whitman boy.*

Samuel tousled Mark's hair, an act he never tired of, and climbed into the new Ford they'd bought earlier that year. Renee kissed the boy on the forehead and hugged Michelle. Michelle and Mark both waved and reentered the French Quarter apartment as Samuel pulled away from the curb and headed toward where Delbert was standing.

Just as he'd planned, Jones stepped off the sidewalk, waved frantically, and started moving toward them as they drove in his direction.

"Mr. Whitman, Mr. Whitman," he called as they neared the corner and pulled over with the window down.

"What's the problem, Delbert?" Sam asked as Delbert stepped over to his driver-side window.

"My worthless piece of junk Stutz broke down just a ways up the street," Jones said, shaking his head. "Can you give me a lift back to my place? My cousin's there, and he's good with automobiles…"

"Well, we're sort of in a hurry, Delbert. We really need to be rolling. Isn't there anyone else you can call to come get you?" Samuel asked.

"It won't take ten minutes, babe," Renee said. "We've got that much time. We can drop Delbert off and then get on with our errands before you even know it."

She smiled and Samuel nodded at the backseat. "What are you doing out this early in the morning anyway, Delbert?"

Jones scooted the package under a blanket, still wrapped and addressed to William Wallace, over to one side and climbed into the backseat of the sweet little Ford.

"Stayed all night after a party in the Quarter, had a little too much to drink I guess. I feel horrible."

"Delbert, Delbert, Delbert, what are we ever going to with you?" Renee laughed.

Samuel pulled the coupe away from the curb and headed on up Dauphine, not paying any attention to the Pierce Arrow that turned off Toulouse Street behind them.

"I know. I know. I'm sorry," Delbert said and ducked his eyes away from Renee. "I think I'm going to be sick. I really don't feel well. I'm dizzy as hell."

"Hang in there, Del, we're almost there." Samuel said glancing in the rear-view mirror as he rolled to the curb in front of Delbert's place.

The Pierce Arrow passed and parked on the other side of the street. Delbert got out of the car and walked around to the driver's side, and for a moment, he contemplated backing down from the plan he'd been made a part of. But his fear overcame his conscience and he just said, "Thank you Samuel."

He walked up the little stoop and pretended to have trouble with getting the key in the lock.

"You okay, Delbert?" Sam called to him.

"Dizzy...can't get the damned key to work... Gonna be sick..." Delbert sat down on the steps to his apartment.

Samuel looked at Renee. "No good deed goes unpunished. Wait here while I get the poor drunk bastard inside, then we go. He can puke, lie down, or do whatever he needs to after he's inside."

"I'll help," Renee said.

Samuel waved her back in the car and got out and started toward Delbert. "You just wait here; we are not gonna stay with him. I just gotta get him inside. He's a big boy."

Sam turned the key, and Delbert slung his arm over Sam's shoulder to mount the steps to his apartment.

The driver had kept the big Pierce Arrow's motor running, and after Samuel entered the apartment with Delbert, two men got out of the car, crossed behind the Whitman's Ford, and nonchalantly walked up to Renee's passenger-side door.

One pointed a pistol at Renee's face through the window as the other stood behind the back of the shiny black Model A.

"Not a sound, sis, or we drop you and the hubby both when he comes out," growled the stocky-built thug holding the snub-nosed .38 pistol.

As soon as he stepped through the door, Samuel felt the gun barrel press behind his ear, and the door quietly closed behind him, but he remained still as Delbert stepped away from him in the dimly lit room.

Sam could see a man he did not know, Pierre Toussaint, sitting in the dark across from where he had entered the apartment with Delbert. Even in the dim light, he could see the other gunman who had leveled his .38 at Sam's chest.

"We have your lovely wife outside, Mr. Whitman," Toussant said evenly. "My boss would like to see you at his place, so we took the liberty of taking her as well. Don't be stupid, and you both will be fine."

Delbert Jones immediately stepped further from Samuel toward Toussaint's side. "I am so sorry, Samuel... They made me trick you... I am so sorry. Please, please forgive me," Jones began to whimper.

Samuel Whitman completely ignored Jones's sniveling. "Who the hell are you?" he said to the dangerous-looking man sitting in the shadows.

The tall, well-dressed man rose and pointed what appeared to be a Smith and Wesson .38 straight at Samuel.

"All in due time, Mr. Whitman," he said. "Let's join your lovely wife and take a little ride to see the man in charge of all this."

In his jacket pocket, Sam could feel the little .32 he'd kept after so many years. He'd decided to take it with him that morning, since he might me re-entering hostile territory. He wondered if he could pull it before this guy, or one of the other two, shot him dead. And if he did, what would the men do who held Renee outside. He opted to remain still for the moment.

"Well, don't just stand there, Melvin, see if he's armed," Toussaint snarled. "Then take him outside to the car with his wife. Delbert, quit your incessant blubbering and shut up. Get in Mr. Whitman's Ford with Hendricks."

"I'm sick, Pierre," Jones blubbered. "Don't make me go. I can't... I'm really sick. I think I may throw up or pass out."

Toussaint backhanded Delbert hard in the face with his left hand, never lowering the .38 or taking his eyes off Sam. "Get your worthless ass in the car with Hendricks, or I'll break your neck right here, right now, you pathetic little shit."

The big man behind Samuel removed the little .32 from Sam's coat pocket, and they all went out the door, Delbert sobbing like a child.

Outside no one was in their car, Renee was missing, but Sam quickly saw her across the street in the front seat of the Pierce Arrow between the driver and a second man.

Toussaint motioned Delbert Jones and one of the gunmen toward the Ford. He pressed the gun into Sam's ribs as they crossed the street and got in the back seat behind Renee and the others. The gunman who'd taken Sam's .32, went around the back of the car, and got in the driver-side rear seat on Sam's left. He, too, had his gun pointed at Sam's ribs.

"Samuel, what's happening?" Renee asked, trying her best to sound calm.

"Don't worry, Mrs. Whitman, just behave and be quiet," Pierre said evenly. "My employer wishes to speak with your husband for a moment about personal matters, then you'll both be back on your way to wherever you may have been headed."

Sam watched Delbert get into the passenger seat of his Ford, where another man took the wheel and flipped a cigarette butt into the street.

"How about you, at least tell us who your boss is?" Sam asked. "After all this isn't how I'm usually called to a meeting, you know?"

Toussant just smiled.

"All in due time, Mr. Whitman, just know for now that Jimmie, the ugly brute next to your Mrs. Whitman there, has a large gun aimed at her pretty heart, and I want a peaceful, quiet drive to where we are going."

Sam quickly realized the depth of their trouble and figured McBride had found him at last. "It'll be peaceful," he said. "I guarantee that. Why don't we just leave my wife here? I doubt your boss has any interest in her."

"No, I doubt that he does," Pierre smiled an ugly smile. "But she's quite handy for keeping you calm and peaceful. Don't you agree? Don't worry. You'll both be fine."

Knowing Samuel needed her to be calm and strong, Renee put on her best face and said, "Let's just talk to the man, babe, find out what he wants from you."

"Smart lady," Toussant winked at Sam.

But Samuel knew a liar when he met one, and he began to look for a way out that would not result in any harm to Renee.

No one else spoke a word as the Pierce Arrow pulled away from the curb with the little Ford following closely behind.

64

THE MORNING AFTER the Pearson bust went to hell, Brant and I sat with Jaxon Moon in his office.

"We lost two good men last night," Jax said. "And Josh Jones is hanging on by a thread. It looks like Clay's gonna pull through, but he's still in serious condition."

"Jesus, I'm sorry Jax, I said. "I still don't know how it went so wrong. I thought we had everything sewed up so nice and tight. It literally makes no sense for anyone to go to such extreme measures in this case."

"I thought we had it wrapped," Jax said as he sipped his morning coffee. "But now we have to figure out what went wrong and get the bastard responsible for this."

"No way it was a random hit, even on a piece of crap like Pearson," Brant mused. "Only someone with serious cash hires a shooter the class of the guy we ran into last night."

"Somebody wanted Pearson out of the picture; that's fairly obvious," I said. "He wasn't simply collateral damage."

Jax laid his chin in his right hand and leaned forward on his desk, looking down on the first reports from the night before. "The smart money would have to be on Marlon Landry or Mason McBride, just based on the expense involved."

"But who knew the particulars of the location or the circumstances of the operation?" Brant asked. "The gunman knew some things, or he was awful lucky, and from my experience with guys like him, I doubt any luck was involved."

"Besides y'all, Chief Boyer, Dani, and Clay," Jax said. "I brought in several need-to-know guys to lay out the trap: Darrell Lackey, the

SWAT commander, Jonesy from DEA, Deputy Chief Martin Monroe from NOPD. They're all stand-up guys, worked with 'em all before. And for what it's worth, I honestly can't imagine any of them being involved."

"There's Marlon Landry to some extent," I said. "Plus Pearson's crew was well aware of the details. God knows any of them could have given out the time and place to anyone interested."

"We have to consider the probability good old Larry communicated a good deal of info with his criminal cohorts as he gathered up the drugs and money for payoff," Jax agreed. "Maybe someone in that crowd decided he was expendable and better dead than talking to the law if it all went south."

"True, but I can't imagine any of Pearson's peers having the connections to bring in a guy like the caliber of the shooter," Brant put in. "For me the quality there points to Marlon Landry or the McBrides. Who else is going to have the know-how to reach a guy like this one, plus the money to pay him?"

"Like I said, it makes sense to me," Jax sighed. "But we haven't got one shred of proof against either Landry or one of the McBrides. We don't even know who the shooter was yet."

"Landry, of course, has all the necessary contacts to bring in a pro, and he could've viewed hitting Pearson as a simple matter of insurance," Jax offered, putting his feet up on his desktop. "But the shooter taking up a position on the second row of train cars bothers me. How did he know we'd just have men on the first row?"

"As much a pro as that guy was, he could have simply made an educated guess," Brant suggested. "And if Pearson talked to Benjamin McBride about needing money for the payout, he definitely has the money and the need to keep his name completely out of any muck and mire."

I was listening and weighing the motives and advantages gained by both of our principal suspects when the phone on Jaxon Moon's desk rang and he answered.

"We can't hang out here forever," I said to Brant as Jaxon spoke into the receiver. "We're not getting paid here, and you know we have work to do back in Oklahoma, big guy, plus this pretty much kills our only lead."

Brant nodded in agreement. "How is Will taking everything?"

"He sounded tired," I answered. "But he's fine, pretty thrilled neither one of us got killed. I told him we were okay, and the most of it was over." I sighed. "Told him I'd call him back with more details later tonight."

Jax hung up the phone. "The shooter is a total spook, guys. We got nothing on him, no prints in the system, no photos, no DNA, absolutely nothing. He doesn't even seem to exist."

"Figures," I said. "He was even more expensive than we thought, probably international."

"That's not a bad guess for an Okie," Brant tried to smile. "Maybe Interpol will have some lead or recognition of the guy."

Jax looked tired. "Let's hope. We're not quitting on it ever, but it doesn't look too good for the home team right now, men. We've hit the wall for the time being."

"Yep," I conceded. I can't see anything that's gonna help us any too soon."

Jax looked like he badly need some sleep. I knew Brant and I both needed some.

"Nope, things are about to get slow," he said as he stood and looked out his window for just a second or two. "And maybe that's good."

It looked like dancing the heels off my boots was out of the picture. I thought I'd see if Dani was more interested in a quiet meal maybe with Brant and Maggie before we left.

Brant and I both stood.

"As much as I hate to say it, buddy, as soon as you clear us, I think we're gonna head back to red dirt country and take care of business there," I said. "Guess we need to stop by Leslie and Marie's place though and say so long first, but we do need to get back soon, Jax,"

Brant took Jax's hand and drew him into a hug. He did likewise with me in turn.

"Well, I guess all good things gotta come to an end," Jax smiled weakly. "It's been real, boys, hope to see you again before too long. Heck, we'll probably call you as witnesses against Brown and Anderson just so we can hang out, maybe play some golf or fish a little bit."

"I don't think you'll get a complaint out of us on that," I smiled. "Brant sucks at golf, but he'll take some wild hacks."

"Like you can even hang with me on the course," Brant laughed. "Custer had a better chance at the Little Big Horn."

"Maybe we better just go fishing," Jax grinned.

I shook my head. "No hope for him there either, can't even bait a hook."

"Whatever," Brant sighed.

"Bring your dad if you can, Mick. We'll leave him and Dad to discuss old war wounds," Jax said. "I'll get Jeff, and we'll play a couple of rounds and then take the whole crew fishing."

"I just hate leaving things unanswered," I said.

Jax smiled. "Me, too, bud, but with what we got, that's all we can do right now. Guessing doesn't count for much in court. If this was Jeopardy, we'd have a chance. At least you guys solved Mr. Wallace's part of the mystery."

"For the most part I guess," I said. "We'll never know exactly how those final hours went down for John William Wallace. We have Mr. Postier's account, and that's about as good as we can get, better than I expected actually."

"Well, will be glad to know his father went down fighting I think," Brant said. "We Okies do not like going gentle into that good night."

"I like the Dylan Thomas reference there, big guy," Jax smiled. "And if nothing else, I have definitely learned that much about men from Oklahoma."

"You got our numbers, boss," Brant said as we moved toward the office door and Maggie's desk. "Maybe we can catch one more lunch before we roll."

Jaxon Moon managed a real smile. "Well, I guess there are still a few great places to eat that y'all haven't managed to get thrown out of yet."

Brant moved ahead of me to set up dinner plans with the lovely Miss Comeau, and I looked Jaxon in the eye. "You know we're brothers now, man, you need us, you call."

"The slightest ripple in the pond, and you gentlemen will be my first calls," he said. "Whoever hired that shooter is at the top of my list to hook, I promise."

I shook his hand again.

Brant was sitting on the corner of Maggie's desk, waiting on me when I turned the corner.

"Let's go see your kinfolks, buy Will some Dixie beer, declare victory and another case solved by our detective expertise," he grinned and stood up to go.

Maggie stood, too, and came around the desk for a hug.

"I'm glad you two cowboys avoided serious injury," she said and gave me a little kiss on the cheek. "Hope to see you and Dani for dinner tonight, Mickey."

I smiled. "If Dani is up to it, maybe we can all grab a bite at Arnaud's before it's time for us to roll back to Oklahoma."

"That would be great," she said. "I'll see you later, Brantley, regardless, right?" She winked and returned to her desk.

As we exited to our rented Toyota parked on Camp Street, I looked at Brant. "Bud, you better hope Dani's in the mood for a meal, or I might just steal your woman."

"Keep dreaming," he laughed. "Let's just take this crap car back to Hertz and get the Jeep."

"First we have to drop by Leslie and Marie's," I grinned. "They've got John William's ashes divided like Dad asked. We'll pick them up and let them know Dad is gonna try to make it down here soon."

"Steal my woman," he laughed again. "I'm telling Leslie how rude her cousin has been to me."

"Let's not," I said as we entered the little Toyota and pulled away from the curb.

65

THE FONTENOT PLACE EAST OF LAFAYETTE, LOUISIANA, SEPTEMBER 1930

PIERRE TOUSSANT'S *Pierce Arrow turned off the highway and onto a drive leading up to the big plantation style house with the Whitman Ford trailing right behind but then they turned on a dirt road leading away from the house toward a barn and some stables.*

Sam Whitman was certain now that something bad was happening, but he was hoping against all hope that he was wrong. Maybe this was a case of mistaken identity.

Unable to figure out the circumstances, Renee looked back at Samuel several times but said little. Surely there had been a mistake of epic proportions.

"Odd place to talk," Samuel said as the two vehicles bumped slowly down the path. "And you still haven't told me who we're supposed to be talking to yet."

"That would be Mr. Marcel Fontenot," Toussaint said.

"I don't believe I've ever met the man," Samuel said. "What does he want with us?"

"I believe he wants you dead, Mr. Whitman, or should I say, Mr. Wallace," Pierre smiled like a cartoon snake. "At least his associate, Senator McBride, does."

Samuel felt the knot grab his stomach and squeeze as Renee gasped, "Oh, God, no."

The Pierce Arrow came to a halt.

"Shut up, sis," *the stocky-built guy to Renee's right said.* "Or I'll have to shut you up."

The unmistakable gravity of the situation was frightening, but Samuel tried to remain cool. Of course his greatest fear was that Renee might be harmed.

"Listen, she's got nothing to do with the problems between me and McBride," Samuel Whitman said as he began to morph slowly back into John William Wallace. "Don't hurt her, and I'll make this easy. I swear McBride wouldn't want her hurt. He just wants me dead."

"Let me think about it," Toussaint grinned and opened his door. "Okay, I thought about it. She's a witness. Now get outta the car."

He jabbed John in the ribs with the gun.

The stocky-built guy got out of the front passenger side, pulling Renee with him. The silent thug sitting on Sam's left slid out the rear passenger door, holding a Smith and Wesson .38 just like Toussaint's on the painter as he followed him out of the car. But the painter was gone. The man who lunged out of the back seat was John William Wallace, cowboy, U.S. Army Panther, warrior.

He caught the thug's wrist on his gun-arm and delivered a savage head butt under the chin as Toussaint fired from the other side of the back seat, striking John in the back. He spun the stunned gunman and took the gun as Pierre poured two bullets into his own man.

Dropping the dead man, Wallace fired once into the face of the driver, trying to exit beside him and two more into Toussaint, still sitting in the backseat.

The punk driving the Whitman Ford appeared from out of nowhere and fired at John from behind, striking him in the upper leg. He went down on one knee but turned and shot the kid they called Hendricks in the chest.

The gunman holding Renee took advantage of the opening and aimed his snub-nosed .38 over the Pierce Arrow's long hood at the wounded fighter, but Renee struck his arm, causing him to miss. She yanked free and began attacking with full fury, clawing the man's face with both hands.

The stocky criminal had Renee between John William and himself as she ripped at his eyes, blocking any chance for John to fire at him.

"Renee, run!" *John screamed as he rose dragging himself toward her and the gunman.*

Then John heard the shot and saw her fall as he lunged around the front of the car with a primal scream.

He shot Renee's killer in the face but went down under his own weight.

He saw lights coming from the big house they passed by earlier as he crawled to Renee. He cradled her head on his lap, and she lifted her hand to touch his face.

Toussaint exited the car bleeding heavily, taking aim at John, but John fired first, striking Pierre Toussaint for the third time. In anger John pulled the trigger on the .38 twice more only to hear the clicks of the empty chambers as Pierre Toussaint rose to his feet.

He tried to throw the useless weapon at Pierre's face, but Toussant's final shot dropped John dead right beside his wife who reached for his hand in the last moment before everything in their world went dark.

66

BACK IN DURANT, Janie and Dad were waiting at our offices on Main Street when we arrived.

"I guess we got a lot more than we bargained for, boys," Dad said from behind my desk.

Brant, Janie and I sat around the desk with a Styrofoam cooler full of cold *Dixie* beer as we looked at the brass funerary urn sitting on the desk, the painting hanging on a wall above a bookshelf.

"I suppose Arcelus Monroe's gone from the family plot?" I asked, winking at Janie and Brant.

Dad took a long pull on his beer. "Good riddance to bad rubbish," he said. "There's still so much we'll never know. But at least we know he went down fighting."

"From the wounds found in the bodies and what Mr. Postier told us, he and Renee put up a good fight and made their killers pay a heavy cost," I said.

"Yep," Brant tossed in. "Postier told us that Toussant died as a result of his wounds not long after Delbert Jones got him back to New Orleans."

"I hope the bastard suffered," Dad said. "Now, son, make yourself useful and get Janie another *Dixie*. Hers is almost gone."

I laughed. "That is damn good beer, can't believe they don't have it here."

"We'll have to go back for the trials, and I sort of promised Janie a week in the Crescent City this fall, guess we can pick up more," I said. "Obviously these two cases aren't going to last."

"But Leslie and Marie and Tommy Moon really want us to bring you down there for a little vacation, Uncle Will," Brant smiled. "How's that sound to you, boss?"

Dad stroked his beard. "Reckon a couple of days off wouldn't hurt. I've been working my ass off while y'all played all over the Big Easy, and I haven't seen Tommy in years."

Brant walked over to the oil painting again and looked at the six-point star. "When do we start the big treasure hunt?"

"Oh, good Lord," Janie said in mock distress; at least I think it was mock distress. "It'll be after my trip to New Orleans, that's for damn sure."

Dad laughed out loud. "The boss has spoken."

Janie kissed him on the cheek. "That's just one of many reasons I love you so much, William Matthew Wallace."

"Meanwhile we'll have to get us a couple of hunting leases around Hartshorne for deer season," Dad chuckled. "But I reckon we can wait 'til fall to find gold, can't we, boys? We've got lots of time, especially since I've decided this terminal crap is for the birds, don't think I'll die just yet."

"That's good to know," I said. "I'm happy to put off reclaiming my desk for a while."

"Nope, I'm afraid not, you get it back in the morning," he said. "Janie fixed me up while you two were dragging ass back up here. I'm retiring again, taking a vacation to New Orleans for a couple of days. Brant can drive me down to DFW, and Leslie has promised to pick me up when I land."

"Surprise," Janie laughed.

Brant laughed, too, and finished a beer off. "That's unexpected; why don't I just drive you back down to New Orleans, boss? You might need a bodyguard."

Dad handed him another beer. "I doubt it, boy. Besides you're gonna be busy here. I hooked you fellas up with a couple of big cases, and Deb and Wayne Ray are still hung up on the Republican."

"Well, at least here's to some paying clients, guess we won't go broke," I said and lifted my bottle.

"One more round, I reckon, looks like we're back at work tomorrow," Brant said. "But I am off that congressman's case, right? That bastard's a sick puppy. How much more dirt on him can his old lady want?"

"Yep, we got security for Daniel Letts' re-election campaign coming up, and apparently Dad has booked us solid somehow," I said.

"Especially since the Republican race just got interesting," Janie smiled slyly. "Mason McBride just announced that he's out for 'health' reasons, and they don't have a serious contender to face Daniel now."

"That's plumb awful," I laughed. "I hate to hear Mason is in poor health. He looked fine when I saw him earlier this month."

"It was sudden," she laughed.

"Think I'll contact Nola Munson again at Big Mac," I said. "See if she can help with any info on the exact area of that logging camp before the break."

"You looking for outlaw gold or an opportunity to talk to a pretty woman again?" Janie smiled.

"I can see a pretty woman just by walking through that front door right up there," I said, winking at her.

"You better not forget it either, buddy," she laughed. "Or I'll have to adjust your eyesight."

Dad twisted the cap off another *Dixie* and quickly switched the subject. "You and Brant are welcome for the help, son. Janie and I tried to keep the business afloat while y'all played. And by the way, who all thinks Mason McBride hired that heavy hitter you boys had to tangle with down there?"

"I'd say just about anybody with the last name of Wallace," Brant laughed.

"To be honest," I said. "I don't think he was involved, but his son, Benjamin, may be another story."

Brant handed me another beer. "I think they're both in on it some way or another, but I doubt we can get an arrest warrant with the proof we have, which would be none."

"You don't always get what you want," Dad said.

"But sometimes you get what you need!" The rest of us chimed in with perfect Mick Jagger imitations.

Ron Wallace is an Oklahoma native and currently an adjunct instructor of English at Southeastern Oklahoma State University, in Durant, Oklahoma, where he was born and raised. His father served as a police officer there, rising to the rank of captain. He is the author of ten books of poetry, five of which have been finalists in the Oklahoma Book Awards with *Renegade and Other Poems* winning the 2018 Oklahoma Book Award.

Influenced by the styles of Robert B. Parker, Peter Bowen, and James Lee Burke, his novel, *A Secret Lies in New Orleans* is the prize-winning poet's first venture into prose, although a second book is nearing completion.